The Odyllic Stone

Alex Scheuermann

To my loving family
Who have given me
all the support
a person could ask for

ACKNOWLEDGMENTS

I have always been a fan of the fantasy genre, since I was little. The thought of magical powers and fighting enormous monsters never fails to capture my imagination. The idea for this book came from wanting a story that explored the birth of magic. Many of the fantasy stories I have read take place in an established world where magic is already widespread, but what if nobody knows how it works because it had never existed before?

Special thanks to my loving wife Elizabeth, who has listened to me ramble about my ideas for years. She is my first reader, my rough draft editor, and always encourages me. Thanks to my parents Nancy and Richard for serving as beta readers and supporting me throughout the writing process. Also, thanks to my editors Hollyanne Jordan and Matt Keefer for providing valuable feedback on everything from characters to prose. Thanks to Kyle Simpson for his high-quality suggestions on story improvements. And thanks to all my other friends who provided their thoughts along the way.

CONTENTS

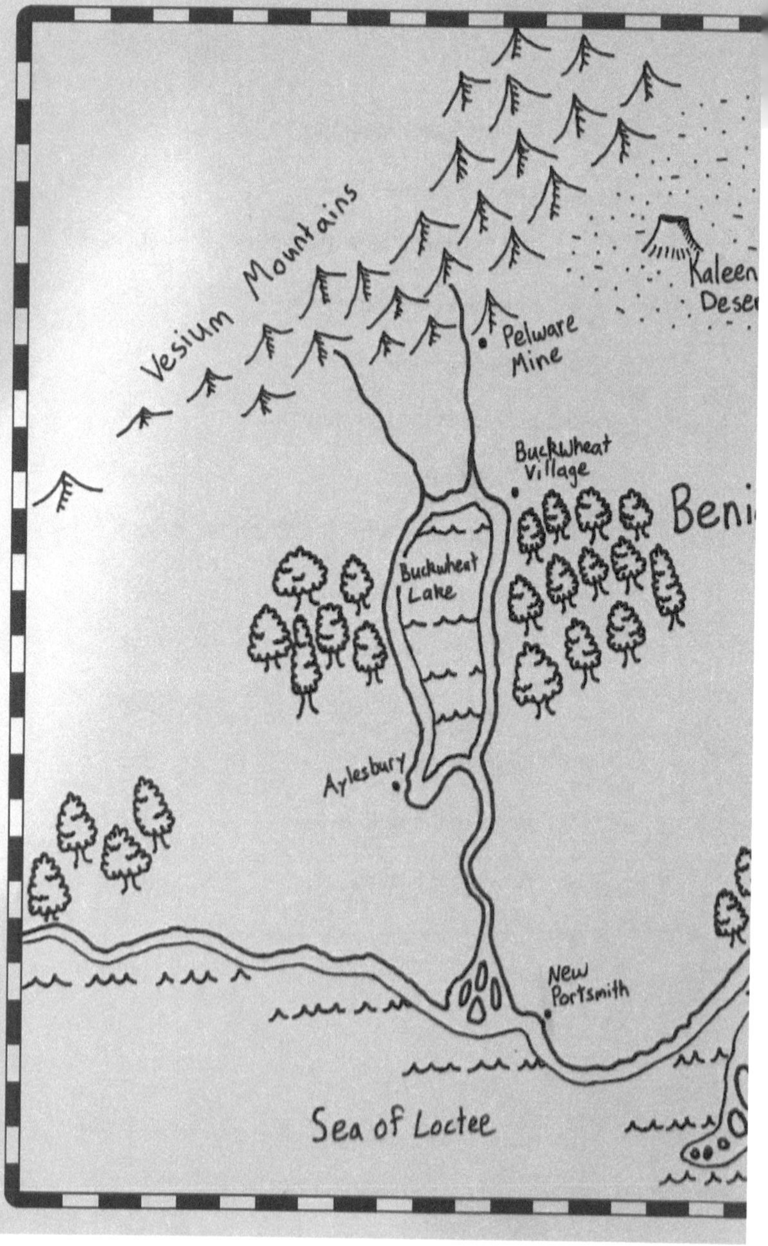

Vesium Mountains
Kaleen Desert
Pelware Mine
Buckwheat Village
Buckwheat Lake
Beni
Aylesbury
New Portsmith
Sea of Loctee

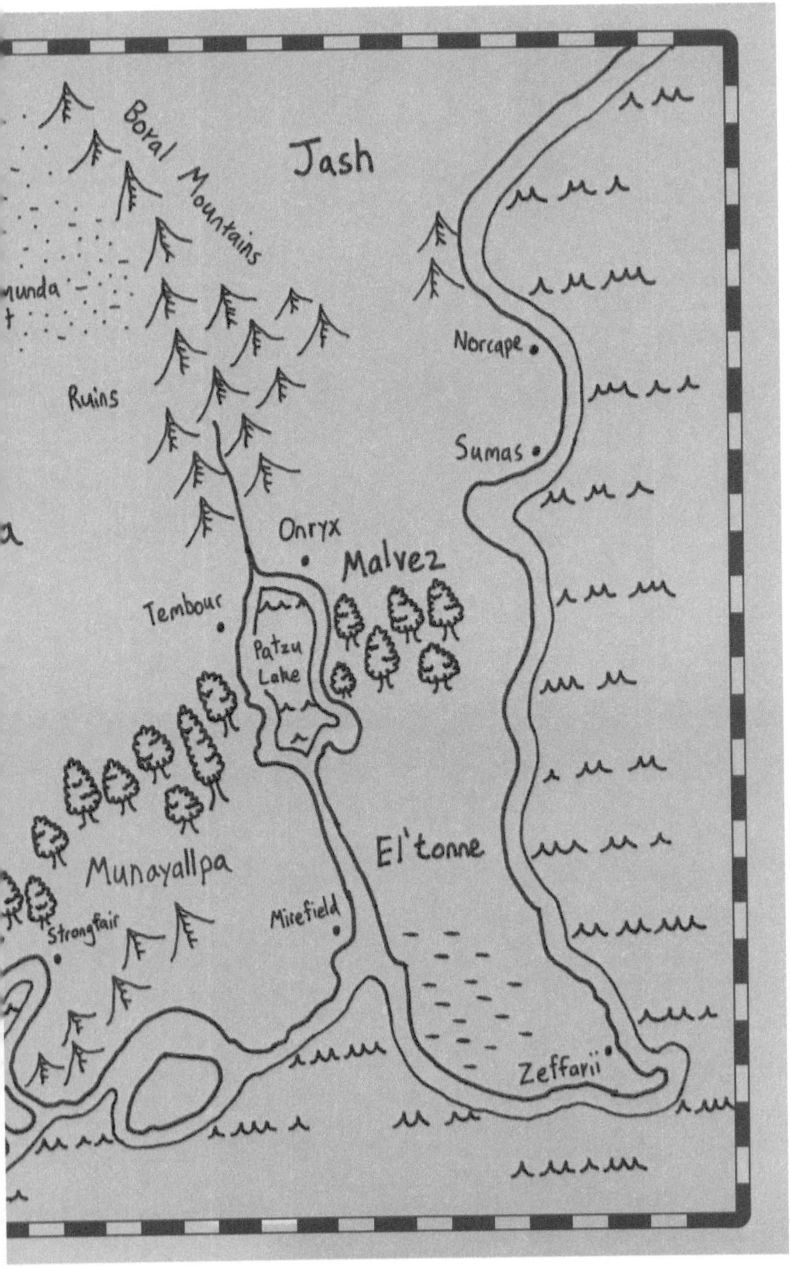

Jash
Boral Mountains
munda
Ruins
Norcape
Sumas
Onryx
Malvez
Tembour
Patzu Lake
Munayallpa
Strongfair
Mirefield
El'tonne
Zeffarii

Alex Scheuermann

1 MONSTERS AND MALADIES

"But mail *is* important," Aster argued as the miner pushed him along the earthy tunnel. The cold, damp air slipped under his shirt, chilling his core.

"Quit yapping and move," the miner said, shoving Aster away from the entrance.

Aster lifted his messenger bag as he ducked under the wooden beams. The metallic air burned each breath. "It's my responsibility to make sure Hannes gets this letter."

"Trust me. I'd rather be in here with you." The miner's teeth chattered as he held the candle up at a fork. "Left," he said, directing them down that path.

"I'll be quick!"

"Stop arguing, Aster." Zinnia's slender fingers grabbed his arm. "Something's not right outside. Didn't you see how nervous everyone was?"

Aster rolled his eyes. "There's always some kind of commotion at the mines. Last time it was about a collapse or something. I just need to put the letter in his hand and then we can leave."

"I wish you didn't drag me along," she muttered, half to herself.

"Here. Sit." The miner pointed to a makeshift bench of fallen rubble and handed Zinnia the candle. "Don't leave until I come get you. Got it?"

"Yes. Fine." Aster lifted himself onto a boulder.

Zinnia sat cross-legged on the ground, placing the candle between them.

"Good," the miner grunted and hurried back the way they came.

Aster listened to the shouts from outside. *We'll be home late,* he thought. *Hopefully Dad won't blame me.* He watched a frown settle across Zinnia's pale face. "You see what all that was about?"

"No, my eyes were on the mountains when we got here."

"Too bad... could be something interesting..."

"Could be something dangerous."

"Whatever it is, I want to see."

"How can you be so relaxed? This is terrifying."

"This was supposed to be our adventure! Pelware Mines on the first day of spring, but instead we're just holed-up in this dirty tunnel."

"The mine-shaft is plenty interesting. Normally, they'd never let us in." She held up a gold nugget the size of her finger. "Look what I've found!"

"Zin, leave it. We could get in trouble."

She glared back. "It's tiny. They won't even notice. Why are you always such a goody-goody?"

The candlelight glinted off the newfound treasure as she stuffed it into her pocket; the same khaki breeches she always wore because, in her words, 'It's easier to escape the woods in pants.'

"You'll be rich… if we make it out alive," Aster joked.

Zinnia jumped to her feet, her bobbed chestnut hair bouncing on her fair cheeks. "Don't be mean, Aster. You don't actually think…"

"There's definitely something outside. Maybe a bear got one of the workers while they were slacking off."

Zinnia's eyes widened.

I shouldn't have said that. Aster raised his voice emphatically. "Relax. It's not a monster. Unless... a boulder beetle traveled here..."

"From Munayallpa? That's way too far. Even if they do exist, I doubt..."

The shouting stopped.

Aster strained his ears, listening to nothing but the occasional vibration of the ground.

"Do you think it's over? I don't want to look." Zinnia's voice had fallen to a whisper.

Aster dusted his pants and slid off the stone. "We need to get home."

"But that man said to stay here..."

"Follow me with that candle. This place is a maze." He marched forward.

Zinnia grabbed the small copper dish and hurried after him. "Why do you always walk so fast? You know I can't keep up with your long spider legs."

"We both know you'd have sat there all day if I didn't set the pace."

A seam of light acted as their guidepost, and after stumbling in its direction for a few minutes they reached the exit. Zinnia grabbed the back of Aster's shirt as he threw his weight against the heavy oaken slab and stepped into the sunlight.

Zinnia cupped her pale hands over her eyes, letting as little light through as possible. Her bobbed brown hair swayed in the breeze.

As Aster's eyes adjusted, he could see the shacks that the miners called home, framed by the snowy mountain peaks. At their center was a heavily worn table and cooking pit, overflowing with coals. Two burly excavators stood around their mine-cart. *Idling when the boss is away —shame on them.*

A set of mine-tracks led to the boss's quarters where the miners would take the gold for weighing.

Zinnia sighed. "Looks like they've already forgot about us. The miners are out working."

"Good. We should find Hannes. We've wasted too much time here."

"Why aren't they moving?" Zinnia waved to the workers. She frowned when they didn't wave back.

"Lunch break?" Aster glanced at the rushing mountain stream—one among many tributaries that fed Buckwheat Lake.

"No. They're just standing there." She crept closer.

"What does it matter? You're not their—"

"Th... they... they've been turned to stone!"

Aster turned. "Not funny Zin."

"I'm serious!" Zinnia's finger shook as she pointed.

Two miners were frozen in place, terror carved into their stony faces. Their hands were outstretched, shielding them from some unseen horror.

"That's... impossible." Aster rushed to the men. One had a familiar dimple above his unshaven chin. *The miner from earlier?*

Zinnia ran her fingers across the man's shirt. "The fabric is normal, but his body is solid."

Aster knocked on the cheek of the second miner. His knuckles scraped against hard rock.

"Stop that! Be more respectful." Zinnia scowled at him until he pulled his hand back.

"I was just double checking... Sure enough, these two are petrified. I've never heard of anything that could do this. Do you think Jash... actually, never mind. There's nothing we can do here, let's get moving."

"Let's go home." Zinnia's voice was barely a whisper.

"But the letter. Besides, we could help."

"These men are stone."

Aster tightened the strap on his messenger bag. "Dad will be disappointed if I don't deliver it. I promised."

"He'll understand."

"Come on." Aster balanced himself on the mine-track, taking step after step around the bend. "If Hannes isn't in the head house, I'll just leave the letter."

Zinnia let out a squeak but followed.

The ground sloped down, leading to the main office which was propped against the cliffs. Aster had never been inside, but he'd heard that this building covered the primary mine-shaft.

As they crept closer, Aster thought he heard a shout from inside. On the second story, two figures darted across the window.

Zinnia's breathing quickened with every step forward.

This is too much for her, Aster thought. "Stay here and I'll check on things."

"Alright." Zinnia barely got the word out before she darted back up the hill, ducking behind a mine-cart full of gold ore.

If there's a monster and I save them, word will get out about my bravery. Aster mustered up his courage and stepped inside.

The room was split in half by the iron tracks with a wooden table near the door and a sturdy oak stairway on the far side. At the base of the stairs, an unusually large rooster stood, transfixed on the second-floor landing.

All this commotion caused by an irritated bird. Laughing, Aster called out, "Oi Hannes, you owe me five gold coins for saving you from the angry chicken! I know they can get mean, but I wouldn't expect you miners to be scared of it."

A panicked voice replied, "Don't catch its gaze!"

Aster's eyes snapped back to the bird. A fleshy red comb crowned its head with lobes hanging below a short, pointed bill. Its body was covered in dark brown feathers with two bare, clawed feet that had gouged the wooden floor. The creature stood taller than the chairs scattered about. Its wings were like cowhide pulled over a campfire to dry. Three sets of bones running through each, segmenting the translucent skin. A long serpentine tail whipped back and forth behind the monster, shimmering a faint green. And thanks to Aster's shouting, it stepped in his direction.

A miner emerged from the depths of the tunnel, lantern held aloft. He yelled out, "Hey, my shift's over, where's my replacement? I ain't working an extra hour again today, blast it!" He stomped towards the stairs, oblivious to the creature in front of him. "Fletch, who's up af'er me today?"

The bird turned to face the noise, stretching its dark wings. It hissed like water across hot coals, causing the hairs on Aster's arms to tremble.

The miner dropped his lantern and darted towards the exit, but the bird lunged after him. He hadn't made it more than halfway across the room when the monster pecked him. He shrieked and tumbled to the floor, clutching his leg which melted like hot wax.

The bird hopped backwards and fixed its gaze on the miner, puffing out its feathery chest.

Aster could only stare.

Every breath the miner sucked in was long and strained. "Can't feel my foot," he whimpered.

His leg re-hardened as a deep gray blob. It looked rough, no longer like skin.

His arms changed next. Starting from the edge of his shirt, down to the tips of his fingers, the gray spread. He howled for the last time as his face became a stony mask, frozen in permanent agony.

Then he was still.

Aster's thoughts were racing.

The monster's head rotated until a beady eye landed on him.

Aster's legs trembled as he backed up in terror. His foot snagged on a loose board, and he fell with a crash. Face down, Aster could hear the scratching of nails on the timber floor. Without looking back, he hoisted himself up and raced out the door.

"Somebody help!" His knees wobbled with each step.

Another hiss escaped from the beast as it stalked him out of the building. Its claws clinked on the metal track in pursuit.

Zinnia screamed from behind the mine-cart on the hill.

Aster could feel its stare on his back, burning like a lit pyre. He fell to his knees, head swimming. With his last shred of consciousness, Aster prayed for warmth in the afterlife.

The screech of metal wheels broke him out of his stupor. He opened his eyes to see a mine-cart careening down the track towards him.

With a sickly crack it slammed into the bird, carrying it backwards. Feathers danced through the air.

The burning ceased and Aster collapsed.

"… Aster, Aster, Aster are you alright?" Zinnia's voice was incomprehensible at first.

"Wh… what happened?" Aster asked, vision blurry.

Zinnia was doused in sweat and her hands trembled as she clutched at the front of his shirt. "I was so scared. When that monster caught up to you and you started turning gray, I thought you would die! But the mine-cart was on the same track, so I loosened the brake..." The words tumbled out between her shallow, panting breaths.

"I'm pretty sure you just saved my life. I owe you big time." Aster patted her shoulder reassuringly as he checked that the monster truly was gone. Blood was smeared across the tracks and feathers were scattered atop the gravel.

The two men who had been stuck on the second floor rushed over to help. The larger man was Fletcher Abberton. Aster had met him twice before. His arms were as thick as a woodcutter's with a clean shaven face and dirty-blond hair. But most memorable of all were his stories. Fletcher could make a walk around the lake sound like an adventure in a faraway land. He wasn't all talk either. Mayor Gilroy swore up and down that Fletcher was an honest man.

That made the other man Hannes Heartford. Aster had never spoken to him before, but seen him in passing. He had pale skin and an abundance of facial hair. His accent was so thick that it made him difficult to understand. Whenever he'd asked where Hannes was from, he could never get a straight answer. Aster's father guessed he'd grown up somewhere in the Boral Mountains, north of

Tembour.

Fletcher shouted to a side door. "Come out. We've got work to do."

Two miners cracked the door cautiously.

"I need you to search for the remains of the beast inside the tunnel. It can't have gone far. I doubt it'll survive long after an impact like that, but be careful."

The men grumbled, causing Fletcher to add, "Do it now. Imagine if we're wrong."

The two men ducked back inside the storeroom, came out with lanterns, and crept down the dark tunnel.

Fletcher shook his head and helped Aster to his feet. "I've never seen someone as reckless as you, Aster Rutherford."

Aster grimaced.

"You saved us all." He turned to Zinnia, pausing for an introduction.

Zinnia stared past him, blankly.

She's still in shock. "Zinnia Hollyhock, daughter of Watson."

Fletcher replied, "Of Buckwheat General Store? Thank Viridus's great bounty that you two happened to come here today."

Hannes Hartford, the short, heavyset man, peered around nervously. In a thick accent, he said, "Let's discuss inside the 'ouse."

The four of them made their way back to the head house, past the gruesome statue, to the foot of the staircase. Zinnia gasped at the stone man clutching at his leg. Her eyes fixated on the tunnel as she edged around the room, following the others to the second floor.

The group found their way to a grand table, where they each took a seat. A map of trade hubs along the Haverhein River lay across its surface.

Fletcher brushed stray dirt off the table and asked, "So why are you two here anyways?"

"Postal delivery." Aster plucked a letter out of the satchel he was carrying and presented it to Hannes.

Hannes took the letter and muttered "T'anks," as he tore it open. He leaned back as he read, keeping Aster from sneaking a peak.

Fletcher cleared his throat. "Well thank you for your delivery, and for helping us out with the cockatrice."

He paused as Hannes looked up from the letter. They exchanged a knowing glance.

Fletcher continued speaking, but his words were more methodical this time. "I know you're probably excited to tell your friends about what happened here today, but I need you to keep it a secret," he said sternly. "In return, we'll give you each a gold coin." He motioned towards Hannes, who reluctantly pulled out a leather drawstring bag, extracted two gold coins out of it, and placed them on the table in front of the wide-eyed couriers.

"But what about the stone men?" Zinnia blurted out. "What will we say when we arrive home late? What's a cockatrice, and where did it come from? I don't think it died, what will you do about it?"

"Don't worry," Hannes said. "We shouldn't cause... how you say... a commotion in town."

One gold coin each? Aster had never owned this much money in his life. *I could buy a year's worth of honey-cakes.*

Fletcher dismissively waved his hand. "We'll take care of the beast and our men. It would be unwise for us to tell you more about the cockatrice. The less you know, the better... for your own safety. As for your delay, let's just say it was a wolf. Snuck into camp and caused a little commotion. That's what you should say to anyone who asks."

He took the coins off the table and gestured for the two to open their hands. After placing one gold coin in each of their palms, he said, "We will be visiting Buckwheat Village in two days for our regular shipment and I don't want to hear any mention of a monster or of stone men when we get there. Understand what I'm saying?"

Zinnia bit her lip. "But—"

Fletcher Abberton, of all people, knows how to handle a monster. "Yes sir. We'll keep it to ourselves."

"Well, you'd better get going or it'll be dark before you make it back." Fletcher shook both their hands. "And remember our agreement."

Aster directed Zinnia out of the house, making their way back towards the mountain stream that marked their path home.

Zinnia stopped to re-examine the stone men as they passed. She ran her finger across the man's hardened hair and asked, "Why are we keeping that monster a secret?"

Aster shook his head. "Probably to avoid a panic. It's gone now anyways. Fletcher and Hannes can handle themselves. Besides, not even Lavender would believe you."

"I don't know... that thing is dangerous. What if it comes back?"

"You're always such a worrier. There's no way we'll see a monster like that again." He tried to sound upbeat, but one look at Zinnia's terror-stricken face quieted him.

They walked down the worn path in silence. Two wide wagon-grooves in the ground cut through the underbrush.

Aster normally liked to keep an eye out for foxes, but not today. *Maybe Zinnia is right. After all, we did save them. Should Gilroy hear about what happened? But it's too late now, I've already given my word.*

"Do you think..." Aster trailed off as he looked at Zinnia. The beginnings of tears were forming in her brown eyes. "Hey, do you still have that nugget?"

She nodded but didn't look up from the bubbling stream beside their path.

"Fletcher found a fist-sized piece of gold in the stream around here. That's how the mine came to be."

Zinnia sniffled. "Everyone in Buckwheat knows that story."

"Well did you know that they had been exploring the Vesium Mountains for a different reason? They were after a gem that supposedly has power over nature itself."

"Always with the tall tales." Zinnia wiped her eyes. "But no, I haven't heard much of Fletcher's explorer days."

"It supposedly sits on the top of the Lost Peak. And Sir Ian Pelware's expedition was looking for it..." Aster rambled through the story for the rest of their journey back.

As the sun ducked behind the trees, Aster spotted the pale water of Buckwheat Lake through the foliage. They were home.

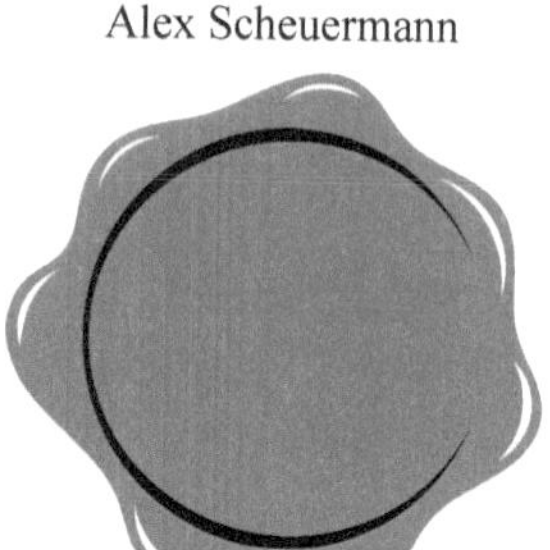

Beryl Rutherford,

It's been too long since I last wrote. Spring is finally here. Buckwheat Lake has melted, and we've started getting visitors again.

I had an experience today that I'm not sure about. Would you hide what happened to keep the peace? Or tell the truth and be a hero? I suppose it would be hard to prove and certain people would be angry. Why's it so difficult to make everyone happy? I guess you can tell which choice I made. What would you do?

Dad has been in poor health so I've been in charge of the postal service. Everyone says that I've been doing a good job, but it's tougher than I expected and dull at the same time. At least I get to leave Buckwheat from time to time.

Zinnia is well, but I think today frightened her. I said some things that I regret. It's been so long that the words just slipped out. She said nothing, but the look on her face was enough. I didn't mean to hurt her by picking at old wounds...

How are you doing? Have you made any new pieces that you're particularly proud of?

I'll write again soon.

Sincerely,
Aster Rutherford

2 THE QUARTERMASTER

Aster woke up and stretched in front of his window. The sun's rays sparkled across the lake as a ship with bright blue sails arrived at the docks. *Yesterday was unbelievable. If Zin wasn't with me, I'd have sworn I'd dreamed it all.* He shivered at the thought of the cockatrice's fanned wings. *I'll think twice before another delivery to Pelware.*

He wandered into the kitchen and made himself some honey-bread for breakfast. Aster swore he could taste a hint of crisp apple under the sweetness. Next batch would be even better once old man Gilroy's apple orchard was in full bloom.

On his way out the door, he picked up three silver coins his father had left out.

First stop was Rowan Goodwin's shop for herbs. Inside, Rowan was in the middle of conversation with a sailor from the Benia Trading Company. He was looking down his wrinkled nose at her. "My apologies, but we are running short of chamomile today."

The young woman sighed. Her tight auburn braid swayed as she put her hands on her hips. A short-bow and quiver of arrows rattled against her back. "You don't have any to spare? Whitlock will be disappointed..."

"Quite a few villagers are sick, and this is what we use to calm their stomachs."

"It's the captain's sleeping aid. What's wrong with the villagers anyways?"

Rowan bent down to rummage through a side drawer. "They've been complaining of numbness in their fingers. Sometimes they're too dizzy to walk straight. Stomach irritation, too. Hugo says it feels as if he's had too much mead."

Aster winced at the mention of his father's illness.

Rowan stood back up with a small bag in hand, eyes wide. "The villagers don't want to say it, but I know the truth—we've been cursed! Damn blue-eyed freaks from Jash did something. I'm sure of it!"

Aster joined them at the counter. "How could the people of Jash curse our village? They live about as far North-East as you can get. The Trading Company doesn't even ship that far."

"Aster, good timing. Your father's got it worse than most, so I'm sure you'll agree with my explanation. I reckon the blue-eyes cursed the snow way up in the mountains. Those pale skinned bastards have an unnatural affinity for the cold. A trek to the peaks is easy for them. They curse the snowfall and the winds blow it all the way here to Buckwheat Lake!"

Aster nodded. *Another one of Rowan's tirades. I should've kept my mouth shut.* "I just wish we could find some sort of cure for it."

Rowan calmed a bit. "It'd be best to find a doctor and bring him to town. Curse or not, my herbs can only dull the suffering."

The sailor turned. Freckles dotted her rosy face. Her arms were toned. "Actually, I know of a doctor from New Portsmith who may be able to help. We'd be happy to take you there if you'd like. It's our next stop."

"You're from the Benia Trading Company? I saw you

dock this morning."

"Yup, you're talking to the quartermaster of the Blue Skies and our ship has plenty of space. We can always use a little extra muscle, if you're willing to work." She looked him up and down with a playful grin.

Aster's cheeks flushed. "I appreciate your generosity, but I can't just leave Buckwheat Village. My father would be furious."

"But do *you* want to leave?"

Every day, Aster thought, but he felt Rowan's watchful eye and opted for a shrug.

"Suit yourself. But if you change your mind before midday tomorrow, come find me. I'll be at the Toasted Oak . Oh… and my name's Kara, nice to meet you." With a wave of her hand, she left the shop.

Kara. Aster stared after her until Rowan cleared his throat, holding out a pouch of finely ground chamomile, lavender, and poppy seeds. "Thanks. Dad will appreciate it."

"You're both welcome. A piece of advice before you go: Don't get mixed up with that sailor, no matter how pretty she may be. It'll take you away from Conflag's fiery path."

I doubt Conflag would fret. "I'll keep that in mind." Aster stopped with one foot out the door. "Wait, is Lavender around?"

Rowan's ever-present scowl deepened. "She's at home, in no shape for guests."

"Oh, I'm sorry. Tell her I said hello." Aster hurried to his next stop, the Buckwheat General Store.

The General Store was a charming place for young and old alike, located on the west side of town, close to the pier. An ideal spot for hauling supplies to and from the boats that dock there. The building's roof was high and slanted to one side. Two large windows enticed passersby from on opposite sides of a heavy wooden door. Aster could spend hours looking in at the jars of honey, rows of candles, and the other trinkets on the shelves. It was the most beautiful structure in all of Buckwheat, and one of the oldest.

He struggled to open the door. It was heavy, but Aster consoled himself with the suspicion that the hinge wasn't properly oiled.

"Hi Aster!" Zinnia's voice rang out from behind the front counter. "Dad is helping to load some crates onto the trading ship, so I'm in charge. No crazy adventures for me, at least not today."

Aster laughed. "Don't worry Zin, I'm here on official business. Has your father finished that wax stamp for us yet?" His eyes darted around the writing supplies. "I need a bundle of paper as well. Ink, too." *Dad would be in a foul mood if we ran out.*

Zinnia perked up. "Actually, he just finished it! This thing's a work of art. Dad even melted down that gold nugget for the accent on the handle." She carefully placed a hand carved letter seal on the counter. The handle was spruce with a small golden bee inset on one side. On the flat end, a simple honeycomb shape had been delicately carved into the surface. The letter 'B' sat in the middle; a bee atop its hive.

Aster turned it over in his hand, examining the craftsmanship. "It's beautiful."

"Aren't you glad I brought it back?" Zinnia grinned and puttered to the storeroom to grab the other supplies.

"I still don't approve," Aster shouted into the next room, happy she couldn't see his smile.

I just hope Dad will be around long enough to make use of it. Aster sighed. "Zinnia… I've been thinking about my father a lot lately. He has good days and bad days, but it is starting to seem like the bad days are coming more often. I wish there was something we could do about this illness."

"You've been saying that for months now. Last week you were complaining about Lavender being sick at home. I want everyone to get better, too, but what can we do? Rowan is the only one around with any sense for medicine."

"And he thinks it's a Jashian curse."

Zinnia peeked her head out from behind the door. "Is that impossible?"

"No, but... you know how he is with his superstitions."

"Unless you've a better idea, I'd believe a curse."

"There's a doctor in New Portsmith."

"New Portsmith?" Zinnia scoffed. "That's the other side of Benia! Are you gonna swim there yourself?"

"No," Aster conceded. "Maybe I'll send him a letter. Though it could be my chance to finally leave."

Zinnia handed him the paper and ink. "And you've been saying *that* for years."

"I'll figure out the details. But I'm already late, so I'd better get moving." Aster gave Zinnia three silver coins and placed the purchases into his messenger bag.

"Just don't ditch your postal duties for the next ship that docks."

He grinned and waved goodbye, heading out the door and down the dirt path.

The Village Postal Service was a small two-room building with a red sign under the eaves that read 'POST'. Inside the main room were two baskets, one labeled 'local' and the other 'foreign'. A small desk sat in the corner with stacks of parchment, two quills, and a bottle of black ink sitting on top.

Aster grabbed the bottle from the desk and held it up to the light, shaking it. He replaced it with the new one, then examined the contents of the baskets. 'Foreign' was empty. *Dad must've already given those letters to those sailors.* The basket labeled 'local' had three letters in it addressed to Buckwheat villagers.

In the back room he found his father sitting at a table reading an official-looking document. He was dwarfed by crammed bookshelves that crowded the room. Mostly dull books about politics or financial ledgers, but two of the shelves were dedicated to the absurd and fantastical: Aster's favorite since childhood.

"Good timing, we just received a tax report from the latest BTC shipment. Gilroy asked us to make two copies, one for his personal records, the other for the archive. Can you do that for me?" Hugo held out the paper.

Aster froze. Dad had never asked him to so much as touch a government document before. He'd always handled it himself, alone. In fact, he had lectured Aster for being in the same room while he was reading an official document.

"Aster?" The report quivered in his hand.

What's wrong? Aster's eyes darted to the wastebasket. It was full of crumpled paper, but he had cleaned it out yesterday. "Sure thing, Dad." He took the report, eyeing it suspiciously, but it turned out to be filled with boring tax calculations. "Did you need me to deliver those letters as well?"

"Please do. Did you pick up the supplies?"

Aster nodded. "Stopped by the General Store on the way here."

"So dependable, just like your mother..." He held out his hand.

Aster placed the seal stamp in it.

Hugo turned it over looking at the intricate design. "They really outdid themselves with this one. It's magnificent. A true symbol of Buckwheat. Use it well," he said, handing it back.

"For me?"

"Yup."

Aster stared at the gift. It had been almost a year since he started taking on his father's responsibilities—notarizing documents, mediating trades, and the other duties of a Postmaster. "Thanks, Dad." *I'm starting to be recognized. Even that curmudgeon, Rowan, can't help but admit that the village is better off with me in it.*

"Well, you have been. I couldn't have kept up with it all without you."

"I'd better get back to work, then." Aster stepped by the wastebasket and allowed the tax report fall to the floor.

"Oops," he muttered and swiped the topmost crumpled page from the basket while picking up the fallen sheet.

"See you tonight," he said, stepping out the door.

Outside he unfolded the discarded page. It looked like the tax report, but was riddled with illegible words and numbers. *He's getting worse.*

Aster spent the rest of the afternoon delivering letters, copying documents, and helping customers. Despite his worry, he found himself smiling. It wasn't every day that his father acknowledged his hard work. He couldn't wait for an excuse to use his new stamp, so he practiced his technique on a dozen blank pages. Each press into the molten wax felt divine—like he was a real Postmaster.

By the time Aster finished his postal work, the sun had set and the town was fading in the twilight. His thoughts drifted to the sailor he had run into earlier. *Kara. I should stop by the tavern and see if I can find her.* Truth be told, he didn't know much about New Portsmith. *At the very least, she'll be able to tell me about the doctor who lives there.*

Inside the Toasted Oak, he was welcomed with a cloud of smoke and the smell of alcohol. His stomach soured, reminding him why he didn't come here often. Polished logs supported the upper floor, rows of boxy lamps dangling underneath. There were a few rooms upstairs that Aster had never seen himself. Five tables surrounded a small stage where the local bard was singing 'The Fall of the Last Empire', a popular tune. The tavern was especially busy tonight, crowded with sailors.

Whitney Fulton was serving wine to a rowdy group at the closest table. At the bar, Don was handing stew to two more sailors. Aster waved to him before he recognized Kara's auburn braid—she was deep in conversation with a muscular man with blonde hair and a well-kept goatee.

Aster grabbed the stool next to her and waited for her

to notice him. Up close, he could see a dozen freckles scattered around her nose and two silvery studs in each of her ears. Her skin was slightly tanned, no doubt from all the time she spent in the sun.

Kara nearly jumped out of her seat, greeting him with a beaming smile. "Hey! Aster, right? Can't believe you decided to come along with us. Didn't really take you for the courageous type."

What a brash assumption. I might be the bravest person in Buckwheat. "Uhhh… not really. I was hoping you could tell me more about that doctor. Maybe I can send him a letter asking him to come to Buckwheat?"

Kara laughed. "Nothing but a guppy, ain't ya! First thing's first, I don't want to give you the wrong impression here. I'm no charity. How 'bout you buy us some of Buckwheat's famous mead and I'll tell you all I know about the guy."

"I've read all about New Portsmith, thank you!"

"If you say so." She mimed drinking from a cup.

Aster hesitated, then untied his coin pouch from his belt. He loosened the drawstring and dumped the contents onto the table. Two copper coins fell out with a thud.

Kara frowned. "You aren't going to get far with that kid. Three copper a pint for the good stuff."

Should I ask Don for a favor? No, that'd be embarrassing. He tapped his pockets in desperation and uncovered a single gold coin. *From Pelware—how'd I forget?* He triumphantly placed it on the table.

Kara's eyes lit up and she flagged down the barkeep, Don. "That's more like it! Barkeep, three pints of mead and a loaf of fresh bread!"

Don lifted the gold, turning it over in his hand until he was satisfied that it was real. He looked at Aster with eyes that asked how a postmaster's son came into gold, but said nothing. He shrugged, changing the coin with nine silver. "Coming right up."

Thrilled and horrified that he had spent so much money on booze, Aster slid the coins into his pouch with a hope that no more money would be squandered tonight.

Kara took a swig of the freshly poured mead and said, "Let me introduce you to my companion." She pointed to the blonde sailor on her left. "This here is Peter Keeton, first mate of the Blue Skies and the most skilled wielder of weapons this side of Munayallpa."

Peter looked Aster up and down, stroking his goatee. "You're not from around here. How'd you end up in this backwater village?"

"I get that a lot. My dad brought me here when I was a baby. Haven't left since."

"Hope you don't end up bein' a burden, Aster." He lifted his cup to his grizzled mouth, leaving Aster scowling.

Kara took the loaf of bread that Don brought back, breaking it in half. She offered a piece to Aster, who shook his head. "So, about the doctor... his name is Malvin, and he lives on the outskirts of the farming district in New Portsmith. His medical skills are legendary. They say he cured the city of a plague a few years back."

"Really?"

"I don't doubt it. I've seen his skills first-hand. During a delivery to El'tonne a few years back, Peter came down with a nasty ailment. I'll spare you the details—seriously gross, puss everywhere—by the time our ship arrived back in New Portsmith, Peter was on death's door. Our captain pulled some strings with the Council of Elders who connected us with Malvin. That man worked a miracle. As you can see, our Peter is still alive and kicking."

"Mostly." Peter shrugged.

"What would we ever do without you, Peter?" She elbowed him hard in the side.

"Probably nothin'. As in nothin' would get done."

Aster cut in. "If this doctor's as good as you say, we should summon him here. I'll draft a letter tonight describing our plight. Could you deliver it when your ship reaches New Portsmith?"

Peter lowered his cup, sloshing mead onto the table. "I wish it was that easy, kid. Malvin's been gettin' more reclusive as he's gotten on in years. He doesn't see just anyone."

"But—"

"What I'm tryin' to say is, if you send a letter, you won't hear back. You oughta go there in person and plead your case. Even if you get him to agree to help, what does this town have to offer him? I'm not sure there's enough gold in this entire village to pay for a doctor like him."

"How much does he charge? Like, ten gold?"

Peter choked back a laugh. "We don't come here for less than a fistful. And I ain't even a doctor."

The truth of that statement stung Aster. A single gold coin was the most money he'd ever owned. In the village, people traded with one another, but never with outsiders. *The Hollyhocks might be able to pay, what with all the visitors to the General Store. Or the Fultons because of this tavern. Would they though? Neither has someone sick.* Aster frowned into his full cup.

"Hey now, don't look so glum!" Kara broke his silence. "I doubt that old coot needs money anyways. Talk with Malvin first. Save the pouting for if he says no."

"I suppose you're right." Aster sighed. "I wasn't expecting it'd have to be in person… I need to talk this over with my father."

He listened to several boisterous sailors singing and clinking mugs. After a moment, he said, "The mayoral summit takes place in the capital and Gilroy will be there to represent Buckwheat. That sweet-talker can strike a deal with anyone. Maybe he can talk to the doctor." *The summit isn't until the autumn harvest, but the sick villagers are managing so far. In fact, Lavender has been complaining of numbness in her fingers since summer, so it's not like there's a rush.*

"Suit yourself," Kara said as she flagged Don over for another round.

Aster gulped down the last of his mead, happy to be

done with it. The flowery aftertaste dried out his tongue. He liked it slightly better than ale, and he'd bought it, so it would be a shame to waste.

He thanked Kara and Peter for their information and headed out of the tavern. *I'll talk to Gilroy tomorrow. A doctor is exactly what Dad needs... what everyone around here needs. Gilroy will take care of things, like he always does.* Aster strutted towards his house on the far side of the village.

The path was dimly lit, but Aster knew the way by heart. His mind drifted back to the cockatrice from the day before. He could hardly believe a monster like that existed, and he wouldn't if he hadn't seen it with his own eyes. *Are there other extraordinary creatures in this world? Beyond Buckwheat Village? Outside Benia? Maybe there are places in Arathanon where nobody has been, where countless monsters thrive.* His father's stories seemed more real than ever before. Goosebumps spread across Aster's arms; it was terrifying yet exciting.

A scream echoed across the buildings, ripping him from his fantasies. It was desperate—a call for help. Aster changed course, sprinting towards the shrill noise.

As he passed the last house on the east side of the village, he pinpointed the source; the clearing before the oak forest.

"Keep those white hands off me! Don't hurt me anymore!" A strained feminine voice rang out.

Beyond the lantern-light of the village, Aster could barely see. He began to run, trying to get there before it was too late. Every now and again he glimpsed a shadowy figure a few paces in front of him.

"The blue eyes are like ice! Burning my fingers! Burning my toes!" The voice was close.

"Stay away! Stay away..." It faded into sobbing.

Aster slowed to catch his breath. He could make out a tree or two of the forest. The figure that he had been trailing had stopped at the edge of the clearing. All of a sudden, light flooded into the scene. The shadowy figure had lit his lamp box.

Lying in the center was a teenage girl dressed in a beige nightgown. Aster recognized her—Lavender Goodwin. Her ever-present smile was twisted in pain. There were scratch marks running down her arms and legs and splotches of blood in her nightgown. Leaves tangled her long brown hair.

Aside from her, the clearing was empty, but the long shadows from the nearby forest played with Aster's fears. When the man with the lamp stepped closer, Aster recognized Rowan Goodwin's wrinkled face.

"By the fires of Conflag, what are you doing here, Aster? Did you see who did this to her?" Rowan asked with rage in his voice.

"No. I heard screaming, and I ran over to help. I think I was right behind you," Aster said defensively.

Rowan looked Aster up and down and then nodded. "Go help Lavender. I'll see if there's anyone lurking in the trees."

Aster hurried over to the girl. "You're safe now, Lavender." He grabbed some spare cloth from his bag and tied it around her bloodied arm. None of the injuries looked life threatening. "What happened?"

"Here before, here again, you can't stop them," Lavender replied. The light danced upon her bruised face as Rowan moved between the trees in his search.

"Who did this?"

Lavender flung her arm out, smacking Aster in the chest.

He flinched and let go as she started convulsing; legs kicking as if they were fending off invisible beasts, arms beating the ground.

Rowan hurried back over. "Conflag have mercy! Not again." He rushed to her side, supporting her head on his lap.

Is she going to be alright? Aster had never seen anyone so out of control. She was like a wild animal caught in a snare.

Rowan held Lavender tight until she stopped shaking. He relaxed his grip when she weakly squeezed his arm.

"This has happened before?"

"Twice before. Flailing and uncontrollable. This is the second stage of the curse. I wish I could've caught the bastards. To think the Jashians have infiltrated our forest… You heard her screaming about blue eyes, did you not? I told you it was them!"

"You mean this could happen to my father?"

"Not just him, but the whole village. I've been treating most everybody for the symptoms, but none have it as bad as my poor Lavender." Rowan looked down at his granddaughter again with concern. "Help me bring her home. I'll come back to the forest and search for Jashian footprints in the morning."

Each of them supported a shoulder of the weakened girl and helped her back to her house. It was late by the time they got Lavender cleaned up and in bed.

Aster hobbled home.

Sleep didn't come easy. He tossed and turned, trying to think of anything other than Lavender thrashing on the ground. *The same could happen to Dad. Why would anyone curse this village? Are the Jashians really involved?* He rolled over, trying to get comfortable. *What else would this curse do to a person? How can I stop this?* These questions rippled over and over in Aster's head.

I need to leave. I need to find help. Besides, I don't belong in Buckwheat. This is my chance to be anywhere else. Zinnia would come too, if I asked. Just as his thoughts stopped making sense, exhaustion overtook him, and he fell asleep. Monsters tormented his dreams. Strange men with white hands clawed at his legs. Giant birds chased him through desolate fields of sand. He tripped and fell into an ocean where no land could be seen.

Aster woke with a start, beads of sweat dripping down

his face. His feet were cold and wet. The birds outside called for mates; dawn was fast approaching.

He laid in bed until his back ached. It wasn't the uncertainty of leaving that kept him there, but the apprehension of actually going through with it. *I've got to leave and find that doctor. It can't wait till autumn.*

Shoving his belongings into his messenger bag, Aster gathered anything he could think of that he might need on a long journey. As he pushed the front door open, a voice called him back inside.

"Aster, you're not getting on that ship," Hugo said from the kitchen. "Zinnia told me that you're looking for a doctor. I appreciate your concern, but it isn't your responsibility."

Aster poked his head into the room and began to protest, but his father continued. "The world is a dangerous place. It'll chew you up and even if you manage to make it out, you'll be scarred for life. Mementos of your missteps." Hugo absentmindedly rubbed his knee, an old injury that never fully healed. He complained about it every chance he got.

"Dad, you know that I was always going to leave the village."

Hugo's face reddened. He stood, but collapsed back into his chair. "Aster, you're not going anywhere. Buckwheat Village is safe. Out there isn't."

Aster could feel his father's anger, even though the man looked pitiful. "I have to do this, for everyone but especially myself. I don't fit in with the villagers anyways. Remember when they refused to even look at me?"

"Are you still on about that? You won them over. You're part of Buckwheat just like everyone else." He gestured widely with his arm, but quickly let it drop. "Drop this fantasy. Don't go."

"This isn't a fantasy! I've got a reason, a greater purpose... This is my chance to help everyone—to be a hero!"

"I won't allow it."

"You can't stop me! Look at yourself. You can barely stand."

"Aster! If you leave, I can't protect you."

"I've been an adult for two years now. I don't need your protection."

Hugo slammed his arm on the table. "Then why do you still act like a child?"

Aster's head throbbed as he turned to leave.

"Wait." Hugo called through wheezing breaths. "I don't approve... but... if you have the chance you should visit your mother in Strongfair. It would do you both some good after all these years apart."

He never mentions Beryl. He must be worse off than I thought. "Uhhh sure. And... don't overwork yourself." Aster left with a wave.

That went better than expected. He walked down the path toward the docks, thoughts of his mother invading his thoughts. *What does somebody say to a parent they've never met?*

He brushed the thought away to focus on the task at hand. *One more stop before the ship, I'm going to convince Zinnia to come along.*

Outside the General Store he found Watson hauling a box of empty glass bottles.

"Zin's still at home," Watson said in a gruff voice.

Time was short, so Aster nodded and rushed across the street to the Hollyhock household. He burst through the door and found Zinnia eating pottage, spoon halfway to her mouth.

"Zinnia!" Aster exclaimed, barely inside the room. "So much happened yesterday, but what's important is that there is a doctor, Malvin, who could help the village. Please come with me to New Portsmith today to convince him!"

"Aster calm down. What's going on?" She placed the spoon back in her bowl and raised an eyebrow.

"I found Lavender thrashing in the woods last

night…." Aster sat down at the table beside Zinnia and told her the story of the day before.

Zinnia's face was pale. "You're sure it wasn't a monster?"

"No. There wasn't anything there." Aster rubbed his temples. "Despite what Rowan says, I think it's just a symptom of the illness."

"Poor Lavender… maybe I can convince Dad to cook for them tonight?"

"That would be nice. I'm sure Rowan would appreciate it. But aside from that." Aster looked at Zinnia expectantly. "Will you sail with me to New Portsmith to bring a doctor back to Buckwheat?"

"This is so sudden…" Zinnia bit her lip. "I…I can't," she stuttered. "After what happened at the mine, I could barely get myself out of bed. And besides, I freeze when I'm stressed. And now with Lavender…"

"But you were brilliant with the cockatrice!" Aster threw up his hands. "It just won't be the same without you. How can I possibly do this alone?"

"Sorry Aster… I… I'm sorry." Zinnia shook her head and looked at the floor. "To tell you the truth, that monster scared me so badly."

"Because of your mom?"

Zinnia squirmed in her seat.

"Sorry… I should've known. But I thought I'd ask."

"I don't think I'd be much good if something scary happened again. The nightmares I've been having are bad enough without a sea monster joining in." She forced a smile.

"It's alright. You've got plenty to take care of here. You can be our base of operations in the village! We need somebody to look after things while I'm away and you are the perfect person for that job. I'll write you every chance I get." Aster returned her smile and added, "I'll be back before you know it."

He left before she could notice his disappointment. *I've just got to do this alone. Zinnia can't always fight my battles for me. Besides, it's unfair for me to expect her to come—she's always been more of a homebody. I'm an idiot for bringing up her mom again.*

Aster had only taken ten paces toward the docks when he heard his name being called.

"Wait up." Fletcher waved him down. "Where are you off to in such a hurry?"

"Actually, I'm on my way to New Portsmith." He stood taller, whether it was to convince Fletcher or himself of his readiness, he wasn't sure.

"Wow, I didn't think the Buckwheat Postal Service delivered letters that far south."

Not wanting to get into a discussion, Aster cut the explanation short. "Special request. Very important."

"It's a coincidence, but could you do me a huge favor? I've got a letter for a woman named Calantha in the market district of New Portsmith. Could you deliver it while you're there? I was planning to hire a courier, but since you're heading that way." Fletcher's voice lowered to a whisper. "And based on the incident with the cockatrice, I know you're trustworthy." He offered the letter discreetly, keeping it close to his body until Aster reached for it.

"I guess I can do that." Aster agreed, tucking the letter into his bag.

"You're a lifesaver! Come find me when you get back. A delivery like this is worth five gold at least. I'll make sure it's worth your time. Oh, and one more thing. Don't tell anyone. Got it?"

"Why…" Aster looked towards the docks, where the last of the supplies were being loaded onto the Blue Skies. "Never mind. I understand."

"Thanks Aster! I really appreciate it." Fletcher concluded their exchange with a nod.

Aster hurried to the ship. It was a grand vessel with light blue sails furled as it sat aside the village pier. Its figurehead was odd: A whirlpool with a menagerie of fish caught in the flow. The hull looked almost new and there was hardly a barnacle in sight, as if it had just completed its maiden voyage.

Next to the ship, he found Kara counting barrels on the docks. "Well, well, well! Guppy decided to leave his pond after all?" she said, half paying attention to Aster.

"Yes. Please take me to New Portsmith to find Malvin."

"Sure thing. Welcome aboard the Blue Skies. Let me introduce you to the most important person on the ship." She waved over a clean-shaven man with jet black hair, cut nearly to his scalp. "Aster, meet Patrick Bartlett, our cook." She clapped him on the shoulder affectionately.

He reached his hand out to Aster and said, "Everyone calls me Pat. If you have a hankering for a snack, come find me."

Kara nudged Aster up the gangplank. "Now hop on. You'll meet the captain in a few days when we pick him up. Oh, and for payment, we've got plenty of chores around the ship. We'll get some muscle on those arms in no time." She winked at Aster as he boarded.

The Blue Skies looked even bigger up close. Two masts jutted out of the main deck, which seemed like they could touch the clouds. Crates and barrels of all shapes and sizes were strapped down with heavy ropes and netting. Aster got goosebumps as he marveled at the sailors scurrying about.

Zinnia Hollyhock,

It's only been a week since I left, but I've decided to write to you about my travels.

Riding on a merchant ship is an unusual experience. It's as if an entire town is living together inside one floating house. The sailors spend most of their days drinking, gambling, and teasing each other, but I've no interest in those kinds of things. Aside from that, there isn't much to do since the lake is calm and the currents are steady. The sailors keep telling me to enjoy it while it lasts, but I'm not sure what to make of that.

We are taking a short break in Aylesbury before we begin down the Haverhein River. Mostly for food, but I saw them load lumber as well. Aylesbury reminds me of home, except with more fish and less honey, so a bit disappointing. I ran into a fisherman that was heading to Buckwheat Village to sell some goods and he offered to bring this letter to you. I hope it finds you well.

Please keep my father in good spirits while I'm away and keep an eye on Lavender. If you help Dad deliver letters from time to time, he'd appreciate it. Even if he won't admit it, he can't manage alone. I'll find the doctor as soon as we reach the city and be home before you know it.

Your friend,
Aster

3 THE DOCTOR OF NEW PORTSMITH

The Blue Skies drifted towards the mouth of the Haverhein River. Without wind in the square sails atop its mast, the waves slowly rocked the boat back and forth in the light of the evening.

Once Aster had gotten situated, he realized how beautiful the ship was. It was a 80-foot-long cargo vessel with a mostly flat hull. Kara had said that the Trading Company ships were designed for river travel, but they would sail coastal waters too—provided the weather was good.

The crew was in no rush to proceed; they were preoccupied with the latest round of coin drop.

"C'mon Aster, stop being so stingy with yer coin," Carter, one of the rowers, egged him on. He couldn't have been much older than Aster, but his muscles bulged through his sleeves. It made Aster feel inadequate.

"You've been watching us play for hours now. Might as well try your luck," said Kara, holding out a plain brown cup to Aster.

"Fine. I'll try once." Aster scooted close to their table. "Though I'm sure I'll just lose my coin."

Kara laughed. "That's what I like to hear!"

Aster cautiously eyed the items on the table. "Explain

the rules to me one more time."

"Coin-drop is simple: You take five coins and drop them in the cup. Put your hand on top, shake it, and then flip it onto the table. The winner is the one with the most coins stamp side up. In a tie, we re-cup and flip again."

Aster took five copper coins from his bag and tried his luck. Slowly he pulled the cup off the table, his hand trembling from excitement and fear. Every coin showed the letters 'BTC'.

"Blast it! Loctee smiles upon you today." Carter said as he revealed two stamps while Kara only had one.

Aster grinned triumphantly and scooped all the coins on the table to his side. "I suppose I could play another round." Coins jingled on the table as the three of them played again. "Tell me about Loctee. In Buckwheat we rarely hear about the other gods."

"The great wanderer," Kara replied. "Didn't you see him on the bow of our ship?"

"A swirl of water is your god? I'd expect something more menacing. Like the Divine Conflagration, who spreads his heat and light as far as the eye can see." Aster pulled back his cup, four stamps this time.

"Once we make it to the ocean, you'll get a taste of what Loctee is capable of," Carter grumbled as he showed two coins with letters face-up.

Kara shook her head. "If you believe all that god nonsense."

From atop a stack of supply crates, a voice interrupted their conversation. "Conflag is just some bird."

Aster looked up at the middle-aged man with an impeccably kept blonde mustache. "Not just any bird, a vulture. The Divine Conflagration is an ancient spirit who lives inside the sun. He was so wise and so powerful that he lifted himself up through the sky and landed there unscathed. He radiates energy and warmth to all living things." Aster grinned as he revealed five stamps.

"Spoken like a priest. Didn't think they had schooling in those backwater towns."

"My dad taught me everything I know."

"Except sarcasm, clearly."

"Stop it, Tristram." Kara scowled at him.

The man scoffed and leaned back with his feet up.

"Don't mind Tristram. He's always in a foul mood. That aside, you did say something interesting," Kara said. "You know how to read. The captain can, but the rest of us never learned. How about you give us a few lessons? We'll consider it payment for taking you to New Portsmith. Quartermastering would be easier if I could read ledgers. People are always trying to stiff me."

"Sure, I know a thing or two. My dad practically taught our entire village, so I know a few teaching tricks. Especially if that means I don't have to come up with gold for payment." *My luck continues!* "Alright, one more round and then I'm done for the night."

"Better make it double then!" Carter slapped the table. "Give me a shot to reclaim my losses." The trio began their final round of coin-drop with ten coppers each.

Aster had one more thing on his mind before heading to his bunk. "The plan is for us to pick up the captain tomorrow morning before we make it to the Haverhein, right? What's he doing in the middle of nowhere anyways? Why isn't he already onboard?"

"Curious about Captain Whitlock?" Kara said, placing her cup onto the table. "To be honest, we don't know either. Only that he had business to take care of."

Carter cut in with a laugh, "Rumor is that he's visiting a lady friend! Pat says he saw the capt'n talking up some traveler a few weeks back, when we were drinking at the Beached Whale. Best pub in all of Benia, by the way. She wasn't much to look at, a portly lass, but she gave ole Whitlock loads of attention. They left together and we didn't see the capt'n again till the next day. Since we were passing by her place, he had us drop him off for a few days and do our pickup in Buckwheat without him. Lazy sod, but I can't fault him for stopping." Aster and Carter had their cups on the table as well now.

"I see." Aster lifted his cup to show the stamps of six coins. "What kind of man is Captain Whitlock?"

Carter grimaced as he revealed three face-up coins. "The capt'n is a good man. Quick to anger, but he's reliable. He makes this whole trading operation run smooth. It'd take four men to do the work he does for the BTC."

Kara lifted her cup showing five stamps. "Son of a sea-snake! Good man when he's not slacking. You'll get to meet him in the morning. But let's keep this drinking and gambling to ourselves. The captain would give us a hard time if he knew—says it only causes fighting."

"Sure." Aster scooped his winnings off the table with a yawn. "I'm off to bed now, we'll have to play again sometime."

"Loctee will be on my side next time," Carter grumbled.

Aster jumped into his bunk and fantasized about filling his pouch fat with coins, before drifting off.

He awoke the next morning to the sounds of sailors scurrying about on deck. He dressed quickly and left the living quarters, to see what the commotion was about.

The crew had dropped anchor and the Blue Skies had come to a stop. Less than a hundred meters away, Aster could see the bank of the lake.

This spot was overgrown with shrubs and grasses hanging over the edge of the water. Amid the dense foliage, four boulders sat half submerged. Kara and Pat climbed into a rowboat and paddled to shore. Just as they reached the nearest rock, a man walked up to them.

He was twice as wide as the other sailors, with long black hair tied back, and a navy-blue coat that reached his knees. Kara and Pat saluted him, then they all hopped into the rowboat and made their way back to the ship.

The man approached Aster after boarding. "You must be Aster. Name's Wilbur Whitlock. Good to meet ya."

Kara peeked her head over the side of the ship as she climbed the rope ladder. "I told the captain that we'd take you to New Portsmith."

"Aster… best you keep to your bunk. I'd feel bad if a kid like you got into trouble. Shipping vessels aren't the safest of places." He considered Aster for a moment, before barking orders to his crew to pick up the pace. The mood onboard shifted, and everyone set to work with haste. After the rowboat and the anchor were pulled out of the water, the Blue Skies sailed once more.

Aster caught up with Peter as the first mate was throwing a weighted rope off the side of the ship. "Is there anything I can do to be useful?" Aster asked, as he looked overboard, curiously.

"Hmmm… I guess you could help me with the soundin' line. Not that I really need the help. Actually, why don't you scour the deck with the holystones? That'll give you some salt." His rope went slack, and he muttered to himself, "Still pretty deep here," then he began pulling the rope back out of the water, wrapping it around his arm.

Aster scratched his head. "What are holystones? And what do I need salt for?"

Peter chuckled. "It's a type of sandstone. You use it to clean the wooden planks. It's tough work, but hard to mess up."

"Sure, I'll do it!" Aster looked around for the holystones.

"We keep 'em below deck. Across from the bunks. Kara can show you, if you have trouble."

Aster bounded down the stairs and returned with the sandstones, thankful he found them quickly. "Is this how you do it?" He got on his knees, rubbing the stone back and forth across the deck.

Peter looked over. "Yeah, good enough. Be sure you scrape with the grain of the wood." He threw his rope back into the water. "I'll be impressed if you finish scrubbing this side of the ship by nightfall."

Many hours passed as the ship made its way down the Haverhein River. Aster was drenched in sweat and his arms felt like jelly. He had only gotten halfway done with scrubbing—due to ample breaks. *I hope this earned me a bit of credibility.*

The forest began to thin out as they rounded a bend. A series of large marble pillars surrounding a flat-topped hill came into view. Most of the pillars were heavily worn. Some were missing altogether. When she saw the structure, Kara skipped to the bow of the Blue Skies and said, "Captain, can we stop here for the night? Last landmark before the sea."

"And yer favorite spot. Drop anchor. We rest here for the night," Captain Whitlock bellowed.

Kara clapped her hands together. "Pat, cook up some of the trout we caught this morning!"

Pat stuck his head out from the galley. "Sure thing. If I remember correctly, wild ramsons grow in this area. That'll add a bit of flavor."

They anchored near the shore and the crew marched around the deck grabbing supplies and preparing the rowboat. Tristram jumped off the side into the water. Aster had tried speaking to him twice since they met, but each time he'd come up with one task or another that needed to be done immediately.

Kara had shrugged it off when he asked. "A ship's carpenter is always busy," she said, but Aster didn't think that was a good enough reason for the cold shoulder.

Pat held Aster back from the rope ladder. "Mind helping me with the perch? Can't carry it all by myself." He led Aster to one of the oak barrels in the hold. It was filled to the brim with water and contained more than a dozen live perch. The two of them gathered the fish and brought them to the kitchen to clean.

Pat motioned in the direction of the shore with a butcher knife he'd just grabbed off the table. "Now could you start a fire for me out there? I'll join you as soon as I've gutted these things. Would be a great help."

"Sure, I'll get right to it." Aster replied as he hurried back to the deck. He had been growing bored of the daily life on the ship and was excited to be able to explore the ruins before nightfall.

When Aster made it to shore, he gathered some tinder and sticks from underneath a grove of trees on the opposite side from the ruins. In the center of the pillars, there was a ring of stones surrounding a pit of ashes. This wasn't the first time this place had been used for a fire. Aster placed the wood he had gathered into a tepee shape on top of the ashes. He was satisfied with his design, but didn't have a way to light the fire. *Better ask Kara for a light.*

He found her beside one of the well-preserved marble pillars.

"Hey Aster, look at this. It always fills me with a sense of wonder." She directed him to an upright stone slab with an elaborate scene carved into its surface.

Sections had been chipped away, but Aster could just make out a faded blue orb in the middle. Small lines radiated out from it towards many unusual looking creatures. One appeared to be a goat with many horns, another looked like a large beetle. A set of long wings missing it's body in a hole near the stone's edge. On the bottom right side, one of the animals looked like the cockatrice he had encountered at the Pelware Mines.

"What does it all mean?" he asked.

Kara shook her head, "The people that built this place disappeared hundreds of years ago, and so nobody knows exactly. Could be that in the center is the Odyllic Stone. It's funny how some myths persist across generations."

"There's something written here." Aster pointed to a few marks chiseled into the corner. "But I can't seem to read it."

"Looks Munayallpan."

"Can you read it?"

She laughed. "Not a word."

"But..." Aster shrunk back.

"Just cause I can recognize the letter of the BTC's biggest trading partner doesn't mean I can understand this scrawl."

"Can anyone in the crew translate?"

"Nope. Captain knows a lick of Tonné, but the rest of us are un-learned as they say."

Aster hung his head. "Too bad... wonder what it says."

Kara just shook her head.

Anyways, I've got a job to do. Can't disappoint Pat. "Can you give me a light?"

After the campfire had burned a while and the coals were hot, Pat brought over the trout. One by one he stuffed them with wild ramson leaves and skewered them on long pointed sticks. When he was finished, he placed them flat above the hot coals and periodically turned them for an even roast.

In the meantime, Pat simmered a thick herbal sauce in an iron skillet. The crew ate well that evening and talked a bit more about the people who built the ruins.

Zinnia would like this place. Aster thought back to the times when they marveled at the foreign architecture from his father's books.

Peter had walked away from the rest of the crew for a few seconds when his booming voice called from the riverbank. "PIRATES! Protect the ship!"

The crew jumped to their feet and rushed towards the Blue Skies. Sure enough, two torches waved back and forth on the deck of the ship.

Captain Whitlock was already in the rowboat, halfway back. Peter dove into the water, swimming to join him in defending the ship.

With the captain and first mate gone, Kara took charge of the rest of the crew. "Looks like they've already taken out our guards, so the rest of you lot better get swimming! If we lose the ship here, we're done for!"

There was a yelp from behind. Aster turned around just in time to see Carter clutching at his chest as the blade of a saber pierced through him. Blood trickled down, glistening in the twilight. Once the pirate withdrew the sword, Carter crumpled to the ground.

Aster screamed. He had never been more terrified in

his life. There was too much happening all at once.

The pirate took a few steps closer to him and brandished his saber, shining with blood, enjoying Aster's fear.

Aster wondered how he kept getting himself into situations like this. He was a postmaster's son, not a warrior. He didn't know the first thing about how to defend himself. "Run. Run. Run." He repeated to himself over and over until his legs wobbled. He took two steps backwards and then turned to run back to the pillars.

It was too late: The pirate grabbed Aster's wrist, a vice-grip holding him in place.

"I'll give you anything you want, don't hurt me!" Aster cried out.

The pirate replied in a gruff voice, "I'm taking your gold and your life." He pointed his sword at Aster's chest.

A twang echoed from somewhere behind Aster. He cried out as a searing pain cascaded up his left arm. *I'm dead. I'm dead. I'm dead. Conflag warm me.*

He looked down, surveying the damage. He was whole —aside from a deep gash in his arm. *I'm not dead. The pirate missed his mark.*

The pirate seemed distracted, but he lifted his blade once again.

Aster ducked, using his good arm to block his face. Instead of another blow, he heard a twang and the saber crashed to the ground. The pirate clutched at fresh arrow feathers sticking out of his shoulder and backed away, disappearing into the woods.

Kara ran up, bow in hand. "Shit, Aster, you alright?"

His shirt had a gaping hole, and his arm was crimson. The grass underneath him was wet with blood. Aster opened his mouth to respond, but his head swam. He stumbled, feet tangling and fell sideways into the dirt.

Kara pulled Aster up and ripped off the rest of his

sleeve for a makeshift tourniquet. She tied it tight across his bicep. "Don't die on me Aster," she muttered before rejoining the fray. She needed to deal with these pirates before she could help him further. *Drown pirates. Ruthless bandits with no consideration for others.*

There were skirmishes all around. At least a dozen pirates had ambushed them on the shore. They needed to secure the beach quickly and get over the Blue Skies. *How'd they find out about the gold?*

Pat was closest to her, his back against one of the marble pillars. He was barely defending himself with his cast iron skillet, deflecting two pirates' swords with the thick metal. He looked pathetic, but then again, he never claimed to be a fighter. Most of the time, he would hide in the galley if things got heated on the ship.

Good thing I'm here, then. Kara drew her bow and fired.

The arrow grazed the chest of one of the assailants, turning his attention to her. He had scars all over his face with an especially deep groove across his left cheek.

She fired two more shots, but the man ducked them as he approached.

If it was anyone but Pat, her arrows would have flown true. *Deep breaths. Calm down.* Kara dropped her bow and pulled a knife from the sheath at the small of her back.

The pirate swung his cutlass at her; Kara stepped back each time. *Focus on this one. Pat will be fine now that there's only one of them.* She needed to find an opening, but it felt like fishing in a puddle against his long blade.

Pat was able to capitalize on her distraction. He slipped to the other side of the pillar and dove for the fire pit. The charred sticks, left over from dinner, were scattered around. Pat grabbed one in each hand.

He's fighting with sticks? Kara sighed. If she didn't know better, she'd have sworn he'd lost his mind. But Pat was smarter than he let on… usually.

The pirate had followed him to the center of the stone

platform, laughing.

Pat bellowed as he charged, trying to skewer the pirate. But the man deflected the makeshift spear with his sword and broke it with his empty hand.

He threw the broken piece in the pirate's face, knelt, and stabbed the other spear into his thigh, causing the man to howl in pain.

The pirate whimpered as he pulled the wood out of his leg.

But Pat was already on him. His elbow smashed into the man's nose, who dropped the sword in surprise.

Then Pat had the sword in hand, brandishing it menacingly. "Leave or I'll roast you next."

"Shit on the plan, this was supposed to be easy coin." The pirate limped backwards into the darkness.

Kara glanced in the other direction to see that Tristram had stationed himself on the riverbank, preventing the pirates from swimming to the ship. With a flaming tree branch in hand, he thrashed at the pirates each time they got close. After a few attempts, they had enough of Tristram and split, running in opposite directions. He could only chase after one, so the other dove into the water, heading towards the Blue Skies.

I need to take control. With Whitlock and Peter both heading to the ship, we need a leader here, on shore. She dropped down to her knees after the scarred pirate swung, thrusting her knife into his leather boot. She'd have to thank Pat for that idea.

His body shook with pain and rage. As he leaned down to pull the blade from his foot, Kara sprung up, driving her elbow into his chin. Stunned, he fell to the ground and dropped his cutlass, which Kara picked up and placed against his throat.

"Call them off," she growled.

The pirate grumbled something unintelligible.

"I said, call them off or die," she ordered once more, pressing the blade further into his neck. *Don't call my bluff.*

"… Fine. I'll do it," the grizzled pirate muttered in a guttural accent. He took a deep breath and yelled, "Retreat! Retreat!"

The remaining pirates around the camp froze and without a second thought, fled to the forest.

Kara looked around, content with her victory. "One more thing before I let you go, who are you and what were you after?"

His jaw clenched, pointing in the direction of the river. "Liosam. We're after yer gold, 'course."

She removed the blade from his throat.

He backed away, then turned and ran to the thicket.

She let out a deep sigh. *I'd thank Loctee's luck… if I believed in that nonsense.*

Aster woke up in his bunk on the Blue Skies. His head was spinning, and his arm, now wrapped in a clean bandage, throbbed.

Pat was sitting beside him. He looked over when Aster came to, his brow furrowed. "Feeling alright, Aster?"

"Not really. What happened to the pirates?"

Pat tapped his fingers on a mug filled with water. "Drink this. Will help with the blood loss."

Aster took it and gladly sipped.

"Kara worked some miracles, that's what. She and not only managed to save you and me, but also beat their leader in a fight and forced him to call for a retreat. I'm shocked how well it went, given her principles and all."

"What do you mean?" Aster asked after his second swallow.

"Kara doesn't kill. It has to do with her father… uh it's better if she told you herself. Not my place."

"Oh…"

"But back to the pirates, the group that we tussled with on the beach was a diversion while the others commandeered our ship. They'd somehow gotten wind of our gold. But by Loctee's Luck, Peter and Capt'n were able to throw them off. A feast worthy victory… except for poor Carter."

Pat rubbed his eyes. "He was too young. We gave him a water burial. May Loctee bring him calm seas."

Aster felt a pit in his stomach. When Kara and Pat were busy Carter had taken it upon himself to keep Aster company. His first friend on the Blue Skies… dead. *I guess Dad wasn't lying about the dangers.* "I'm so sorry. Carter was a good guy."

"A fine sailor, too. He'll be missed."

Aster winced as he propped himself up, swinging his legs off the bunk.

Pat scowled at him. "Where do you think you're going? Should take it easy. Can't have you collapsing up on deck."

He reluctantly pulled his legs back in. "My arm's not too bad." Another look from Pat silenced his protests.

Aster stayed put for about three hours before deciding that he'd waited long enough. He left the sleeping quarters to see how the rest of the crew was doing.

Tristram was pacing in front of the captain's quarters, inspecting the door for damage. When he noticed Aster, he smirked. "How you feeling, Lantern? Glad we didn't have to amputate that arm."

"Who's Lantern?"

"You."

"Huh? What're you talking about?"

"Not too bright and you need to be carried." Tristram chuckled to himself.

Aster clenched his teeth and pushed past him. *Jerk. What did I do to deserve that?*

Kara was at the stern, gazing out on the gentle current of the river that pushed the Blue Skies forward. She had a small brass compass in her hand and was deep in thought.

"Thanks for saving my life earlier," Aster said as he put his hands on the railing next to her.

Kara spoke with melancholy in her voice. "I'll always

do what I can to protect our crew. After a scrap like that, you're crew too."

"Tristram doesn't think so. He's calling me Lantern."

Kara chuckled. "Okay that's pretty clever. Didn't think he had a funny bone in his body."

"Can I ask you something?"

Kara shifted her gaze from the water.

"I felt like a burden today. Back there, I froze. I didn't know what to do. Can you teach me how to fight?"

She looked him up and down before responding, "No."

Aster's mouth fell open.

Kara couldn't help but crack a smile as she continued, "I'm rubbish at teaching. But Peter's a top-notch fighter. We'll convince him to show you the basics." She pocketed the compass and led Aster down the steps.

They found Peter in the captain's quarters. He was hunched over a map of the river, plotting their course. The room was decorated more than the rest of the ship. Five wooden chairs sat atop an intricate blue rug. A saber was mounted to the wall above a locked chest in the corner.

"Plotting landfall in New Portsmith?" Kara slid into one of the chairs.

Peter muttered, "Looks like we lost a half-day at the ruins, but we ought to make it to the capital in a week. Should be plenty of time for the delivery."

"Good to hear. The BTC would beach us otherwise."

She motioned Aster forward. "We were hoping that you could help train Aster to fight. He wants to be able to defend himself after... you know..." She pointed at his bandaged arm.

Peter looked up from his map with one eyebrow raised. "Bad idea."

"C'mon. We haven't even reached the sea and he's already got a battle-wound. Call it a favor to me."

"If ya say so. Got a weapon in mind?"

"I've always wanted to learn how to use a broadsword," Aster blurted out excitedly. "I've read a few stories about Picari the Lionhearted who always carried one around with him."

Kara laughed. "We don't have any broadswords on the ship. They're pretty useless onboard 'cause even if we get into a scuffle. Not much room to swing a two-hander."

"How 'bout we start with a knife?" Peter pulled out his blade and laid it on the table. "Good for lots more than fightin'. Dawn tomorrow, we'll start trainin'."

"Thanks so much! You won't regret it."

"I already do." Peter shook his head. "But since Kara's agreein' to take over my helmsman duties…"

Kara shook her head no.

"I won't have time otherwise."

She sighed. "Fine… but Aster: You owe me."

Aster nodded, smiling. He owed her more than he could ever think of repaying. *If only everyone was as kind.*

The sky was still dark as Aster made his way onto the deck of the ship. He'd nearly fallen out of his bunk, dreaming about swinging around a broadsword. Back home his father wouldn't let him near anything sharper than a letter opener.

Peter had moved a few barrels out of the way to give them extra space for practice, but it was still cramped. Like everywhere on the ship, space was for storage. If there was room to move about, it was because the sailors needed quick access to some pulley or compartment.

"Good, you're up. While the sun is risin', I'll give ya the basics."

Aster nodded. He was only half awake and practically all his muscles were stiff from the day before. Not to mention his arm, which he dared not move.

Peter slid a knife off the nearest crate and handed it to him. The handle had a reddish hue beneath its deep brown. The blade was straight and about the size of Aster's hand. "You can keep this. I've collected plenty over the years. Won't miss it."

Peter began by showing Aster how to hold the weapon. "You've gotta treat the blade like part of your body. More you use it, the more it'll be that way. Now try to use the blade to block mine." As he slowly moved his dagger forward, Aster jerked his sideways, crashing into the other knife.

Aster's injured arm screamed, and the knife dropped. The blade pierced the deck near his feet.

Aster held his breath and stared at Peter wide-eyed.

"Welp. That coulda been bad. Gotta hold it tight. It's a part of you now." Peter said cautiously, watching Aster cradle his arm. "On second thought, let's focus on your footwork for now."

"Most've the time, footin' wins a fight anyways," he added. "Stay on the balls of your feet and take a step forward for me."

Aster did.

"Now back."

"What's the point of this?"

"Step back."

Aster pulled his feet together.

"Again," Peter commanded, leaning back on the barrels.

Aster stepped forward and back once again.

"Quickly this time."

"Can you please tell me why we are doing this?"

"I'm trying to judge your balance and quickness. And to be honest, you're as graceful as a beached whale. But that's nothin' that practice can't fix. Now quit yappin' and start movin'."

It took over an hour before Aster felt confident with the movement. At this point Peter added the next step, trying to throw Aster off balance. After a tumble and a bruised shin, he got the hang of it. They weaved and dodged each other's blows until it looked like they had mastered some bizarre dance.

Finally, Aster had had enough and stopped them. His

body was exhausted, so he sat down with his back to a barrel to take a well-deserved break.

Peter leaned over him. Aside from a bit of sweat, he didn't look tired at all. "So, you've takin' a shine to Kara?" Peter asked as Aster caught his breath.

"She's been kind to me, but to be honest, I don't really know a thing about her."

"I know a bit of her past. She grew up on a farm outside of New Portsmith. Her family sells what they can in the city, but they're still very poor. When Kara lived with them, she'd help her uncle with organizin' the harvest and bringin' it to sell at market."

"Really?" Aster couldn't picture her working on a farm.

"I reckon that's why she's so skilled with her quartermaster duties. Loads of practice back home. Her little sister, Janna, is—as they say—gifted. Kara joined the BTC to help pay for her schoolin'. In any case, don't think she's got a man back home, so you're welcome to try your luck."

Aster's face went scarlet. He stood. "Thanks for the lesson. I'll rest up a bit and we can get back to it tomorrow." He backed away, tripping over a coil of rope, as Peter smirked. Catching himself on the railing, he avoided falling on his face, but his wounded arm screamed from the sudden movement.

"Loctee drown me. Not only useless in a fight, but also an expert at getting in the way."

Aster hadn't noticed Tristram sitting cross legged behind him, hands busy with rope. "Oh, sorry Tristram. What're you doing here?"

"Splicing." He held up the frayed ends in his hand. "Those pirates cut a few of our lines so I've got to fix 'em," he grumbled.

"Anything I can help with?" Aster asked, scooting the coil of rope back towards Tristram.

"You know what a fid is?"

Aster shook his head.

"How 'bout tapering?"

Again, Aster shook his head.

"Any knots? The bowline perhaps?"

Aster shrugged.

"No? Then get out of my way, Lantern. I swear one of these days I'll have enough coin for that house. Then I'll never have to deal with this shit again."

Peter burst out laughing. "With our wage, you'll be an old man before that happens. Aster, don't worry about him, he's always like this. Come find me in the mornin' and we'll pick up where we left off."

Aster slinked back to his bunk and lay down, closing his eyes. *I can't do anything right on this ship. They're all so crass. What can I do to get these sailors to like me?* He considered it for a while until his thoughts drifted back to home. *Dad would've known what to do. He always did. Back before he got sick, he used to read to us—Zinnia, Lavender, and all the others in front of the fire until late at night. I miss that.*

Aster and Peter continued to practice each morning for six days as the ship meandered down the calm waters of the river. In the evenings, he had a few of the crew join him for reading lessons—his only skill that interested the others.

Aster wrote letters on loose paper from his messenger bag. One by one he flashed them to the crew, reciting each. "And this one is S. It makes a *sssss* or *shhhh* sound like in sailor or ship. Sometimes it makes a *zuuhh* sound like in treasure. Oh and it can make a *zzzzz* sound too. Like in poison or music."

Kara ran her hand down her braid. "How do you know which to use when?"

"It's not easy. Most of the time, I've heard the word before I've read it, so I can remember which sound it used. Other times, I'll get it wrong and Dad would correct me."

Tristram grumbled. "Yer dad ain't here, Lantern. Not much good to us now." The others nodded in agreement.

"Why isn't it simpler?" Kara asked. "Why not one sound per letter?"

"Uhhh... I'm not so good with the history. But Dad would say that Benian is a thief's language."

Kara tensed up. "That's awful."

"No, not like that. He says that it took words from several other languages and mixed them all together. That's why sometimes it's one way and others it's different."

"Like Munayallpan?"

"Yeah. I guess."

Tristram shook his head. "I think I'll leave the reading to the captain. Lantern's teaching skills are just not good enough for us *uneducateds*."

Aster scowled as Tristram went below deck. A few joined him, but others stayed for the rest of the lesson.

Kara picked reading up quickly, but the others struggled. She kept the papers from Aster after each session and continued to practice by herself. By the end of the week, most everyone was able to read simple words for objects found around the ship.

The Haverhein River widened as the Blue Skies approached the Sea of Loctee. The first thing Aster noticed was the faint sulfurous smell: It reminded him of finding an abandoned blue jay egg as a child. After one week of caring for it in the place of its mother, Aster accidentally crushed it. The egg was rotten, explaining why it had been abandoned, but the scent lingered in Aster's memory.

This smell was slightly different—less putrid. It emanated from streams that had split off, creating small islands filled with greenery. The cries of water birds alternated between the grasses which grew taller than a full-grown adult in places.

The captain carefully maneuvered the ship to the

center of the main flow as they weaved back and forth. Eventually the green islands were replaced with sand banks and Aster was able to see the bottom of the river in places. He marveled at the skill of the crew in handling such treacherous terrain, where one wrong move could beach their vessel. The Blue Skies picked up speed as the river widened.

"Low tide must be in an hour or so," Kara mentioned to Aster.

"How can you tell?"

"The strength of the current. And the depth of the water here. If it was closer to high tide, most of these sand banks would be submerged."

"I never knew..." Aster looked out over the expanding blue.

"See that rock over there?" Kara pointed towards shore. A square boulder, as big as the ship, sat nestled in the mostly sandy beach. "That's our marker. Once we pass it, we're in the Sea of Loctee."

Being on the ocean was a much different experience than the river. The Blue Skies swayed back and forth in the waves and Aster could hardly keep his balance walking on the deck.

Kara noticed him stumbling around and called out sarcastically, "Break into the mead already? Plenty of time for that after we get to port."

Aster crossed his arms and stomped up the stairs towards the bow of the ship. By the time he'd made it up, his stomach turned and his spit tasted metallic. He ran to the railing to vomit over the edge.

Kara could only laugh as she watched.

After a few rounds of unproductive retching, Pat brought Aster a cup of water. "Took me three trips before I stopped getting sea-sick. The city's just a stone's throw from the river. In the meantime, sip on this."

After what felt like an eternity later, a voice rang out from the crow's nest. "Land, ho!"

Aster turned his eye to the front of the ship and saw the

rocky shore on the horizon. New Portsmith came into view. White stone castle walls surrounded a dozen buildings that were taller than any structure Aster had seen in his life. At its center was a golden monolith that held a single bell above everything else. On the left was a series of docks and on the right a grand city climbed atop the seaside cliffs. At their highest point outside the walls, a lone tower sat against the blue sky—a vibrant olive silhouette.

Aster stared in awe of New Portsmith, his nausea completely forgotten.

The ship reached the docks, where a dozen other vessels were anchored. Half of them were cramped fishing boats, typical of back home. There were four other trading ships, about the same size as the Blue Skies. One ship was jet black with bright yellow sails, lacking a figurehead entirely. The last ship was larger than the rest, with violet trim and sails adorned with golden crowns. Kara had mentioned it in passing: the Council of Elders vessel, though they rarely left the city.

The crew tied the ship to the closest pier. Tristram secured the sails while others began hauling boxes off the ship.

Captain Whitlock was discussing plans with Kara.

Aster eagerly listened in.

"Kara, you and Peter are in charge of the shipment. Bring it to the usual spot in the BTC headquarters. Make sure to watch as they count it all, so they don't rip us off again. I'll find Carter's family and let them know the bad news. Poor lad had only been with us a year." The two nodded somberly and parted ways.

Aster followed Kara down the gangway to ask her advice. "Where can I find Doctor Malvin?" He didn't want her to know, but the massive city intimidated him.

The docks themselves had over a hundred people moving about their business, loading and unloading ships. There was an inn just off the water with two merchants in front, peddling their wares. The only time Aster had seen this many people in one place was during the harvest festival back home.

"Follow that path through the market center, and just past the city walls is the farming distri—" Kara was interrupted by a loud chiming that caused Aster to jump.

"What was that?"

She laughed and pointed to the tall golden building at the center of the city. "That's just the clock tower. It'll ring each hour to tell you the time. You should visit it."

"I will. Not sure how you can just ignore that noise." He adjusted the strap of his bag on his shoulder, trying to shake off the initial shock.

"I guess it is pretty startling if you've never been here before, but it makes a good landmark. You always know where you are in the city if you find the bell. Anyways, like I was saying, Malvin's house has a bright yellow roof, and it's just past the pigpens. Dunno why such a skilled doctor lives in the outskirts, but that's where you'll find him."

She patted him on the shoulder. "In any case, I'd better start unloading our shipment. If we don't deliver it before this evening, they'll lecture us for being late. And don't forget to meet us at The Beached Whale later tonight. Pay day is always a lively time." Kara pointed to the inn across from the shore. "Oh and one more thing: If that bell starts ringing non-stop, then beeline for the inn."

"Why?"

"Means trouble's afoot. It's only happened to me twice, but both times I was glad to have taken cover." She waved goodbye, leaving Aster nervously staring at the clock tower.

After regaining his nerve, Aster wandered down the path to the market center. The further away from the docks he got, the more merchant shops he could see. Each was a small wooden stand with baskets full of food, clothes, tools, and everything else a person could want.

His head spun as he tried to find his bearings around all the bustling people. They pushed him around as they rushed from cart to cart, as if they didn't have a moment to spare. There were more people here than Aster had seen in his entire life.

To clear his head, he stepped out of the bustle at a stand selling cured fish. The bright red fins had caught Aster's eye. *Fish can get this big?*

"This one's called a red snapper," the man behind the table explained, "It's delicious. Only found in the reefs of El'tonne. Yours for only five silver. Come now, you won't find a better price. Four silver—take it or leave it?"

Aster shook his head and backed away from the forceful merchant.

Vendors of different booths called to him, trying to get his patronage and coin.

Overwhelmed by all the attention, Aster quickened his pace. *Why would somebody need all these clothes, or fish, or any of this?*

By the time he reached the outer walls of the city, Aster's legs ached. He let out a deep sigh, happy to be out of the crowd. A massive wooden drawbridge, spanning the briny moat, connected the city to the fields outside. Houses interspersed many animal pens. The furthest had a distinctive yellow roof. *That must be the doctor's place.*

When he had finally arrived at the house, he knocked on the door nervously. *What do I say to convince him to help a tiny village like Buckwheat?* Just visiting this massive city made all of Aster's problems seem small by comparison.

The door opened and a man looked out. He was emaciated with dark circles under his eyes. His gray hair was tied back into a ponytail. He wore a nondescript brown tunic and no shoes.

"Are you Doctor Malvin?" Aster asked, uncertain if he had found the right house.

The man glared at Aster. "Who wants to know?"

Aster took a step back and rushed into the speech he had been preparing in his head for weeks. "Hello, my name is Aster and I'm the postmaster's son from

Buckwheat Village. My father and several other villagers are seriously ill, and we were hoping that you could help us cure them. I don't really have any money to pay you for your services, but I would do anything to make up for it. Please help us!"

The man studied Aster carefully. "I can't." Then he closed the door.

All the stress and exhaustion from the journey hit Aster as he replayed the last minute again in his head. *I've messed up my only chance at saving the village. If only Zinnia was here, she would have known how to convince the doctor.* By now tears were rolling down Aster's face. He kept picturing his father writhing on the floor like Lavender had. *No, I've come too far to give up now.* He slammed his fist on the door.

The door to the house opened again. "Boy, you're being obnoxious." But Aster's puffy eyes tempered his demeanor.

He let out a heavy sigh. "Fine, I'll hear you out. Buckwheat Village, that's the small town in far North Benia, right? Up the Haverhein?"

Aster wiped his tears in disbelief and stared at the man.

"Well come in and tell me about this sickness, boy. I haven't said I'd help you yet. But I'll listen."

Aster nodded and followed the man inside.

He felt as if he had stepped into a lord's manor. A bright red coat of arms hung above the table with a ferocious cat embroidered in gold on its center. The fireplace was adorned with two paintings that appeared to be Malvin when he was younger.

"You said your name's Aster? Please take a seat and describe the symptoms."

Aster took a seat at the round table next to the fireplace and told the doctor everything he knew. "It started a year ago, some of our villagers started to get sick for no reason, puking and complaining that they couldn't feel their fingers or toes. My father has trouble writing sometimes because of this. They also have fits of dizziness and have to sit down for hours at a time. Right before I left, Lavender had an episode where she started convulsing on the ground, saying things that made no sense and experiencing some kind of vision. Rowan Goodwin is our village's medicine man, and he believes that this is caused by a Jashian curse. He mentioned something about the snow… I didn't really understand it. In any case, he uses chamomile to soothe the stomachs of the sick people."

Doctor Malvin stroked his short white beard a few times and said, "Very interesting. Those aren't common ailments. I would need to run some tests on the sick villagers."

"Please, you have to come help us." For a moment, Aster was filled with hope.

"I wish I could, but traveling outside the city is impossible for me. You see, I'm a prisoner in my own house. In my youth I was an asset to this city, and they repaid me by making me a Lord. Little did I know that this meant that I was at their beck and call. Now they don't let me leave the city at all."

Aster's head slumped.

Malvin's eyes drifted to the coat of arms on the wall. He sighed. "Well, we can try one thing. It's a long shot, but you can go to the Council of Elders and plead your case. Ask them to permit me to travel to your village and research this illness. Perhaps they'll feel pity and grant your request."

Perfect! The Council will surely understand. "Are they nearby?" Aster dreaded going back through the maze-like city.

"The clock tower—I'm sure you noticed it on the way in. On the ground floor, you can arrange for a meeting with the Council."

Aster thanked Malvin repeatedly as he stepped back outside, but stopped after remembering the letter from Fletcher. "Oh, one more thing, do you know where I might find someone named Calantha? I have a delivery for her."

The doctor squinted at Aster and said, "Boy, you are full of mysteries. I've purchased herbs from her before—some rather hard to come by in Benia. Not sure what you could be carrying for that eccentric naturalist, but I'll tell you what I know. Last time I saw Calantha, was at her stall in the market center. You should ask for her there." He looked down and added, "Try not to get your hopes up with the Council. They always seem to let me down."

Kara and Peter had managed to haul a cart full of gold to the BTC's headquarters. It was carefully concealed inside five wooden crates for transport, to avoid prying eyes.

Kara spotted Vincient, the master of shipping, deep in discussion with an odd-looking man. The stranger stood out, not only because of his towering presence and the perfect hairlessness of his asymmetrical head, but also due his dark skin, the color of mulled cider.

A Munayallpan, she thought to herself. *I haven't seen one here in years.*

Vincient was still speaking as they approached. "Yes, we can have the order delivered to you in Strongfair within a week. And yes, it will be the finest quality in all the land."

The Munayallpan man only nodded.

"Actually, looks like our shipping crew has arrived just in time. Let me introduce to you Peter Keeton, first mate of the Blue Skies, and Kara Reeves, the quartermaster. They will be transporting the material on their ship."

The gruff man stared at Kara, expressionless, for so long that she started to question whether he would speak at all. Vincient nodded impatiently, keeping his eyes on the man, who finally responded in a rumbling voice, "Name's Chert. Pleasure."

Vincient jumped forward and forced Chert into a handshake. "It's great to do business with you, as always.

But, if you'll excuse us, we have other matters to take care of."

Vincient pulled Kara towards her cart as Chert ambled out of the building. Without a word, he led the group down a curved ramp into the basement. Two guards in full plate armor, each armed with a shining broadsword, greeted them.

Vincient stood in front of an enormous steel door, turned some knobs and then cranked the wheel until the door slowly opened. Kara and Peter strained as they wheeled the heavy cart inside. The door swung closed behind them.

The three of them stood inside the vault beside organized stacks of jewels, silver, and other valuables. On the left side of the room display cases lined the wall, filled with relics of immeasurable value, some that she swore she had only heard legends about.

Vincient's mustache twitched as he let out a breath of relief. "You should've asked for guards to help transport this from the docks. Oh well, it's safe now."

Kara nodded as she pried the lids off the crates. "It's all here. I counted it before we got off the ship. Please double check while we are in here so we don't have a repeat of last time."

Vincient glared at her, "You were ten bars short, I checked four times! Not my fault you miscounted at Pelware."

Kara turned away to hide her scowl. She knew he was going to say it, but it still annoyed her. *All three hundred and twenty bars were loaded onto the cart in Pelware. And three hundred and twenty bars made it aboard the Blue Skies in Buckwheat. I don't miscount.*

She wandered over to the nearest display case as Vincient pulled the gold bars from the crates to examine them before marking a number down in a ledger. Inside the glass box, a golden, bejeweled crown was perched upon a marble visage. Next to it sat a plaque with the words 'The crown of Federyc, last king of Benia'. Kara was excited to finally read these words thanks to Aster's lessons.

"Why're these here and not on display?" She asked Peter.

"If I didn't know any better, I'd say for security. But it's probably to keep people from rememberin' the monarchy."

"Then why keep it at all?"

Peter shook his head. "My coin is on vanity."

"Of the Council?"

"Hush." He tilted his head toward Vincient, who was still blissfully counting bars. "Emmeline's decision, I'm sure."

A short while later, Vincient called them back. "It's all here. I'm glad you didn't run into any trouble. This was the biggest shipment yet; Shaheed was nervous the whole time you were gone."

Peter somberly corrected him. "Actually, we got ambushed by a group of pirates on the Haverhein. Managed to spot 'em in time, and chase 'em off. Carter didn't make it, may Loctee rest his soul."

"Sorry to hear that," Vincient replied, shaking his head. "Carter was a good man. I assume that's why Whitlock isn't here right now... but no point in dwelling on the dead." He handed Peter a sack with their payment inside. "As you overheard, your next assignment is to deliver an order to Strongfair. I'll arrange a packing crew to load it on your ship tomorrow morning."

"So soon?" Kara eyed the bulging sack. *The others will be disappointed.*

"Yup. Best to work while there's work to be done."

The three discussed the logistics of the shipment. When they finished, Vincient led them back out of the vault.

Peter and Kara stopped back by the Blue Skies to distribute wages. With their duties completed for the day, the crew headed to the Beached Whale for supper and relaxation.

Kara stopped beside the whale sculpture in front. "I'll be back soon. Have to stop by the postmaster."

Peter pushed open the inn door. "Your usual pay day ritual?"

"Yup." She fingered the bag of gold coins in her pocket as she ducked under the wooden handrail. *Half for Janna.* She smiled to herself. *Another year. Two at the most and I won't need to send more money.* She was proud of her sister for finding her own way to escape the farm.

The clock tower was twice as tall as any other building around, built out of marble and adorned with gold—a grand monument, obviously dear to the people of New Portsmith.

Aster entered underneath an archway and found a clerk sitting at a small desk behind a metal gate with an elegant set of stairs on the other side. "Hello. May I speak with the Council, please?" Aster asked the short, mousy-haired woman.

She looked up from her paperwork and said, "Yes, please fill out this form and I will find you a time-slot."

He wrote a few lines about himself and the purpose of his meeting with the Council, then handed the form back to the woman.

She looked it over, then pulled something out from a nearby drawer. After jotting a note down, she stamped his note before placing her note back along with Aster's form. "Your meeting has been scheduled for six weeks from now," she said, her attention no longer on Aster.

"Sorry, what do you mean? Can I see them now?" he asked, scratching his temple.

"The Council is very busy in preparation for the election. I set the meeting to discuss your doctor with them for six-weeks from now. Please don't show up late or you may miss your chance."

"Can't I talk with them sooner?"

"I'm afraid not. They have many obligations and only so much time for provincial issues."

Aster's heart sank at the news. *Is there anything Kara could do to help speed this up? After all, the BTC must carry some influence here.* He thanked the woman behind the counter and exited the clock tower.

The sun was beginning to set as Aster headed back to the market center. Finding Calantha was the last thing that he needed to do. He stopped at a stall selling wildflowers, because it reminded him of home. There, a kind looking old man was packing up his supplies for the evening.

"Excuse me, do you happen to know where I could find Calantha's shop?" Aster asked the wrinkled shopkeeper.

He looked up from placing a basket of flowers in his handcart. "Aye. She's not allowed here no more."

Nothing was going right for Aster today. He let out a deep sigh as the shadows grew on the ground.

The old man continued, "But they say she lives in the green tower on the hill, just outside the city. You should check there." He pointed east.

Aster thanked the man for his information and left the market. *It's too late in the day to find a way to the tower. I should meet back up with the others.*

As he approached the Beached Whale, he could hear a ruckus inside. It was mostly familiar voices—cheerful and very drunk. The light from the latticed windows flickered across the whale sculpture out front. Aster stepped into the doorway and stood in awe of the place.

This inn was more than twice the size of the Fulton's place. Two floors were lined with bedrooms. Anyone who peeked out of their room would be able to see over the balcony into the dimly lit dining area.

Pat yelled to Aster from the bench of the closest table. "Over here! Come celebrate with us on this glorious day!"

He took a seat between Pat and Kara. "What's so special about today?"

Kara smiled at him and said, "It's pay day. We

completed our delivery." The table loudly cheered at Kara's words. "Your food and drink are on me tonight, so let's have some fun!"

Aster was swept up in the mood of the sailors. He happily flagged down the barkeep and ordered some crab stew and a pint of the famous Portsmith Wine—always wanting to sample the local cuisine. Back home, the villagers were always excited when they could get their hands on a barrel of this wine.

Aster devoured the stew; it was the perfect combination of salty and savory with big chunks of potato and carrots at the bottom. He had forgotten about eating while he wandered the city all afternoon, and soon found himself ordering a second helping. The wine wasn't his favorite—it was bitter and left a dry feeling on his tongue, nothing like the mellow sweet flavor of mead.

"Don't go and eat all that pumpkin pie," Pat called over to Kara. "You'll get fat. 'Sides, I can make it better."

Kara glared back. "It's been over a year since you made pie for us. And this reminds me of home. I'd eat it every day if I could."

"I know, just got to pull your leg from time to time." He chuckled into his cup as he sipped.

Peter had been sitting at the bar away from the group, but stopped by Aster to give him the details of their next voyage. "Noon tomorrow we set sail for Strongfair. Best finish your business in town before then." He rolled his eyes at the rest of the drunken group, then joined a cloaked figure in the corner of the room at a small round table.

Aster could only make out the soft glow of a pipe, passed between the two.

As the food was cleared from their table, Aster remembered to ask about the Council. "I was able to find Malvin and he agreed to help me."

"Oh, that's great!" Kara replied.

"But... he said that I need to convince the Council of Elders to let him travel to Buckwheat Village. And they said they can't see me for another six weeks. Is this normal? Is there any way to see them sooner?"

Kara scowled and shook her head. "The Council is known far and wide for their pointless bureaucracy. Best bet is to wait for the appointment."

Pat spoke up from Aster's other side, "Actually, six weeks is pretty good. Once I had to wait four months to speak with them about a land purchase—less than a quarter acre. Consider yourself lucky."

Aster stared into his half-empty cup. *That means I won't get back till summer. I hope Dad can hold out until then.*

After a few songs and rounds of liquor, it had gotten late. Most of the other tables were empty. Tristram was going around to the stragglers trying to convince someone to play coin-drop.

Kara was deep in conversation with Aster about her family back home; her face flushed from the wine. "My little sister, Janna, is attending school in Tembour. She'll be a fine scholar some day! Last time I saw her, she was studying the histories of the Great War between Benia, Jash, and Malvez. Don't get me wrong, I love working on the Blue Skies, but the reason I'm here is to make enough coin to send home to her."

Aster said, "That is really kind of you! Are you from Tembour as well?"

Kara replied, "Nope, we grew up in a small farming village about halfway between New Portsmith and Tembour—Wildflower Farms. It doesn't show up on any maps. I'm glad I left and get to travel the world. The life of a farmer is dull."

Aster nodded in agreement, thinking back to some of the small farms around Buckwheat Lake he had delivered letters to. "All this talk of family reminds me—you said that your next delivery is to Strongfair? That's where my mother lives. It would be nice to meet her. Seeing that I have six weeks till the Council meeting, would it be alright to continue traveling with you guys to Strongfair?"

Kara put her arm around his shoulder.

Aster's wound pulsed, but he forced himself not to flinch.

"Of course! As long as you can hold your own in the next scuffle. Wouldn't want you fainting and leaving me to take care of things again."

Aster scowled. "I can take care of myself." He didn't know if it was from the wine or the stuffy inn, but his face felt hot.

Laughing, Kara added, "I heard that you almost took care of your toe the other day… but I'm willing to help train you up a bit more. Come up to my room and I'll teach you a proper grip." Before he could reply, she leaned in and kissed him.

Aster had never been kissed before and was having trouble keeping his thoughts straight. He could see all of Kara's freckles atop her rosy cheeks while her soft lips were pressed against his own. The next thing he knew, Kara was leading him by the hand to her room upstairs while Pat was giving him a silly look and a thumbs up from the table below.

Before opening the door, Kara looked out in both directions and locked it securely behind them. "I was trying to figure out a discreet way of doing this, but that was the best I could come up with." Kara's jovial expression was gone.

Aster stood awkwardly in the center of the bedroom as she pulled paper out of her pocket and held it up.

Kara's eyes softened again. "Sorry for leading you on like that, but I needed an excuse to get you alone with this letter. I think I know what it says, but I need to be absolutely sure. Can you read it to me?"

Aster's ears buzzed in the quiet room, which was slowly spinning in circles. He hesitantly took the letter from her and held it under the lamp-light, squinting to keep the words from dancing around the page. "Comrades, meet me on the ship at sunrise. The company is loading new cargo and we'll be leaving tomorrow. What happened on the Haverhein was not acceptable. Not a single scratch on anybody this time! Signed, W.W."

Kara frowned as Aster finished reading.

"What's this? Why's it so important?" Aster folded the paper and handed it back to her.

She stuffed it back into her pocket and unlatched the window, peering down to the cobblestone street. "Aster, please don't leave this room tonight." Without another word, she jumped out, leaving Aster alone and confused.

Sleep didn't come easily to Aster that night. Between thoughts of the doctor, his mother, and the events with Kara, he couldn't calm down. From the bed he could see her belongings strewn about the room, which left him wondering what he'd done wrong.

When morning finally arrived, Aster had barely slept at all. Kara hadn't returned either. He let out a sigh and pulled a sheet of paper from his bag. *A letter to Zinnia—that'll organize my thoughts.*

After he finished writing he got ready for the day. *I need to deliver Calantha's letter before the Blue Skies sets sail. And give Doctor Malvin an update on what the Council said. Come to think of it, I should probably see him first.*

Aster made his way there without any stops this time, trying to ignore the overwhelming din of the city, but the regular bell chimes continued to make him jump. When he knocked on the door of the yellow-roofed house, Malvin invited him inside.

Aster didn't bother to sit at the table, instead he stood just inside the hallway. "Doctor Malvin, I went to the clock tower like you said and tried to get a meeting with the Council. But they are making me wait six weeks!"

The doctor didn't look surprised. "Typical bureaucrats. Glad you went instead of me. They would've made us wait even longer. Good news is that I don't think we need to rush to your village. From what you've told me about this sickness, I think it will be a slow progression. Waiting for your meeting is best for now."

"If you say so. Since we've got time to spare, I'll be traveling to Strongfair. They say it shouldn't be more than a two week trip."

"Safe travels. And don't be late."

Aster chuckled as he grabbed the doorknob. "I'll be back in New Portsmith with plenty of time to spare." With that, he said farewell and made his way back into the city.

Aster stopped at the center of the market square, looking up at the clock tower. He had walked some distance from Malvin's house before he realized that he didn't actually know how to get to Calantha's place. *I remember seeing the olive spire on the right side of town when the Blue Skies was approaching the city. I passed on the left side of the clock tower to get to the doctor, which means I need to head straight under the clock tower from here.*

Satisfied with his plan, Aster rushed underneath the gilded timepiece. The sun had fully risen as he entered the residential district of New Portsmith. The streets zigzagged around the modest homes of the city folk. Each looked moments from toppling over, but they were so close together that they seemed to be propping each other up. Judging by the dirt in the streets and the stink in the air, this was the poor part of town.

People trickled in and out of the houses, more than could possibly fit inside. Kids dashed around playing some kind of game with a ball and two sticks each. He turned down an alleyway that looked to be a shortcut, beside a house with a particularly run-down door, but then he stopped. It was a dead end—fenced off and littered with torn paper, scraps of cloth, and other trash.

A hand grabbed Aster's shoulder, causing him to jump.

"Spare some coin?" It was a beggar in ragged clothes.

"Uhhh sorry, I'd better be off." Aster shook himself free from the man's grip and looked to the sky for the golden tower he had been using for reference.

"Come boy I know you've got spare copper," the beggar had hobbled towards him with a wild look in his eyes.

Aster panicked and ran. He sped back past the neglected door, took a left at an empty wooden cart, and down a somewhat larger street where merchants were milling about.

When he finally paused to catch his breath, the golden tower broke the skyline directly in front of him. *This makes no sense. Am I lost?* His pulse quickened as he pictured the Blue Skies setting sail without him. *How will I manage in this city without money? I'll end up like that beggar; stealing just to feed myself.*

He took a step backwards in panic, only for his boot to catch a loose brick. He tumbled to the ground.

Aster lay there staring at the sky, squinting towards the sun, just starting his worry anew, when he noticed something out of the corner of his eye. He turned to see an olive spire piercing the sky, towering above the monotonous brown and gray roofs of the buildings around. *I'm close.*

Following the beaten cobblestone road, he reached the edge of the city. The gate stood open, identical to the one he passed through to see the doctor. Beyond it was his destination, the olive-green tower.

By the time he reached the place, he was out of breath. The tower had been further away than it looked. The bottom was the same architecture as the rest of the city, but two floors up, plants had taken over. The olive color was from the vines that weaved across its surface, fiercely gripping the mortar. Thousands of coin-sized leaves faced the sun as if they were praying to Conflagration. A square board covered the arched entrance, held up by vines seemingly sewn through the wood.

Aster knocked loudly on the makeshift door. "Calantha, are you there?" he yelled.

There was no response. Aster tried again. After several moments of silence, he gently pushed the door open. To his surprise, the vines held firm acting like a hinge.

Inside was empty except for a few chairs around a

table. A set of spiral stairs worked their way to the upper floors. *What kind of person would live in this half-destroyed tower way out here?*

Every hair on Aster's arms stood as he made his way up the stairs. The second floor was empty like the first, except there was a lone red flower, atop a pile of soil, in the center of the room. It had been watered recently, judging by the droplets on its leaves.

"Calantha? Are you home?"

There was no response.

By the time he had made it to the third floor, the air had gotten warm and humid. Vines covered the walls. A single hole in the wall, let the sun's rays fall onto the floor.

Aster looked around. *This is practically an indoor garden.* On the left were a few plants that he recognized, but on the right, there were many he had never seen before. Across the room was an enormous pale pink flower. Its petals were so large that it brushed against both the floor and the ceiling. The shape reminded Aster of a king's throne, designed to draw all eyes.

Curious, he crossed the room. The flower smelled sickly-sweet, like lost fruit left to rot. Each one of its petals was pristine.

His leg stung as it brushed against a short bush covered in thorns. Thankfully it was only tender, not bleeding. The plant that pricked him had many small buds at the end of each stem.

"It's a sunset rose. Vibrant orange and yellow flowers will bloom in a few weeks."

Aster jumped and turned around. He'd thought he was alone, but sitting on the lowest petal of the giant flower was a woman with ear-length pale blonde hair. Her skin was fair, almost the same color as the flower behind her, and she wore a long flowing pink dress.

"Where'd you come from?" Aster asked, his heart thumping in his chest.

"Oh, I was perched here watching you the whole

time," the woman replied.

Aster swore she hadn't. "Are you Calantha?"

The woman studied Aster for a moment. "Yes, I am her. But more importantly, who are you and why have you intruded into my lair?"

Something about this person made Aster uneasy, but he was determined to see his task through. Steadying his trembling hand, he reached into his bag and pulled out a letter. "My name is Aster, and I was asked to deliver this letter from Fletcher Abberton."

Calantha was motionless, eyes fixed on Aster. "Normally, I shy away from unexpected visitors, but you seem as harmless as a fly. Besides, Fletcher would not contact me without a significant finding." In a single swoop, she lifted the letter out of his hand, broke the wax seal, and began to read.

"Oh my, this is quite interesting." She finished the letter and placed it down on the petal next to her. "And you must be the same Aster from the mines with the cockatrice?"

He stiffened. *That was supposed to be a secret.* "Yes... Who are you exactly, and how do you know Fletcher? And why do you live way out here?"

"The best answers in life are the ones you figure out for yourself," she replied pensively. "Although, I suppose I should assure you that I am an ally." She nodded, appearing to convince herself of something. "I met Fletcher several years ago in a valley of the Vesium Mountains. I was analyzing some of the unusual flora that grows in that area. In particular, I was in search of a strain of fireweed that gives off a flickering light in the dark. That is rather unusual, I might add. Fireweed is named after its tendency to grow in the ashes of forest fires, not for any bio-luminescent properties. Aside from its elongated raceme, the common man would think it was any other flower.

"But I digress; I had just found the fireweed in question, when a boulder rolled down from the cliff side, nearly crushing my specimens. At the origin of the commotion was a small group of adventurers, swinging pickaxes at the mountain. The team was led by Fletcher Abberton. Suffice to say, he was very interested in my work and invited me to collaborate on their expedition. I have been in communication with him ever since. He is a good reference for me on inorganic materials. And I have been assisting him with unusual organisms."

Aster struggled to piece together Calantha's story. "But Fletcher retired and settled into his mining operation. Why does he need your help? Does it have to do with the cockatrice?"

"Fletcher has not informed me of the specifics. Please take me to Pelware Mine and we shall find out for ourselves."

"Uhhh… I don't know if I can just invite you onto the ship. And besides that, we aren't going to Buckwheat yet. Our next stop is Strongfair."

"I will convince your captain otherwise. Take me with you at once."

Everything about this situation struck Aster the wrong way. *The gold coin, the warning from Fletcher, and now this bizarre person demanding passage on the Blue Skies, which is setting sail soon.* His heart raced. "What time is it? I need to be at the docks now or I'll miss the boat!"

"One moment and then we can depart." Calantha sprang off the petal and glided up the stairs.

Leave without her. She'll only cause trouble. Aster inched his way to the ground floor, feeling guilty. He stopped with a hand on the makeshift front door.

Calantha returned with two satchels filled to the brim. The slightly smaller one had a vine sticking out as if it was hastily stuffed with plants.

Aster frowned at the small bags and looked back at her delicate dress. *She claims to be an adventurer, but she clearly doesn't have sensible clothes. Oh well, no time to argue.* "Let's go."

They hurried out of the tower and into the city. Just as

they had passed through the southern gate, Calantha directed Aster down a dark alley to the left. "This way is a shortcut to the docks."

After endless winding passages and turns through corridors that reeked of old fish, the duo emerged at the edge of the ocean cliffs, overlooking the docks. The square sails of the Blue Skies rippled in the breeze in the same spot that Aster had left it the day before. "Conflag's warmth, we aren't late."

Aster was completely out of breath by the time they made it to the pier. Tristram was just hauling the last barrel of drinking water onto the ship.

Peter stood, arms crossed, at the bottom of the gangplank. His head was on a swivel, scanning the crowd.

Aster ran up to him. "Sorry for making you guys wait. I hope it's alright for Calantha to join us? She needs to go to Pelware with me."

"Have you seen Kara? She hasn't shown up. The rest of the crew is ready to go. We're only waiting for her."

Aster blushed. "Not since the Beached Whale."

Peter tapped his foot impatiently. "Hurry onboard. We need to leave as soon as she gets back."

As they stepped onto the ship, Aster heard Kara's frantic voice behind them. "Sorry I'm late. Needed to take care of something."

"What were you doin'?" Peter grumbled. "You should've been here hours ago to load the cargo. I was forced to take care of it."

"I'll tell you later. Thanks for covering for me." She hurried on board, only pausing for a moment to whisper in Aster's ear as she passed. "No matter what happens. I need you to trust me and follow my lead."

Before he could ask what she meant, Kara had jumped into action, untying ropes and preparing to embark. Peter pulled in the gangplank and the Blue Skies began moving out to sea.

Aster found a place on the quarterdeck to watch. He had learned a lot from Kara about what it took to set sail, but he knew to stay out of the way.

They had just lost sight of the city, when a cacophony of voices erupted from the captain's quarters. From inside Whitlock muttered, "Hush. Steady."

Peter scratched his head and knocked on the door. "Need somethin' Capt'n? Things are smooth out here."

"Blast it." Whitlock sighed. "Alright, go now."

There was a cheer and the door swung open, smashing Peter in the face. A dozen pirates, brandishing swords burst from the room.

The crew was caught unaware and easily overpowered. One by one, their hands were bound in rope. Aster could only watch as two pirates forced him against the stair railing, restraining him as well.

Peter was already up, knife in hand, cornering two against the main mast. A swift palm strike and both men's swords clattered to the deck.

"Enough Peter." Captain Whitlock stepped out of his quarters and patted his pristine blue coat. "Put yer knife down, or I'll tell my men to stop playing nice."

"Your men? What's goin' on?"

"Sorry Peter, but I've got other plans now. And they don't concern you."

Peter looked to the rest of the crew. Nobody else had fought back; they didn't have a chance. He shook his head and let the knife fall from his hand.

With the crew immobilized, Whitlock began directing the pirates. "Change course. We are heading for the cave."

Aster, Pat, Kara, Peter, Tristram, and the others were barricaded in the living quarters while the Blue Skies turned around, sailing into the open ocean. The hatches were bolted shut and two pirates stood guard at the door, brandishing their swords at anyone who got close.

Aster's head swam as he sat on his bunk. There was too much happening and all he could do was watch the others scurry about the room. In the commotion, he had lost sight of Calantha. *Did she manage to avoid capture somehow?* He hoped so because he couldn't stomach the alternatives.

Pat and Kara huddled in the corner, whispering to each other. Tristram got into a heated argument with Peter and kept slamming his fist against a support beam.

The two pirates keeping guard were growing increasingly irritated at the commotion. Finally, the scarred pirate pushed Peter aside and grabbed Pat's shirt, yanking him away from Kara. He jabbed his cutlass against Pat's throat and screamed, "Enough! Whitlock said you might try to scheme your way out. The next person who so much as whispers gets their throat slit."

Kara stood and the pirate pressed his blade into Pat, drawing a trickle of blood. She whimpered and sat back.

The pirate smiled, showing two missing teeth. "Glad you understand. This won't be like what happened on the Haverhein." He hurled Pat to the floor and stomped back to his post.

Kara helped Pat up and pressed a cloth against his neck, frowning. She looked towards Peter, who just shook his head and lifted his shirt showing an empty sheath.

Tristram sighed and slumped into his own bunk.

Aster studied the crew's reaction. *An order from the First Mate: Nobody do anything stupid. Wait for the right moment to make our move.*

But the pirate's threat was sufficient enough. The crew sat in silence through the night, with only the sounds of the sea and occasional heavy footsteps from above to remind them of their delicate situation.

Kara didn't sleep a wink. Her stomach was in knots, and she couldn't stop her bound hands from shaking. *Please work, please work, please work.* Her glorious plan seemed less so by the minute. *If only I'd told Pat sooner.* She had given him the gist yesterday before the pirates shut them up, but it wasn't enough. *Peter will fight back. People will die.* She couldn't bear a repeat of what happened to poor Carter.

Through a porthole, Kara watched the Blue Skies sail alongside a stretch of steep coastal cliffs. *West? Why are we heading west?* The ship passed a rocky outcropping that almost resembled a tree, then turned, moving between the stone branches into an especially large sea cave. The waves sloshed against the rocky sides as the ship swayed back and forth between them. As they floated deeper into the cave, the water calmed. The pirates tied the ship to a lone wooden walkway in the center of the pool, then simply waited.

The anticipation was cruel. Kara gritted her teeth. They could try and fight back or submit and do as they were told. Both options were shit. They were dead either way.

The scarred pirate burst through the door and prodded each crew member out of the sleeping quarters and onto the dock. Kara recognized the man's face, Liosam. On the Haverhein, she thought he was their leader, but he must really be second in command.

A different pirate climbed down, grumbling to himself as he gave a report to Captain Whitlock. "All that's down there is wood. I don't see the gems anywhere."

The captain pointed at Kara. "Bring her closer. Where'd you put the jewels that we're carrying to Strongfair?"

She snickered. "I lied to you. Why would we be delivering riches? It's all cherry wood..." *It's not much, but I hope it ruins your plans, traitor.*

The captain scowled and fixed Kara with a hard stare. "Why lie?"

She tilted her chin up, looking down her nose at him. "I found your note."

The captain barked with laughter and planted his hands on his hips, eyes skimming over the captives, pausing briefly on Aster before moving back to Kara's face. "So, you've learned to read? I should've been more cautious..."

Kara gave no answer.

Whitlock grumbled and started pacing. "Shit, how can

we salvage this? I guess we need to complete this delivery, take the payment, and then avoid New Portsmith like the plague. We'd have been much better off with the gold... too late now." He flicked his coat behind him twice, then yelled, "Tie 'em up in the jelly room and grab our stash! We won't be coming back here again."

Kara's eyes darted to Peter. *Anytime now, he'll make a move.* But his shoulders were slumped, and he wore a sad, defeated expression on his face. *That's not like him, but it's probably for the best.*

Liosam led the captives to a corner. He pried a boulder away with a piece of driftwood, revealing a cramped passageway into a secret part of the cave. An eerie green glow pulsed from within, faintly illuminating the way.

One by one, Captain Whitlock forced each crew member through the opening.

Pat was last. He resisted the captain's hand and faced him. "Why are you doing this?"

Kara froze and turned her neck. *Please, Pat. Don't.*

Whitlock sighed. "It ain't you that I've a problem with, it's the BTC. We've all seen the wealth that they've got in the vaults. Why's it that we're always short-sheeted? Barely enough pay for any of us. I'm weary of it all, so I'm taking my fair share and disappearing." He pushed Pat's head into the opening this time. "Now keep moving. I'm trying not to get you hurt... if I can help it."

A few steps in, the passage branched to the right, opening up into a chamber with a high ceiling. Kara was stunned when she saw the source of the green glow above their heads. Over a hundred thin crystalline strands hung from the ceiling. They circled three domes on the roof, each the size of a ship. One-by-one they pulsed with a mysterious glow as if there were torches hidden inside the transparent shapes.

"Are those sea jellies? Can they get that big?" Kara asked aloud.

The nearest pirate shook his head. "Must be. We found this place by accident and the light was useful, but we never found out what those things are."

The crew was taken to the side of the room and tied wrist-to-wrist around a boulder. The pirates picked up a lone, rusted chest and hauled it back towards the ship.

Captain Whitlock placed a cloth sack full of food and eight waterskins at Pat's feet. "This should last you a few days. We're leaving the rowboat here for you as well. I hope you can make it back to New Portsmith before you run out."

With that, the captain followed the pirates out of the room, leaving his former comrades to fend for themselves under the pulsing glow of the sea jellies.

Kara let out her breath. *At least nobody died.*

Zinnia Hollyhock,

It feels like a lifetime has passed since I left Buckwheat Village. New Portsmith is wondrous! The buildings tower above you like mountains, and at the center of the city is a golden clock tower that chimes every hour. It was startling at first, but the sound is hauntingly beautiful. The city is a maze though; I don't know how anybody can find their way around.

On to the good news! I found Doctor Malvin and he's agreed to examine the villagers. Unfortunately, we need to seek permission from the Council to do so. That will take a few weeks. I don't understand government.

Tomorrow, we will be traveling to Munayallpa while we wait. I'll try and find Mom while we are there. I've imagined it more times than I can count, but right now my mind is drawing a blank. What should I say to her?

I had a new experience. My mind goes fuzzy when I try to think about it. Kara kissed me. I was so happy at the time, but it was really a trick to get my help reading. I don't understand. Does she actually have feelings for me? I wish you could sit me down and explain how women think.

In any case, I'll be back in Buckwheat with Doctor Malvin before too long. I miss the simple life at home.

Your friend,
Aster

4 SIDETRACKED IN STRONGFAIR

"So, Captain Whitlock betrayed us?" Aster said, breaking the silence in the dim green glow of the sea cave.

"Yup." Peter replied as he tried to reach his hidden knife. "Blast it! They tied us up too tight. I can't cut us free."

Aster struggled against the ropes in vain; the fibers cut into his skin. He winced in pain. "What do we do?" He turned to faced Kara. "Is this what the letter was about? You said you had a plan?"

She sighed. "I *had* a plan. Until we ended up inside this cave."

Peter stopped straining against the ropes. "Plan? What're you talkin' about?"

"Well, we found Whitlock's note, so I arranged for—"

"If you knew he'd betray us, why didn't you warn me?" Peter voice shook.

"I didn't know who to trust! What if you were in on the scheme?"

"After all we've been through... I thought we were friends!"

"You'd been with Whitlock since well before I joined. Plus, you ditched us at the inn to smoke with that stranger. How would I know that he wasn't one of them?"

"He's the opposite of a pirate! That man is..." Peter paused awkwardly, "An old friend... In any case, me and the capt'n didn't see eye-to-eye on some of his earlier under-the-table moneymakin'. Small stuff like dodgin' the port tax or smugglin' the occasional box of Zeffarii red sand. Guess he knew I wouldn't take his side in this."

Pat interrupted. "Enough. Can we focus on getting out of here? Plenty of time for bickering after that."

Kara and Peter quieted down and for a minute, the only thing anyone could hear was the crashing of waves against the rocks outside. They continued to struggle against the ropes to no avail.

Tristram's stomach rumbled, causing him to scowl at the cloth sack at Pat's feet. "What good's that food if we can't even get to it?"

Aster's own stomach clenched in agreement. *Come to think of it, I haven't eaten since the Beached Whale. I was all over New Portsmith, talking to the doctor and Calantha, and then we spent last night restrained on the ship.* He stretched his foot out towards the sack to see if he could reach it.

He stopped and twisted his head to look at each crew mate. "Did any of you see Calantha today? I know that she got on the ship, but I don't see her here."

"Huh? Who?" Kara shook her head.

An airy voice rang out from the opposite side of the cave. "I am here, Aster."

Calantha was seated atop a smooth rock, her silky dress cascading down onto the floor. She had a notebook in one hand and was gazing at the ceiling, writing intently as she studied the crystals above. "Based on the luminescence and the micro-movements I've observed over the last few minutes, these crystal jellies must be living creatures. How fascinating! I wish there was some way to get a closer look at them."

Kara gasped. "Who are you? And how'd you get past the pirates? Actually, hold that thought. Untie us first."

"Yes, I suppose there is not much more I can learn

from down here." Calantha carefully put away her notes, crossed the chamber, and with a flick of her hand freed the crew from their confines.

"Thanks," Kara said with uncertainty. She dusted herself off and addressed the group. "The faster we get out of here, the more likely we can take the Blue Skies back and give Whitlock what's coming to him!"

Aster wasn't as optimistic as the others. "I don't think we can all fit in that tiny rowboat. Would four of us travel back to New Portsmith to get help while the rest stays here?"

Kara grinned. "Remember the plan I mentioned earlier? He should be here by now. C'mon let's go."

Pat scooped up the food and water as Kara led the crew to the boulder that had been rolled back in front of the cave entrance. It took three of them, but they managed to move it enough to squeeze by.

When they had all filed back into the main chamber of the cave, the rowboat greeted them as promised, gently rocking in the ocean waves. Beside it approached a trading ship: Aster recognized it from New Portsmith. The plain white sail bobbed up and down as it made its way beside the dock. More than twice the size of the Blue Skies, it made the cave look small by comparison.

"Perfect timing," Kara yelled. She waved as she rushed down the wooden walkway.

A man in a crimson hat climbed down Jacob's ladder and hopped onto the pier.

Peter sighed. "Vincient. Thank Loctee! Never thought I'd be this happy to see you." He turned to Kara. "Guess this was your plan?"

"Yes, Kara showed me Whitlock's letter," Vincient replied. "We decided I would trail the Blue Skies after it left New Portsmith. It wasn't easy sailing just out of sight the whole time. When your ship entered this sea cave, we went a bit further and found a section of rock to anchor behind until we saw the Blue Skies leave. Didn't know what we'd find in here..." He looked around at the crew, clapping a hand on Peter's shoulder. "What next? Do you want a lift back to the city?"

Peter tapped his foot on a loose board and grabbed his goatee. "Any chance you could take us to Strongfair? If we are quick enough, we might be able to take the Blue Skies back."

Vincient sucked his teeth. "I suppose I must, now that I'm involved. Shaheed wouldn't be too happy if we lost one of his precious ships… not to mention the cargo. But I need to be back in New Portsmith in a week—we have a shipment from Zeffarii that I must be there to accept."

He held his hat and jumped back onto his ship, grabbing the ropes of Jacob's ladder to climb aboard. "Everyone on board the Gull's Perch!"

As Aster and the crew followed Vincient, Kara directed Tristram to the rowboat. Two of them brought it around the dock and hauled it up. Soon enough, they were on their way east.

The next day Aster caught sight of Calantha on the bow. She was staring at a group of seabirds building nests on the shoreline. With all that was going on, he wanted to be sure that she met with Kara. Hopefully, there would be no concerns having her aboard after she rescued them from the cave.

He found Kara on the lower deck, half-asleep in a chair. She looked exhausted. Her normally neat braid was loose and frayed. There were dark circles under her eyes.

Aster almost let her be, but she spoke when he got close. "Everything alright?"

"Yeah... didn't want to disturb you, but I was hoping to introduce you to Calantha."

Kara rubbed her hands down her face and stood. "Good. I've got to thank her." She followed Aster onto the bow, where Calantha was still staring towards land.

"Now that we are out of that mess, I'd better introduce

myself. My name's Kara Reeves and I am… was the quartermaster of the Blue Skies. I guess we'll see if that stays true. Anyways, your name is Calantha, right? Thanks for untying us back in the cave."

Calantha smoothed her floor-length eggshell-colored dress as she turned to face Kara. "Calantha Coronatus. It was my pleasure to assist you in that beautiful sea cave. Now I am certain in my decision to join you on this journey. Thank you for allowing me to travel with the crew. Though I suppose there is no possibility of going straight to the Pelware Mine."

"Unfortunately we don't have our ship anymore."

"After the mutiny?"

Kara ran her hands through her hair. "Is it mutiny if the captain is the one to rebel?"

"Mutiny of the ship? No. Mutiny of the trading company? Yes."

"You think?"

"Some say I think too much. But let us leave those types of questions to philosophers."

Uhhh… sure."

Calantha pressed her thin lips into a smile. "All this excitement reminds me of the first time I left home. Not very rational, I know. Sentiment more than anything."

Before Kara could press further, Aster chimed in. "I'm glad you finally had the chance to meet. Calantha, you have to tell us how you evaded those pirates. I was worried they'd killed you."

She paused before responding. "It is a combination of the way the light reflects off your person and a mimicry of movements in a slight breeze. The unobservant mind will consider you part of the background."

After seeing the confused looks on Aster and Kara's faces she followed up. "In essence, I can hide if I do not wish to be seen. It is a rather mundane type of illusion."

"Impressive! Can you teach us to do that too?"

"I am afraid not. It is my heritage, for better or worse."

"At least show us again."

"Very well."

The air around Calantha shimmered as if it was steam and the brown deck bled into her dress.

Aster blinked and Calantha was gone.

Kara put a hand over her mouth. "How?"

"I'm not sure if I could explain it another way." Calantha's voice hung in the air behind them.

Aster whipped his head around and watched Calantha re-materialize. "Wow, I wish I could turn invisible," he muttered.

"It is closer to sleight-of-hand. It can be taxing to keep up."

"Strangest thing I've seen," Kara said.

"I suppose. Do you mind telling me more about yourself? A young quartermaster is not a common sight."

As they talked, a dark rain cloud filled the sky above them. The water became choppy, which caused Aster's stomach to turn sour. He leaned over the edge of the bow to catch some fresh air and settle his nausea. *I guess Carter was right, ocean sailing is nothing like the calm waters of the Haverhein. It was bad before, but all this from a little rain?* In front of the ship, there was a patch of water that was so still it was like looking through the window of the Hollyhock's store.

By the time that the boat had crossed into the glassy water, Aster saw something pale white beneath the surface and froze in fear. Below him, a colossal skeleton drifted by. Its elongated mouth led two paddle-like fins, which connected to a long chain of vertebrae. The rib cage was big enough to hold an entire ship inside. Aster recognized this ivory skeleton as that of a whale, from his father's book *Fascinations of the Sea.* But this one was so much larger than he'd ever imagined.

Looking closer, he could make out a swarm of pink crustaceans that appeared to be picking flesh off its ribs. There were schools of other odd-looking fish swimming around as well. A few spots on the skeleton—including the creature's jaw—appeared to have fine red hair that swayed in the current. A moment later, it slipped completely below the ship's hull.

Aster ran to the stern to continue gazing at this bizarre sight. He was so transfixed that he didn't notice Kara calling out to him. Just as the skeleton drifted out of sight, a thought crossed Aster's mind. *Bones don't float like that. Why's that skeleton not sunk on the bottom of the sea?*

His hairs stood on end as the whale skeleton produced a deep rumbling noise and several high-pitched clicks. It lunged out of the water and gracefully arched its way back in with a moderate splash.

"What was that?" Aster asked aloud, dumbfounded, but nobody else had witnessed the creature.

Later, Pat said he had heard the splash and Kara caught its cry, however nobody believed his story of the skeletal whale.

Aster had watched the rocky cliffs give way to fine sand beaches, but the view was beginning to bore him. He'd already felt useless on the Blue Skies, but the Gull's Perch was even worse. Nobody would let him help with chores, and because they already had a full crew there wasn't room to lay about. He had taken to lounging atop a supply crate beside the hatchway.

On the third day, Vincient climbed down from the crow's nest and gathered the ship-less crew around. "I just caught sight of the mountains of Munayallpa, which means we're close. We need a plan for taking back your ship. The Munayallpans aren't the brightest, but they'll catch onto us sooner or later. What I mean is, we need to be quick. If it comes down to Whitlock's word against ours, I don't think we'll win. He still has all of the paperwork showing he's Captain of the Blue Skies."

Kara nodded. "Whitlock can't have docked more than a few hours before us. He's itching to sell the cargo and then disappear, so we should split up. One group takes back the ship, and the other intercepts the deal. If we restrain the captain, we could take back the money before anyone notices."

Peter fingered his knife. "It's risky."

"We can't let Whitlock get away with this!" Kara's frustration was palpable. A few other crewmates grunted in agreement.

Vincient tapped the brim of his hat. "The plan is fine. But the details are what matters. And unfortunately we have to take the Gull's Perch back to New Portsmith now. After my delivery arrives, if I haven't heard from you, I'll return to make sure you didn't get stranded... again."

Kara thought for a moment. "Peter and Aster should go after Whitlock. Aster can read or write any documents for us, and Peter has already met our trading partner, which gives us some credibility. And he's the best equipped to take on Whitlock. The rest of us will rescue the ship. We'll need all the hands we have for that."

"You sure about this? Shouldn't I help take the Blue Skies?" Peter asked, thrusting his knife forward in the air. "Fightin' is almost certain."

"I considered that, but I think we can manage without you. Plus, you're the only one who can handle Whitlock one-on-one, if it comes to that."

"True. Well, I'll do my best to keep this one alive." He slapped Aster on the back.

The comment didn't sit right with Aster, who watched anxiously as the city came into sight. *What a disaster. I never thought my first visit to Strongfair would turn out like this.* His stomach turned, though not because of Whitlock. A childhood of loneliness teased the edges of his mind. *Is this really where she lives?*

Strongfair was unlike anywhere Aster had ever seen. The entire city was a shade of brown or yellow which made it stand out from the blues of the ocean and the green of the western forest. The earthen buildings were at most three stories tall and filled the landscape in tight clusters. Wooden logs provided a framework for the bizarre structures. Some looked like they were piled on top of each other. They all had a uniform texture, as if sculpted out of the clay beneath them. To the east, houses were built into the mountain cliffs.

Behind the docks was the city center. Its centerpiece was an enormous water fountain with a hundred stone faces carved upon its sides.

As they docked, Aster saw familiar blue sails a few boats down, furled but distinct from dozens in plain white.

Aster and Peter marched into the city as the rest of the crew followed Kara to the Blue Skies.

"Buyer's named Chert," Peter told Aster as they made their way past the fountain. "Vincient said that he owns a stonecuttin' shop on the east side of town. Let's ask around."

Beyond the fountain was an elaborate sandstone path that led to a domed building, etched with geometric drawings of animals and studded with gemstones. Each side of the path was crowded with merchants peddling their wares.

Aster was struck by how much quieter it was here than in New Portsmith. There were nearly as many people scurrying about, but instead of merchants yelling over one another, the occasional low-pitched voice was all that could be heard. More than anything, the ground itself pulsed—a rhythmic beat from the bustle.

He followed Peter to the closest booth, which displayed a series of intricately sculpted vases—embossed with patterns of spiraling turquoise lines. Judging by the line, the booth was quite popular. Unlike the chaos of New Portsmith, things here were orderly and slow. Each customer received the shopkeeper's full attention. Half of the conversations were in Munayallpan, a language that Aster recognized but didn't understand.

When they finally got to the front, Aster eagerly addressed the clean shaven merchant. "Excuse me. Can you point us in the direction of Chert's stone cutting shop?"

The man looked away from them but said nothing. His eyes darted down the path, to the domed building, then swerved somewhere to the right.

Aster glanced around for a more knowledgeable merchant.

Peter reiterated Aster's question, speaking slowly, "Do you know the way to Chert Penya's stonecuttin' shop?" The man still didn't respond, so Aster stepped towards the next booth.

Peter grabbed his shoulder. "Wait. Give him a second."

The man pointed to the side of the path, "Take a right at the split. Third huddle on the left."

"Huddle?"

"It's their word for a group of houses," Peter answered.

They thanked the merchant and hurried on.

When they were out of hearing distance, Aster blurted out, "What was that about?"

Peter's voice dropped to a whisper. "Munayallpans are a bit dense. Gotta speak slowly and give 'em time to think."

"Oh?" *I hope he didn't think I was being rude.*

They found the shop exactly where the man said it would be. Made of red sandstone with three wooden supports, it was unique even for Strongfair. The sign above the door was a simplified picture of rock being cut out of a quarry. Around the back, Aster could see several tall stacks of brick, stone, and wood in different colors.

Peter entered first, hand hovering over the knife in his belt. He relaxed when he recognized the bald man behind the counter. "Hello Chert, good to see ya again. Nice shop you got here. Did you happen to talk to Capt'n Whitlock today? We need to find him to… discuss somethin'."

Chert stroked his hairless chin, leaving the room in silence for too long before uttering, "Yanapa. No."

"Wonderful, we'll wait for him." Peter scanned the room. "Why don't we take a look out back in the meantime?" He tilted his head to the door.

Aster gave Chert a weak, "Hello," then backed out of

the room, waiting for Peter outside.

Peter led him to a pearly white pile of stone behind the shop. "Yer givin' me a look," he said when he'd found a shady spot.

"Didn't want to wait inside?" Aster knew that they needed to be quick, but he found himself wishing they'd slow down a bit.

"Ah don't want Chert overhearin' us. Need to let you in on the scheme." Peter talked Aster through his plan to confront Whitlock, pointing to the main road and then over to the nearest alleyway.

Once he was satisfied that Aster had memorized the details, he followed the shade to a pile of reddish bricks, and sat facing towards the port.

I guess we've got some time to kill now, Aster thought. *Now's my chance to ask.* "Back in the cave, Kara mentioned that you've known Whitlock for quite some time. How did you end up on the Blue Skies?"

Peter's eyes grew distant as he stared down the busy street. "I was with the capt'n even before the Blue Skies. It's a long story... but I guess I could tell 'ya."

"It must've been ten... no, nineteen years ago... Loctee drown me, I'm old. Those were the final days of the monarchy. I was a personal guard for King Federyc, responsible for the protection of his majesty durin' the People's Rebellion. You head of it?"

Aster nodded.

"Times were tough then; the king was young, and his family presumed dead. There had been unrest brewin' for years, during his father's rule. The rebels used the chaos to their advantage. I'd single-handedly foiled two assassination attempts. But too many wanted him dead."

"You were a soldier?" Aster studied the man's worn face.

Peter grinned. "Bit more than that. Royal guard."

"You? No way."

"I thought I was pretty good at it. My commander had a tough time keeping it from goin' to my head," Peter chuckled.

"No wonder you're so good with a blade..."

"Lots of trainin'. Anyways, Whitlock was a smuggler who could always find the finest wine, ale, and other less savory goods. The night I met him is forever burned in my memory.

"It was late in the evenin' during a blood red harvest moon. The king had the last shipment of mead for the season delivered. But the problem was this mead wasn't for sale, if you catch my meanin'. So that's how we came to rely on Whitlock. Delivery went off without a hitch, but there was no celebration that night. I found Federyc dead in his room just as it got dark."

Aster's mouth opened in shock. He had heard about the king's assassination, but not the details. "How'd they get away with it?"

"We did a thorough investigation. The former mead owner never even noticed it was missin', so Whitlock was our number one suspect. I was tasked with trackin' him down and determinin' his guilt. I caught up with him by the spring, but I there was no evidence that he was part of the assassination. In the end we never did find out who killed Federyc."

"And you're sure it wasn't Whitlock?"

"No. Whitlock's a scoundrel, but he didn't kill Federyc. They chalked it up to politics. Didn't matter who did it in the end."

"That's sad. What happened next?"

"I"m afraid that was that: With the king dead, the rebellion had succeeded. The empire fell, and the people got what they wanted: New rulers they dubbed the Council of Elders. They claimed it would give the citizens of Benia more representation, but I still have my doubts." Peter shrugged.

"And you?"

"Time passed and with the empire gone, I was no longer needed as a guard. I ended up stayin' on Whitlock's ship and helped guide him to a more respectable future as a merchant. A year or so later, the ship was falling apart, and we were so short for gold that we had no choice but to join up with the newly created Benia Trading Company. They gave us the Blue Skies and an endless amounts of business. We were a great team back then. I wish he would've just talked to me instead of this..." Peter remained lost in thought.

Aster shifted uncomfortably, unable to come up with a reply. *This man should be a hero—was a hero. Now he's forgotten. Perhaps a footnote in some old history book.*

It was another hour or so before Whitlock arrived with the wood. An exhausted mule pulled a cart that looked like it was about to tip over.

Peter touched Aster's shoulder. "Not yet."

The former captain directed Chert to unload the lumber, not lifting a finger to help. One by one the Munayallpan lifted the reddish beams and placed them in a tight stack in the yard. After Chert finished, he handed Whitlock a bag.

Aster leaned forward from their hiding spot only to be pulled back by Peter.

Chert and Whitlock shook hands and Chert ambled back to his shop, closing the door behind him. Whitlock dumped the bag of gold coins into his palm and started to count them.

"Go."

You deserve everything that's coming to you, traitor. Aster dashed forward, putting himself between Whitlock and the cart. His hands shook as he lifted his knife and raised his voice, in an attempt at intimidation. "You aren't going to get away with this."

Whitlock jumped and dropped the coins. "Aster, what in Loctee's dark blue sea are you doing here? How'd you get out of that cave so quick?"

"Vincient brought us here. Now I'm here to stop you and take back the coin."

The portly man looked around and grinned, showing a single gold tooth. He pulled out a cutlass from under his coat and pointed it at Aster. "You shouldn't have come alone. Stay put." Keeping the blade raised, he bent over and gathered the coins from the ground.

Intimidate, don't fight. Aster repeated the plan over in his head, but his knees were still trembling. "The other's are taking the Blue Skies. You have nowhere to go."

Whitlock glanced towards the port. "You and I both know yer rubbish with that blade."

Aster gripped the knife with both hands, knuckles turning white. "You sure?"

Faster than Aster anticipated, Whitlock thrust his cutlass forward.

Aster to jumped back with a squeal.

Whitlock used the distraction to sprint down the nearest alley in the direction of the docks. He'd barely made it past the first awning when there was a loud crack that echoed against the buildings.

It worked! Aster let out a breath and sheathed his weapon.

Sure enough, Aster found Peter holding a wooden plank and Whitlock, face-down in the dirt, unconscious. "He acted exactly as you said he would."

Peter laid the plank against the sandstone wall beside him and took the cutlass and the coins from the ground near Whitlock. "Yeah, he's predictable. I've known him for a long time, like I said..." He trailed off as a large shadow joined them in the cramped alley.

Peter hid the cutlass behind his back. "It's not—"

"Loud noise means thieves," Chert bellowed, putting his fists up.

Aster readied his knife once again. *This is my chance to defend myself.*

Chert took two steps forward.

Aster thrust the blade forward, but Chert was beyond reach.

Like a branch falling from out of an ancient tree, Chert brought his arm down, crashing into the side of Aster's head.

"It should've been me," Kara muttered under her breath as she hung underneath the pier. She couldn't help but worry about involving the newcomer in arguably the most important part.

"Don't be thick, Calantha will do fine. Remember, they know our faces." Pat lifted a crab off of his leg and stared at it thoughtfully before tossing it in the water.

Tristram ran his fingers up a length of rope that he "liberated" from a nearby crate. "Any chance I get paid extra for this?"

"Doubt it," Kara replied. "Hush now... She's coming."

The boards creaked as Calantha led a half-dozen pirates off the docks. "Yes, it is fortunate that I found you, helpful gentlemen. I just couldn't lift the gold myself. I left it in my room at the inn."

"Glad to help." One of the pirates chuckled.

"Right this way." Calantha led them down an alleyway, out of sight.

"Now!" Kara swung herself up onto the pier and dashed towards the Blue Skies.

Tristram followed closely behind. "I only see one of them over there, but I'd guess there's another on board."

"Three to two, I like those odds," Pat added as he ran alongside.

The pirate saw them coming and pulled out his sword. "How'd you get here so quick?"

Pat lunged at the man, feinting sideways.

Kara kneed him in the stomach, then jumped back out of his reach.

The man doubled over as Tristram whipped the rope over his head, lassoing the man, pinning his hands to his side.

"Nicely done," Kara said as she hopped onto the gangplank and boarded the Blue Skies.

Pat followed suit as Tristram tied the pirate to the pier.

Kara kicked open the door to the captain's quarters and found the last pirate: a woman that she didn't recognize. Tattoos covered her arms. "It's over. Surrender the ship."

The woman looked from her to Pat. "The man outside?"

"Alive. Our friend is tying him up now. He'll be here in a second."

"And the noble with the gold? Another friend of yours?"

"Yup."

She shrugged and lifted her hands. "Fair enough. No sense in dying for it."

Pat tied her hands and escorted her off the ship, leaving the two restrained on the pier. "I'll get the others," he said as headed back into town.

"Tristram hoist the anchor. We may need to leave quickly. Keep an eye out." Kara ducked into the hold to check on their supplies. Aside from the wood, everything was still there.

The footsteps above and the sound of Pat's voice, made her smile. *The rest is up to Peter.* She climbed back up and grabbed the wheel. "Keep your weapons ready."

Calantha returned to the pier, out of breath, yelling at the top of her lungs, "They have seen through our ruse. We are no longer safe here!" With the bottom of her long dress in hand, she dashed aboard the ship. Six pirates and four Munayallpan guards were on her tail.

Not guards too! If we fight them, we'll never have another peaceful day in Strongfair. Kara swore under her breath before yelling orders to the crew. "Ready the sails! We've got to go!"

Pat rushed over to her. "What about Aster and Peter?"

Kara looked down into the rolling ocean waves. "We can't stay."

"Okay, we'll just circle round to pick them up?"

"No, they'll recognize the Blue Skies if we stay close. Only choice is to return to New Portsmith. Maybe Vincient can lend us a different ship? Peter will take care of Aster in the meantime."

"I don't like it," the cook grumbled.

By then Calantha had dashed up the gangplank while Tristram freed the ropes, leaving the pirates and soldiers yelling profanities from the dock.

"Got a better idea?" Kara stepped up the stairs to the steering wheel, with Pat following.

"Not without getting a message to Peter."

"We're out of time." She spun the wheel and the Blue Skies pulled away from the dock.

"Peter will take care of them." Pat nodded reassuringly.

I hope so. For a moment, Kara wished that her friend had put up a bigger fight. *Being in charge is stressful.* The sails caught a gust of wind and she directed the ship away from Strongfair, leaving Aster and Peter behind.

Aster awoke tucked into a woolen bed in an unfamiliar house. Judging by the sandstone walls, he was still in Strongfair. The light shining in from the lone window was a deep red; the sun was setting. His head throbbed as he sat up. *So much for defending myself.* He found his knife sitting on the dresser next to him, so he stashed it back in its sheath under his belt before leaving the bedroom.

There were a couple other rooms in the hallway, but he followed the soft chatter to the kitchen, where he found Peter, Chert, and a younger Munayallpan girl sitting together around an intricately carved granite table.

"What happened?" Aster asked, careful to keep his distance from the Munayallpan who had downed him.

Chert stood and rummaged around in his cabinets, causing Aster to jump out of his way.

Peter laughed and gestured for Aster to take a seat. "After you got clobbered. I managed to explain things to Chert, and he calmed down. He's sorry about hittin' you, so he's lettin' us stay here for a while."

"Oh uhhh thanks." His ears got hot as he thought about trying to stab the man. "And Whitlock?"

"He got away, but we've got the coin. And I don't know what happened with the Blue Skies. It ain't in port anymore. I went to find it after we got you situated. No sign of the crew either. I'm guessin' that they caused a bit too much of a ruckus and had to scram. So, we'll be spendin' a few days in Strongfair while we're waitin' for them to come back for us."

Chert had returned with a bowl of deep brown liquid and handed it to Aster. "Yanapa, Aster. Drink xocoatl. You feel better."

He swallowed a bit and was surprised by the combination of nutty, spicy, and sweet flavors of the drink.

Peter grinned. "Pretty good ain't it? They make it from the xoco beans that grow in the hills."

Aster let his muscles relax. *And Chert doesn't seem mad. But the Blue Skies missing is a real setback. I should have plenty of time before the Council meeting and it's not like I could get back to Buckwheat any faster. I'd better make the most of things here.* "So, I guess this means we've got some time to kill?"

Peter nodded. "By the way, this is Chert's sister, Sienna." He tilted his head to their silent companion.

"Hello, nice to meet you," Aster held out his hand.

Sienna looked up at him with her hazel brown eyes, but returned to her food without acknowledging Aster.

Did I do something? Aster squirmed in his chair for a moment, then let his hand drop back to the table. "Since we've got nothing better to do, my mother lives around here somewhere. It would be nice if you could help me find her."

"So that's why you looked out of place in Buckwheat Village. I guess you do look like the locals." Peter smoothed the tip of his goatee and raised an eyebrow.

Aster sighed. "Chert, do you happen to know of anyone named Beryl Rutherford?"

Chert was quiet for a few seconds before speaking up. "Beryl very famous. Best jeweler in Munayallpa. I take you to guild in morning."

Aster tensed up. *That's too soon. I'm not ready.*

The artisan's guildhall didn't look special from the outside— a rectangular sandstone building with a flat roof. The walls weren't even decorated, unlike the majority of houses nearby.

Aster followed Chert and Peter inside. Despite the press of people, their voices never rose above a murmur. Like ants devouring dropped food, the artisans swarmed around them, hawking their goods. Each hand held a new treasure: A beautiful emerald ring, a ruby bracelet lined with pearls, and a glittering opal pendant were among the many items that caught Aster's eye. But before he could decline any of the jewelry, Chert raised his calloused hand above the throng and said in a booming voice, "We're here for Beryl."

The mention of this name was all it took for a pathway to open up through the busy room. Three of the guild members pointed to a vivid orange curtain in the far corner of the room. Chert led the way while Aster and Peter gawked at the merchants and their dazzling wares. Chert pushed aside the curtain revealing a modest bedroom.

Only two pieces of furniture fit inside this room; a simple bed and an oversized oak table which crowded out the possibility of anything else. The table was covered with uncut stones, scraps of gold, and various oddly shaped tools. Aster was certain each served a single, dedicated purpose. The three men could barely wedge themselves in the room.

A woman sat cross-legged atop the quilted bed, inspecting a light blue gem in her hands through a jeweler's loupe. Her skin was darker than Aster's, and she wore many pieces of finely-crafted jewelry—probably more than all the jewelry Buckwheat, combined. One ring in particular stood due to its poor quality it was compared to the others: It was plain silver with a faded red stone in its heart—twisted and off-center as if made by a child.

Beryl spoke without breaking her gaze from the gem. "Kapchi and welcome to the jewelers' guild. How may I help you?"

A wave of excitement and fear washed over Aster. He had been too caught up in the events of the last few days to give himself the chance to prepare for this meeting. From the time he turned ten years old, he had had vivid dreams about his mother visiting Buckwheat Village to see him. Each time, she would give a grand apology for not being there for him and swear to stay forever. His father would console him each morning after the dream dissipated.

Aster was face-to-face with his mother for the first time in over fifteen years. *What do I say to the person who abandoned me?*

"Are you looking to have a jewel appraised? Or perhaps commission a piece?" Beryl asked, nonchalantly.

Aster thought about growing up reading her letters. He thought about his father's many stories of life in Munayallpa: fantasies of adventure in exotic places, but also tear-filled nights. When he was younger his heart would dance at every knock at the door only to be let down when it wasn't her. "I'm... your son, Aster."

She placed the piece and loupe down on the bed and looked up. "So, you've finally come. I'm glad to have the chance to see you. In your letters, you always talked about the grand adventures that you wanted to go on. I figured it was only a matter of time till you left Buckwheat. You've gained the courage to break away from your overbearing father. And you've found your way to me."

She seemed sincere, but Aster was taken aback. "He may be a bit overbearing, but at least he didn't abandon me to play with shiny stones."

After a few seconds of uncomfortable silence, Beryl spoke again. "Mighty Ochress temper my heart. That was the hardest decision of my life. I've spent every night questioning my choice."

"I don't understand. You made the choice to do what? Become the leader of this crafting guild? Why was that so important to you? Was it really better than raising your son? Even if that was your choice, couldn't you have visited us from time to time?" Aster added one final question before turning away with tears forming in his eyes, "Do you regret it?"

Beryl picked the gem back up from her blanket. She sighed deeply, rolling the loupe between her fingers and thumb for a moment before she bent to examine the gem again. "It's not that simple."

He shot back at her, "Then make it simple. Do you regret abandoning me?"

Beryl's eye twitched. "I... all things considered; I think it turned out... well."

Aster's stomach dropped. It was the worst thing his mother could say. Choking back tears, he muttered, "I've heard enough. Let's go." Peter and Chert, shifted towards the door, shadows on the wall no longer.

Beryl called out after them, "Wait, Aster! I can't bear to have this be our final conversation. I'll tell you everything... Please meet me here at sunrise tomorrow. I need to show you my choice."

Aster brushed aside the curtain as he stomped through the busy guildhall and out onto the street. *She's a disappointment. Just like I always knew.*

Back at Chert's house, Aster kept to himself for the rest of the day, refusing to join them for dinner. After sunset, he left his room to sit alone outside on the front stoop and look up at the stars. They were brighter here than in New Portsmith, but not as bright as they were in

Buckwheat Village.

The door swung open, and Chert stepped out. "How you feel?"

Aster kicked at the ground. "Like my chest was crushed. How can someone be that cruel?"

He squatted down next to Aster. "Chert thinks you go back. Talk again."

Aster dug his fingers into the sandstone step. "Why? You heard what she said—she doesn't care."

"That's not what Chert heard."

"What do you know about it?" Aster snapped. "She wasn't around when I needed her growing up. She chose to stay in Strongfair, instead of Buckwheat with her family."

"Chert's dad not around much." He gave Aster a rough pat on the back. "Great man. Not great father. One day of pain better than lifetime of regret. Chert knows."

"So?"

"You may not get another chance."

Aster's heart thumped in agreement. *Even if I hate every minute of our talk, maybe I need to hear her side of things. It was an accident that I ended up in Strongfair to begin with. At least it could give me closure from that miserable woman.* "Thanks Chert, I guess I should hear her out."

They sat around for a while longer until Chert went to bed. Aster was exhausted from the emotional drain of the day, so he followed suit to try and get some rest.

Aster woke up throughout the night, disturbed by a rhythmic snoring from the other room. After turning over a dozen times, he gave up on sleep and got out of bed well before dawn.

The air had grown cold in the absence of the sun. He dressed quickly and retraced his path back to the guild hall where he waited an eternity for his mother to arrive.

There were a surprising number of people leaving the building—mostly artisans. *Did they stay here all night? Don't any of them have families? When do they eat? The artisan lifestyle seems unhealthy.*

It was nearly midday before Beryl appeared with a large drum strapped to her back. Aster had considered giving up multiple times, but he stubbornly convinced himself to keep waiting.

"You're late," Aster said, trying not to lose his patience.

"Kapchi, my son. I'm sorry, but I had to take care of something." His mother was oblivious to his anger.

Aster shook his head. "I just hope you have a better justification than you did yesterday."

She examined him carefully. "Yes, I believe so... please follow me. It's a bit of a walk, but we can talk on the way."

Aster nodded and followed her through the city toward the eastern mountains. They loomed over the city, casting early morning shadows. It was as if daytime needed their permission to exist.

As the buildings became more and more sparse, Beryl spoke. Her voice strained against every word. "For all of this to make sense, I need to start from the beginning. I don't know my parents. As far back as I can remember, I lived in the streets, alone and without purpose.

"I tried not to steal, but begging only goes so far. The Mogul filled up most nights leaving me nowhere to go. Yes, they would prioritize children, but there weren't nearly enough beds for all of us. And I never managed to get there on time.

"One day, after a particular streak of bad luck with food, I came across an old artisan who was selling silver rings. They sparkled brightly in the hot summer air, each with a unique gemstone in the center of the band. I must've been fourteen at the time and I'd already learned the best way to separate merchants from their wares."

A leech and a thief. Rowan Goodwin would gloat if he knew.

"Since my clothes were always grungy and my hair unkempt, everyone could tell I was up to no good.

108

Merchants would keep a careful eye on me while I was around. But they also had great pride in their goods. They thrive off of conversation about their trinkets. So, I began hanging around these silver rings asking questions.

"I learned that this man had founded an artists' guild and made every ring himself. This struck my curiosity because I couldn't imagine where a person would find such beautiful stones. I had only seen them on the hands of nobility, never considering how they came to be. The man became a different person when he sensed my genuine interest.

"His name's Argil Barros. He dedicates his life to trekking through the mountain streams in search of precious stones and materials. There was something about the excitement in his voice and his tales of exploration that drew me in. My thoughts of stealing were quickly forgotten. His tales became part of my routine. I spent every morning at his stall to learn about the latest big find or magnificent creation.

"After a few weeks like this, I must've earned his trust, because he invited me to join him for his next material hunt."

They passed the last house and the dirt path twisted and turned between the trees. The mountains towered in front of them, full of scrub brush. The land here was no longer flat like it had been in Strongfair.

Beryl adjusted the straps on her drum and began climbing up the rocky path. When she pulled herself onto flatter ground, she started speaking again.

"Looking back, he must have been thrilled to find someone who would listen to his stories. We ended up finding a river in the mountains that had a variety of rocks littering the riverbanks. I spent the entire afternoon pulling stones from the water, breaking them open to see if there were treasures inside. The repetition was frustrating at first, but when I opened a very plain piece of sandstone, I fell in love. It was my first gemstone. In the sun, the opal shimmered like blue and green waves of the ocean.

"When we made it back to town, Argil arranged a feast in celebration. That was the best day of my life."

I see where your priorities lie.

"Months passed and we continued to scour the countryside for materials together. Eventually, I became his apprentice, and was offered a position in his guild. Its charter was to pay respect to the god Ochress through discovery and craftsmanship of all things that come out of the ground. Ochress is the god of minerals. Argil believes this is the ideal way to show our devotion.

"Argil gave me everything I could ever want: food, a trade, and a place where I belonged. I happily made these beliefs my own."

But not how to be there for your family.

They had hiked to the foot of the mountain. Aster fought to maintain his footing as they ascended the slopes. Lifting his legs became a struggle and he needed to stop frequently to catch his breath. Halfway up there was a small clearing below a free-standing rock outcrop.

Aster found a smooth boulder and took a seat. The parched air was exhausting.

Nervously, Beryl examined the area. "We can't stop here. The tor is a hunting ground for boulder beetles."

Aster jumped up and his eyes darted around the rocks. Sure enough, just beside a shadow on the hill, a stone about the size of a man's head was inching up the slope. If it wasn't for his mother's words, he wouldn't have noticed the dull gray creature with spindly legs.

Beryl walked back over to him. "Clever animals. They collect boulders by rolling them up the hill. They'll wait for days, perfectly still, for a small animal to pause underneath to spring their trap, crushing the unsuspecting victim. Usually it's birds or rabbits, but occasionally they get a deer. I heard a rumor of a man getting killed by one a while back. They say some hikers found him half eaten with a crushed skull."

Aster felt a twinge of childlike glee alongside the horror of her words. *They are real! And I got to see one with* my *own two eyes*! He lingered a moment longer, observing the creature's gray carapace before continuing on.

The next segment of the path was the greenest. Aster had to grab hold of roots growing out of the cliffs and pull himself from foothold to foothold.

Beryl traversed the terrain naturally, only breaking stride to wait for Aster to catch up. She effortless continued her tale while climbing, never seeming to run out of breath. "Years later, an unusual man arrived in town from New Portsmith. He had bright green eyes that reminded me of my opal. I don't know if you've noticed, but in Munayallpa most everyone has brown eyes. Green eyes are exceedingly rare in southern Arathanon. He wanted to know everything about Ochress and since I was so enchanted by his eyes, I volunteered to teach him.

"That man was your father, Aster. We fell in love, swore our vows of union, and I gave birth to you. We were happy for a while. If I could point to anything, I would say that the death of the king of Benia was the first hint of trouble for us."

"The king?" Aster stopped to pant with his hands on his knees. "Why did that matter?"

"Your dad took the news quite hard. He was worried about his family back at the capital amidst the turmoil and birth of the new government. He must've sent out two dozen letters that night. It wasn't long before he found a merchant ship willing to take him back home.

"He returned much later a changed man. Paranoia around strangers was the worst of it. Some nights he would wake up screaming about being found by some monster. He used to lock himself in our room, studying maps of Arathanon, trying to find the best place to hide. Buckwheat Village, he decided, was the ideal location for safety. He even made sure that there was interesting geology nearby for me. At the time, there were rumors that Sir Ian Pelware was planning to build a mine in the mountains nearby.

"He spent two weeks begging me to move to Buckwheat with him. If circumstances were different, I probably would have gone, but the day after he found Buckwheat Village, my life changed. Argil was out on his own when he had an accident. During a climb, he lost his footing and tumbled down the side of the mountain. It was two days before we found him, and his leg was never the same after that. Knowing he would never be able to climb again, he retired from the guild and entrusted it to me. Guildmaster Beryl. It was everything that I never knew I wanted."

Artistry over family. At least there was a reason. Aster had never felt that strongly about work. Even though being the postmaster was something he enjoyed, he'd give it up in a heartbeat to stay with his father.

The steep cliffs evened out as the two approached a small cavern entrance, partially obstructed from view by a lone desert-willow tree. It tenaciously held onto the side of the hill with tiny leaves and pink flowers blowing in the breeze.

Beryl paused beside it and continued her story. "Stay as guildmaster or go with my husband: I spent so long agonizing over that choice. Too long. After a late night working on a pendant, I came home to find you two gone. Your father always used to look after you during the day so that I could work... Or maybe he was being overprotective. In any case, he left a note. It said, 'I love you. Please come to Buckwheat Village with us.'"

So, it was Dad that left. It made sense given that Beryl stayed in Strongfair, but Aster had never given it much thought. He never asked Dad why.

"I was devastated. I felt betrayed. He forced me to make a cruel decision. I went into the mountains to clear my head. The moon was full that night, perfect for seeing the glimmer of rare gems—to palliate my mind. I stumbled a bit in the dark and ended up on a different path than normal.

"When I looked back towards the mountainside, it was

the most beautiful sight I've ever seen. The moonlight reflected off the surface of a thousand multicolored gems that flowed as a river of stars. I collected as many as I could carry, but I needed to find the source. By the time I had climbed up to the cave entrance, the sky was bright, and the sun was moments from rising. That's when I saw it. That's when I knew I couldn't leave Strongfair."

"But what did you find that made you so sure?"

For the first time since they reunited, Beryl smiled. "My son, come see my biggest secret with your own eyes. It gives my life purpose." She stepped into the cave.

Aster hesitated outside. He looked down to where the rocky slopes met the frothing ocean. Waves splashed against the side of the cliffs, spraying a mist into the air. *The reason that I never had a mother is inside.* He took a deep breath to try and calm his nerves. *It doesn't matter how large or how beautiful this gem is, I'll never forgive her.* Aster squeezed his leg and forced himself to follow.

The interior was deceptively large compared to the tiny entrance. The walls around the opening had been chipped away. Scraps of jagged stone littered the floor. Aster noticed why a bit further in. The walls were sporadically covered in gemstones. Even the untrained eye could recognize them.

"Well, this is an impressive find. You've got to be wealthy now, but I'm not sure why this stopped you from joining us in Buckwheat?"

"My son, you shouldn't judge a stone by its luster only. Its clarity is also important. And for that, you need a deeper examination."

"What are you talking about?" Aster grumbled.

"Look carefully and listen." Beryl said, gesturing to the wall behind him.

Aster focused. He could hear a deep whooshing noise followed by a slight breeze coming from somewhere above. A clear crystal on the wall sparkled as it crossed a beam of light from a crack near the entrance. "A giant diamond?"

Beryl shook her head, eyes fixed on the ceiling.

It all finally clicked together in Aster's head. The crystal was moving. The wall itself was part of a larger structure that captured his mother's attention. It was a face. "What is that thing?"

"This... is Mother Ochress." Beryl whispered, tears in her voice.

Fear overtook Aster, and he bolted out of the cave, only stopping to catch his breath after he was a safe distance away. He'd never seen a living thing that massive in his life.

Beryl caught up to him. "Her size is quite terrifying, but she won't harm you."

Aster began to regain his wits. "That thing could crush us with one hand! Is that really a god?"

Beryl pointed back towards the cave. "Come and let me introduce you to her. Truthfully, I'm uncertain if this is Goddess Ochress herself or one of her servants. Either way, we must be reverent and respectful." She took Aster by the hand and led him back towards the cave.

Aster pulled back at first, but there was something about the sincerity in her eyes that won him over. And he needed to know. More than anything else, he had to understand why.

At the center of the cave, Beryl removed the straps from the drum she had been carrying and placed it on the ground. She sat cross-legged holding it between her legs and began to strike it with a regular rhythm while chanting a prayer to the goddess in front of them.

Mighty Ochress, eldest of the four, ruler of earthly riches,

dweller of dirt, clay, and stone.
In the language of earthquakes
we honor you and your creations.
Walking thy land, scaling thy mountains, polishing thy gems,
are how we show our devotion.
Please grant us thy favor.

After speaking these words, she stopped beating the drum and stillness filled the room. "Now ask," she whispered.

"Uhhh... please help me find what I'm looking for. I mean a doctor. Actually, a cure for the village would be better. Help me find that."

Aster was focused on the face in front of him, motionless, until the ground started to shake. It intensified so suddenly that he tumbled to the floor. There was a loud crash from the entryway as a stalactite broke free of the ceiling and splintered onto the entryway.

The shaking stopped and the room returned to silence aside from a whistle of wind. Excitedly, Beryl jumped up and rushed over to the shards of rock. She picked up the pieces one-by-one, examining them carefully before throwing them aside. Finally, she held up a black stone, distinct from the rest.

She looked back towards her goddess and bowed her head until her hair touched the smooth floor. "Kapchi. Thank you for your gift, Ochress." She stowed it in her pocket, retrieved her drum, and guided Aster out of the cave.

When they were back in the fresh air and late afternoon sun, Aster asked, "What was that?"

Beryl pulled the stone out of her pocket and held out to Aster. "It's a blessing from Ochress. That was the first time that she has ever responded. And I've never seen a mineral quite like this. It looks like onyx, but is darker and heavier. I must bring it back to the guild and examine it."

The path became a dusty red color under the setting sun as they returned to Strongfair.

Aster was lost in thought the whole way back. *If Conflag asked me to abandon my family to serve him, would I have done the same?* His head swam with questions.

He was surprised how quickly they made it back to the guildhall. Outside the door, Beryl stopped to hug Aster. "I hope you understand now why I had to remain here without you. I found my purpose in life: to serve the goddess who had revealed herself to me. The goddess who gave me my mentor and my guild. I needed to stay and spread the blessings of the earth and elevate Munayallpa to a center of worship. And for Ochress' sake: Please do not mention what you witnessed to anyone."

She stared at Aster expectantly.

"I don't really know what to make of all of this. Was that really a god? Even if it was, you choose this god over your family. I can't say that I agree, but I think I understand. I'm not angry anymore. Thank you for sharing your secret with me. I'll keep it safe."

She smiled. "Please come visit once more before you depart Munayallpa." She waded into the crowded guildhall.

Aster stared after her in the twilight.

Peter had checked the docks each day in search of the Blue Skies. Occasionally Aster joined him, but on other days he would assist Chert in his shop. After two weeks of waiting, Peter returned in a particularly bad mood. "Loctee drown me, I don't think they're comin' back. They should've been here by now. Somethin's wrong. We need to get back to New Portsmith as soon as we can."

Aster nodded. "My meeting with the Benia Council is in two weeks, so we can't stay here much longer."

Chert placed his ledger back on the desk. He surveyed his shop with hands on his hips. "Chert will take you home. Jasper will watch shop. Head out tomorrow."

"Who is Jasper?" Aster asked.

"Chert's brother."

Aster glanced in the backroom, not expecting to find anyone.

"Not here. Tomorrow home. Leave message with Sienna."

"That's very kind of you. In that case, I need to stop by

the guild hall and say goodbye to my mother." Aster placed the rag he had been using to dust on the nearest counter and headed out the door.

Aster pushed past the artisans hawking their jewelry more confidently than his first trek to the guildhall. He parted the colorful curtain at the rear and found Beryl hard at work.

"Hi, Mom. We are heading back to New Portsmith tomorrow. I wanted to say goodbye."

Beryl looked up from her desk and waved him closer. "Kapchi. It was wonderful that you came to visit me. I have something for you."

She lifted a gold chain necklace off the table and fastened it around Aster's neck. A heavy black pendant hung down from its center. It contained a golden inlay of a semicircle with its flat side down. "Here in Munayallpa, we show our devotion through works of art—Kapchi. This is the gift we received from Ochress. I have cut it and adorned it with the symbol of the Goddess herself, transforming it into a prayer. You should take it; may it serve as your guide in times of hardship."

Aster could barely hold back tears, muttering a simple, "Thanks." He hugged her so tight that all five of her necklaces dug into his skin. *I should ask her to come back home. No, after all she's told me, I've got to respect her decision.*

He pulled away, hiding his reddened face as he left her room. When he stepped back into the bustling guild hall, her voice rang out once more. "Come back soon!"

Beryl was nothing like he had expected. Much more kind and understanding than he had ever thought. But devoted, too. Aster had always pictured her as an unmotivated person, simply unwilling to leave Strongfair. She wasn't. She was driven by a divine calling. Something that Aster couldn't wrap his head around. The gods had always felt out of reach for him. He believed in Conflag, but seeing one up close was different. *I'll be back some day.*

The next morning, Aster joined Chert and Peter for breakfast before they departed. After Chert had served everyone, he took a seat at the table. In unison, he and Sienna raised their bowls above their heads and said, "T'Och," before taking a bite.

Fork in hand, Peter watched the ritual. They had gotten used to it by now—a prayer for their food. He smirked as he shifted his attention back to Aster. "We'd better hurry up so Aster can reunite with his love-bird, Kara."

Aster blushed which only caused Peter to tease him more. "Don't be coy, I saw you two back at the Beached Whale. Don'cha think she's pretty?"

Aster stammered. "Well... yeah, but nothing happened! She only used me as a diversion to foil Whitlock's plans. Guess it worked if you were fooled as well..."

"Hmmm," Peter stroked his goatee. "In any case, you'll get another shot when we meet back up. Tristram tried his hands with her once. Let's just say that she ain't shy in sayin' when she ain't interested. But I reckon she won't be sayin' anything like that... for you." His lips twisted in a knowing smirk.

Chert interrupted, saying, "Time to go."

Aster stood, happy to leave the topic.

The three men cleaned up, grabbed some supplies, and walked down to the shore where Chert's modest dinghy waited for them. The small boat barely big fit them.

There were bird droppings on the seat. Aster's knees pressed against Chert's tree trunk legs. He hoped that the pungent smell was a missing fish head under the seat and not his companions.

Chert handed him an oar. "Help row." The men each traded off paddling the craft as they bobbed up and down on the waves. The wind shifted and Chert raised a ragged sail. The boat picked up speed as they headed back to the capital city of Benia.

It was more than a day before they saw the clifftop olive tower that marked the eastern side of New Portsmith, which seemed to glow a vibrant green in the sunlight. A welcome beacon after the turbulent waves.

Aster had never been more exhausted in his life. They hadn't brought much food for the trip, and he had declined all of it. Between the smell and the swell, he couldn't eat. *Being on the ocean is the worst.* He clenched his stomach and spit overboard.

As the three men arrived at the docks, they recognized the familiar shape of the Blue Skies among the ships there.

"Glad we found them. Now we can find out why they couldn't come back for us," Peter commented as he helped Chert secure the boat to the pier.

Just beyond the water, Aster recognized the large oak whale sculpture of the Beached Whale inn. He never thought he'd feel this happy to step foot in that place again. There was a commotion outside. Instead of merchants, a young man stood atop the railing, surrounded by a crowd of people.

They got close enough to hear. "Come one, come all. Purchase the news of the week. Come read about Jash's declaration of war on Malvez. Could Benia be next? The spring festival of Viridus will begin tomorrow, so read about all the wonderful events planned for this year. Discover the motives of traitorous Kara Reeves!"

At those words, Peter shoved the crowd aside and grabbed the man by the shirt, forcing him to answer questions. His face was white by the time he had returned.

"What happened?" Aster asked.

"Loctee, drown me." Peter clenched his teeth. "He says that Kara Reeves was found guilty of mutiny, the murder of Captain Whitlock, and disturbin' the peace of our allied nation of Munayallpa. She's scheduled for execution by hangin' the day after next."

Zinnia Hollyhock,

It's been a strange turn of events since I last wrote. We were deceived by the captain. He stole our ship and left us to die. We escaped thanks to Calantha, who is still very much a mystery. She managed to hide from the pirates and cut us free thanks to some kind of stealth. She tried to explain it, but I couldn't follow. In any case, we ended up chasing the captain to Munayallpa.

Strongfair is so different from Buckwheat Village. The land itself is brown and orange! That's where Peter and I caught the captain. It didn't work out as expected though; we got stranded here without the rest of the crew. Luckily for us, one of the locals, Chert, let us stay with him. He banged me up a bit at first, but we sorted things out.

That's how I finally got to meet Beryl. It was weird. I was so angry at first, but I heard her out. It wasn't what we thought. I can't go into it in this letter, but she had a divine calling. That and Dad left her pretty abruptly. I don't know Zin. I ended up forgiving her, but part of me is still hurt that she didn't move to Buckwheat with us. I wish you were here to talk it over with me.

I hope all is well in the village. Show my father this letter and tell him I miss him. After a few more days in New Portsmith, we'll be heading home. Tell the Fultons to stock up on honey cakes for my return!

Your friend,
Aster

5 RESCUING KARA

Aster could barely keep his balance as he navigated around the chairs of the Beached Whale. To his horror, the ocean waves persisted on land. It was as if the building was slowly rocking him back and forth. An awful feeling. Peter dashed ahead to the corner table, leaving Aster to stumble from chair to chair. Chert followed, keeping a close eye. *He found Pat and the others. That was quick.*

"Glad we found you here," Peter addressed the crew. "What happened in Munayallpa? And why's Kara on the choppin' block?"

Pat nearly fell out of his chair at the sound of Peter's voice. "Loctee bless us! You made it back."

"Yeah. Thanks to our new friend, Chert, who gave us a ride. Errr, rather, we both gave Aster a ride seein' as he doesn't have the muscle to help much. But that ain't important now."

Aster caught up to them and dropped into a seat. Holding onto the table for dear life.

"You're right, we've got bigger fish to fry." Pat nodded before saying, "Let me catch you up. In Strongfair we took back the ship, easy enough, but there must've been a lookout we didn't spot 'cause the guards were on us too quick. Kara made the right call to get us all out of there.

"We planned to come back for you, but things didn't work out that way. We stopped to borrow a different ship and pick you up. When Kara and I found Vincient, I shoulda known something was up. Vincient is normally a talker, but he was quiet. Seemed meek, nervous. He had us wait in the headquarters while he prepared the new ship. He returned with three soldiers. They took Kara away."

"Shit. Vincient say why?"

"I tried to get the story from him, but he could only mutter something about being sorry and that there was nothing he could do about it. We ended up waiting a few days for Kara to return only to find out that she was on trial for the murder of the captain. We all knew she was innocent so we went to the clock-tower to share our testimony with the Council. They gave us the run-around at first, but we finally convinced them to give us an appointment three days from now." Pat smacked the table. "The afternoon after the execution."

Peter grimaced.

"Yeah, I don't think they intended to talk with us in the first place. I don't know what's going on, but there ain't much left we can do. We even tried to visit Kara at the barracks, but they said that she wasn't there. An hour ago, Tristram left to do some investigating. Calantha is back home. Said she needed to water her plants. So Peter, you got any bright ideas for how to get us out of this mess?"

Aster spoke up. "I'll clear her name."

"You got a plan?" Pat itched his stubble. Scattered black hairs marred his typically smooth shave.

"I'll talk with the Council tomorrow. I'll tell them all about Whitlock's betrayal."

"Don't think they'll let you in. Took us three days to even get a meeting on the books."

"I've already got a meeting with them." *A stroke of good fortune.* "Booked it weeks ago to get permission for Doctor Malvin to travel to Buckwheat Village. I was worried that we wouldn't make it back in time, but everything worked out."

"I hope you're right, Aster. This whole situation is making me uneasy." Pat glanced at Peter who shrugged. "In any case, let's order you a bit of food and you can rest up. Traveling in a small boat is tough work and you've got lots to do tomorrow. Say, how about I join you at the Council? That way I can back your story up with some BTC credibility."

"That would be good. Thanks Pat."

Peter had already eaten half the carrots off of Pat's plate, by the time their food arrived. Chert lifted his plate into the air with a "T'Och," and began eating.

Aster hadn't realized how hungry he was. The room had settled and so had his stomach. He gulped down the ale and devoured his roasted Tembourian game hen. The simple, earthy flavors reminded him of home.

His stomach was full and the siren song of a clean, warm bed was too much for Aster to take, so he retired early. As he made his way to the rooms upstairs, he noticed Peter and Pat in a heated discussion, but he was too tired to care. *I'm going to free Kara tomorrow. That'll raise everyone's spirits.*

Early the next morning, Aster readied himself for his meeting. Pat was waiting downstairs. After a quick breakfast they headed down the cobblestone road towards the city center, taking a different route than Aster had been before. They passed an enormous anvil in front of a building where black smoke billowed from the chimney. *City armory? Is this where the soldiers get their plate mail from?*

Lost in thought about the lives of weapon-smiths, Aster mindlessly followed the path toward the sparkling apex of the city. Before he knew it, they had arrived at the clock tower.

Once inside, Aster saw the mousy woman he had

spoken with before. She was leaning back in her chair, lazily flipping between pages. "Hello. We are here to speak with the Council."

Without looking up from the papers, the lady replied, "Sorry. They aren't taking any visitors today."

"But I have an appointment."

"If you'd like, I can reschedule you for first thing tomorrow?"

"Tomorrow is too late. I need to speak with them today," Aster's words burst out, causing the woman to look up.

Pat grumbled and cleared his throat. "Loctee drown all of this bureaucratic nonsense. Listen: This poor boy arranged this meeting to help his village a month ago. Ain't there anything you can do to get him in front of the Council today?"

She pulled out a calendar and studied it before slowly nodding to them. "Yes, I think I can, if you are patient... On second thought, you should wait here," she said, pointing to Pat. "It will go more smoothly if it's just him."

Pat scowled but took a step back.

The woman placed her papers down and guided Aster to the stairwell. "My name is Olivia. You're Aster Rutherford, correct? What's the name of your village again?"

"Buckwheat Village."

"Being in front of the Council can be daunting; I hope you're ready. Let me know if you need a rest on the stairs. I climb them so often that I sometimes don't notice."

Sure enough, Aster had to stop twice to catch his breath before they reached the tenth floor.

Olivia paused in front of the ornate golden doors. The high ceilings arched upwards, pearly white with gold inset. A floral perfume permeated the air and the patterned tiles echoed with every step.

Olivia whispered, "We need to wait until they are finished. Then I'll introduce you."

Aster caught his breath and marveled at the grand

hallway. The conversation in the other room was audible from where he stood.

"Why must we continue with this farce?" The raspy voice of a woman echoed from the other room. "I say we do away with it starting this year."

"No. We shall have it again, just like every year. The ritual calms the citizens. Helps them feel like they have a say in what goes on," a high-pitched, nasal voice replied.

"They didn't seem to mind with the child king," the woman countered.

A third voice, deep and gravely, interjected, "Now Emme, you know that's not true. He was assassinated."

"Not soon enough."

The last voice, distinct with a foreign accent—almost Munayallpan, but with inflections that Aster didn't recognize—added, "I'm not about to spend good coin on this."

The lady raised her voice authoritatively. "Things have been running smooth lately, I suppose we wouldn't want to upset the balance. It's decided. We will continue as we have."

Olivia took this statement as her cue to interrupt. She shoved the massive door open with her entire body and led Aster into the center of a round room under a high domed ceiling. The floors were marble and accented with polished red stone that Aster didn't recognize. On the far end of the room, three men and one woman sat on excessively tall, golden chairs atop the dais. One chair sat empty on the left side—for an absent fifth council member.

They stared down at Aster and Olivia, like hawks examining their prey.

Olivia raised her voice, "Wise and just Council of Elders, I introduce to you Aster Rutherford. He is here to seek the Council's decision on behalf of his home, Buckwheat Village."

The woman at the center frowned, her wrinkles pulling her already low cheeks below her chin. "I thought we said no visitors." Her stern voice gave Aster goosebumps.

"Apologies, Elder. This poor boy had an appointment for today. And he's traveled a long way from home."

"We were in the middle of important business."

Olivia bowed. "Consider it a personal favor to me. I did help convince Elad to—"

"Very well. But cancel all other appointments this week."

"Yes, ma'am." She then turned to Aster and said, "You speak to the great Council of Benia: Emmeline Dolloway, Elder of Tradition and former advisor to the king; Archbishop Nicholas IV, Elder of Faith and high priest of the Order of Conflagration; Shaheed Iman, Elder of Economy and owner of the Benia Trading Company; and Rufus Henderson, mayor of New Portsmith."

Aster's head spun as he stared up at the most powerful people in all of Benia. Archbishop Nicholas was the most intimidating. His face was lined with wrinkles and his stick-like arms minuscule in the billowy amber robes. But it was his crooked nose that was most disconcerting—thin and beak like. *What a small question I'm bringing them, compared to their usual affairs. Will they care?*

Olivia must have sensed his intimidation, because she gave him a nudge of encouragement.

Aster rubbed his goosebumps. "Hello, Benia Council. I need your help with my village. There is a sickness that we can't overcome. We need Doctor Malvin. He told me to get the Council's permission for him to travel to Buckwheat Village and perform an examination. So please, will you allow Dr. Malvin to travel with me?" Aster was trembling and out of breath, but happy he articulated his request.

In a gravelly voice, Rufus spoke first, "Buckwheat is one of the furthest villages. Malvin would be gone for at least a month." Rufus was the only Council member dressed practically. *I bet Gilroy gets along with him well, when he visits.*

Archbishop Nicholas added with a nasal hum, "We still

have a full stock of his medicine. We could manage without him. How much tribute did Buckwheat offer last harvest?"

Shaheed patted down his crimson shirt, startling the dozen necklaces that lay there. He waved a bejeweled hand in the air, two rings on each finger. "Five hundred gold. A reasonable amount, for its size."

Aster stared at the man's dark skin. *There's no way he's Benian.*

Emmeline peered down at Aster, studying him. "Another consideration is Malvin's temperament. He's been refusing to teach our representative. We still need him and he knows it, yet he keeps putting us in impossible situations. Last time it took us the entire winter to retrieve him. I suppose we could send a guard to keep an eye on him—"

Rufus interrupted with a deep cough. "It's important to note that this village is strategically located near the Pelware Mine. If the village is impacted, it would substantially slow our flow of gold."

Shaheed added, "My comrades, please recall the *efficiency* improvement we made some years back. It would be unfortunate if Malvin were to hinder that."

Emmeline gave a decisive hum. "Oh yes, I had forgotten about *that*. I say, it settles this matter. Aster Rutherford, we reject your request. Malvin must remain in New Portsmith."

Aster couldn't follow their discussion, but understood the verdict well enough. "Why? We need him badly. The villagers are in danger!"

"All Council decrees are final."

Aster's fists trembled. "If you will, I have one more topic to discuss," he said through gritted teeth. "What about Kara Reeves? She is innocent and should be released."

"State your reasoning."

Aster described to the Council the events of Captain Whitlock's betrayal and the confrontation in Munayallpa.

Emmeline perked up. "Well now you have said something interesting, Whitlock is stranded without coin or vessel in Strongfair? That explains things. Baxter will flush that relic out of hiding."

Aster's shoulders relaxed. "So now that you know Kara is innocent, will you cancel the execution?"

"No. There's a small chance that Whitlock will return to New Portsmith."

"But Kara has nothing to do with that!"

"She is still serving her role. Besides, the Council does not make mistakes."

"You can't do this. She's innocent!"

"You are dismissed. Olivia, take this boy away and fetch Baxter as soon as you can. We have a new task for him."

Olivia grabbed Aster's arm and directed him out of the room. She stopped on the stairs and said, "Sorry that the Council couldn't give you what you wanted. I wish you the best of luck in finding another way to assist your village."

Aster couldn't find the words to say anything back. He stared at his feet all the way to Pat, where he told him about the Council's decision on both topics.

"Ouch. Sounds like you got trampled in there." Pat put a hand on Aster's shoulder. "I wish they'd have let me join. I would've given them a piece of my mind."

"They're a bunch of useless egotists! It was like they didn't even hear what I was telling them."

"Well, don't worry 'bout it too much. Peter had an inkling it'd turn out this way. Let's get back to the Beached Whale and figure something out."

Everyone was there when they arrived at the inn. Calantha had returned from her tower and was deep in discussion with Chert about the life cycle of a xocoatl plant. Tristram was also back from his investigation with no news to report. Pat directed everyone to a long table in the back where Aster recounted his meeting with the Council.

"We're beached! There's no option but to rescue Kara," Peter concluded. "Good thing I found us a contact who knows where she's being held."

Tristram slammed his hands on the table. "That's treason! We shouldn't be discussing this."

Pat glared at him. "We can't let Kara die. She's family, and we all know she aint guilty."

"I don't like it any more than you do, but the decision has already been made. We need to grieve and move on."

Aster crossed his arms with a huff. "I'm not leaving without Kara."

"Shut up Lantern, the adults are talking," Tristram snarled.

"Be nice to Aster." Pat glared. "He's as worried about Kara as the rest of us."

"I'll not hear it from the cook. Don't throw your lives away for this hopeless plan."

Pat kicked back his chair, which crashed to the floor. "I won't sleep another peaceful night unless we do everything we can to save her." He grabbed the table so hard his forearms bulged and reddened.

Tristram stomped to the door. "This isn't right. Anyone who doesn't want a noose around their neck should come with me. Leave these fools to their hopeless plan."

The inn fell silent, giving Aster a queasy feeling. One by one, the rest of the crew stood and followed Tristram, leaving Peter, Pat, Aster, Calantha, and Chert alone at the table.

"There's so few who stayed." Aster put his head in his hands.

Pat shook his head. "Most of the others don't want trouble. They could lose everything."

"You could too."

"I've already lost everything once. I'd do it again for a friend."

"The others are cowards."

Peter waved the thought away. "Nah they're makin' a reasonable choice. As much as you don't like Tristram, he's got a solid head on his shoulders. He's in the BTC for the coin. What we're doin' could leave us worse than coinless."

Pat eyed Calantha and Chert and asked, "And what about you two? You've no fish in this barrel."

Calantha stirred as if pulled from watching a performance. "I do not fear my face on a wanted poster. I am journeying with Aster for the time being, so I will assist him as best I can."

Chert made eye contact with Aster. "Kara is nice lady. Like family. Chert will help."

Peter seemed satisfied. "That's that. The five of us will stop this execution. Aster, we need you for the first step. My informant is a member of the Order of Conflagration. It wouldn't be out of place for you to visit the cathedral, unlike the rest of us. Find a blonde novice named Martha. She knows where Kara is being held."

Aster gasped as he arrived at the north entrance of the Cathedral of Conflagration. He had only ever seen this building as an illustration in the sacred texts his father had read to him as a boy. There was a splendor that drawings couldn't capture. A large steeple soared above the red stained-glass windows, which depicted scenes of fire and lightning. Carved vultures adorned the walls. Gargoyles crouched atop the fine stonework.

The entire population of the city could fit inside during the hour of worship, but today only a few elderly men lingered to make offerings in front of a looming marble statue. With a smooth crooked neck, the bald, birdlike head stared down at them. It was cloaked with feathers that danced in the firelight. The Divine Conflagration— identical to Deacon Arnit's painting.

Novices in burgundy robes tended the holy fire at the center of the room. One of them had long blonde hair, visible from inside her hood. She prodded the coals with a forked fire iron.

Our contact. Aster shuffled down the aisle. "Are you Martha? I was told that you could help me."

She turned to him, holding the glowing red poker safely away. She was younger than Aster expected. Most likely a first year of the Order. "Yes, I am. But I don't do favors for heretics."

"Huh? I'm devout."

Martha pointed to Aster's chest, where the black pendant rested.

"This is only a gift. It's... it's a long story." Aster tucked the pendant into his shirt and his mind drifted back to the giant stone creature in the cave. Truth be told, he wasn't sure what he believed anymore. Had he actually met a god? He'd never experienced anything of Conflag that was quite as real. Kara's face appeared in his mind, pulling Aster from this musing. He didn't have time for a crisis of faith. He could sort out his beliefs later, when her life wasn't at stake.

"I've prayed to Conflag since I could speak. In Buckwheat Village, there is no other god. In the summer months, during the longest day of the year, we hold a festival for the Divine Conflagration. Our people provide offerings of wood, fish, grains, and fruits to the bonfire. The morning after, the local priest will take the ashes and bless us each with a symbol of lightning on our backs."

Martha looked into his eyes. Aster could see the reflection of the holy fire dancing back and forth in hers.

She grabbed his hands. "If you're truly a servant of Conflag, then pray with me."

Aster raised both their hands into the air and closed his eyes. They spoke in harmony.

Divine Conflagration, Lord of Forces,
Dweller of the dry deserts,
In the language of fire,
we praise your vigor.
The spectacle of lightning, and the warmth of the
hearth.

We are in awe of your gifts.

As your servants, we worship your everlasting might.

Aster thought he could feel his pendant moving, as if pulling him back towards the door he came in. He dismissed the feeling as guilt.

When he opened his eyes, Martha was staring at him, expectantly.

Oh right. He pulled a leaf of paper from his messenger bag.

She smiled. "I can write it for you if you need."

"No, I'm just finding the words to say." A proper prayer to Conflag required a note, one's wishes turned to ash to reach God above. *But what to say. To cure Dad? Or rescue Kara? Conflag is neither a healer like Viridus nor a finder like Loctee.*

He leaned over a pew, placing the paper on its seat. *I should ask for Conflag's strength. To help me help those I care about.* He scratched a few words onto the page and then folded it crosswise three times.

Martha opened a palm to the fire at the room's center.

Aster felt the warmth on his face as he pointed the tip of the paper at the hot coals. It ignited before touching. He bowed in reverence, until the flame licked his fingers. Aster flinched but held the paper until it burned through. *"Worth the pinch of pain," as Dad always says.*

"I apologize for doubting you." Martha cooed. "A worshiper of Ochress wouldn't have caught my misdirection. So, brother of Conflagration, how can I help you?"

"I'm looking for a woman named Kara." Aster said, glad to have won her trust.

"Ah yes, I've been expecting you. I'm told that she's being held in the ruins of the former castle. Specifically, the dungeon, below the rubble. That is where they keep the prisoners of special value. It hasn't been used since the death of the king."

"Thanks." Aster turned to leave. "Wait, is that all?"

"There will be eight guards. Two or three around the

cells. The others patrol the grounds."

Martha stuck her poker back into the coals. "May the holy fire guide you in your quest."

Aster thanked her again and hurried out of the cathedral to rejoin the others. *I should be more careful with my necklace. Wouldn't want others to get the wrong impression.*

Back at the Beached Whale, Aster found Peter at the back table, nervously smoking his pipe. "She's in the castle ruins," Aster said, dropping into the chair between Calantha and Chert.

"Keep it down." Peter scowled. "We're doin' somethin' illegal, remember?"

"He wasn't that loud," Pat countered, scooting his chair closer. "That's near the northern edge of the forest. Easy as fish in a barrel."

Aster looked around for eavesdroppers. "So what do we do?"

"In the hours before sunrise, we sneak in and break Kara out of her cell," Peter stated confidently. "I remember the old passageways, assuming they haven't collapsed."

"That's it? Shouldn't we come up with a backup plan?"

"Backup plan is to fight our way through the front. It's not like we've got time to figure out somethin' better. She'll get the gallows in the mornin'."

Calantha clapped her pale hands together. "A rescue mission! How exciting."

"I need to see Malvin beforehand," Aster said. "Maybe he'll have pity on me and give me medicine to take home or something."

Peter shook his pipe at Aster. "Best you keep him light on the details. If he squeals—"

"He's a kind old man. He wouldn't."

"This is why Tristram calls you Lantern. Just don't."

Aster leaned back with his arms crossed. *No need to be mean about it*

After everyone parted ways in preparation for the night

ahead, Aster visited Dr. Malvin to let him know the bad news.

The old man answered after the third knock. "Welcome back. I take it that you've finally talked with the Council? Come in and tell me all about it." He stroked his ponytail uneasily as he showed Aster to the table.

"It didn't go well. They were concerned that you'd run away. Also something about your refusal to teach their representative."

"That ingrate couldn't tell his left shoe from his right," Malvin grumbled.

"Why do you hate the Council so much?"

The doctor sat on the tabletop. "How to put this... I dislike following orders barked at me from above. When I was young, my mother died of the plague. Ever since then, I have devoted my life to medicine. I never want anyone else to suffer the way she did. After the fall of the king, I allied myself with the Council to lend my services to all of New Portsmith."

"Oh, I'm sorry to hear that."

"It was a long time ago. Anyways, this alliance came with a cost. I was to charge each patient a modest fee and a portion would go into the Council coffers. The partnership worked great for all of us, for a time. The people were directed to me for treatment, so I saw more patients than ever. And the Council made a substantial amount of coin. Each year the Council asked for more and more payment.

"I was very wealthy at this point and didn't notice until a small boy broke down in tears in my chair and told me that his father was on death's doorstep because he had lost Conflag's favor. They had saved up enough to have the boy examined, but didn't have the coin for the father as well. I made a complimentary house visit to this family. They all had a bad case of indigo blight, even the mother.

"After a bit of experimentation, I found the cause to be a fungal infection caused by spores inside our imported cotton. The spread could be controlled with proper hygiene, but here in the city, some folk don't have that luxury. Mild cases are quite easy to cure with some herbal paste, but the father needed to have the boils removed surgically. The family all recovered, one of my greatest successes! But at the same time, that was the beginning of the end for me.

"You see Aster, I was so inspired by this family that I came up with a new idea—a pauper's clinic. Like I said, under the Council's direction, I had become unbelievably wealthy. Coin no longer mattered to me, so what better way to help this city than to help those who couldn't help themselves?

"I stood in front of the Council and presented my idea. They were appalled. Why would I help the cur of the street? Who would pay for my services if I was giving handouts? I had done the calculations. With the coin that I had already received, I could pay for my medical supplies for years to come. That was not what concerned them. They were fretting over the profits that I had been passing to them. After much discussion, they forbade me from it."

Aster rolled his eyes. "I'm not surprised."

"I'm a rather bullheaded man. Maybe it is because my father was a farmer who spent long hours tinkering with his grindstone. Maybe it's from something else. But once I see a problem that needs fixing, I cannot let sleeping dogs lie. I started the pauper's clinic in secret, against their wishes.

"Within a fortnight, they found out. Someone broke in, stealing anything of value and breaking the rest. The only thing left was a copy of our agreement, carefully laid atop this very table.

"So I ran. Opened business in Tembour. They found me and dragged me back. In the end, I moved to the edge of the city to give myself an illusion of freedom, but I'm not free. My skills and person are subjugated. No longer am I a servant of Loctee. I'm a slave to a man-made god."

Aster shifted uncomfortably. "How awful. I couldn't convince the Council to free my friend Kara, who is to be put to death for a crime she didn't commit. We are planning to take matters into our own hands before dawn tomorrow."

Malvin raised a silvery eyebrow. "What about Buckwheat Village?"

"Don't know. Maybe we can bring my father to New Portsmith and you can help him here?"

"At best, it sounds like you'll have trouble showing your face here."

"I don't have a better idea."

Malvin's eyes filled with fire. "No, enough is enough. I'm coming with you. I've been planning an escape from this prison of a city for over a year now. The soldiers that watch me know my schedule. Each morning, I take a walk around the city. There's a loose stone in the walls near the docks. I can disappear through that before they notice. Which ship is yours? I can meet you there just after sunrise."

Aster's heart pounded. "The ship's called the Blue Skies. The only one with two square blue sails. You can't miss it."

Malvin turned his back and rummaged through a drawer. "Come here and open your bag."

Malvin dumped the drawer's contents into it: surgical tools, small vials of liquid, and other odds and ends that Aster didn't recognize. "Take these with you. I'll need them later, but I can't carry them on my walk without attracting suspicion."

Aster barely latched his bulging bag before he was shown to the door.

"Now, I have many things to take care of here. We can talk in more detail when I see you again tomorrow." Malvin disappeared into his bedroom, muttering to himself.

Aster left, staggered back to the inn, his heavy bag clinking against his leg with each step. His luck was finally turning around. They just needed to free Kara and sail back up the Haverhein. *I'm so close. I'll be a hero.*

Aster awoke to three knocks on his door followed by Peter's gruff voice. "It's time."

It was still dark outside. Everyone clutched their cloaks close in the cold and salty breeze. They were as much for hiding their persons as they were for keeping warm. Very few townsfolk were out at this hour. Every once in a while they would pass a soldier patrol as they made their way northeast, to the castle ruins.

They passed through the outer gate without incident. The guards didn't give them a second look.

They crept along the edge of the forest until a chest high wall was illuminated by Peter's lantern. "This place used to be such a grand sight," he reminisced. "Over on the right, that pile of rubble was the tallest tower in the entire city. On the left, that was the banquet hall. Doubt there's much to see there anymore. This place has since been pillaged for anythin' of value. I always would ride through the gate and give Tommlin, the gatekeeper, a hard time about the stupid helmet he had to wear—Wait!"

Peter held his hand up, stopping the group. "I see light over there. Should've known they'd have a watch if they're keepin' prisoners. If it isn't caved in, there should be a back entrance in the forest." They backtracked and entered the treeline to the east.

A figure approached them from the clearing before they made it more than a few steps.

"We may be dead in the water." Pat clutched his cast iron pan as if it would protect him.

"Hide. Maybe they didn't see us." Peter extinguished the lantern.

Aster found a tree with a thick trunk and crouched down next to it. His heart beating faster by with every breath.

A voice called out to them. "Peter, Pat, you guys out here?" It was Tristram.

"What in Loctee's deep blue sea are you doing out here?" Peter's voice was nearly a growl.

"I had a change of heart," Tristram said sheepishly. "I know I made a stink at the inn, but after thinking about it a bit, I decided to help."

Aster could barely make out his mustache in the moonlight. "What, that's it?"

"It's Kara. She'd do the same for me."

Pat slid his pan back into his backpack. "I, for one, am glad you're helping us. Could use all the hands we can get."

Aster disagreed but didn't protest. *We're better off without this curmudgeon.*

Navigating the forest was tough at night. With only the moonlight to show them the path, they stumbled across roots and vines.

After more than a handful of cuts and swears Peter stopped them. "Hopefully we're deep enough that no one will see the light," he said as he reignited the cotton wick.

Chert grumbled. "Light attracts other attention too."

Peter pushed ahead. "It'll be fine, we're almost there." He paused at a small creek, walked up and down it twice, then jumped over the flowing water.

The place was alive with the buzzing of crickets and the croak of frogs. Calantha dashed ahead of the group and fell onto her knees on the bank. "Oh, I didn't know this paradise was so close to my tower! There are so many species of insects here. It is like a festival of miniature proportions."

The others, wary of the mud, followed Peter's lead across. It wasn't until Aster called back to Calantha that she joined them on the other side.

"Found it." Peter shone the light into a small cave in the side of a hill. Glowing red eyes stared back. He yelped and jumped back. A young boar trotted out with a squeal, freezing when it noticed them.

"Careful now," Pat said as he lowered his pan towards the beast.

Feeling confident, Aster stepped forward. "I'll take care of this," he said, pulling out his knife.

The boar snorted.

"Get away from it." Peter tried to pull Aster back. "They're aggressive little—"

It charged, tusks flailing.

Aster held his knife out, but panicked and stepped to the side at the last second, dodging its jagged tusks.

The boar dashed into the woods and away from the noisy group.

"Nice moves, Aster," Pat said.

"That was very stupid," Peter countered. "We are lucky that it was a small one, otherwise we'd be pickin' your guts from the forest floor." He shrugged. "I guess you're not as flat footed as when we first met."

Pat cautiously peered into the tunnel. "Alright, it's clear."

One-by-one, they squeezed inside. Peter led the way, brushing spider webs out of his face as he went. Aster and Calantha were in the rear. They squeezed through the dirt walls before the passageway opened up. Stonework replaced dirt at a fork.

"Hmmm. Right, I think," Peter mused, looking down each path one at a time.

Just as they had taken the right turn, a voice called out from the opposite direction, "Hey! Who's there?"

They ran, but the soldier caught up.

"Nobody's allowed here."

Calantha leaped forward, pulling her hand out of her bag. With a flick of her wrist, she scattered something into the air, covering the soldier.

The man stopped, studying his armor, which turned a vibrant shade of green. Tiny vines sprouted across his chest, on the cobblestone floor, and in a few crevices on the walls as well. Before Aster could blink, the vines had grown, filling the entire space before finally blooming with miniature lavender flowers. The soldier struggled with all his might, but couldn't break free of the vines. He cried out, only to be silenced as the plants twisted over his mouth.

"What did you do?" Aster asked, gawking at the soldier.

Peter shoved him forward. "Keep movin'."

When they had gotten a good distance away, Aster asked again.

Calantha smoothed her pristine dress. "They are called Brejo Clemantis vines. A rare species of fast-growing vines from the Panta Marshes. I discovered them myself, a few years back. Quite unusual in that they are able to grow large in a short period of time—typically a few days to cover a wall."

"But they grew faster than that."

"The secret to the accelerated growth you just saw, is to mix their seeds with bone meal from the Kaleenmunda Desert. There is something extraordinary about the fertilization abilities of the bone. I must confess that I do not know enough about it myself."

"Could you show—" Aster walked into Chert, who'd stopped.

"Shhhh! The prison is on the other side of this wall," Peter whispered from the front. "Ready your weapons." He pushed the wall open, revealing a row of cells surrounded by iron bars.

It all happened in the blink of an eye. Two guards who had been sitting idly at a table at the front of the room, jumped to their feet, chairs crashing to the floor. Tristram and Peter rushed them, swords in hand. At the back of the room, Chert lunged at a third guard who was still half asleep.

Aster spotted Kara's auburn braid and rushed over to her cell. Before he had reached the iron bars, all three guards were on the floor. The surprise entrance had worked overwhelmingly in their favor.

Kara was sitting on a pile of straw with her back against the stone wall. "What are you doing here?"

"We're here to save you." Aster pulled at the door, but

it didn't budge.

"What?" Kara rubbed her back as she stood.

"Your execution is hours away. We couldn't convince them that you were innocent, so we had to break you out."

"No... My trial is today."

"Huh? But the Council said—"

"Aster, enough." Peter grabbed the cell lock. "Kara, they lied to you. We don't have time to be discussin' the details. It's time to cut and run."

Pat bent over the bodies at his feet, rummaging through their pockets. "Drown me, where's the key?"

Chert lifted a sturdy iron key into the air, stolen from the unconscious guard next to the stool. He tossed it to Peter who unlocked the cell.

"Thanks." Kara dusted pieces of straw off of her pants.

Pat paced back and forth in front of the false wall. "We can't go back this way unless we're going to cut through those vines. And that soldier is still in there too. We should go out the main entrance."

"Wait! Unlock me too." A grizzled woman with patchwork clothes and unkempt hair called out from the furthest cell.

"Who are you and why should we free you?"

The woman stood and cleared her throat. Her appearance was ragged but her manner was stately. "I am Sir Josselyn Helisent and my only purpose left in life is to seek out the king's murderer and bring them to justice."

Peter's jaw dropped. He flung her cell open before the others could react. "Joss? What in Loctee's name are you doin' here? You look awful."

"Peter?" The haggard woman ran her hands through her short blonde hair and attempted to straighten out her rumpled clothes. "I owe you for this, Peter. I will not forget." She stepped out of the cell and bowed her head low. "As for why I'm here; the Council decided they didn't need me anymore. A fate crueler than death, they locked me in this dungeon. I've been stuck here for almost a year."

"We have to move. Now's not the time to catch up."

Leading the way up the stairs, Peter scoured the dark hallway on each floor for any signs of movement. Instead of a fourth floor landing, they found themselves stepping outside into the grass. The stairs should have kept going, but everything above was now rubble. The sun peeked out from beyond the horizon, giving everything a dark orange glow.

"We've got to hurry back to the ship." Pat glanced back and forth, jumping at the slight breeze.

Peter marched forward. "Yeah. I'm kinda surprised the executioner hasn't shown up yet."

They crept out the remnants of the main gate, and hugged the castle walls until they were back in the forest.

Calantha spoke up. "We can regroup at my tower. It is on the eastern cliffs." She pointed in the direction with a slender finger.

"Good enough for me." Pat was trembling. Barely noticeable, but Aster was sure of it. He'd always thought the crew of the Blue Skies was fearless, but it was comforting to know he wasn't the only one a bit nervous by all of it.

They kept along the tree line and dashed towards the coast, stopping to watch a wagon pass.

When they arrived at her tower, Calantha slipped upstairs to tend to her plants, leaving the others to talk among themselves. Peter gestured to Josselyn. They stepped outside for a private conversation.

"Well, I guess I'll start off by thanking you all for saving me," Kara said to Aster and the others. "It sounds like I was in over my head and didn't even know it." She looked at Chert. "So how did you end up involved in all of this nonsense?"

He scratched the divot on his head. "Lending a hand."

Aster added, "He saved us in Strongfair and even helped us sail back."

"Thank you for your help, Chert." Kara smiled.

A horn blew from the direction of the castle ruins.

Peter stuck his head inside. "Time to go."

Aster hopped out of his chair and grabbed Calantha from upstairs. They rushed out to the eastern gate, which had two guards as usual.

"You going to vine them too?" Aster asked Calantha as they got close.

"No. That would cause more of a commotion." She waved as she walked under the suspended pickets. "Morning, Daniel. These gentlemen are with me."

A short guard with a face full of dirt or freckles waved back. "Mornin', Calantha. You know I need to inspect your belongings. We go over this every time."

She stepped past him. "So sorry. We are in a hurry today."

"But—"

"I will make it up to you. Maybe another bouquet for your wife?"

"Ugh fine." He palmed his helmet in frustration, muttering, "queer woman," under his breath. The second guard just laughed at him, causing Daniel's cheeks to redden.

Calantha led them through the city back roads, down the seaside stairway, to the docks. Malvin was waiting for them, sitting underneath the mast of the Blue Skies.

Aster ran up to him. "Doctor Malvin you made it!"

"Thanks, Aster. I'm ready to leave this city behind. Let's go to Buckwheat Village!"

Josselyn scowled. "You aren't heading for Tembour?

"Nope." Peter replied as he pulled up the anchor.

"If that's the case, I think I'll stay behind. I wish you luck. And Peter, I owe you more than I could ever repay. Thank you for giving me my purpose back." She saluted him before stepping off the gangplank and disappearing into the city.

"Hey Aster, give me a hand with the ropes," Pat called out. "Now that we don't have the full crew anymore, you'll need to pull your weight to keep us afloat. Less mouths to feed will be nice though."

Aster helped Pat untie the Blue Skies from the pier. They ran back up the gangplank and pulled it up behind them. As the ship pulled away, three soldiers ran across the wooden planks, pointing at their ship.

"Close." Pat wiped his sweaty forehead. "We barely escaped in time.

Aster hoisted himself onto a supply barrel. His heart hadn't stopped racing since the forest. He was giddy. Every day was an adventure on the Blue Skies. And as long as luck was on their side, he was happy to be part of it.

Once the sails were out and the course was set for the Haverhein river, Peter called a meeting inside the captain's quarters.

The room was spacious compared to the rest of the ship, with a wooden table at its center. But the best part was the balcony with a superb view of the sea. Peter was leaning over a golden key as he waved everyone inside. "Now that the rescue is over, there are a few matters we need to agree on. First, we need a new captain."

Tristram pulled at his mustache. "You were first mate, which makes you next in line."

"A ship'll run aground without a loyal crew, but the captain also needs to be a man worth followin'. I'm not cut out for that job."

"You sure, Peter?" Pat asked. "You've got more experience than the rest of us. And we all trust you with our lives."

Aster couldn't help but agree. Peter could be distant at times, but he'd always come through when they needed him. And he was always willing to help when asked.

Peter shook his head. "I'm no leader. I've screwed up too many times to trust myself."

"Really? Name one time."

Peter pulled at his goatee. "That time I got sick and almost died."

"You getting sick isn't a screw up."

"How 'bout the time I got us lost at sea for a week."

Kara laughed. "That was my fault. I bought us that awful map. We would've made it to the pickup spot if the shoreline was drawn correctly."

"Well... I can't think of anything, but don't put your coin on me bein' captain. It ain't goin' to happen."

"If you say so." Pat picked up the key and grinned. "Then I think Kara should be our captain. She's always kept us out of trouble and kept the ship well supplied. If anybody is worthy of the Blue Skies, It's Kara."

Aster nodded.

"Hold on," Tristram said. "What about me? I could do it."

"After that stunt with Kara, I don't think so."

Kara eyed him. "What stunt?"

Tristram looked down, focusing on a knot in the table, circling it with a finger.

"Well that settles it," Peter declared. "Captain Kara, you're in charge."

Tears welled in Kara's eyes as Pat handed her the key. "Thank you so much. I'll do my best to steer us well." She held it against her chest. "You'll still be first mate though, right Peter?"

"Of course! You'll need all the help you can get. I'm just not cut out to be givin' orders. That's all."

"Good. Thanks."

Peter spoke up once again. "Now that's out of the way. All of you here are crew." He nodded to Aster, Chert, and Calantha. "We've been through some rough seas and that means we're a team. Comrades. Family."

Aster watched Malvin lean back against the timber wall.

"And on a grimmer note, we are all traitors. We have violated the laws of Benia to rescue Kara. That makes us wanted men. I don't know how the Council will react, but we need to watch our backs from now on."

Aster felt the mood turn somber. The capital barely ever sent representatives to Buckwheat Village, so he wasn't terribly concerned, but he understood what it meant for the others. There were things they would never be able to do again without worrying about ending up in a jail cell. But of everyone there, the person who had the most to lose was Calantha. After all she and her plants lived in New Portsmith. But she seemed the least concerned, smiling with her hands clapped together on the side of the room.

"Enough of that." Pat pushed on the door. "We need to celebrate our new captain." He rushed to the kitchen and brought back a pint of mead for each of them. "Here's to Captain Kara Reeves and the new crew of the Blue Skies." He raised his mug into the air. Peter and Kara followed his lead and seconds later so did everyone else. Aster, Kara, Peter, Pat, Tristram, Calantha, Chert, raised their drinks.

Malvin hung back, eyeing his cup suspiciously, not participating in the revelry. "I'd be more concerned," he muttered under his breath. He shrugged and took a few sips of the mead.

Captain Kara. Aster sipped his drink. *And a doctor. Everything turned out well in the end... surprisingly. Now I can relax. Dad and the others will be healthy in no time.*

They arrived at the Haverhein river delta without incident. The familiar pungent smell of the salt marshes greeted them. Kara called out from the bridge, "Traveling upstream is always tougher. Tighten the sails. Lucky for us, it seems the wind's in our favor. Peter, keep an eye on our starboard side. I don't want to get stuck in the shoal."

Tristram grumpily showed Aster how to tighten the mainsail. It was more complicated than Aster expected. But after a flurry of words like draft, boom, and jib, he discovered that his job was mostly to pull a certain rope tight. *It's not like I'm learning to be a sailor.*

Each of them jumped about their tasks as Kara slowly steered the ship between the islands until they reached the mouth of the river. The current had slowed down considerably, and the sky was growing dark. Tristram anchored the ship in a spot protected from the swell of the ocean. Everyone slept soundly that night as the adrenaline of the day wore off.

The next morning, Aster found Malvin, arms folded over the railing, staring at the trees drifting by on the riverbank. The vibrant green pines dotted among them reminded Aster of home.

"It's been a long trip for you. You excited to be back in Buckwheat?" Malvin asked, wrinkles pulling against his fatherly gray eyes.

"Yes and no. I'm ready for the sickness to be done. And to see Zinnia again. But if I'm honest, leaving the village was... exciting. I think it was good for me in a way. And I got to meet my mom."

"Hmmm..." The older man looked as if he had more to say, but kept it to himself.

Calantha glided up the stairs and nodded to the doctor. "I suppose that you have finally fulfilled your wish, Malvin." Her voice was airy, barely audible over the wind.

"Yes, I guess I no longer need your help with those herbs. But tell me, what business do you have with this obscure northern village? I must say, I was surprised to see you here."

"You two know each other?" Aster asked.

"Yes." Malvin smoothed his ponytail. "There was a big fuss when she first arrived in New Portsmith. Half the men wanted to marry her. The other half thought she was a witch."

Elegant was the word that came to mind every time he looked at her pale dress. "I can see why."

Aster's comment earned a chuckle from her. "Uninteresting brutes, all of them."

"And Malvin?"

"I found that Calantha was an expert at botany. It can be hard to acquire the proper herbs. Half the sellers can't tell a poppy from a windflower."

She nodded. "See? They truly are brutes. I would never make such a careless error."

"But why are you on the Blue Skies?" Malvin asked

again.

Calantha daintily placed her hands on the railing next to Malvin. "I am meeting an old friend. He has made a breakthrough in our research project. Perhaps it will be significant enough to gain the recognition of the Collective."

Malvin stroked his short gray beard. "You are as cryptic as ever. What exactly are you two researching?"

Her face lit up and she made a circle with her arms. "We are trying to find the birth of the Fourth Age: the catastrophe that destroyed the greatest civilization that had ever lived. The event that led to the world we live in today."

Malvin looked back out over the water, watching a school of bass dart back and forth among the rocks. "I didn't realize you were so interested in history. You always struck me as more practical than that."

"History is practical. If my theory is correct, the catastrophe will repeat. Imagine all of the novel discoveries that could be made. Why, it could be the foundation for an entire new field of study."

Malvin smiled weakly as she rambled on about her research. Aster couldn't understand much of what she was saying, so he slowly backed away to see what the others were up to.

On the other side of the ship Aster found Peter and Kara on the bridge. She was clutching the wheel, carefully adjusting the course of the Blue Skies to keep it in the deepest channel of the river.

Peter was pacing back and forth, spinning his knife around his hand playfully. "Kara, I've gotta say, seeing you back on the ship puts a smile on my face. I was pretty worried about you."

She looked over her shoulder. "It's only thanks to you that I'm here. Though, I'm still nervous about what will happen to us now. After we get Aster back to Buckwheat, what are we going to do? It's not like we can continue to work for the BTC."

Peter laughed, "No, we can't. I'm sure we'll figure it out. Worst case, I know a guy in Zeffarii who will pay us some coin to do a bit of work for him."

Kara scowled. "I'm not a smuggler."

Peter shrugged. "I don't like it any more than you do, but we're already wanted men. And it's better than starvin' to death. Besides, Red Sand is legal out there, so it wouldn't be smugglin' exactly. I'm more worried that the Blue Skies wouldn't be able to take us that far. It's not really built for ocean trips." He stopped to watch a sea bird flying overhead. "It don't matter much, new currents will open up to us before we know it."

She smiled at him, pulling the wheel slowly to the right as they approached a bend in the river.

Aster asked, "Hey Peter, I was wondering, who was that woman that you rescued? You seemed to know each other pretty well."

He walked up to the bow of the ship, adjusting a rope that had come loose. "You mean Joss? She was the commander of the King's Knights. A lifetime ago, she was my superior. They used to say that she was the strongest warrior in the whole world."

"Really? She was in rough shape when we found her. What was a commander doing in a cell?"

"It's all politics. Do yourself a favor and never get involved in that nonsense."

"He kinda is," Kara sighed. "We all are."

"No. It's not the same. Joss was at the center of things. We're just jetsam to them."

Eight uneventful days passed as the Blue Skies made steady progress toward Buckwheat Lake.

Underneath the mast, Tristram was teaching Aster about types of knots. He handed him a short piece of rope as he demonstrated on his own. "Lantern, this one's the most important one. It's called the bowline knot because it is used to hold the main sail towards the bow of the ship. Here, practice tying it a few times on this spare rope. Once you've got the hang of it, it'll be your job to do it right."

He watched Aster try it many times, while correcting his mistakes.

Ever since they rescued Kara, Tristram had opened up to him. Aster was glad he didn't feel the need to avoid him on the now much emptier ship, though he wished he'd drop the nickname.

Kara called to them from above. "All hands on deck! We've got to yield to another ship."

The crew sprang into action as Kara maneuvered to the left until the hull was nearly touching the mud on the bottom of the river.

She yelled across the water, "Stand-on!"

A ship, nearly identical to the Blue Skies, began slipping past them. The sail of the vessel was vivid green.

Tristram waved at the rowdy men and commented. "The Green Flash, our sister ship."

The man behind the wheel waved back and yelled to them, "You guys are too early. You'll be stuck in town with nothing to do for a while." Kara smiled and waved back, saying nothing.

After they had passed, Kara centered the Blue Skies and continued up the river which widened more and more.

By the evening of the second night after entering Buckwheat Lake, Aster noticed flickering lights reflecting off the water. Then, one by one, wooden houses came into view. He didn't often see them from this angle, but they were easy to recognize. *Buckwheat Village. Home at last.* His thoughts drifted to Zinnia and his father. *I hope they're doing alright.*

Tristram had Aster tie the ship to the pier. It took three tries before Tristram redid it himself. "Guess we need to give you a bit more practice, eh Lantern?"

Since it was already late, Peter led them to the Fulton's inn for the night.

Whitney flagged him down the moment he walked through the door. "Aster, you're back!" She placed a tray of empty glasses on the nearest table to hug him.

"Hi, Whitney. I brought a doctor. Can he stay here?"

"Absolutely. Everyone can stay for free. It's the least we can do." The crew thanked her as she led them to their rooms.

Aster ducked out of the inn, leaving his friends to rest for the night. He couldn't wait another night to see Zinnia and his father.

As he walked back down the familiar path to the Hollyhock's shop, he felt as if the village had shrunk: Each house was shorter than he remembered. Less impressive, too. As he passed the mayor's house, he remembered the time when he was young and couldn't sleep for two days because he had been so excited to tour Mayor Gilroy's manor—the largest residence in town. All the children had been invited inside as a part of the summer solstice festival. But compared to the towers of New Portsmith, it now seemed underwhelming.

Further down the path, the light from the Buckwheat General Store spilled onto the dirt. *Oh good, I made it before they closed.*

He easily opened the large door to the front of the shop. The familiar smell of scented candles and honey greeted him. Zinnia's curly brown hair bounced up and down as she stacked fresh bottles of mead on the shelf.

"Zin, I'm home."

She jumped, nearly knocking a bottle off. "Aster!" She ran over to him and embraced him, squeezing with all of her strength. "You feel heartier."

Aster laughed.

"I was so worried about you after your last letter. You went all the way to Strongfair? And were attacked by pirates! What a wild journey."

Aster pulled a new letter out of his bag and handed it to her. "Here. This is the next one. I guess I was a bit overzealous when I wrote it, but it seems silly now that

I'm here in person."

"Your letters have been keeping my spirit up. In fact, everyone is excited to hear about your journey. The villagers talk about you like you're some kind of famous adventurer!"

"Ha! Not really. Kara and Peter have been taking care of me. They are the toughest people I've ever met."

"So, did you find Doctor Malvin? Is he here now?"

"Yes! The doctor is resting up at the Toasted Oak. I'll take him to see Lavender and the others in the morning. How are they?"

Zinnia frowned. "She's had a few more episodes since you left. They are getting more and more common. Several others have caught the sickness as well. Rowan lost sensation in his fingers a week ago and even my father is having fits where he isn't able to move. It mostly happens in the morning when I'm around to help, but I worry that he may get hurt. It's hard getting out of bed some days... the stress of it all."

"Malvin will cure everyone. Just give him some time."

"Thank Conflag..." Her eyes glazed over as she stared at the neatly arranged shelf.

"Zin?"

She shook her head and perked back up. "Also, you got to meet your mom!"

"Yes, but it wasn't what I expected. I found out that she chose to stay in Munayallpa to become a priest of Ochress instead of coming to Buckwheat Village with Dad and me. She didn't paint Dad in the best light."

She put her hand on his back. "Oh, I'm sorry."

"In any case, I'll come find you tomorrow and introduce you to the crew. I'm sure you're excited to meet them all. I want to catch my father before he's asleep."

Zinnia nodded vigorously and gave Aster another hug before he went back outside.

It was late, and Aster's eyelids were heavy. He finally made it to his house. Inside was dusty and unkempt.

Aster followed the light into the bedroom. He found

his father in bed, reading.

"I'm home."

Hugo's face lit up as he tried to get out of bed. "You're safe." His voice was hoarse and weak.

Aster hugged him and motioned for him to stay seated. His arms fit all the way around his father, which was a first.

Hugo wiped a tear out of his eye. "Did you have to take so many risks? It sounded like you were always in some sort of trouble."

Aster sighed. *Already? I just got here.*

"Oh, but let's not talk about that now. You finally got to meet your mother? How is she?"

"She seems to be doing well. I never realized how influential she is in Munayallpa. But I did get the chance to learn a bit more about her, which was nice."

"You couldn't convince her to come live in Buckwheat? I was hoping that talking to you would persuade her more than I ever could."

"No," Aster lied. *How could I ask her that after what she showed me? After what she said had happened?*

"A shame." Hugo interrupted himself with a coughing fit, holding his chest tightly until it subsided. He wiped phlegm off of his mouth, then asked, "Did she say anything about me?"

"A bit. She told me the story of how you two met. And the story of when you left..."

"By Conflag she was beautiful. I'd always bring her fresh flowers." He coughed once more.

Aster smiled and held his father's hand. "A true gentleman. How are you feeling today, Dad?"

"I'm fine."

No you're not. Aster looked at the sweat-stained sheets. "When's the last time you got out of bed?"

Hugo frowned. "Few days..."

Aster scowled at his stubborn dad.

"You brought a doctor?"

"Yes, Doctor Malvin. With the amount of trouble it

took me to get him here, he'd better be the best doctor in all of Benia. Finally, we can get back to normal."

"Judging by those dark circles under your eyes, you've been pushing yourself pretty hard. Why don't you get to bed? We can see what this doctor has to say in the morning."

Aster agreed and left his father to rest. He frowned as he tidied up the kitchen, wiping the dust of the table with a wet rag. *Dad will be back to his usual boisterous self in no time.*

Aster woke at first light. His body wouldn't let him go back to sleep. He couldn't tell if it was excitement or nervousness.

When he got to the Toasted Oak, Don Fulton made him sit with everyone for a breakfast of wild berry porridge. It was hearty and warm, a welcome change from the rations on the ship.

Peter grumbled under his breath and picked the berries out of his.

Just as they had finished their meal Calantha asked, "When will I be able to meet with Fletcher?"

Aster pointed behind him, in the direction of the mountains. "Fletch lives about a half-day hike north of town. After we bring Malvin to his patients, we can go see him."

Calantha frowned. "I was hoping he would be here already. No matter. We shall leave immediately."

Aster shifted uncomfortably in his seat. "I need to spend some time with the doctor. He's the whole reason I left the village to begin with."

"Yes, yes, you did mention that. I can be patient for a while longer." Calantha pulled a bound notebook from under the table and started flipping through the pages at a lazy pace. She was in her own world.

The rest of the crew prepared for the day. Malvin was

the first to be ready, but Kara and the other sailors had insisted on coming along too, so Aster waited silently with him, watching him inspect his tools.

The doctor looked professional today; his white button-up shirt was smoothed and tucked in. His black medicine bag had gotten a fresh coat of wax. He looked stern, almost frowning as he stared at the odds and ends.

The right man for the job. I need to thank Kara for helping me find him. Without her help, I couldn't have done it.

After a bit of prodding, the others joined them downstairs and Aster showed them to the Goodwin's household. Old and plain, the style most other houses in the village had adopted.

Lavender was in bed in the furthest room. Rowan led them to her, giving Peter and Chert cautious looks.

She was paler than the last time Aster saw her. She'd never had muscle but her arms had thinned. Now, Aster doubted she could lift herself out of bed.

Doctor Malvin placed his bag on the nightstand and lifted her gown to place his ear on her back.

The others crowded in, filling the kitchen. Chert was stuck in Rowan's bedroom, peering around the door frame to get a look at the doctor's work.

"Brown vial," Malvin instructed as he placed two fingers on his patient's wrist.

Aster poured out his messenger bag onto the bedside table, which caused Malvin to flinch. He shoved the ink bottle back. *Not that.*

The doctor grabbed one filled with a thick brown liquid and dabbed some on her skin. Kara, Peter and the others leaned in.

Pat yelled from the back, "Is she cured yet?"

Malvin glared at him. "I appreciate all of your support, but this is a slow and delicate process. It will take me days before I know what is wrong with her, let alone find a treatment."

No one said a word.

"Entertain yourselves elsewhere," Malvin commanded.

The crew gawked and didn't move.

"That means go away. Leave us." Malvin pointed to the door.

Rowan, who had ended up scrunched into a corner of the bedroom, took the opportunity to shoo everyone out of his house.

Malvin called after them in a softer tone, "When I'm done here, I'll take a look at the other patients, and I'll find you when I have news."

After the door closed behind them, Aster turned to Calantha. "Well, I guess we can go to Pelware now."

Calantha beamed.

Peter spoke up, "I'm not comin'. I've been there enough helpin' them move supplies 'round."

Pat eyed Tristram as he flicked his wrist forwards and backwards, causing all three to nod vigorously. "We're staying too," he added. "Good chance for some down time. Plus, we haven't gone fishing in weeks."

Kara shrugged. "Fine, but don't lose the ship this time."

Pat laughed. "We'll be more careful."

Peter just shook his head.

Kara, Chert, and Calantha followed Aster towards the northern path. Before they had made it beyond the last house, Zinnia rushed past with a crate of glass bottles in her hands.

Aster shouted after her, "We are going to the mines. You should join."

"Busy!" She waved him off, before looking at the others, which stopped her in her tracks. "Let me get these to the store first. Why are we going to Pelware this time?"

Aster shook his head. "I'm not really sure, to be honest. Calantha needs to meet with Fletch." They all looked at Calantha, but she had leaned down, touching the petals of a small yellow flower on the side of the trail, oblivious to their attention.

Chert took the crate from Zinnia and together they

walked her to the general store, leaving Calantha on the trail.

She hadn't moved from the spot when they returned.

Just after the group lost sight of the village, Zinnia picked up her pace so she could walk next to Kara. "So, you're Kara, right? What do you do on the ship?"

"Oh, I'm the captain now."

"The captain! How'd you get so important?"

"Peter, our First Mate, didn't want the responsibility, so they asked me to do it." Kara shrugged. "It's a lot more pressure than I thought, if I'm honest."

"That's... actually pretty impressive. So, what are you doing with Aster?" Zinnia squinted her eyes, staring at Kara's face.

"I've been helping him."

Aster added. "Speaking of. Thank you so much for all —"

"That's not what I mean. You kissed him, right?"

Kara's freckled face turned bright red, and she looked away.

I can't believe she just said that. Aster shot Zinnia a dirty look. "Why don't we talk about something else?"

Zinnia sulked to herself and nobody else said a word. They finished the hike in an awkward silence.

Once they arrived at the base of the mountain, they noticed the stone miners, still standing with shocked expressions in the open. Kara, Chert, and Calantha all took a closer look.

Calantha pondered out loud, "So this is the power of a cockatrice. It is quite an unusual transformation. Where does the energy come from to make their flesh change states like this? Why does it not affect the clothes they were wearing? I have so many questions. I would love to be able to research these monsters more closely. I hope Fletcher has a live specimen."

Aster didn't. He'd rather be stuck in another Council meeting than see one of those monsters again.

Kara and Chert lingered, unable to pull their eyes from

the petrified men. It took Calantha daintily clearing her throat to pull them away. Aster lead them to around the mountain bend to the head house.

Fletcher was inside, busily poking at a map of the mines. "Great to see you again Calantha, I'm glad you were able to make it." He offered them seats around his grand table. "Aster and Zinnia, I see you are both doing well also. I don't mean to be rude, but who are your friends here? Are they trustworthy?"

Aster introduced them. "This is Kara Reeves, captain of the Blue Skies. And Chert. Actually, Chert, I still don't really know what you're doing in Buckwheat with us."

Chert grunted. "Chert looking for lost chalice. Is black as night and can't hold water."

His comment drew shrugs, but Fletcher pressed on. "Kara Reeves. Yes, I remember you. I think we met briefly once or twice before, for shipments. Well, if you're all friends of Aster, I'll trust you, but you must swear to secrecy."

Kara laughed. "It's not like I've got anyone to tell anyways, so sure."

Fletcher stared at Chert, expectantly.

"Won't tell."

"Good. The reason that I asked for you to be here, Calantha, is related to an incident we had. One that Aster and Zinnia were involved in. But before I go into detail, have you learned anything interesting?"

She flicked out a notebook and paged through it. "According to the literature, Charles Benia was able to find the Odyllic Stone with the help of something he called his guiding star. I have been surveying the constellations and each star in the sky while perusing the texts, but I cannot make heads or tails of which one he used as his guide. His descriptions do not match anything up there, as far as I can tell."

Fletcher nodded. "That's alright. It doesn't matter anymore. I found a different lead. We've been noticing an increase in monster activities coming from the

Kaleenmunda Desert. It was dumb luck that Zinnia managed to slay the cockatrice that stumbled across our mine. After they left, I retrieved its corpse and extracted its scent gland."

Aster interrupted. "But what's so special about a cockatrice's scent?"

Fletcher shifted his weight awkwardly from side to side. "Do you know what happened to Ian Pelware in the end?"

Aster shook his head.

Kara leaned her chair back. "They say he died in the desert."

"That's only half true. The last letter I received from his expedition described a den of beasts with the power of petrification, somewhere in the Kaleenmunda Desert."

Zinnia gasped. "A cockatrice got him?"

"Precisely. I've gone looking for this place a few times. But I've finally found it! I didn't dare get close to those horrid creatures, but with their scent I believe that we could safely reach Pelware's final camp."

"I see." Calantha flipped through the pages of her notebook, stopping on one to read. "These creatures are driven by their sense of smell more than anything else. It could trick them long enough to let us sneak past."

Kara raised an eyebrow. "But why do you want to go there? To pay respects?

Fletcher scoffed. "No. His final letter also mentioned an ancient map. Our theory was that this map pointed to the final resting place of Charles, the first king of Benia; a man responsible for eradicating an entire species and bringing about the end to the Golden Age."

"How exciting!" Calantha clapped her hands together.

"There are fragments of an older society all over the world, now in ruin. Over the years, we found a few relics of theirs. Each and every one of them are scientifically advanced beyond our wildest dreams. I dare say that it will be hundreds of years before we match them in any single discipline. I have reason to believe that the greatest of these relics rests in Charles' tomb."

"So, you think that you will find this map in the cockatrice den?" Aster asked.

"Exactly," Fletcher replied. "I traveled with Ian enough that I know how the man thinks. If we go to this den, I'll find the map. But I can't do this alone. I need a team. Will you all join me? If the statues outside are any indication, this will be dangerous."

"Chert will come."

It was the fastest Aster had seen the bald man respond to anything. "I should stay home with Dad." He looked at Kara who shrugged.

"Nonsense, you're coming!" Fletcher stood and began collecting supplies from a chest, shoving rope and other tools into a large backpack. "You and I are a lot alike, Aster. And this is your chance for adventure. Real adventure, like you've always wanted. The chance to make a name for yourself in this uncaring world. This will be a big discovery—the tomb of Charles Benia! Your name will be known across Arathanon."

Zinnia Hollyhock,

I'm writing to you from aboard the Blue Skies again. In all likelihood, I will be handing you this letter in person. We are currently in the middle of Buckwheat Lake on our way home with Doctor Malvin.

It was like a fairy-tale. We infiltrated castle ruins to rescue Kara from certain death! I even managed to protect everyone from a wild boar with my new knife fighting techniques. I cannot wait to tell you about these stories in person; they are much more exciting told than written.

Right now, I feel on top of the world. I was able to have adventures, to see wondrous sights, and I even accomplished my mission of bringing the doctor home. I will be sad when this experience comes to an end, but at the same time Buckwheat Village is all I can think about.

The biggest surprise of my journey was how much I stuck out. New Portsmith was noisy and uncaring, and the style and customs in Strongfair were alien to me. I had secretly hoped that I would fit in there seamlessly, but that wasn't the case. Perhaps after everyone is healed, I could visit Munayallpa once more and learn about my heritage.

Your friend,
Aster

6 SECRETS OF THE KALEENMUNDA

The Toasted Oak was quiet when Aster arrived. Most of the chairs had been placed upside down onto the tables. The place had a clean smell, pleasant compared to its typical smokey musk. Don Fulton looked half-asleep as he absentmindedly wiped the bar down.

Fletcher waved Aster over to their table. "So, just the six of us then?"

Kara stifled a yawn. "Yeah. I asked the guys if they wanted to help out, but they weren't interested in risking their lives for some old map. And I made the mistake of telling them when you wanted us awake."

Fletcher frowned. "I was hoping for more muscle, but it'll be fine. We do need to pick up a few more things before we go. The Kaleenmunda is brutal for the unprepared."

Zinnia excitedly piped up, "Our store has everything you could want for a journey through the desert. I'll even give you a discount!"

"Very good, but first: Barkeep, a duck egg sandwich."

Don scuttled over, rag on his shoulder, wetting his white shirt. "Anyone else?"

"That sounds great. I'll have that too," Kara replied.

Calantha raised a hand, letting her silky sleeve fall

down her slender arm. "Porridge for me please."

"Porridge," Chert grunted after Don stared at him.

"Just the berries for me, please." Zinnia flashed him a smile.

Aster stood. "I've already eaten, so I'll meet you guys there. I need to speak with my father before we go. He was still asleep when I left."

Truth be told, Aster wasn't sure why he'd agreed to join the expedition. But after Kara had said she'd join, how could he refuse? Knowing that Pat and Peter wouldn't be there to make faces at him made it all the more worthwhile.

"Make it quick." Fletcher pointed at him. "We need to leave in the morning."

"Yeah," Aster replied automatically, but his mind had already moved on.

When he arrived home, Aster found his father sitting at the kitchen table eating a bit of honey-bread. He struggled to hold his cup which kept sloshing water to the floor.

"Feeling good today?"

Hugo put down his drink with both hands. "Much better. Whatever the doctor gave me has calmed my stomach. I think I'll try and take a walk later. The fresh air will be good for me."

"That's wonderful to hear. Soon you can take as many walks as you'd like." Aster joined his father at the table. "I wanted to let you know that I'll be leaving for a bit, to the desert this time. Fletcher expects we'll be gone for a fortnight."

"Another dangerous journey? I wish you were happy staying here in the village where it's safe."

Something in his tone irritated Aster. "You're not going to try and stop me?"

"It's not like you listened to reason last time. You are too fanciful, just like your mother... stubborn like her too."

Aster palmed the table. "I got you a doctor."

"For that I'm grateful. But someone else could've gotten him. Gilroy?"

"Never mind. I don't want to get into that again." Aster felt his pulse quicken. "Speaking of Mom, I've been waiting to ask you something."

Hugo stared at him.

"Don't take this the wrong way..."

"Go on. I'm not some frail old man."

Aster swallowed, feeling his tongue scrape against his teeth. "What made you leave Beryl behind and move us Buckwheat? That's the only thing that doesn't make sense to me."

It took his father a full minute to collect his thoughts, shifting his weight from side to side. "Promise me that you will keep this a secret. Even from Zinnia and the rest of your new friends."

"They wouldn't tell."

"Promise."

"Fine, I promise."

Hugo took a deep breath. "I was a... diplomat... in Munayallpa, reporting back to King Federyc's inner circle... Improving relations between the two countries was my primary task."

"You've mentioned that before."

"Yeah but I didn't mention that my job was also to arrange... economic deals."

"So?"

"So everything went swimmingly and our countries grew closer than ever. I loved the culture and food of Munayallpa but most importantly, I loved your mother."

Aster shrugged. "I'm not seeing the point."

"I'll get there if you stop rushing me." Hugo stifled a cough. "When the king died and power began to shift, some of the old guard began to disappear. It was all speculation at first, as to what was happening, but when the Benian soldiers made their first arrest in Strongfair, that's when I knew. I needed to hide, to protect everything I cared about. My family... you. Strongfair just wasn't safe.

"I found a small village in North Benia that could be

the perfect escape. Away from prying eyes and very remote. They needed a postmaster, which was easy for me to learn. It also allowed me to keep an eye on all messages to and from the village. We were safe."

"Except..."

"My only regret is that I wasn't able to convince Beryl to come with us. But moving to Buckwheat was the right choice; who knows whether we would have survived otherwise."

Aster shook his head. "But why didn't you tell her the truth? From her perspective you were acting crazy. She may have been willing to come along."

"Fear, mostly. I was afraid of assassins from the rebels. I was afraid of anybody finding out that I was connected to the old king in any way."

"Really? I don't think I've ever seen you afraid of anything... except me leaving Buckwheat."

Hugo sputtered into his napkin. "It's true."

"No. I think you were also afraid of mom. That your entire relationship was built on a lie. It would've broken her heart if she found out."

"I truly did love her... do love her. She wouldn't have forgiven me."

"And why did you take me?"

"Aster, my son. You carry the family name. I couldn't leave you there. If the rebels ever made the connection to the name Rutherford, they could target you just as easily. I pleaded with Beryl to change your name, but she had no interest. And I couldn't push the subject without making her more suspicious."

Aster felt sorry for Beryl. Yes, his father may have had his best interests at heart, but he could've explained himself. He had made wild choices and kept her in the dark. "You should've just come clean about your connections with Benia."

"Believe me, I spent many nights thinking the same thing. But I was scared. And that's just how things happened. It's no good to be stuck in the past when there's nothing you can do to change it."

"I suppose... Thanks for trusting me with your story. I'm sure it wasn't easy for you to tell."

"Actually, I'm happy to finally be able to share it with you. It was a burden to shoulder alone. And I half expected I'd be taking it with me to the pyre."

"Maybe you should talk to her... Strongfair isn't that tough to get to..."

Hugo frowned. "I... Will she be angry?"

"I'd be angry."

"I'll think about it," he concluded with a sigh.

"You should. I've got to go now."

Hugo stared right through him. "Be careful in the desert. Bring plenty of water. Stick with Fletcher."

Aster lingered at the door. His dad was different... almost vulnerable. He couldn't tell if it was the sickness or the talk of Beryl.

Outside a cool breeze swirled around Aster, bringing the familiar scent of freshly caught fish from the docks. He arrived at the General Store just as Fletcher and the others were leaving.

"Hey Aster. Good timing. We got everything we needed thanks to Zinnia. She had a rather nice map of the desert and plenty of waterskins."

As she walked out the door, Kara added, "Zinnia also wanted you to have this." She handed him a light brown traveler's cloak. It wasn't new, but it was sturdy and free of holes. "We each purchased one, but since you weren't here yet, she used her own coin."

Calantha rubbed her cloak between two fingers. "They are ugly. Uncomfortable too."

Kara let out a booming laugh. "These will actually provide some protection, unlike your silk dresses." Calantha scowled but kept quiet, so Kara changed the subject. "Hey Aster, you might want to go inside and talk to Zinnia. She doesn't seem herself. Strangely quiet, like a merchant caught with contraband. She's hiding something."

"No, she would never." He had known Zinnia since they were children, and she was always sincere. "I'll check on her and we'll catch up with you soon."

Fletcher added, "Don't be too late; we have two day's journey ahead of us before we even get to the Kaleenmunda." With that they left him beside the window's yellowed panes.

Aster entered the shop. They were alone among the bottles, candles, and other familiar wares. "Thanks for the cloak, Zin."

Her head popped up from under the counter. "I just kept picturing you wandering the desert in nothing but your tunic and turning as red as an apple. I know that you tan easily, but the sun is more powerful out in the desert... something about the sand."

"How bad could it be? After Munayallpa, it's hard to picture any place hotter."

Zinnia rolled her eyes. "Just make sure you wear it."

"I know you'll be giving me an earful the whole way. I could've used a bit of your sarcasm back on the boat. It gets boring with only grimy sailors to keep me company."

"Oh? And what about Kara? Is she grimy, too?"

Aster scratched the back of his head as he felt his cheeks flush. "Cut it out. That was all a misunderstanding—one that probably saved our lives. She's the smartest person I know, except for maybe the doctor."

"That wasn't a 'no'. I hope grimy Kara keeps you entertained." Her forehead wrinkled as she looked past him, at nothing in particular.

"What do you mean, Zin? You're being weird right now. What's wrong?"

"I... I can't go with you."

"Why not? Are you feeling sick?"

"No, that's not it, Aster." She crouched down below the counter, her face hidden by the wood. "Ever since our encounter at the mines... I keep having nightmares of birds flying in the sky, only to land as grotesque monsters."

"It's happening again?"

"I can't even go out after dark. The thought of leaving the village is too much for me. Sometimes I'm so scared that all I can do is lock the door and cry in my room. I want to be fearless like you, but I'm not. I can't trick myself into going."

Aster leaned forward just enough to see her face. "Zin, this is your chance to be a part of the adventure. Who knows when we'll get another?"

"A cockatrice isn't the only monster out there. It isn't safe. I would just curl up into a ball and die on the spot at the first sign of trouble. I'm sorry, Aster. Go without me." Zinnia eyes turned glassy as she fixated on a cobweb in the corner between two bottles.

"It's alright Zin. I'll keep writing... Though there's no postmen in the desert. Keep an eye on the doctor and help him out if he needs any supplies."

She sniffled. "Thanks, Aster. Be safe out there."

Cloak in hand, he hurried out of the store to the edge of the village. *I should've spent more time with Zinnia. It's been a long time since I've seen her like that...*

Aster caught up with the rest before they had passed Gilroy's apple orchard. Kara gave him a questioning look when he came close.

"Zinnia is staying. She's got to take care of some things at the shop."

"Is that so?"

Aster couldn't meet her eyes. "How long till we get to the desert? I've never been that far myself, so it must be more than a day."

Fletcher cleared his throat. "Two. We need to make it to the sand's edge by nightfall. After that it gets harder."

Aster grunted in acknowledgment.

Chert took the moment to bend down and stuff a few apples into his pockets. "For later," he said aloud. A pair of honeybees passed by his face, causing him to jump. He quickly rejoined the group.

The orchard gave way to rolling hills of hay and barley. Aster stumbled as he pushed through the tall grasses, crickets chirping in the undergrowth. Twice Calantha paused to examine an insect that flew by.

The pace Fletcher had set for them was too much for Aster. By the time they set camp, his legs burned from overexertion. They found a dirt clearing and made a small fire, positioning their bed rolls around it. Aster's stomach grumbled as he sat cross-legged warming himself in the cool evening.

"Apple?" Chert grinned and tossed him one.

"Guess you had the right idea." Aster munched on the fruit as Fletcher handed out dried pork. They chatted into the evening about what they would find in the desert until sleep found them.

Another strenuous day of walking passed, and they found themselves at the edge of the Kaleenmunda Desert. The ground was flat and only a handful of trees could be seen. They looked as if they were barely clinging to life—withered and brown.

Kara looked out over the sand and said, "We should rest here. The next leg will test our strength."

Fletcher nudged Aster forward. "We aren't stopping yet. If we go a bit farther today, then we'll reach the oasis by nightfall tomorrow for sure."

"No, we should stay here. Look, Calantha is exhausted already. And Aster hasn't been able to keep up for hours."

"That's a silly reason. Who put you in charge of this expedition anyways, missy?"

Kara clenched her jaw. "I'm the captain of this crew."

"Well, I don't see a boat nearby, so you can—"

"Enough!" Chert slammed his foot on the ground. "We stop."

Kara gave Fletcher a smug look. He sighed but placed his pack on the ground and started to set up camp.

The morning air was already making them sweat. Fletcher insisted it would get worse, so they wrapped themselves in their new cloaks to keep the sun off.

Aster found that walking through the deep sand was difficult. Each step he took pushed him backwards slightly as the sand compressed beneath his feet. He trudged forward, trying to hide his heavy breathing from Kara.

"A little rest, please," Calantha panted.

Looking back, Aster could still make out the tree line where they had camped the night before. *This will be tougher than I thought.*

After stopping for a minute or two, Calantha said, "It is far too hot out here. I feel as if I may turn to dust."

Aster chuckled in agreement.

The sun was brutal as it beat down on the travelers, causing Aster to wonder if they had brought enough water with them for this trip. He shook his waterskin and heard a reassuring slosh.

After several hours and many more water breaks, Chert pointed out a grove of dried out trees blocking their path. The roots twisted and turned, a maze tying them all together. When he had gotten closer, Fletcher stumbled over an unseen nodule further away from the rest, catching himself just in time.

Kara marveled at the dead growth. "How could these possibly be living out here? I've only ever seen them by the sea, but I haven't seen water anywhere."

Calantha stepped closer, chipping off pieces of the bark. "These mangroves have been dead for years. I suppose the dry air has preserved them."

Fletcher briefly ducked into the tangled labyrinth before reappearing with his head shaking. He pulled out his map and then directed everyone on an alternative route. "No point in getting lost in there. Going around is our best bet."

They continued to trudge through the powdery sand. Calantha was the worst off of the bunch. She had been trailing behind again, making the others wait for her to catch up. Aster had been grateful for each stop, whereas Chert and Fletcher had barely broken a sweat. Thankfully, the heat seemed to be slowing Kara down as well.

Finally, when their shadows had grown to twice their height, Fletcher had them set up camp for the night. "We should start a fire before the light goes out. The desert can be cold without the sun."

Aster couldn't imagine this place cold. But sure enough, as he helped Chert unpack their sleeping mats a breeze began that pulled the sweat right off him. Before long, a steady fire burned, protecting them from the cold air at their backs.

Aster took this downtime as an opportunity. *I should try and get to know Kara better. We've been traveling together for a long time now and I only know bits and pieces about who she is.* He circled the fire and sat cross-legged to her right. "Kara, what are you going to do after this is over? I mean... do you think that you can work for the BTC after what happened in New Portsmith?"

She pulled a brass compass out of her pocket and stared at the needle that flicked back and forth. "I'm trying not to think about it. To be honest, I never imagined that I'd have avoid the capital."

"Yeah..."

"I guess what worries me the most is my sister."

"What's wrong with your sister?"

Kara sighed. "Nothing. I've been sending her my pay. Without it, I worry about the cost of her schooling."

Fletcher chuckled from the other side of the fire. "So much for being a captain."

Calantha nodded to herself. "Proper education *is* expensive."

"I'll have to find something else. I can't let Janna down."

Chert scratched his bald head and said, "Munayallpa always needs shippers."

Aster was drawing circles in the sand near his feet. *This wasn't supposed to turn into a group discussion.* "Yeah, you could start your own shipping company. You'd be great at that!"

Kara sighed again, "I wish it was as easy as you say."

Fletcher stood and stared at Aster as if daring him to quip.

Am I that obvious? Aster squirmed, feeling the sand tickle his leg.

Fletcher inched around the fire.

"C'mon, Fletch. Not funny."

He leaned down and pointed an ice axe at Aster. "Don't move."

Aster froze. *What did I say?* The others stared.

Fletcher didn't blink. He stared for an uncomfortable amount of time. Then he lunged.

Aster flinched.

With the axe, Fletcher knocked a pale-yellow scorpion off of Aster's leg. It skittered out of the light faster than he expected.

"The black one's sting hurts for days, but these guys will only hurt for an hour or so. After that, we'll find a spot to bury you."

Aster's skin crawled and everyone looked around them for other invaders.

Calantha let out a disappointed huff when no other scorpions could be found. Her eyes scanned the ground at every rustle and breeze.

They continued chatting around the fire as the sky turned pitch black.

Aster had every intention of staying up as the others slept. A little alone time with Kara was all he could think about, but his tired body betrayed him. Between the soft cackle of the fire and the warm sand, he relaxed, resting his head on his messenger bag. His eyes were only closed for a second, or so he thought, but when he opened them again, the sky was bright blue.

The next day was more of the same: hot sands, dry air, and not enough water to drink. By midday, they had come across a particularly large sand dune. From far away, it had looked like any other, but what hinted at its scale was how long it took them to actually reach its base.

Once they were there, Aster swore it was taller than the golden clock tower in New Portsmith.

"We're close now. Up and over." Fletcher didn't sound tired at all, much to Aster's irritation.

Each step caused an avalanche of shimmering granules as their feet sank under.

Finally, a chance to steal Kara's attention. Aster trudged ahead, surpassing the others and yelling back, "Kara, I'll race you to the top."

She put her hand above her brow, looking at him as he ascended. "What are you doing? Don't waste your energy."

He ignored her and continued up. Fletcher was about to call out to him when Aster lost his footing and tumbled all the way back down.

As he passed his friends, his bag flew up into the air and landed beside Chert, who saved it from following his fate.

Fletcher shook his head. "Idiot," he said under his breath.

Kara laughed so hard that she had to sit to keep from falling herself.

When Aster finally made it back to the rest, sand covered his face, and stuck to the sweat on his arms. *At least she thinks I'm funny.* He laughed at himself before he pulled out his waterskin and tipped it into his open mouth. Nothing came out.

"No water?" Chert shuffled over to him, handed him the messenger bag, and gave Aster his own halfway full container.

Aster hid the waterskin under his cloak as he drank in an attempt to hide from snide comments.

They walked up and down over a dozen other drifts until their legs were sore, and their heads swam with exhaustion. Finally, they stumbled upon a welcome sight: It was a modest little oasis with date palm trees dotting the edge of a lukewarm pool of water. There were reeds growing from the shallows and a few wispy strands of dried scrub brush at the water's edge.

Aster had been hopeful that they would find a bit of food, but the only fish to be found were minnows that darted between the foliage. Still, he was overjoyed at the chance to refill his empty waterskin.

Fletcher set up camp on the bank of the pool, unrolling his hefty sleeping bag on a fine patch of sand.

"Dinner soon?" Aster asked as he threw his bag down, claiming a spot of his own.

"Yup. Was thinking soup. Could slice up some of those reeds for a bit of extra fiber." The burly man emptied his pockets and three brown mushrooms fell in the sand. "And these."

Aster frowned.

"They're fine. Just rinse the sand out. Mushrooms are my secret ingredient. You never know how dull things taste until you're stuck at a dig site for a season, eating the same roots day in and out."

"And three mushrooms will last the whole dig season? I'm doubtful they'll feed one of us."

Fletcher laughed. "They're for flavoring the soup. We packed plenty of provisions for this trip. Their dust is the secret—well, the spores to be exact. Find a cool, damp spot and you'll have more mushrooms than you need. Learned that from the forest back home." He looked to the desert sands around. "Not that that'll help us here."

"Whatever you cook, start now. I think my legs will give way without food."

Fletcher shook his head. "Hugo never taught you how to take care of yourself, huh?"

"Sure he did."

"Hmmm... you're welcome to start the soup, then. Chert's got the pot."

"Alright, I will," Aster replied. Truth be told, he'd never cooked anything more complicated than a fish over coals or spreading honey on bread. His dad had taken care of cooking until recently. Since then Watson Hollyhock would send Zinnia over with servings.

Chert was busy collecting palm fronds when Aster caught up with him.

Keeping his voice low, so Fletcher wouldn't overhead, Aster asked, "Could you tell me how to make stew?"

Chert shrugged. "Maybe different flavors in Munayallpa. But first boil water." He dragged the fronds back to the shore and arranged them in a careful pile.

Aster lifted the pot out of Chert's bag and filled it in the shallows. Before long, they'd gotten the fire blazing and a hearty pork and reed stew going. Fletcher made a show of adding his three mushrooms. When Aster finally got a bowl, he had to admit that they did add to the flavor.

Morning came and Aster pushed himself to open his eyes. The night was cold and he couldn't seem to fall asleep after the fire had died down. *It's going to be a long day.*

Fletcher gathered everyone around the map they had purchased from Zinnia. "Not much further now. Here's where we spotted the cockatrices," he said pointing to the edge of a canyon. "Should only take a few hours to get there. I guess I should give you this now."

He pulled out a vial of pale-yellow fluid from inside his backpack. Popping the cork out with his teeth, he poured a bit into his palm and slathered it all over his face and clothes. When he was finished, he passed the bottle to Aster, gesturing for him to follow suit.

Aster gagged as he lifted it past his face. "What is this stuff?" It smelled sickly sweet, and strongly of urine. *No way am I walking around with this on my clothes.*

Fletcher smiled wide. "Our secret weapon. This is distilled cockatrice pheromones extracted from the beast that you encountered in the mine. It's the only way to enter their domain unharmed. You saw the havoc one of these creatures can cause. Just beyond these waters is their brood. Must be over a hundred of them."

Aster's eyes grew wide as he hurriedly applied the fluid to his arms. *Better than a run-in with another cockatrice.*

Calantha took the bottle next, and fanned the fumes towards her face. "Beautiful! There are complex tones in here. Ammonia is the foremost component—most likely for territorial markings. And a hint of cadaverine. I wonder if it is from the corpse's decomposition, or instead used for attracting mates. So many exciting possibilities! You did an excellent job at extracting this, Fletcher."

"All thanks to the notes you left me."

Kara held her nose while applying it to herself. Chert was unfazed by the smell, humming to himself as he dabbed it all over.

After they finished, Fletcher spoke again, "Two more things before we leave: We're looking for any signs of the Pelware expedition. If you see any stone men, or the remnants of their campsite, let me know. Second, stay quiet and keep your distance from the monsters. They should treat us like part of their crackle, but if they are frightened, they may attack anyway. I'll try to help if anyone gets in trouble, but... just don't let it happen. I suppose we could attempt to break its line of sight, but there's no evidence that'll work."

"And you're sure this stuff will work?" Aster asked, lifting his stained pant leg.

"Nope. Never tried it before."

Calantha cleared her throat. "It works in theory. Fletcher has extracted the correct chemicals. The confounding factor is the creatures reactions. We've never had a live specimen to test on."

Aster grimaced. "Comforting..."

"They only write songs about people willing to take a risk." Fletcher lifted his bag onto his shoulder. "C'mon, we'll be the only people alive who've done this."

With that they left the comfortable waters behind. There was nothing in sight past the dunes, only desert. After a few hours of walking, the ground became more solid beneath their feet: It reddened in color and began to incline until they found themselves standing atop cliffs that dropped down into a wide canyon.

Fletcher led them along the ridge until they spotted pearl-white pillars sticking up out of the red sand. Partially-demolished houses with collapsed walls dotted the landscape, a few with their roofs caved in. Their surfaces had long since worn away. Only the marble walls remained of whatever town had once been here.

Just like the ruins on the Haverhein. Aster ran his hand down the stone. *The material looks almost identical. Their sharp-cut shape is strikingly familiar.*

Scattered among the broken-down buildings were clutches of eggs, each the size of a man's head and speckled with brown and red spots. A long snake-like creature was wrapped around the nearest clutch, keeping it warm. When it noticed the travelers, it lifted its head and stuck out its tongue, smelling them to see if they were a threat. Aside from a pair of scaly black wings, it could have passed for an abnormally large cobra. After a minute of considering the newcomers, it lay its head back down to rest, unconcerned.

"Those are basilisks," Fletcher explained in a whisper. "I wouldn't have guessed it before I found this place, but they appear to be the same species as the cockatrices. See how they're paired up?"

Calantha perked up. "How very interesting. The basilisks warm the eggs and tend to their young. And it looks like the cockatrices hunt for food. If they were not so dangerous, I would love to study their life cycles in more detail."

Kara quietly said, "Seeing that this smelly stuff is working, how about we split up? If we don't, we won't be able to search all this before nightfall."

Everyone agreed. After some negotiating gestures, Fletcher took Calantha down a path to the ruins on the left. Aster, Chert, and Kara explored the rubble near the cliffs.

Just as the trio lost sight of Calantha and Fletcher, a hiss echoed from a door-less building to their left. A muscular cockatrice burst out, featherless wings flapping as it cut across the path in a cloud of sand.

Chert put his hands up, stopping Aster and Kara in their tracks.

The beast paused and glared at them, tilting its bird-like head from side to side.

Aster's heart raced. He backed away.

The cockatrice followed. Its wings folded delicately to the side as it strutted across the sand.

Chert pulled Aster behind a rectangular house and into a side road. They hurried away while it was out of sight, listening to its clucks fade behind them.

The road ended abruptly in a circular crater, where the sand had crystallized into jagged spikes leading away from the epicenter.

The crater made Aster's hair stand on end. "Let's look over there instead." Aster pointed to a circle of houses around a dried out well.

They found nothing interesting, only broken buildings and monster nests. Worse, the cockatrice from before had caught up with them.

The wind picked up. Kara pulled her cloak up to her face to stop sand from getting into her mouth. "Nothing here either," she said, looking behind a partial stone wall. "Chert, why are you checking inside each of these houses? None of them are big enough for a fire, so I doubt Ian's crew made camp inside."

Chert stuck his head out of a round home with a missing roof. "Ruins may be place to find chalice. Munayallpan names in the stone."

Aster pulled out his waterskin and took a careful sip. He leaned over the well to look inside before he turned and asked, "What's so special about this cup? If it can't hold water it sounds rather useless to me."

Chert's face scrunched and his eyes went wide. He waved his arms back and forth in the air.

Aster stared at him, trying to figure out how his question had offended, but whirled around when he heard a hiss coming from behind. The cockatrice was only a dozen paces away and it began to kick at the ground with its massive talons. *A territorial display, if these beasts are anything like Buckwheat's chickens.*

It raised its leathery wings into the air, head jutting forward and it hissed. The sound itself was terrifying. It brought back memories of the mine.

Aster backed up, trying not to anger it, but keeping the cockatrice in sight.

The air had thickened with sand. Aster found himself in an unfamiliar alley with the beast slowly following. Kara and Chert were right behind, careful not to catch its attention.

Aster's mind was racing at this point, expecting to feel the burning cockatrice gaze once more. *What is it doing? I thought that they weren't supposed to attack because of the pheromones.* He continued backing up, and after a few more paces, his questions were answered. After stepping backwards one more time, his foot found no ground. The cockatrice had led him to the cliffs. Unaware, Aster lost his balance.

The world spun. His arm smacked against the cliff side, then he landed with a thump as his shoulders caught between two rocks. His head had, thankfully, not collided with the rock.

That was bad... Aster lay face-down. His arms and left knee throbbed, but he could wiggle his toes and open his hands.

"Are you alright?" Kara's voice called down from above.

Aster grunted as he lifted his chest. "I got pretty banged up, but I'll be fine. What about the cockatrice?"

"It whistled a tune as it watched you fall, looked pretty pleased with itself, then left. I don't know if it even noticed us."

"That's good. Maybe it'll leave us alone. So, what

now?"

"These cliffs are too steep to scale. We'll get Fletch and see if there's another way down. Stay here and wait for us."

"I'll try. Just don't take too long. I may need to find shelter if the wind gets any stronger." The sky had yellowed ominously, making Aster uneasy.

A glint of gold caught Fletcher's eye. He leaned down and carefully dusted the sand away, revealing a simple ring. When he tried to pick it up, he found it was still attached to a hand made of stone, fractured at the wrist.

Based on the amount of detail around the nails, this has to have belonged to a person, not a work of art. The wind and sand have eroded most of the structures around here, but this hand is still in fairly good shape, which means that it isn't as old. Very interesting.

Calantha interrupted his thoughts, pointing to the sky at a wall of haze moving towards them. "A dust storm is approaching. If we found shelter nearby, it would help us twofold: as protection and as an ideal spot for our search."

Fletcher scanned the area, his eyes landing on a small opening in the side of a lone hill. "There." He trudged forward with Calantha in tow.

The entrance was a short tunnel with a sharp turn. Judging by the faded patterns on the wall, it was enough to keep the inside safe from the abrasive sands. The tunnel ended in a single domed room which contained a half-buried fire pit and three statues.

The Pelware expedition. Fletcher recognized Ian instantly. His long beard and leathery skin gave him the look of a beggar, but in truth he was extremely wealthy.

He glanced at the other two men. One was Munayallpan and the other was Benian with a missing hand. *Here are the two victims. Clearly a cockatrice had found its way inside. We were right.*

"It looks like Ian has indeed been killed here. Probably the most interesting thing to happen to the man." Fletcher scowled and tipped Ian's short statue over. It fell face-first into the sandy floor.

Calantha made a simple noise of acknowledgment. She was preoccupied, scrounging through the remnants of their belongings. After digging inside a half-rotten chest, she squealed in delight, and held up a creased map. "This must be it! The map of King Charles' grave." She turned it from side to side. "But this does not make any sense. There is no ocean that looks like this."

Fletcher took it from her. *She's right. The land masses aren't recognizable. I thought... I thought his tomb was somewhere in Benia, but this map looks more like a peninsula.* He ran his fingers through his hair. "His tomb is on an island in the center of a bay, but it's unlike any island that I know of. Even considering falling sea levels, the position is wrong. It can't be Buckwheat Lake. And the shape is wrong to be Patzu Lake. No wonder Ian couldn't find the king's remains."

Fletcher handed the map back to Calantha before spending a few more minutes rummaging through the chests. *Nothing else is here, but we found what we came for. Plenty of time to puzzle over it later.*

Fletcher turned to leave but stopped. *A good man would pay respects. Besides, today he gave me what I was looking for.*

He scrounged around, finding a long stone and burying it halfway into the sand at the entrance to the cave. Half under his breath he said, "A memorial to the notion of Sir Ian Pelware." *More than he deserves.*

He took no more than a dozen steps back towards the ruins before the sandstorm became unbearable. The air howled as they were pelted with sand. Fletcher wrapped his face in as much fabric as he could.

"Wait! Listen." Calantha yelled over the buzz, stopping him in his tracks.

Through the noise, they could just barely make out

Kara's voice calling to them.

"Over here," he shouted.

After what felt like ages, Fletcher managed to follow her voice to a house that was mostly intact. "Where's Aster?"

"He fell. We need to go after him."

Fletcher's skin was being rubbed raw by the sand. "Going out now is a bad idea. We need to wait for the storm to pass."

Kara waved them into the building. "We can come up with a plan in here."

Aster lay with his head in a gap between two stones, clutching his bleeding leg. His pendant had fallen out of his shirt and started tapping against the rock. *That's odd, the wind is blowing the other way.* He brushed himself off and sat up to inspect his wounds. *Nothing serious, thankfully.* He wiped blood off with his cloak.

He hopped down onto the sand. *I need to find shelter before this gets worse.* The only thing he could make out were the cliffs to his back, everything else was obscured.

Which way? On the left, he felt a presence watching him through the haze. The smell that followed was a hundred times worse than that of the cockatrice pheromones. It was the scent of rotting flesh, fermenting and decaying. Aster covered his face to keep the stink out. Then he felt a searing pain. As if he had stayed in the sun for too long, the left side of his body was itchy and hot.

Whatever is over there is bad news. Aster took his knife out and carved an arrow into the rocks before wading through the wind. It wasn't long before he was out of sight of the cliffs.

A gust knocked him over, but when he stood, he couldn't remember which way he was facing. The sands swirled around him, and everything looked the same. He was lost.

In the beige desolation of senses, there was one feeling that was consistent: Ochress' pendant. No matter which way he was facing, it seemed to pull him towards the same direction. He stumbled forward, guided by his mother's gift.

Aster focused on putting one foot in front of the other. His exhaustion had caught up with him and all he could think about was finding shelter.

Hours went by in a monotonous blur until Aster slammed headfirst into a sandstone wall.

He fell backwards in shock, and landed on the soft ground, laying there, nearly delirious.

In front of his face, the necklace slowly floated upward until the gold chain was drawn taut. In awe of this nature-defying sight, Aster grabbed it and let it go, repeatedly testing its behavior. *The pendant is leading me.*

The wall was porous with plenty of footholds. Aster stood, slipping his hand into a crevice and pulling himself up. It was curiosity more than anything that drove him up with the pendent hovering just below his chin.

As he scaled, the pull grew stronger. His arms were weak and his legs wobbled by the time he heaved himself up onto a landing. It was an opening, larger than him but not by much, which hooked to the right, hidden from view. A weathered blue door stood at the back. *Odd place for a door.*

Aster's necklace strained towards it, like a hound eagerly chasing a fox to its hole. He pushed at the faded door with all his might, but the hinges were rusted shut. Leaning closer, he found that the door was only barely connected to the surrounding rock, polished by the years.

Aster dug his knife into the rock and dislodged the hinge. Scraping his fingers between the sides, he pried the door open, jumping back as it landed with a thud, now only a doormat to the cave beyond.

Inside was a passageway lit with a faint green glow. *Like the sea jellies,* Aster marveled. At the end of the tunnel was a large circular room with an ornate stone coffin to one side.

A mural covered the walls and ceiling. Green scaled creatures on two legs looked down from the clouds while ocean waves destroyed the land below. A glowing blue orb shone light on the scene. Humanoids with fins dotted the sea, oblivious to the storm. A small village of what looked like Benians cowered behind a dozen Munayallpans, whose spears defended them from something unknown. That portion of the wall had been damaged by a cave-in; its artwork lost to the ages. Fragments of painted blue stone lay scattered on the floor.

More interesting than the painting was the source of the light at the room's center. A transparent green orb sat atop a marble pedestal, illuminating the ancient artwork.

Aster reached out and touched the surface, which was as smooth as a glass bottle. He gingerly lifted it out of its stand. *It's so light. Too light.* His pendant fell flat against his chest, no longer pulling him towards it.

The orb was a microcosm unto itself. Inside was a miniature forest filled with lush trees and tall grasses. A tiny river flowed from a picturesque hill to a lake surrounded with speckles of white flowers.

No matter which way he turned it, the scene remained upright. *Not sure how this is possible, but I'd better not break it.*

He placed the orb back in its resting place and then examined the carved stone coffin. "Charles, First King of Benia" was engraved under the bust of the legendary founder. *Then it really is the Odyllic Stone...*

Aster legs wobbled with exhaustion. *I just need a moment to think.* He sat, leaning his head against the mural. *Fletcher will be thrilled. Now what did they say the Odyllic Stone could do?* He meant to close his eyes for a second, but before he knew it he had fallen asleep in the pale green glow.

Fletcher leaned over the disintegrating marble table, scratching his scalp absentmindedly. Both maps were spread out in front of him, one plain and understandable, the other still hiding its truth.

The companions had rested through the night inside the two-room house, not daring to make the trek while the sandstorm raged.

A suitable path into the valley... a gradual slope down. He tried his best to focus but the siren's call of the tomb kept diverting his eyes to the ancient map. *I'm closer than I've ever been. Ian was here for a reason.*

Kara paced back and forth in the room, occasionally poking her head outside. "The sandstorm has been over for an hour now. Let's search for Aster."

"I need more time. This map doesn't have any detail about the cliff gradients, so we'd just be guessing where the way down is." It was mostly the truth.

"Hurry. He could be hurt."

"He said he was fine, right?"

"Yeah, but he was outside during the worst of it."

Chert wandered over and observed the maps over Fletcher's shoulder. After a minute he spoke. "Map upside down."

"No, it isn't. See, the cliffs are to the north where we found them yesterday. Plus, the compass rose is drawn in the bottom corner."

Chert shook his lumpy head and replied, "No, other map is upside down."

"How do you know? There's hardly any detail..." Fletcher rotated the burial map. It was barren compared to the one he had purchased from the Buckwheat General Store. "Even if this is correct, I don't see how this helps us,"

Chert paused, considering his words carefully before responding, "Before lake. Now is desert."

Fletcher's eyes darted back to the illustration of rolling waves. Sure enough the island at the center of the map was perfectly aligned with the mesa beyond the cliffs, which themselves roughly matched the outline of the bay. "The older map shows three sand beaches leading to the water. If that's true, then these places should be gradual slopes down into the valley." He pointed at the new map. *Which means that the tomb is somewhere on the mesa.*

"What a marvelous discovery," Calantha added. "The terramorphic powers of the Odyllic Stone must have changed the very properties of the land. This is why we must contain and study this power to prevent similar catastrophes from occurring in the future."

Kara shook her head. "More importantly, it's our way down to Aster."

Fletcher nodded. *It would be a shame if something happened to Aster.* He liked the kid, even if he could be naive. *At least he has a genuine sense of adventure.* That was more than he could say about the rest of Buckwheat Village.

The path into the valley was surprisingly straightforward. Their prediction had been right and the loose sand gently sloped down until they were at the bottom of the reddened cliffs. Kara lead them forward as they watched for hints of marble above. Anything that would suggest they were below the ruins.

Kara was paces ahead when she called the others over. "I found something. These markings look very fresh. I'm sure Aster was here and left them for us, probably needed to find shelter. He should be close by."

Fletcher examined the crude arrow gouged into rock. It pointed northwest into the endless sands. He examined the desert floor. Like a fresh snow, drifts of sand piled up everywhere. "Too bad. His tracks are gone. I think we need to split up. Kara, keep looking among the rocks to the West. Chert and Calantha, head North. Keep sight of the cliffs in the distance. I'll go beyond that. Let's meet back here an hour before sunset. That should give us enough time to walk back to the oasis camp before dark."

"And if we don't find him?" Kara's eyebrows were drawn.

"We will. If he's smart, he'll have stayed close."

With that, each went their separate way in search of their missing companion.

Fletcher was just out of sight of the others when he stopped and pulled out his maps. *They'll find Aster. He's got to be near to those markings. But if he wandered off, he should be near the mesa... And it would be a waste not to look for the tomb while I'm nearby.* Fletcher folded the maps back up and trudged onward.

Time passed without a hint of anyone or anything. Fletcher looked up to see a lone mountain on the horizon breaking up the barren landscape. Its red and yellow striped walls and flat precipice were a stark contrast to the endless sands.

This must be the place. He paced around its base, checking the old map once again. *A cave somewhere on the southern side.* No features stood out. If there was a cave, he couldn't see it.

He flaked off a piece of the sandstone in his hand. *Not the most stable rock for a climb, but shouldn't be difficult if I take it slow.* He grabbed his trusty ice axe out of his bag and drove it into the sandstone. It slid in easily but held firm.

Fletcher quickly scaled the mesa until the color of the rock lightened. *Sun-bleached.* He circled the gradient, looking for a cavern before finally spotting the landing below a particularly large outcropping.

He pulled himself up and stopped to catch his breath. There was a broken-down door, flat against the floor. His heart skipped a beat. *By Viridus' blight, I refuse to believe this place has already been looted.*

His mind raced. *Did Ian find it first? No... we searched their camp. Someone else? How would we not have heard about this great find? That would be a deed proclaimed around the world.*

He brushed his fingers against the holes in the sandstone where the hinges had been. *No, this must be natural erosion. I hope that everything inside is still preserved, spared from the sandstorms.* He stepped across the threshold and into the green glowing room.

With each step Fletcher's heart rate climbed. *I'll be famous. All Arathanon will know of Fletcher Abberton, greatest adventurer of all time. Ian Pelware will be a distant memory.*

His jaw dropped when he spotted the paintings on the wall. *Beautiful! The historians back home will be giddy.*

The soft glow from the orb at the room's center drew his eye next. It wasn't what he had expected. Every other find he had been a part of felt incidental in comparison. *This is what being an explorer truly is.* He marveled at the clarity of the scene within. It was almost as if he was looking at a field located somewhere else.

Don't get ahead of yourself. Confirm that this is Charles' tomb. He tore his eyes away from the stone and spotted the kings bust. He stepped forward to get a closer and kicked something soft.

A body. Fresh. In a familiar traveler's cloak... "Aster? Hey, wake up."

Half asleep, Aster opened one eye. "Fletcher? I did it. I found the tomb. But wait, how did you get here?"

"Chert managed to decipher the Ian's old map." Fletcher was dumbfounded at finding Aster here. "How did you get here?"

"Dunno." Aster face was red from sand-burn and he was barely coherent. "Got lost in the sandstorm and ended up here."

Without the map... The second time he's impressed me through dumb luck. "Well, we've all been looking for you, but now that you're safe, help me document this discovery. But first, have some water. You look dehydrated." He handed over his waterskin.

Aster gratefully chugged the water.

"I've been searching for this tomb for my entire life. It's unbelievable—when even the *great* Ian Pelware couldn't. We need to document these murals. I want a record of every detail, since we can't take the images with us."

Aster was already more lively, with a goofy smile growing on his face.

"I'll be famous! We'll be famous!" Fletcher couldn't contain his excitement. "I hope one day a stranger will buy me a drink when they learn my name..."

"Fletch, what does this say?" Aster pointed to a small plaque under the bust.

Oogoo Amiguh History Verid Zririririri. Fletcher could only make out the middle word. "Something about history. It's strange. Might be Munayallpan. I think I recognize the second word, but... no... this isn't written in Benian."

"I'll try and copy it."

"Make a rubbing," Fletcher instructed. "It's better than trying to match the symbols."

"Do you think there's any truth to the stories? About the Odyllic Stone?"

"Not a chance. In my experience, it's all exaggeration to excite children. The real truth is what it meant to the people of the past."

Aster's smile dropped for a moment, but he grabbed writing supplies from his bag and they got to work.

The two spent hours and used up all of their paper, writing about King Charles's tomb and the history it contained.

Satisfied, Fletcher turned back to the orb at the center of the room. He removed his cloak and wrapped the stone inside of it, holding it against his chest with both hands. "Finally, a discovery that will echo across Arathanon!" He paused a second and handed it to Aster.

"Will this fit inside your mailbag? I have axes, hooks, and a hammer in mine. Don't want them to damage the stone."

Aster's bag was barely big enough. The clasps stretched as far as they could and the cloth bulged at the sides, but it was secure.

"Be careful with it."

"I won't let anything happen to it."

Aster sounded sure, but Fletcher was already regretting his choice.

It was getting late, and they had done all they could do. After they took a final look around, Fletcher lifted the old door and placed it back to cover the entrance.

"Every little bit helps preserve history," he remarked before securing a rope and throwing it off the ledge to give them a quick way down. "I'll need to come back with a proper crew."

The journey back was uneventful. They managed to meet up with the others, only slightly later than planned.

The impatience melted from Kara's face when she saw Aster walking towards them. Fletcher recounted the spectacle of the tomb on their path back to the oasis. Only Chert had thought to ask him why he was at the tomb in the first place, to which Fletcher simply replied, "I had a hunch."

Aster dipped his waterskin into the oasis, listening to the slow glug as it refilled. *I need to be more careful with water out here. The desert can be dangerous.*

Once again, the sun was setting and a cold breeze blew across the sands. He rejoined the others around the fire, excitedly waiting for everyone to settle. Fletcher had described Charles's tomb in excruciating detail except for one thing: the most important find. Aster had played along. *A big reveal.*

Aster couldn't help but stare at Fletcher, who was picking sand out of his boot, oblivious. *Aren't you going to say something?*

He played with the clasp of the bulging messenger bag.

Fletcher noticed him and shook his head.

No? Why? Aster slipped his hand inside and felt the smooth surface of the relic.

"Later." Fletcher voice was stern.

Now's the perfect time. We'll have their full attention.

Besides tomorrow will be busy with the hike back. Aster pulled the stone out of his bag and held it high in the air. "We also found the Odyllic Stone."

Fletcher palmed his forehead and Calantha perked up.

"The what?" Kara leaned around the fire the get a better look.

"The Odyllic Stone. You've heard the legends, right?"

"Can't say that I have."

Calantha cleared her throat. "References to the Odyllic Stone go back to the first written histories. Some scholars say that the stone is synonymous with the first king of Benia, but others insist that it is merely a metaphor for his divine right to rule. Of course, all agree that the stories of what it could do have been exaggerated over time. The most widely agreed upon explanation..."

Aster stared at the orb. The scene inside reminded him of the grass fields back home that were dotted with wildflowers in the spring. The sweet floral smell when the wind was blowing. It was serene. Vibrant. Alive.

It happened all at once, the stone glowed bright, illuminating the oasis and the barren sands behind. The light became unbearably intense; stalks and tendrils shot up from the ground, reaching for the sky. The sands parted, making way for a field of grasses and flowers. Pink and yellow lilies exploded out of the water, spraying the group in the process. It was over in an instant, but the small desert oasis had been transformed into a verdant plain. Before, it had been a sanctuary of life, but now it was unnaturally lush. The stone's glow began to fade, leaving the campfire as their only source of light.

Calantha jumped up and shouted in excitement as she ran over to examine the fresh blooms. Fletcher pulled the orb out of Aster's hands for a closer look. Kara was on her feet ready to take action. Aster and Chert didn't move, stunned by the turn of events.

Calantha was the first to speak. "The rumors are true. You have sufficiently demonstrated its power to control the laws of nature. Not even my Brejo Clemantis vines are capable of growing over this large of an area. And these wildflowers aren't even native to this region. What a delight."

Kara's face was white. "What just happened? How did you do that?"

"I don't really know. I guess I was thinking about plants when I raised it."

Fletcher held the stone to the sky and closed his eyes, straining with concentration. Nothing happened. After he tried a few more times, he passed it around. Nobody was able to reproduce the effect.

"Well, I hope that wasn't a 'one wish' kind of thing," Kara said, as she gripped her elbows.

Fletcher ran his fingers through his dirty hair. "It shouldn't be. I can't recall any descriptions or stories about limitations to its power."

Calantha nodded in agreement. "Neither have I."

The soft smell of the new flowers danced around them as they discussed ancient stories about the stone until they were too exhausted to continue. That night Aster dreamed about magic, monsters, and kingdoms of old.

The next morning, they packed their things and left the waters behind. The journey back through the desert was calmer than the way out. The scorching sun and dry air again tired their bodies and depleted their water, but their spirits were high.

Twice, Aster thought to use the stone to create a new oasis, but thought better of it. *I shouldn't mess around with things I don't know enough about.*

When the desert sands yielded to grassy plains, Aster sighed in relief. They paused for a moment to rest in the shade of a leafy oak tree. Not long after they had passed through Mayor Gilroy's orchard, he spotted Buckwheat Village in the distance.

Zinnia appeared out of nowhere and ran up to Aster, giving him a hug, and welcoming them all back to the village. "Aster! Welcome back! Did you find the map?"

He smiled wide and pulled the Odyllic Stone out of his

bag. "Not only did we solve the mystery of the final resting place of King Charles, but we also located his famed treasure."

Zinnia's eyes grew wide with excitement.

Fletcher swore under his breath, interrupting their reunion. He turned Aster toward him. "Before we go any further, we need to come to an agreement among ourselves. No one else can find out about the stone. Calantha will undoubtedly agree with me when I say that we can't have word getting out before we've had the chance to study it. We must all swear not to reveal the existence of the Odyllic Stone to anyone outside of the five—er six of us," he said after glancing at Zinnia.

"That includes your families and especially your pirate friends," he added, pointing at Kara.

She scowled at the remark. "We aren't pirates."

There were several reluctant nods, but Chert scratched his bald head. "What to say instead?"

Calantha lifted a finger. "We shall tell them that we found the map only. After all, that is what we were searching for in the first place. We should make no mention of the tomb or the stone."

Aster grumbled to himself, but was glad that Zinnia had been included in the secret. At least she would share his excitement.

"Aster?" Fletcher tightened his grip on his shoulder.

"Alright, I won't say anything."

"Excellent. It's better for everyone."

Once Fletcher had gotten everyone's word, he allowed them to continue into Buckwheat Village.

In town, they went their separate ways: Kara to find the rest of her crewmates, Chert and Calantha to the inn to rest, Fletcher to the church to see if he could find any relevant literature, and Aster and Zinnia to the doctor to see if he had good news.

Malvin was finishing up a treatment for Hugo when they caught up with him. Aster opened the door to his father's bedroom as Malvin was putting medical odds and ends back into his black medicine bag.

"Any news?" Aster quietly asked, nodding to his father who was resting peacefully.

Malvin sighed and said, "I have a theory, but I would like to check one more thing to be sure. Don mentioned that there is a gold mine just upriver from here. Could you take me there tomorrow morning?"

"Of course, but I don't understand how that is related to the illness."

Malvin patted him on the shoulder. "Don't worry. I'll explain it after we get there and I've had the chance to run some tests. I would hate to cause a panic prematurely."

They said their goodbyes to the doctor and left Aster's father to rest. Aster walked Zinnia back to her house for the night.

As they walked, Zinnia jumped up and down in excitement. "I just had a great idea. We should use the Odyllic Stone on those poor miners! You said yourself that it has power over nature. It could save them."

Aster thought back to some of the stories about the stone. "I'm not sure that'll work. Actually, I'm not even sure how to control this thing. But I guess they wouldn't be any worse off..."

"I just feel so bad for them."

It's what a hero would do. "Alright I'll bring it with us."

Zinnia grinned and opened the door to her house. "See you tomorrow."

Aster waved her off and walked home. *Dad looked better today. Bringing the doctor home was worth the trip to New Portsmith.*

When morning came, Aster and Zinnia met Malvin for their hike to Pelware Mine. It was a relaxing trip compared to the desert.

When they arrived, Malvin took three vials and filled them with water from the river stream. While he was preoccupied with this, Aster and Zinnia slipped away and returned to the stone men among the miner's cabins.

Nobody was around. *Busy in the mines. Or maybe they've abandoned this place?* Aster wasn't sure. When he was positive that they wouldn't be disturbed, he pulled the orb out of his bag and handed it to Zinnia. It was glowing faintly once more.

"It's your idea Zin, you do it."

"If it works like you said..." Zinnia peered into the clear orb. Tears fell down her cheeks.

"Did it not work?" Aster placed a hand on her shoulder.

"No... sorry. Let me try again." She wiped her eyes with her sleeve.

"What happened?"

"I just had to know. I thought about mom alive..."

"Oh... I'm sorry."

"It's fine. This time I'll focus on the miners." She carefully held it out between the two statues, and closed her eyes. The orb flashed a bright light before falling dim. Tremors rippled across the stone skin. Slowly, color started to creep back into the faces of the men, their fingers twitching back and forth as they gained mobility.

Aster grabbed the stone to hide it inside his bag.

When the whites of their eyes returned, they each let out a horrible scream. "Monster! Light of Conflag, don't kill me." They flinched backward, stumbling over the mine tracks.

Zinnia flatly said, "Monster's gone," repeating herself until the two men stopped and took a good look around.

"What happened? Where'd the beast go? When did you get out of the tunnel?"

Aster smiled at them. "That monster almost did you in, but Zinnia managed to save you. It's long gone, you're safe now. But you should know that you had been petrified for a month or two. I think that—"

"Aster, stop. Oh, what have we done? This was a mistake." She grabbed him by the hand and pulled him back towards the river.

When they were out of sight, she turned to Aster. "I'm

sorry. I was so caught up that I didn't think our plan all the way through. People will talk."

"It'll be alright. Those miners seem pretty confused."

Zinnia fidgeted with her hands in her pockets. "I sure hope you're right."

We didn't break our promise. Aster kicked at dirt clods on the way back to the doctor. *They didn't see the stone. Zinnia is overreacting.*

Malvin stared across the water, ponytail flicking in the light breeze. When he saw them, his demeanor changed. His voice was slower and his word methodical. "Maybe you should sit down."

Aster sat in a patch of grass. Zinnia stayed standing and crossed her arms.

"Your village is being poisoned."

"So, Rowan was right? Jash is trying to kill us."

"Do they own this mine?"

"Well, the Pelware Mine is owned by the BTC. But what's that got to do with anything?"

"If you'll be patient, I'll explain it to you." Malvin looked more melancholy than angry. "Seizures, psychosis, vomiting, numbness in extremities: These are all symptoms of heavy metal poisoning. I ran tests on your father and friends to confirm. When I found out this mining operation was upstream of your village, I knew I had to see for myself. The water you drink and the fish you eat are all contaminated with it."

Aster examined the clear mountain stream. It didn't look poisoned. "How could this happen?"

"It's quicksilver mostly, with traces of lead. I thought the practice had been outlawed years ago, but it seems like this mine is discarding waste into this river. It slowly builds up in a person's body, and when there is enough present, they start showing symptoms. If too much builds up it can be fatal."

Aster felt a lump in his throat as he swallowed. *All of our suffering caused by the mine?* "Now that you know what's wrong, can't you cure them?"

"It isn't that easy, unfortunately. There is no cure for quicksilver poisoning. The best course of action is to prevent further exposure. Some people recover over time, but others may not."

Zinnia cupped her open mouth.

"There isn't anything we can do?"

"Like I said, we need to talk with whoever is in charge of this operation and get them to stop using quicksilver. Or dispose of it better so it won't seep into the ground water..."

Hannes or Fletcher...

"We have the chance to keep everybody else in the village from getting sick. After that, I'll see what I can do. But we need to do our best to keep anyone else from consuming more of it."

Zinnia nodded.

Aster sat in silence. He couldn't believe what the doctor was saying. *No cure...*

Malvin put his hand on Aster's shoulder. "Listen to me. You did good. You've saved a lot of people with your persistence. There are only two people that need special attention and I'll do my best to keep them healthy. I need you to cheer up and help me see this through to the end."

Aster let the doctor pull him to his feet. *No cure for Dad. No cure for Lavender. No cure for Buckwheat.* He felt sick to his stomach.

As they walked back to town, Zinnia's mood had lightened and she tried repeatedly to catch Aster's eye, but he was too upset to acknowledge her. She darted in front of him and said, "Aster, listen. I've got a great—"

He brushed her away with his hand. "No Zinnia, I've traveled for months and now Malvin says there's no cure."

"But—"

"Don't you get it? He says it's in our water. Everyone we know could be affected."

"Aster it's not so bad—"

"Not so bad? You heard Malvin, there's no cure!"

"What if we used—"

"Enough! I spent the whole spring trying to find help and we find out it was pointless. Hopeless. Just let me be."

She shrank away from him and walked the rest of the way in silence.

When they arrived in Buckwheat, Malvin stopped at the Goodwin house to examine Lavender and Rowan.

Aster and Zinnia found the others at the Toasted Oak. Just as they sat down, the door opened and Fletcher joined them.

Aster tensed up. *The owner of the mines. Ignorant of the quicksilver? No, he's too smart for that.* His eyes tracked Fletcher as walked to their table.

"Hello again. Say, where did you put that thing we—"

He kicked his chair to the floor, standing ready. His voice broke as he yelled, "Why is Buckwheat being poisoned by your mines?"

Fletcher's expression soured and he made a stop motion with his hands. "Aster, calm down. What are you talking about?"

"We just got back from Pelware where we found out about the quicksilver you are using. You've poisoned us all!" He said through bared teeth.

"Quicksilver is killing the village?" Fletcher dropped into the nearest chair, fingers massaging his temples. "So, you are saying that this illness is due to our mining activity?"

Aster looked him in the eyes and said, "Did you know about this?"

Fletcher started a few times but couldn't find his words. He took a deep breath and said, "Yes, I knew that we were using it and I also knew about the risks. I don't want to make any excuses, but we thought it wouldn't be a problem."

Aster slammed his fist into the table. "That's not good enough! Lavender and my father are both dying. Malvin says there's no cure. How come you didn't warn Buckwheat?"

Fletcher shook his head.

Aster doubled down, pointed at him menacingly, "Answer me or I'll—"

Kara pulled him back. "Aster, stop. We aren't getting anywhere here. You must be tired. Why don't you get some rest?"

Aster turned his anger on her. "Back off, Kara. It's not like you give a shit about Buckwheat."

For the first time, Kara looked sad. Something that he hadn't seen when they were attacked by pirates, or when they were betrayed by Whitlock, or even when they broke her out of the Benia jail cell. Before she could protest, Aster stormed out of the inn.

Everyone stared at Zinnia as if she had an explanation. She squirmed in her seat as the sailors gave up and went back to their dinner. Fletcher's eyes were glazed over as he poked at his slice of roast beef.

"He doesn't mean it," she said under her breath.

Fletcher didn't look up. "Hmmm..."

"He's just upset."

"I see that."

"Did you really know about it?"

"Yes, but not how bad it is. It wasn't really our choice. Shaheed insisted that we use quicksilver to create an amalgam with gold and... well I'll skip over the technicalities, but it's supposed to be more efficient."

"Can you to stop using it?"

"I'll talk with the men and see if we can come up with something."

Zinnia dropped her voice to a whisper. "While we were in Pelware, we used the stone. Saved those miners. Could it help us too?"

Fletcher went pale. "I should also send a message to the capital about a longer-term solution. Actually, I'll head out now." He grabbed his bag off the table and hurried out.

The Toasted Oak was quiet for the rest of the night and most everyone turned in early for the night, leaving Kara and Zinnia alone at the table.

Zinnia pushed her now cold food back and forth across her plate, absentmindedly. *Why's Aster always so rash? I wish he'd listen to me more.*

Kara spoke, breaking her train of thought. "I'm sorry about Buckwheat."

"And I'm sorry about Aster," she replied.

"You don't have to apologize for him."

"After that, I feel like I should. He's like family."

"Is that right? I knew you were close, but..."

"Yeah I've sort of always looked out for him. He's had a tough life... we all have."

"Ain't that the truth. Say, want to see something my sister, Janna, gave me?"

Zinnia perked up. "Sure. What is it?"

Kara pulled out a weathered brass compass from her pocket and handed it over. "It's from when I first accepted my job on the Blue Skies. So I'd never get lost out at sea. No idea how she could afford something like this."

Zinnia turned it around in her hand and watched the needle spin before settling to North. "You two must be close."

Kara laughed. "I guess you could say that, though Janna's a bit of a brat. Always instructing me on how to do my chores as if she had done them her entire life.

"One time, when I had gotten home late from the market where we were selling corn, she had the audacity to lecture me on the importance of reading books.

"I spent all my time helping around the farm. She never really got that. We didn't speak for a week. Thankfully she's mellowed out since then."

Zinnia cracked a smile. "Kind of like Aster. He can also be a bit of a brat."

"Sometimes..."

"But enough of him, tell me a story of your wildest

adventure on the Blue Skies. Stories of danger or treasure always brighten my mood, something I could really use after the news today."

Sliding the compass back into her pocket, Kara said, "It isn't the wildest adventure that I've had, but it is a funny one. I'll never forget the maiden voyage of the Blue Skies. I was still new to the crew. We were sailing to Zeffarii to purchase some incense for... I want to say it was for the archbishop himself."

"Must've been important!"

"I'm not sure about that. In any case, we were more than halfway there when it was my turn to take watch for the night. If you've never had to keep watch, let me tell you: It's dull.

"I swear that I only closed my eyes for a second, but before I knew it, Pat was shaking me awake. He was the second watch, but something was wrong. His face was pale as he told me to wake the crew. We were about to crash into an island that we didn't have on the map. He told me to ring the bell and yell 'Land Ho' over and over until everyone woke up."

Kara smirked and shook her head. "There was no land. And waking everyone up yelling 'Land Ho' doesn't even make sense. Pat had decided to play a trick since he found me asleep. It was years before they stopped teasing me about that one."

Zinnia laughed. "Pat seems like quite the trickster."

"He's the nicest man I've ever met. But he's not afraid to have a bit of fun at my expense."

The two ladies chatted late into the night about Kara's time on the ship and about their families.

The next morning Zinnia stopped at the Rutherford house to check on Aster.

Hugo was still asleep, judging by the snoring echoing through the kitchen.

I hope Aster has cooled down, she thought as she opened his bedroom door. *I've never seen him that angry before.*

But Aster wasn't there. His room was empty aside from a letter sitting atop his bed, hastily written and addressed to her.

Zinnia,

It's gone. Fletcher took it. I caught him rummaging through my bag in the kitchen. When he saw me, he ran. I'm not sure why, but it seems like he's heading east towards the Boral Mountains. Maybe to Jash. I'm going after him.

-Aster

7 A GREAT LOSS

Frigid spears of rain assaulted Aster's face as he pushed back the underbrush. *I'm an idiot*, he thought to himself as he slowly marched forward, his destination unknown. He shivered and pulled his cloak tight to his chest. *If only I'd listened to Zinnia, I wouldn't be in this mess.* A thorny vine grazed his thigh, clawing the skin open. He yelped in pain as he felt the blood trail down his leg.

"When I find Fletcher, I won't hold back. This is inexcusable," he growled. The soft mud squished below his feet and twice he almost lost his footing. His body was numb from the cold. A delicate tugging of his necklace guided his way.

His stomach interrupted his self-loathing with a bubbling growl: He was starving. *Maybe I should stop to eat?* He didn't have much food left. It had been over a week since he left Buckwheat Village, and he was no closer to his goal since he had left on that godforsaken morning. *I made a mistake. It's my own fault I'm alone in this wilderness.* He pushed himself harder and harder, following the pull from his neck until he broke through the tree line.

Aster found himself in a clearing filled with fallen logs and scrub brushes. At its center were the mossy stone walls of a city. A fracture tore across its middle, leaving two sides off-balance, tilting away from the city center. The trees around him bowed to it, as if praying to its majesty. *I've only heard of small villages to the east of Buckwheat. Why is this here?* As he climbed onto the stone pavement he saw that everything was in ruin. *Fletcher must be inside,* Aster mused, feeling his pendant directing him towards the city center.

Once inside the outer walls he marveled at the size of the place. This city was bigger than New Portsmith, with rows of buildings as far as he could see. Several were bright white, which stood out against gray stone and encroaching greenery.

There's nobody here—probably hasn't been for years. The thought was unnerving to Aster. His head swiveled around, looking for movement. Aside from patches of overgrown weeds swaying from the breeze, the place was still and silent.

In the ruins of a courtyard, Aster's eyes caught sight of a bronze effigy, dented and prone upon the floor. He hopped across the rubble, nearly slipping on the wet stones, grabbing a hold of some tall grass to keep upright.

I need a closer look. The back of the figure had two powerful wings and its skin was roughly textured. Before it had fallen, it must've been standing tall with its sizable chin pointing to the heavens.

Aster looked around until he found the statue's former resting place, an ornate marble base. It was engraved with languages Aster didn't recognize except for a single line near the bottom. *"The enlightened soar above worldly troubles"*— *Quell'est the Philosopher.*

Aster shivered as water dripped down his nose. *It's time to get out of this rain.* Dodging puddles in the pavement, he slipped through an ornate doorway into a room with a high-vaulted ceiling.

He pulled off his cloak and twisted out the moisture. The pendant around his neck continued to pull towards the hallway at the far end of the chamber. He instinctively checked that the paper in his bag had not been soaked in the sudden storm. Then he marched forward, deeper into the mysterious city.

The hallway was unremarkable aside from a textured mural on the left-hand wall: a series of gears attached to a winged figurine, flying through a blue sky. It would have been interesting if it was still functional. He always liked to see how these types of mechanisms worked. It reminded him of the wheels on Gilroy's wagon, but more intricate.

Pressing on, Aster tripped over an indentation in the threshold of the rectangular room, catching himself before falling. He looked back and saw a series of notches in the floor. *A door must have been here once.*

Inside was a scene of nature, masterfully carved upon each wall. A flowing waterfall became a river, which in turn fed the ocean. Trees, flowers, and animal life dotted the surface, but the waterfall itself was most interesting. Lukewarm water trickled over its chiseled surface. The stone was worn around the bottom edge of the opening.

He looked around and found a metal drain underneath the ocean scene. *This city is more advanced than New Portsmith. The artwork in this place is so detailed.* After admiring the animals embossed in their stone paradise, Aster tried to open the closed door at the room's far end. It was sealed shut.

No handles. No locks. It looks like a city gate. Is there a wheel to raise it? He surveyed the room, but it was empty aside from the wall decorations.

A tuna, carved at knee level, caught Aster's attention. The fish protruded from the wall slightly. He ran his hands over the scaly texture of its body, and with a little bit of force, he pressed it into the wall. When he let go, it slid back to its original position. Looking closer, the other animals were the same. Each was raised out from the scenery.

"I bet one of these animals is the key to opening the door," he mused as he eyed a bird flying in the sky just out of reach. A crash shook the room as a wall of stone fell into the doorway that had tripped him. His exit was blocked.

Aster depressed the fish again before running over to the door, anxious to get it open. Even throwing his full weight against it, it wouldn't budge. He ran back to the animal carvings and pressed each one, sometimes twice, to see if they would release him. It took a few leaps to reach the bird, but still nothing changed.

Dejected, he sat cross-legged. His only consolation was that his clothes had dried. *There has to be a way out. Who would make a room this pretty that locks you inside? It doesn't look like a prison.* His stomach made an audible gurgle. *I haven't even eaten today.* He pulled the last apple and slice of bread from his bag and devoured them. *Great. Another mistake I made, not bringing enough food.*

Aster's legs ached and now that he was out of the rain, the weariness was weighing on him. *A little rest may do me some good. Clear my head.* As he lay down, eyes closed, he pictured Zinnia scolding him for taking off so quickly. Then he thought of Kara's dark brown eyes underlined with freckles. *Kara would've been more prepared.* As he drifted to sleep, he pictured himself back on the Blue Skies with the salty spray of the ocean splashing his back.

He bolted upright, eyes wide open. His back was wet. The floor was covered in a thin layer of water. Looking over to the waterfall, he could see that the flow had increased. "Conflag have mercy."

Kara watched as Zinnia opened the rusty cellar door. If it was anything like her family farm it would be cold, cramped, and full of spiders. Back home she avoided cellar chores whenever possible.

Zinnia hoisted up a crate full of jars. The colors of all the pickled fruits and vegetables seemed like a decoration all on their own.

From the stairs Kara lifted the crate out of her hands. "What's all this for? You mentioned some sort of celebration."

"Yeah, the fire festival. I'm surprised you don't know about it. I thought that New Portsmith had the biggest bonfire every year."

Kara placed the box next to the others as Zinnia disappeared into the dark cellar depths. She came back with another box of food. "Is it really that time of year already? I've never been to the festival myself. On the farm we don't worship Conflag."

"Another god?"

"Used to.... haven't for years, though. And after I joined the BTC we were always hauling supplies in preparation for the event but never stayed to participate."

Zinnia ducked into the cellar one final time and returned with four bottles of mead. She climbed the stone steps and placed the bottles down before turning back and locking the door. "I'm excited you'll be joining us. And thanks for helping me out! Usually, Aster would help set up..."

Zinnia trailed off as Kara let out a deep sigh.

"Kara, nobody blames you for not chasing after him. He could've talked to us before he left. That was his choice."

"I was still pretty upset after what he said, but now all I can think of is him lying dead in a field somewhere. I'm the one who took him away from Buckwheat to begin with. I should've gone after him, too." Kara looked east.

"At least Chert volunteered to go. That alone makes me feel better," Zinnia replied as they both strained, one at each end, hauling the heaviest crate towards the center of the village.

"I hope it's enough," Kara said, trying to focus on her task as the wood dug into her fingers. "Are your parent's going to join us tonight? I figure everyone will be there."

"Dad will. Mom passed away when I was still pretty

young."

"I know how that feels. My dad is gone too. It still seems like it wasn't that long ago. If you don't mind telling me, what happened?"

Zinnia stopped, causing Kara to nearly crash into her with the crate. "It was a bear... I don't like thinking about it though."

"I'm sorry." Kara nudged the crate forward until Zinnia started moving again.

The two ladies went back and forth, carrying the crates to the tent set up near an enormous stack of split logs.

Mayor Gilroy directed them to a table on the side where the other supplies were. "Are you young ladies excited for the election?" he asked as they were taking a rest.

Kara shrugged. "I don't pay much attention to politics. Who's running this year?"

Zinnia cleared her throat and answered in a scholarly tone. "Of course Emmeline Dolloway will be trying to defend her seat as Elder of Tradition. She hasn't lost since the Council was first created! Russel Warren is running against her this time. Shaheed Iman and Vincient Harlow are running for Elder of Economy and Archbishop Nicholas is against Grovemother Lucinda Roman for Elder of Faith. The thought of Lucinda in charge frightens me. Did you know that she is the leader of the Congregation of Viridus in Tembour? Also, this year is the first time Sir Josselyn Helisent isn't running for Elder of Defense. They say that she has health problems and had been struggling to fulfill her duties. Baxter Meyer and someone named Scott Alber are running instead, but I've never heard of either of them."

Kara was nodding along until one of the names struck her memory. She waited until Gilroy was out of earshot before whispering to Zinnia, "I met Josselyn. She was in the jail cell next to mine. Said she had been locked in there for years. Something fishy is going on."

Zinnia shrugged. "I don't know anything else. Maybe

we can ask before the vote begins? In any case, we need to go back and check on my father now. He's dead set on joining the ceremony tonight but I need to make sure that he's fit for it. Malvin gave him some medicine and he seems to be doing better, but he hasn't left the house."

Kara wiped the sweat off her brow. "Sure. I should check on Calantha and see if the boys are back from their fishing trip. I can't believe they talked me into letting them sail the Blue Skies without me. If there is so much as a scratch on that beautiful hull, Loctee save them... Anyways, I'll see you tonight."

Kara ambled away from the tent, stopping to watch the other villagers scurry past. It was peaceful here. Most everyone seemed to get along and there were enough people around that it would be a tough target for thieves.

When she arrived back at the inn, Calantha was by herself at the table with notes and drawings strewn about.

Calantha was muttering to herself. "Two... no three uses left. I cannot believe I did not think to pick up more bone from Kaleenmunda. That was a rare opportunity. Who knows when I will come across another merchant who has been there."

Kara tapped Calantha on the shoulder, causing her to jump. "Sorry to startle you, I wanted to see how you were doing."

"Solitude is my natural state."

Kara sat down next to her. "Not that. How are you feeling about this Fletcher business? He was your friend, right?"

Placing her papers down, Calantha folded her hands together and looked up at Kara. "He was a collaborator and our desires coincided for a time. It is a shame that he is at odds with us at the moment." Sighing, she added, "I thought that he was a seeker of knowledge, like myself, but I suppose there is another factor at play here."

"He was just using us." Kara scowled. "I don't blame Aster for chasing him, but he shouldn't have gone alone."

"On the one hand, retrieving the Odyllic Stone is

necessary for my research, but on the other, I question Aster's survival capabilities in the wilderness. I believe it will depend on whether Chert catches up with him or not. That Munayallpan seems quite dependable, so I have high hopes."

"True... maybe more of us should have gone..."

"You said yourself that you have obligations to crew and ship."

"Yeah, but what if he gets hurt?"

"Then he will have to manage that himself."

"You're not very empathetic are you?"

"Where I grew up, self-sufficiency was the law."

"Like an actual law? Actually, never mind... have you seen Pat and the guys today? I was hoping to have a talk with them before the fire festival."

Calantha picked up her papers and put them back into her bag. "They have not returned yet. Would you tell me more about the events of tonight?"

Kara repeated what Zinnia had told her and the two chatted for some time.

Aster tried to control his breathing as he held his bag above his head. The water had risen to his chest, and he had already tried every trick he could think of to stop the water, open the drain, or raise either door. He was out of ideas.

Drowning is the worst way to die. A sentiment from Pat, when he offered to jump into the ocean and catch a fish for dinner one night. Aster was a weak swimmer and there were strong currents that day. *If only I had gills like a fish!*

He glanced at the wall where he had seen the tuna earlier. It was hard to see beneath the sloshing waves, which had lined up perfectly against the carved surface of the ocean. It was beautiful—a kinetic sculpture, merging art with substance. *It's perfect. Too perfect. As if the designer had intended the room to be this way all along.* He waded back over to the fish and dunked his hand under the water to press against the tuna once more.

A loud click echoed through the room as the water started to drain out of the room.

Aster struggled against the flow as it pulled him towards a whirlpool under the ocean scene. Another click, followed by the sound of heavy machinery as both doors opened.

"The fish needed to be underwater!" He waited, letting his heartbeat settle before following his necklace to the open door. *I hate this place.*

The next room was much smaller than the first: A circle of six pedestals surrounded a roaring fire. Atop four were statues of winged humanoids similar to the one he had seen outside, except these were sitting with relaxed expressions carved into their scaly faces. Aster paced back and forth in the doorway eyeing the floors for drains.

When he didn't see any he stepped inside. Upon closer inspection, the fire at the center of the room was odd. Instead of bright flames, it appeared as if sunlight flickered back and forth behind orange tinted glass. To Aster's dismay, it was cold, too. He had hoped to warm up and dry off, but no heat radiated from the hearth.

At the far end of the room was another door. Closed and locked like the last. *Another puzzle?* Aster groaned and turned back to the statues. *Let's see. There are four statues. Two empty pedestals. And this replica fire pit.* The walls around him had a forested scene, with an occasional rabbit or stag behind the trees. A single word, indecipherable to Aster, was scrawled above the door frame.

The scene reminded him of home. Back when Mr. Hollyhock would take Aster, Dad, Zinnia, and Lavender fishing up the river and they would spend the night under the stars. Zinnia would always stay close to the fire and jump at strange noises from the woods. Lavender loved to fetch more wood, so she could spook the group by hooting and hollering beyond the tree line. Watson would always scold her and bring her back while chuckling. *It was so peaceful before everyone started to get sick.*

Aster pulled himself onto one of the empty pedestals. He braced himself as it shifted under his weight, and settled with a metallic click. But the door showed no signs of opening. *Does each empty spot need somebody to sit on it?* Aster hopped off the pedestal and tested how much weight it needed to compress—a lot. In fact, his full weight was barely enough.

His mind jumped to the rubble outside. *Was there any masonry heavy enough for this, but light enough that I could drag it here?* The divots in the floor made him nervous. He kept picturing hours of effort ending in the stone getting caught. *Besides, there's no way I could lift it onto the pedestal even if I got it to this room.*

He turned to the entrance and nearly jumped out of his skin. In front of him was Chert, hands on his knees, breathing heavily.

"Chert! What are you doing here? Is Kara with you?" Aster asked after he recovered from the shock.

"Heard loud crash, so ran this way," Chert said between breaths. "Only Chert. Came to find you and bring you back."

Aster smiled. "Thank you for coming. I... I'm sorry I didn't tell you guys before I left. I just felt so helpless and angry..." He trailed off, looking at the statues once again. "Chert, do you mind giving me a hand here? I think there is some trick to each of these rooms. Sit on that." He pointed to the closest pedestal.

Chert struggled, but managed to pull himself up.

Aster hopped onto the remaining pedestal, resulting in another click. With a rumble, the door ascended in front of them. "That was easy with you here."

"Go back?"

Aster clutched his pendant, which tugged towards the newly opened door. "No, we have to go further in."

Chert blinked at the writing and followed Aster into

the next room.

The walls contained another set of symbols, similar to those on the statue out front. Another closed door blocked their way forward. Aside from that, the room was bare.

"I guess we're stuck. These symbols don't have a translation underneath."

Chert examined the symbols and, one word at a time, recited, "In life, I stay where I was born. In death, I may travel the land. I bathe in the morning and tuck myself in at night. I feel no sadness, but my tears are worshiped regardless. What am I?"

Aster's mouth fell open. "Did you just read that? Is that what it says?"

Chert looked back at the carvings on the wall. "Yes."

Aster's mind raced as he shot down a dozen reasons why Chert would be able to read this text. *The Munayallpans have their own language, but that looks different from this. Firmer corners. This is sharp and distinctive too, but it has an aesthetic flow to it.* "How can you read this? And come to think of it, how did you even follow me to this city in the first place?"

Aster stared. He didn't really know much about the man in front of him.

Chert regarded Aster's confused expression in a silence that lasted far too long. "Dad was treasure hunter. He taught Chert to read letters and told stories of ruins. He would leave Chert to care for brother and sister. One day he came home with chalice. He said chalice held ghosts of the past. He hid chalice again in ruins. Bad men went after him. But he never came back. Chert must find what Dad protected."

Aster shifted his weight uncomfortably. "I'm sorry about your father. I guess I never really asked about your past and I probably should've. Is there anything I can do to help you Chert?"

He flashed a toothy grin. His lumpy cheeks wrinkled as he spoke. "Solve riddle. This ruin—like Dad's story."

Aster paced around the room speaking his thoughts.

"Well, it sounds to me like it must be a god. Would Conflag tuck himself in at night? That sounds odd."

Chert grunted in disapproval, so Aster kept thinking. "How about man? We bathe in the morning and tuck into bed at night. In Buckwheat Village, the dead are turned to ash and scattered upon the winds. But many people don't stay where they are born, and the part about worshiping tears doesn't make sense either."

The big man shook his head, so Aster gave another guess. "How about a tree? It doesn't move from where it is born and when it dies, we chop it down and use it for lumber. It bathes in the sunlight every morning. Could the tears have anything to do with tree sap? I don't think a tree can tuck itself in at night though."

Chert suddenly threw his hand into the air. "Chert knows answer."

What are we still doing here? Tristram thought as he found a seat near Calantha, Zinnia, and Malvin at the banquet table. *Something happened that they're not telling me about. Do they know?*

He saw Peter and Pat duck under the tent flap.

"Glad you made it," Kara yelled out to them, indicating her position among the tables.

"Just so you know, Kara, I won the fishing contest," Pat said as he sat down.

Tristram rolled his eyes. "If we'd been out there for longer, I would have caught up."

"How many fish did you each catch?"

Pat sat up straight and announced, "Four bass and a trout. The trout was a thing of beauty. Golden with a streak of pink across its center. I cooked 'em in a honey butter sauce. They're over there if you want a taste." He pointed to the long table that held a variety of delicious looking dishes.

She turned to Peter, expectantly.

"Three bass... and a half," he said in a monotone.

"What do you mean by a half?"

"By the time I pulled it out of the water, it was only a head. Somethin' must've taken a bite out of it on the way up." Peter dropped his knife on the table for emphasis. "That counts as half!"

Kara chuckled and then pointed to Tristram, who did his best to ignore her.

"Tristram how about you?"

He clenched his teeth and glared at them silently.

Pat spoke for him. "Tristram managed to catch some seaweed. And don't forget that feisty stick—took ages to reel in. But mostly, he just lost bait."

Everyone else burst into a howling laughter, even Calantha chuckled a bit.

Tristram got up to fill his mug with ale. *Just a while longer. Then I'll have the coin.* It wasn't that he disliked any of the Blue Skies crew, more that he disliked work in general. In fact, he had a great deal of respect for Peter— the man was a rare breed. Honest and hard working. Both things Tristram wished he was.

He filled his mug to the brim, patting the keg. *At least the booze here is decent.* Buckwheat Village was tolerable. It had a good view of the lake and was far enough away from civilization to provide a certain peacefulness. But the problem with villages was that all the ladies were taken. Practically the day they came of age they'd be married off.

He watched Zinnia talking with Kara back at the table. She wasn't really his type. The bustier the better. He surveyed the other tables. Everyone else was paired up. *Figures.*

He topped off his mug and returned to the table.

Kara pointed to a pastry on Zinnia's plate and said, "What's that?"

Zinnia covered her mouth, "Honey cake topped with pear glaze. The mayor makes it for special occasions. He has an orchard and is a surprisingly good cook. Do you know how to cook?"

She shook her head. "Only in a pinch. Pat does most of the cooking on the ship. We don't often get sweets though."

Pat added, "Pastries like this would fall apart on a ship. They'd be waterlogged from the sea breeze before we even left port. Believe me, I've tried."

Kara turned to Zinnia. "So your father couldn't make it?"

Zinnia frowned. "No, he had a spell of dizziness so I made him stay home."

"Too bad. This'll be a delightful party." Kara eyed the hog roast on the serving table.

Peter was in the middle of retelling his favorite story about the time he single-handedly saved Sir Josselyn's life by eating an entire wheel of cheese when Mayor Gilroy stepped up onto the makeshift stage.

"Citizens of Buckwheat and travelers alike, I am overjoyed that we have made it through another year and can celebrate again. Before we light the ceremonial bonfire, I would like to say a few words, then invite Deacon Arnit to the stage for a prayer. Finally, there will be a statement from our guest of honor."

Hopefully short, Tristram thought as he leaned back, half-listening.

Gilroy cleared his throat and surveyed the audience. "I know that this year has been particularly unpleasant for us. Hugo Rutherford, Watson Hollyhock, and Lavender Goodwin are so ill that they cannot be here in person. But I want us all to take a moment and thank Doctor Malvin for all the help he has given us so far. And especially the bravery that Aster Rutherford has shown in bringing him to us. It is unfortunate that he cannot be here today, but he has shown courage that most of us do not possess."

He paused as the crowd clapped, with a few people getting up to shake Malvin's hand.

"Finally, I want to remind you of the political purpose of this festival. At the end of this week, Buckwheat

Village will be sending our representative to the capital to vote on the Benia Council members for the next year. I encourage you all to discuss the candidates and their policies among yourselves so that you are ready for the official vote. When you are prepared, please come see me. I will tally them up and announce Buckwheat's chosen candidates. Now I'd like to invite Deacon Arnit to the stage."

An elderly man with graying hair and a long burgundy robe hobbled up. He held his hands in the air and bowed his head solemnly. In a rough and cracking voice, he called upon the group to join him in prayer.

Divine Conflagration,
god of energy,
dweller of the dry deserts,
we present to you this offering of tinder and mirth.
In times of darkness and times of light,
please watch over us and grant us your favor.
As your servants, we worship your everlasting might.

"Keep Conflag in your hearts as you enjoy the festivities tonight. And I expect to see all of you at morning prayer."

Fat chance. Tristram eyed the keg. *Somebody would fuss if I got up for a refill now.*

Gilroy thanked him as he left the stage. "Our special guest for the night is a candidate for the Council of Elders, Baxter Meyer."

Tristram sat up and scanned the tables. A man who had been sitting with his back towards them stood. He ascended the platform two steps at a time.

The Dread Scorpion? Here? Nobody mentioned it to me. Damn. Something bad's about to happen. He checked his belt—only a knife. He'd left everything else at the inn, even his hammer.

Peter grabbed Kara's arm and whispered. "This ain't good. Listen: Baxter is an assassin for the Council. He wouldn't show up unless someone is goin' to die. Kara, my guess is they're after you. Run to the docks and take a rowboat out as far as you can: He won't think to look for you on the lake."

Kara went white. She sank below the table and kept her head low as she slipped out the back of the tent. Carefully, she kept to the shadows and disappeared into the night. Pat left next, heading in the opposite direction. Peter stayed seated at the table, eyes focused on the man.

Zinnia was trembling at this point. "What... what do we do, Peter?"

"Prepare to run."

Calantha and Malvin looked uneasy.

And what am I supposed to do? Tristram pulled at his mustache.

Baxter threw back his black hood, revealing a heavily scarred face. "Hello, Buckwheat Village." Stained teeth chewed each word.

"There are two kinds of people in this world: the weak and the strong. The only way for the weak to survive is to ally themselves with those who are strong. The Council is the most powerful organization in Benia; everyone knows this. If you elect me to this group as Elder of Defense, then I will ensure that the Council is the most powerful organization in all of Arathanon."

Baxter raised his fist into the air. A tattoo of a scorpion was briefly visible on the back of his hand. "They want you dead. Those icy bastards from Jash, the freaks of Malvez, and the swamp people of El'tonne. I'll keep them out. Better yet, I'll wipe them off the map!"

By the time he was finished speaking his eyes had a wild look to them, but none of the villagers seemed to notice: They were too busy cheering.

Malvin looked around and whispered, "Why's he so popular? He's talking about war. Do the people of this town really want another war?"

Zinnia shrank in her seat. "The people who live here have always been afraid of foreigners. We always hear stories of the east's crime and corruption. It's hard not to be wary of them. Even Aster had trouble fitting in here at first. Things have gotten better in the last few years, but old habits never really disappear."

Malvin shrugged and said, "As long as we can get rid of Emmeline, then I'll be happy. All these politicians are the same, but Emmeline is worse than the rest."

Baxter loitered for a minute on the stage, taking in the applause before stepping down and out of sight. Deacon Arnit returned, carrying a torch in his hand. He spoke. "Please bow your heads for the ceremonial lighting of the pyre."

Tristram watched as everyone except for Peter closed their eyes in reverence.

When Arnit threw his torch into the stack of logs, pandemonium ensued. The moment the flame touched the base of the fire pit, it exploded. Wood and flame flew in every direction, knocking over tables and embedding into the houses nearby. Arnit flew backward and crumpled against the stage. Embers leapt onto the tent fabric, catching it ablaze.

Shit. A letter would've been appreciated.

The townspeople erupted in a cacophony of sound and movement as they fled the blaze, pushing through the large opening and into the night.

Zinnia screamed as she pulled herself under her table. Malvin jumped into action, pulling Arnit to safety before tending to the other wounded. Peter had his knife out.

Baxter reappeared, pulling out a short sword and approached Peter. "Where is she? You think you're clever, but I saw her here." He raised his arm and made a chopping motion. Six cloaked figures appeared just outside, surrounding the remaining crew members. "Capture Kara and kill anyone who fights back. We'll deal with the king defender here."

Meaning me, too? Tristram drew his own knife as the fabric above him burned.

Two of the cloaked men turned back to search for Kara. The other four attacked Peter and Tristram, short swords in hand, each taking a swing.

Guess that answers that. Either they don't know or don't care.

Peter deftly dodged and blocked their advances. Tristram took his back, protecting his blind spot. The clink of steel on steel echoed through the village. The two danced between the blows, knuckles white as they gripped their rigging knives.

"Tristram, we can't keep this up for long. Can you break out?" Peter grunted between each strike.

"Don't think so," Tristram huffed.

Baxter stomped his foot on the ground. "Back up you idiots. I'll take him."

The circle parted allowing him to move within reach. He pulled a blade from behind his back and thrust it at Peter, who brought his knife down to deflect the blow. The sword crashed into the small knife, forcing it back, and piercing Peter. Crimson splattered onto the grass.

"Shit! My leg," Peter groaned.

A clang reverberated and one of the cloaked figures fell to the ground. Pat stood above him, cast iron pan in hand.

One of the figures split from the circle, turning his sights on the newcomer. He slashed at Pat as he ducked behind his pan.

Pat backed over a tent stake and fell to the ground.

Tristram pulled an assassin's cloak over his face and kneed him in the stomach. He pushed the man to the ground, watching Pat struggle. "Pat's in trouble now."

A pastry flew out from under the table and smacked one of the attackers in the face, slowing his approach. But it wasn't enough.

The man wiped it off and threw the bench out of the way, exposing Zinnia's hiding spot. "Come here, girl. You just earned a place on the funeral pyre," he growled.

Zinnia crawled backwards, but the man grabbed her arm and yanked her out. She screamed and fainted, her head hanging limp.

Vines burst out of the ground, separating Baxter from

the others. A beast with elongated eyes and a pointed mouth bounded into the tent, slashing at the hooded men with scythe-like claws. It let out a horrid screech that caused the man holding Zinnia to release her and back away in fear. The beast sprang out and pinned the man against the ground. It extended its mouth pincers into his neck, ripping his throat to shreds. Peter seized the chance and drove his knife deep into the heart of the closest enemy.

Tristram tackled the last man, causing him to drop his weapon.

The vine wall started to thin out as Baxter hacked his way through, rejoining the fray.

"Pat, find Kara! I'll keep him occupied." Peter was out of breath and bleeding profusely.

Pat glanced at Zinnia on the ground. "What about her?" The beast perked up at these words and dropped the now-dead body. It jumped on Zinnia, grabbing her in its claws, causing Pat to raise his pan.

What is going on? Tristram plucked at his mustache, head swiveling between the creature and Baxter.

The beast gently raised Zinnia's body and hopped out into the darkness.

"She'll be fine. It seems that beast is helpin' us. Just go save Kara," Peter yelled, moving to prevent Baxter from following.

Pat lifted his faithful pan for a moment before dropping it in the dirt. He bolted toward the docks.

"How heroic." Baxter laughed as he watched Pat scramble away. "Peter Keeton, do you know how long I've been waiting to drive my sword into your flesh? The girl can wait until after I'm finished with you."

"That was twenty years ago. How can you still be mad that I stopped you? It was my job." Peter grasped his knife in one hand as the other held his bleeding leg.

"No... No, I'm not mad that you stopped me. I'm mad that you didn't stop the next one." Baxter pointed his sword at Peter.

"What in Loctee's name are you talkin' about?"

"You let Federyc die! I should've been the one to kill him."

Tristram crept over to Pat's discarded pan. Just like always, he was in the background. Ignored. Might as well have been invisible. But he liked it better that way.

Baxter spat on the ground. "You were too incompetent to protect him long enough for me to try again. Regicide. It was so close to being mine. And not just any regicide; I could've been the man who killed the last king of Benia." Baxter chuckled to himself, but it turned into a snarl as he brought his attention back to Peter.

"You're insane."

"And you're dead." Baxter brought his sword down.

All Peter could do was fall to the side, barely dodging the blade. The weapon sunk deep into the ground, giving Peter a moment to get back onto his feet.

Tristram edged around the vines until he was behind Baxter.

Peter limped over to the tables and grabbed a cup of ale in each hand, leaving his knife behind. Just as Baxter pulled his sword free, Peter threw the liquid in his face.

Baxter hissed as he wiped it off with his sleeve, keeping one eye on Peter.

Tristram crept close and bashed him on the head with Pat's pan.

Baxter dropped to the floor, unconscious, his hair wet with blood.

Peter limped over to the remaining tent fabric and tore it down to restrain Baxter and his men.

I'm going to hear about this later. Tristram pulled a chair over to sit. Most of the flames had gone out, but a few tables were still smoldering.

Kara caught sight of the Blue Skies, rocking atop the shimmering lake. She heard commotion on the docks and could see shadowy figures dart back and forth through the moonlight. *They're already on the ship. Where else can I go?*

She ducked behind two empty crates, hiding herself from view. *The Toasted Oak? No, they'll definitely look for me there. Aster's house? No, I can't drag Hugo into this. Pelware Mine? It's far, but that may be for the best.*

The wooden pier squeaked. Somebody was breathing heavily nearby.

"Let Kara go!" Unmistakably Pat's voice.

The two assassins leaped off of the Blue Skies, drawing their swords.

"Don't come any closer," he said as he rummaged through his pockets.

Kara poked her head over the crates. *What are you doing? I'm not over there. Run away!*

The two men pressed forward until they were uncomfortably close to Pat. He whipped around and sprinted away, towards the dirt road in the village, but he was too slow. One of the men grabbed the fabric of his shirt, holding him in place. With a sword poking into Pat's chest, the man said, "You don't know where Kara is, right?"

Before Pat could respond, the other man caught up to them. "No, he doesn't know. Just kill him." He pulled back his sword as Pat cowered.

"Stop! I'm here, take me instead," Kara yelled as she stepped out of the darkness.

The man in the back laughed. "We don't take requests. Kill him."

Kara dashed forward and threw her shoulder into the cloaked man holding Pat. His grip was too strong, so they fell backwards into the water together. She almost jumped in after them, but the last assassin stepped forward.

Kara pulled out her knife, a meager defense against his blade. *I've got to stop him before worrying about Pat.* She glanced around for some rope, but everything she could see was firmly secured. *Shit.*

He swung his sword at her. She dodged.

He slashed at her twice more, closer this time. She barely stepped away in time.

I can't fight back, he outreaches me.

Pat gasped, pulling his head out of the water for a moment before the other man dragged him back under.

I don't have time to think. I've just got to act and hope the wind is in my sails today. Kara lifted her knife above her head and lunged at the assassin who blocked with his sword. The steel clashed, but Kara kept her momentum, slamming her forehead into the man's nose.

His surprise was palpable, his free hand grabbed his bloody nose.

Kara slid her knife down his blade, cutting into the man's fingers.

"Argh," he screamed, dropping the sword.

She kicked it off the walkway, into the dark water below. *What now?* She hadn't heard Pat in ages, but she didn't trust this man to stay out of their way, even though he was disarmed. *Kill him, it's the only way.* The voice in her head belonged to Peter. *That's what he would do... It's probably right, but I just can't.*

"Get out of here," she shouted to the bloodied man, waving her knife. "Now! Before I finish you."

He put his hands up and slowly edged past her, running down the dock towards the village.

Kara let out a sigh and peered into the water, squinting her eyes to see in the dim moonlight. In the rippling water she caught sight of a black cloak.

Pat surfaced once more, again gasping for air. He swam to the pier between breaths. The assassin behind him still, floating in the water.

"Dead," Pat said as he pulled himself onto the wooden platform. "Strangled him with his own cloak. Serves him right for trying... to drown me." He laughed weakly, coughing up water.

Kara closed her eyes and laughed with him. "That worked out better than expected."

The creak of loose nails was the only warning they got. The other assassin jumped forward and sank his spare dagger into Pat's chest.

Pat groaned and tried to grab the man, but he had already stepped out of reach, leaving the blade.

Weaponless once again, the assassin retreated back towards Buckwheat Village.

Kara rushed to her friend, all caution abandoned. "Oh shit... Pat don't move, I'll get Malvin right away."

She helped Pat to lie down, careful not to jostle the blade, the only thing keeping him from bleeding out. She could feel the warmth of his blood soaking his tunic.

Kara stood, and was about to sprint to find the doctor, but Pat grabbed her leg.

"Stay safe, captain... You'll be a great one." Pat said in a pained, raspy voice. His breathing was strained.

This was my mistake, letting that man go. I should be the one with a knife in my chest. "Pat, you alright? Pat!"

He didn't respond.

Kara knelt down and shook his arm, but he didn't move. "Pat!" Kara screamed at the top of her lungs, tears welling in her eyes.

"Well, Chert what is it?" Aster tapped his foot on the floor, suspecting that Chert was intentionally drawing it out.

"A poppy plant," Chert said with a smile.

Aster tugged on the strap of his bag, contemplating his answer. "Well, like my tree guess, a plant is also stuck where it lives, and if it's plucked it can travel. It bathes in the sunlight, but I don't understand why you think it tucks itself in at night... or why its tears are worshiped. How do you explain these?"

Chert put his hands together, miming petals with his outstretched fingers. He pulled them in until both hands were in fists while saying, "Poppy flowers close at night.

And opium. The rest like your tree."

Aster laughed. "That could be right. Once, Rowan Goodwin showed me how he harvests the oozing bulbs for his medicine. So... what do we do with this answer?" Aster looked around the room again without finding anything of note. "Poppy. Poppy flower," he said out loud, thinking there was some unknown magic that would accept his voice.

Nothing happened.

"Wait!" He directed Chert back into the first room, where he had been trapped in the rising water. "Here. Next to the sheep." Sure enough, one of the illustrations on the wall was a tall gangly plant with four mauve petals.

"I knew this poppy plant was here. By Conflag's flame, I'd better have known it after I was stuck in this place for hours."

The petals depressed as Aster ran his fingers over it. A switch, invisible unless scrutinized. With a distant rumble, the door opened.

Aster and Chert walked back through and into the new room, again with a door at the far end.

Aster groaned. "I'm tired of these puzzles already. Maybe we should just go back?"

But Chert stood transfixed with his mouth open, staring at the center of the room. Atop a plain stone pedestal stood an onyx chalice. Its mouth and the stem were solid black, but the bowl was silver filigree.

"What's the point of that? Those holes are too big to hold anything useful. Wait... is this the cup you've been looking for, Chert?"

Without a single word, Chert lifted the chalice up into the air to examine it in the light streaming down from somewhere above.

Another click opened a new door at the far side of the room. A burly man tumbled in, dropping the object in his hand, which started to roll across the floor. Behind the door, Aster could see rain falling inside, through a large crack in the wall. His necklace tugged him forward.

The man on the floor grumbled and rubbed his head. He squinted in the light of the room, trying to reorient himself.

Aster recognized the hiking boots of the man in front of him. "Fletcher!" He cried out, as the Odyllic Stone rolled into his feet. A small worm was roaming among the foliage inside the orb.

Fletcher dove at Aster before he could get a better look.

Defensively, both Aster and Chert stepped backwards and braced themselves. But Fletcher's eyes weren't on the two newcomers, instead they were fixed on the floor.

The Odyllic Stone! I can't let him have it again. Aster kicked the orb away, but Fletcher rolled sideways, grasping the Odyllic Stone in both hands.

"I thought we were friends," Aster cried out.

Fletcher pulled the orb against his chest. "You forced my hand. Even after I warned you."

"I didn't do anything."

"You did. And the worst part is that you're clueless about it."

"Why'd you do it, Fletch?"

"You're too dense to understand."

"Try me," Aster shot back.

Fletcher stood and dusted off his pants. "Ian Pelware."

"Ian Pelware?"

"My idol was an ordinary man with boring work. And nothing I did was ever good enough."

Fletcher stepped over to the pedestal where the chalice once sat. Keeping his distance from the others, he examined the structure. "Emmeline Dolloway showed me the truth. It wasn't the heroes that were interesting, it wasn't their quests, it wasn't their treasures. It was the stories that were told about them. She said that I would be the most famous person in all of history if I could find the Odyllic Stone for her. It has taken years, but I'm so close now."

Aster sighed and placed his hands on his hips. "It isn't

ours in the first place. But we need it in Buckwheat Village first. Let's go back, and after that you can do whatever you want with the thing."

"How do you even know it'll cure them? You could make it worse. This thing doesn't follow any logic as far as I can tell."

"We have to try!"

"I don't know," he said, looking around the room until his eyes settled on Chert. For a moment he smiled with unfettered joy. "How about we make a trade? If you give me that chalice. I'll give you a week with the stone in Buckwheat. After that, it's mine to take to New Portsmith."

At his words, Chert protectively pulled the chalice to his chest.

"What? Why do you care about this chalice, Fletch? Why are you even here in these ruins to begin with?" Aster asked. *None of this makes sense. Why didn't he go directly to New Portsmith?*

Fletcher held up the Odyllic Stone and walked toward Aster. "Look, why don't you hold onto this again while we sort things out. We've got plenty of time on the way back to Buckwheat for me to explain things to you."

As Aster reached out to take the stone from him, Fletcher twisted his body and elbowed Aster in the ribs, causing him to crumple to the floor. Then he ran, pushing past Chert, out the door they had entered.

In a fluid motion, Chert tucked the chalice into his pocket, pulled Aster up, and they dashed toward the echoing footsteps, back through the puzzle rooms and out into the courtyard by the city walls.

They caught up to Fletcher as he was kneeling next to the fallen statue of Quell'est. Aster cried, "Fletcher! Don't do this."

The Odyllic Stone glowed brightly, enveloping everything in a hazy green. The statue creaked and groaned. Flecks of marble shot off in every direction as its feet freed themselves from the stone base. Using both bronze hands, it lifted itself upright. It was alive.

"Don't let them pass through this gate," Fletcher cried out as he ran out of the ruined city.

The winged statue took three steps and positioned itself on the cobblestone pathway in front of Aster and Chert. Once there, it stopped, motionless.

Aster was too angry to be afraid. He kept his distance from the simulacrum, circling around it until he was near the wall, then dashed through in pursuit of Fletcher.

Chert yelled, "Watch out," as the statue stirred again.

It moved faster than Aster expected, ducking under the gate and picking him up by his leg. With excruciating force, the simulacrum tossed him back over the city walls.

Aster cartwheeled across the rough stones, crashing into a marble pillar. His leg made a loud pop, then throbbed in excruciating pain. The rest of his body was covered in bruises and cuts from the cobblestone. He tried to stand up, but his legs wouldn't cooperate.

The statue moved to block their exit once more.

Chert rushed over to Aster, who winced at his touch. "Right leg broken," Chert said, moving on to examine the other injuries. "Rest is fine." Chert lifted and placed Aster atop his broad shoulders. "Hold on." Chert grunted and walked along the wall, giving the statue a wide berth.

Aster nervously watched their back, terrified that it would pursue them, but it never did.

They hadn't gone far before they found a hole in the wall where a column had fallen over and now decorated the forest floor. Chert carefully climbed over the rubble.

"Will it come after us?" Aster strained his ears listening for broken twigs or another sign of movement.

"Hope not."

Aster winced as he was put down against a tree. "What do we do now?"

Chert rummaged around until he had two thick sticks in his hands. He pulled some fabric off of his sleeves and made a splint for Aster's broken leg. "Go to Buckwheat. Or to New Portsmith. You choose."

"Well, I want to chase Fletcher, but we won't catch him with my leg all messed up. And I made the mistake of leaving without help before. This time, I want to do it right. Let's go back to Buckwheat for help."

"Walk back will be tough."

"I know... I'm ready." *I need to make this right.*

"Good choice."

The two of them rested for a bit longer.

Chert grabbed Aster by the waist and they slowly hobbled west.

Tristram could feel the weight of his eyelids. He hadn't had the chance to sleep. Even if he had gotten to bed last night, he wasn't sure he'd have been able to.

"Shit. This is a disaster," Peter sighed as he rested his arm on the wall of the inn, using his other hand to shield his eyes from the light of dawn.

"Yup." Tristram's reply was half-hearted. The two listened somberly to the sobbing from within.

"Doc said that it pierced his lung. In a bad spot. There was nothin' she could do for him."

"Knowing Kara, she probably still blames herself." Tristram rubbed his eyes.

"I can't believe Baxter got away."

"His ship is still here, so he must've run off on foot. The guy that stuck Pat must've untied the others while we were dealing with that," he lied.

"Loctee drown me, I should've just killed that lunatic." Peter kicked the side of the small house.

"I'm sure Kara is thinking the same thing."

"Don't tell her this, but we must've had Loctee's grace to get out of that with only one death. If Baxter wasn't toyin' with us, we'd be right there beside Pat."

Tristram frowned. "That doesn't make me feel any better."

"It shouldn't."

"So, what now? I was hoping that we were safe hiding in Buckwheat, but I guess that ain't true." Tristram twisted at his mustache. "Shit. I never signed up for this kinda life."

"I've got an idea. But first we need to put Pat to rest and cheer up the captain. I'm not sure if we can sail the Blue Skies with just the three of us. We've done it with four, but even that wasn't easy."

Before Peter could finish his thought they were interrupted by Doctor Malvin, who stepped outside to find them. "Peter, how's your leg?" he asked, peering down at the bloodied bandages.

"I've had worse."

Malvin poured alcohol on a rag to wipe his hands and said, "Looks like the bleeding has stopped. We will need to change those in a few hours to keep your leg from getting infected."

Malvin flung the rag onto a nearby stump. "But that's not what I came out here for. Kara has agreed to the funeral pyre. I know you boys would probably prefer Pat to have a burial at sea, but I don't think we'd be able to manage that right now. Nobody will mind if you speak a few words about Loctee."

Peter took a deep breath to maintain his composure. "Alright, thanks doc. How's Zinnia?"

Malvin shrugged. "Physically, nothing is wrong with her. But I think last night spooked her real bad. After she woke up, she wouldn't leave my room. Even after we told her that the assassins had gone. Whitney moved me into a different room for the time being."

Tristram shook his head. "Poor girl. I'm sure Lantern would've pissed his pants in her shoes. Still can't believe the Council sent an assassin. Thought they were better than that. In any case, I'm going to get some sleep. I was out all night trying to find Baxter. Come get me before the funeral."

Tristram marched back to his room. Inside, he sat against the door and put his hands over his face. *Pat didn't deserve that. Out of everyone, he didn't.* Even though he respected Peter, he had to admit that the man had skeletons. *And Kara's as good as dead anyways—just a matter of time. But Pat was only ever a friend and a chef.*

He banged his head against the wooden door. *Maybe I made a mistake cutting Baxter free?*

It took three days before Deacon Arnit had recovered enough to perform the funeral ceremony. Kara spent them alone in her room, too ashamed to show her face to the crew. But she wouldn't miss Pat's funeral for anything.

Peter, Tristram, Zinnia, Calantha, and Malvin were gathered around the fire when she arrived. Quite a few villagers were in attendance too. She figured it was closure for them too, seeing as there were a few injuries among them. And the trauma of what had happened.

The old man winced as he tossed the torch onto the pyre under Pat's lifeless body. He bowed his head as he spoke. "We gather here today to mourn the loss of Patrick Bartlett. He was a friend to all he met and family to those he traveled with. Although he wasn't a worshiper of the divine Conflagration, I still ask that he be kept warm in the afterlife by the almighty flame. And though I'm not a believer in Loctee, I still ask that he be kept afloat by the god of the sea." Arnit fell silent, and the group watched as their comrade disappeared behind the flames.

Kara clutched Pat's cast iron pan against her chest as she began to cry.

Peter bowed his head in reverence.

One by one, everyone left the ceremony, and returned to their responsibilities. Kara and Peter were the last to leave.

Peter broke the silence. "I'm not good with this emotional stuff, but I know that you and Pat were close. I guess, let me know if you want to talk about anythin' and I'll do my best to listen." He started to walk back to town.

"Wait," Kara mumbled between sniffles. "Tell me the truth, Peter. Is it my fault that he's dead? I was the one who Baxter was after. I was the one on the run from the Council. Before that, I convinced everyone to chase Whitlock to Strongfair. And looking back, I was the one who invited Aster onto our ship, which caused all of these problems in the first place."

Peter frowned. "That's all true, but I don't think you could've known things would turn out the way they did."

"Well, I regret it all! We were employed and happy, then I stuck my nose in something that wasn't my business, and look at where we are now."

"I don't think that's fair to say."

"I don't think it's fair that Pat's dead!" Kara snapped back, wiping tears out of her eyes.

"Look, I know that you're hurtin', but you can't blame yourself. Pat knew what he was signin' up for when he first joined the crew. And he knew the risks when we broke you out of prison."

"I could've come up with a better plan for following Whitlock. I could've been more careful here in Buckwheat. I let the man who killed him go! I'm ashamed to be your captain. We should've chosen you instead." Kara slumped, letting her chin fall against her chest.

"Stop that. I've known a lot of leaders in my lifetime, and you're a good one—a bit green but that's all. I'm not. I've made so many mistakes. My actions changed all of Benia and not for the better. I think you need to trust yourself more, not less," he said, placing his hand on her shoulder.

"But Peter, I don't know what to do. How do we get out of the mess we're in?"

"Let's sail to Tembour. That's where your sister is, right? There's a man there that I want you to meet. He... has experience with avoidin' the law. After you've talked with them both, make a choice. I'll support you, Capt'n, whichever choice you make."

Kara contemplated Peter's words as he walked out of

view. She collapsed into the soft grass and stared at the ashes of her closest friend.

Aster felt rotten by the time they returned to Buckwheat Village. They were both covered in dirt and starving. What little food Chert had ran out after two days on their trek back, leaving them hungry for four. And Aster's leg crackled in pain with every step, but Chert kept pushing forward, even when Aster protested.

"Doctor," Chert panted as he entered the inn, carrying Aster on his back.

Don was mopping up one of the tables. He sighed when he heard Chert's voice. "More trouble? I've had enough for a lifetime."

"Where's Doctor?"

Don turned and noticed Aster hanging from Chert's back. Annoyance wiped from his face. "He should be upstairs in his room. I hope it isn't serious."

Chert grunted in exhaustion and Aster gave a brief wave. "No." He hauled Aster up the steps until they were outside Malvin's room. "Doctor." He pounded on the door.

Malvin's voice responded from the other side. "Yes, come on in. What's the matter?"

The door popped open, and Aster said sheepishly, "I broke my leg. Can you look at it?"

"Yes, of course. I assume you two have just arrived?" Aster nodded, so Malvin continued. "There was... an incident while you were gone. I'll fetch your friends after I've taken a look at your leg, and they can fill you in on what happened."

Malvin prodded Aster's ankle, sending pain pulsing through his body. "Hmmm, seems like a clean break of your fibula. I'll go and get a leather brace to stabilize it. You won't be able to use that leg for weeks, but it'll heal."

"I don't have that long. I need to go after Fletcher."

"Your leg won't heal properly if you don't let it." Malvin started to dig through his bag, before pausing. "Do I remember correctly, was there a willow tree just outside town, on the way to the mines?"

"Uh yeah, there are a bunch of them around the lake, but that's the closest one."

"The bark will help reduce your pain. I'll be back in a bit. Whitney will bring you some food in the meantime."

Just as Aster had finished his meal, Kara burst into the room and hugged him tightly. "I'm glad you are... mostly alright," she said as he winced and clutched his leg.

"Kara, I'm sorry for what I said to you. And I'm sorry that I didn't talk to you before I left."

She frowned at him. "You're an idiot. We could've helped."

Aster timidly changed the subject. "In any case, Fletcher is heading to New Portsmith to give the Odyllic Stone to the Council. We need to follow him."

Kara took a deep breath. "No. We are going to Tembour."

"Tembour? Why would we go there?"

"Look at me, Aster. I am your captain. Now, I'm going to start acting like one. I've got to figure out what is best for the crew, and right now, that is sailing to Tembour."

"But—"

"No, Aster. It's not like you're in any condition to be chasing people right now. Besides, Fletcher will have gotten to New Portsmith before we could make it there."

Aster protested quietly under his breath.

"We were attacked. Pat's dead."

Aster's stomach dropped as she recounted what happened.

Zinnia Hollyhock,

I'm sorry. I should have listened to you. I let my anger take control and didn't want to listen. You were trying to tell me that we should use the stone to cure the villagers. That's why you weren't as upset as I was at Malvin's news. If only I had listened, things would be fixed by now. I'm an idiot.

Thanks for sending Chert to help me. I'm not sure I would be alive still if it wasn't for him. We caught up with Fletcher and I did my best to persuade him. He was not interested in helping us. I got hurt.

Fletcher is heading back to New Portsmith. That's where I'm going next. I don't see another option. I'll make Kara understand.

Your friend,
Aster

8 THE BOSCAGE SCHOOL OF BENIA

Aster hobbled over to the bedroom door as the amber rays of sunset fell upon the hallway of the Hollyhock's house. Watson was feeling well enough to let him inside.

Aster winced, losing his balance as pain rippled up his bandaged leg. Bracing himself against the wall, he softly knocked on the door.

"Zin, can we talk? I heard that you had a rough time while I was gone."

There was a flurry of movement in the room followed by a meek reply. "Aster? I... I don't want to talk. I'm angry with you."

"I just got back to Buckwheat yesterday. I would've come sooner but Malvin insisted that I rest."

"That's not what this is about," she snapped, her anger muffled by the wooden door.

"I see. I've been thinking about this, so I wrote out my thoughts." Aster pulled out the letter he had written her and slipped it under the door. "I wanted Kara to deliver it last night, but we got into an argument about where to go next."

There was a creaking of floorboards and a minute of silence followed. Zinnia's voice was louder when she spoke again. "Aster, say it yourself."

Aster sighed. "Zinnia, I'm sorry. I was wrong."

"Wrong about what?"

"I was wrong to chase Fletcher without telling anybody. It was a poor choice and I have this broken leg to prove it." Aster rubbed his right thigh, looking down at the leather that braced it.

"I accept your apology." Zinnia opened the door and pulled Aster into her room. She closed the door behind them, but not before scanning the hallway. "But that's not the only thing that I'm upset about, Aster."

Her room was dark. A single beam of sun snuck into the room from behind a blanket covering her only window.

The room was musty and disorganized. "Is everything alright?" Aster asked.

"Not really," she whimpered, sitting down on her bed, knees in her arms. "The festival was ruined. There were men with swords. Pat was killed. I've never been more scared in my life." She sniffled before continuing. "You led those men here."

"I didn't mean to. And I brought the doctor too, so that has to count for something."

"We were safe before. Now we aren't." She wiped her wet cheeks.

"That's not fair. If Buckwheat was perfectly safe, I wouldn't have needed to bring Malvin in the first place."

"Your dad is right. There is nothing but trouble out there. Stay here. Let's find another way to deal with the quicksilver."

Aster put a hand on his hips as he leaned back on Zinnia's desk. "I can't do that. The Odyllic Stone is our best chance."

"You could die!"

"If that's what it takes to save Buckwheat, so be it."

"But I don't want you to die." Zinnia hid her face behind her pillow.

"Zin, I've got to do this. I don't see another way. Besides, Kara and the others will keep me safe." He walked over to the window and pulled the blanket down. They both blinked as their eyes readjusted to the light. "You should focus on yourself. I think it would do you some good to go for a walk or something. You've been cooped up in the village your entire life. And now you won't even leave your room. You'll have to face your fears someday."

"Not if I stay here."

"We're leaving tomorrow. I wish you'd come with us. There's so much to see out there."

"How are you going to get around with your leg like that?" Zinnia asked, pointing to his brace.

"I'll manage. There's no time to be waiting around. Besides, we'll be stuck on the ship for weeks. It's not like there's anywhere to go."

Aster opened the door to leave, but Zinnia called him back.

"I'm going to work on it."

"Huh?" Aster turned back.

"I'm going to work on facing my fears. Maybe I'll even have an adventure of my own."

"It would be great if you did. Stay safe. I'll keep writing you." Aster hobbled down the hallway leaving Zinnia sitting on her bed.

He believed that she wanted to change, but it wasn't that easy. She'd made declarations like this before, but all it took was one random incident and she would be back to her room. Not that he blamed her. It had been years since it happened, but her trauma never seemed to fade.

The morning of their departure, fog lay low on Buckwheat Lake. The air was cold for this time of year and everyone was wrapped up tight in their cloaks. Aster struggled to get on the Blue Skies with his broken leg. It took him three tries to walk up the gangway before Chert carried him onboard.

They left without any fanfare. Aster got the impression that after the trouble at the fire festival, the villagers were glad the crew was leaving.

Chert helped untie the mooring ropes and Calantha steadied the wheel so Kara could help Peter and Tristram ready the sails. Aster couldn't find a way to be helpful. He had enough trouble keeping himself upright.

The journey to the ocean was uneventful. Aside from mealtime, now a difficult and somber affair, they maneuvered down the Haverhein River with ease. Aster found it difficult to stay on deck, spending more and more time in his bunk.

A familiar briny stink told Aster that they were near the ocean and less than a day from New Portsmith. He took the opportunity to pull himself out of the sleeping quarters and argue his case one more time. Everyone was scurrying about, preparing the Blue Skies to meet the sea..

It took Aster ages to hobble to the stern, but he was determined. Kara was behind the wheel, carefully navigating between sandbanks. She didn't acknowledge him, so he just asked his question. "Since we are going to be passing by the city, why not just stop and see if Fletcher has made it there yet?"

Kara kept her eyes focused on the bowsprit and the water in front. "Sorry Aster, but I can't discuss that right now. I've got to focus here."

He stepped in front of the wheel, blocking her view. "It's just that we are practically there already, and we need to find Fletcher sooner rather than later."

Kara brushed him aside with her arm. "Aster cut it out, I'm busy here. We can talk after the ship has settled in the sea."

"But it doesn't make sense to me that we are heading to Tembour. What could possibly be there to help us out?"

Kara sighed. "Look, Peter says there's someone there that I need to talk to. Besides, that's where my sister goes to school. If nothing else, it'll be good to talk to her."

"Listen to what I'm saying!" Aster stomped in front of the wheel once more. "My village is in trouble now. My dad might not last long enough for us to go to Tembour."

Kara leaned side to side to get a view beyond Aster.

Then the ship lurched, followed by a loud scraping noise, causing her to wince. "Enough, Aster! Get out of my way. Maybe this time it isn't about you or your village. Maybe I need to figure out how to help myself before I can even think of helping you."

"But..."

A loud pop caused Kara to flinch. "Peter! Peter, take him away. Get Aster out of here."

Peter darted over to see what the problem was. In one swift motion, he hoisted Aster up onto his shoulders and carried him back to his bunk.

"Let me go! We need to find Fletcher! We need to go to New Portsmith!"

"C'mon Aster, be reasonable. New Portsmith is the last place we should go. They'd lock us up before we left the docks."

Aster ground his teeth. "Tembour is worse. There's nothing there for us."

"Hopefully we'll find a bit of perspective."

"It's not your call, anyways." Aster shoved Peter, who fell into somebody's bunk.

"She doesn't want to talk now. Don't you see you were in her way?"

"This is more important."

"Enough." Peter grabbed a length of rope and tied Aster's arms and legs, leaving him immobilized in his bed. "Apparently we've given you too much leniency aboard this ship. You're being a nuisance, so we'll treat you like one."

Aster kicked against the rope, but between Peter's knots and the pain in his leg, it was useless. He was stuck.

A few hours passed and Aster's temperament grew increasingly sour. It had gotten to the point where the crew was avoiding the sleeping quarters to spare themselves from Aster's wrath. Kara fiddled with her compass when Peter stepped up beside her. He held out a hand and pointed his goatee towards the stairs. "It's time to deal with him, Captain."

"I never thought I'd have a problem like this."

"The price of leadership."

"Any advice?"

"There's two sides to every coin. He's got a valid point. But you are the captain. You've taken his side into consideration and come up with the best plan for the entire crew."

"Thanks, Peter." *As much as Aster deserves to be tied up, I can't keep him down there forever. Guess being captain isn't as glamorous as I thought.* Begrudgingly, she pocketed her compass and handed Peter the wheel before trudging below deck to confront Aster.

He looked miserable. Both arms were bound together behind his back and his one good leg was secured to the wooden beam above his bunk. His black hair was plastered to his face, sweaty after all of his struggling despite the cool sea breeze.

"We need to talk," she said.

Aster strained his neck to face her. "Yes, we do." His voice was almost a growl. "How could you let him do this to me?"

"He may have overreacted a bit, but you were becoming a threat to the entire crew. I could've crashed the ship with you standing in the way. Why couldn't you have waited till we made it to sea?"

Aster grumbled and strained at the ropes on his wrists. "I just can't believe that you don't want to chase Fletcher. It'll be too late if they put the Odyllic Stone in some vault in the capital. We don't have a shot of getting it there. Why can't you see that?"

Kara crossed her arms and leaned over him. "I don't agree. We'll have another chance at some point. Better to plan it out now instead of rushing in unprepared."

Aster raised his voice. "You're wrong! We are wasting time going to Tembour."

"I'm tired of arguing this with you, Aster. When are you going to recognize my authority as captain and do as you're told? I've been beyond patient listening to your arguments. But now I've made my decision and you need to accept that." She pinched her thigh using the pain to stay calm in the face of Aster's shouting.

"But what will happen to Buckwheat Village? I'll never forgive myself if we get back and find everyone dead. Lavender Goodwin is in bad shape, not to mention my father. We don't have time to spare!"

"I know, but what about the lives of my crew? Do they not matter to you? Why are you placing Buckwheat above everyone else?"

Aster sat up, straining the rope as much as he could to look Kara in the eye. "I'm just scared to lose them. It took years, but I've finally become one of them."

Kara raised an eyebrow. "I don't understand. Didn't you grow up there?" She untied the ropes, allowing Aster to sit up completely.

"Look at my skin. It's a few shades darker than everyone else's. You don't see people this dark in Benia often. I was a monster that they couldn't get rid of, so they did their best to ignore me. They never even let the other kids play with me. Rowan Goodwin even started a rumor that my father had made an evil pact to conceive me."

"That's awful."

He took a deep, shaky breath. "Thank the light of Conflag that Zinnia was there! She visited me in secret. She helped me become an ideal villager. It took years, but first Lavender, then Mayor Gilroy, and even Watson started to talk with me. Around the time I turned thirteen, I'd finally earned the respect of everyone in the village and was no longer looked down on. Kara, I don't ever want to feel alone like that again. I need to protect those people that I worked so hard to win over." Aster's eyes glistened.

"I see. I'll do my best to help out, but you've got to trust me. And don't *ever* block my view when I'm steering."

"I... I won't," Aster said meekly.

"Good. Then I'll say that I'm sorry that you were tied up." She reached up and slipped the knot off of the beam and untied the two ropes. "I promise that we'll get the stone back soon. Or whatever it takes to help Buckwheat."

Aster was finally able to sit up properly. He rubbed his wrists where the ropes had bit into them.

"In a week or so, we'll pass by Mirefield. It'll take another day or two after that and we'll arrive in Tembour."

"What's it like there?"

"Patzu Lake is smaller than Buckwheat Lake. It's just off the Panta Marshes so the water can be shallow and muddy. The cypress trees make it seem eerie at times, especially in the hours before sunrise. I think you'll enjoy it."

Aster nodded and Kara left the sleeping quarters, her hands trembling as she took the wheel back from Peter.

"How'd he take it? I heard shouting," he asked.

"I think he's calmed down now. What if I'm making the wrong choice?"

"You can't know if a choice is good or bad until you see it play out. But if you do make a bad one, you've got to do your best to make it right, then learn from it."

"Where'd you get all this sage advice from?"

"Mostly mistakes. And a lot of listenin'. You'll get a better idea when we get there."

The sun had begun to set when they arrived in Tembour. They were greeted by the symbol of the city set atop two vertical pillars at the water's edge. To Aster, the intricate mahogany semicircle's tapered edges looked fierce, like the tusks of some enormous creature that could roam the nearby forest. The town itself was constructed further inland than most places with nothing but a lone pier jutting into the lake.

He saw why once they were ashore. Between them and the spattering of houses at the edge of a dense forest, was a massive cypress tree. Its gnarled trunk was twice as wide as the Blue Skies, knotted roots reaching out of the ground everywhere. If it wasn't for the raised boardwalk, it would be impossible to take carts into the city.

"It's supposedly a shrine to Viridus. They say it's hollow on the inside," Tristram remarked to Kara, pointing to the tree.

"It's much larger than I pictured in my mind. Believe it or not, this is my first time in Tembour."

"Really? But you grew up in the next town over. I would've thought you'd visited at least once before."

"No. All of our business on the farm was with New Portsmith. And I never had any free time to travel for fun. Even with the BTC, we've never had a reason to come here. I'm sure we would've eventually." She adjusted her shirt as they stepped onto the shore. "Aside from the humidity, it reminds me of home."

Peter raised his voice as he helped Aster manage his footing down the gangway. "The inn in Tembour is called the Parched Root. We should find it before dark."

The crew finished tying the Blue Skies up and marched down the boardwalk.

Even with help, Aster struggled on the uneven planks. By the time he had made it to the inn, the rest of the crew was already heading to bed. Aster didn't mind. The thought of sleeping in a warm, dry bed for the first time in weeks made him happy enough.

After breakfast the next morning, Peter made an announcement. "Before we're able to meet with my contact. I need to make sure he's willin' to see you. It's a bit of a complicated matter, so I'll be back this evenin'. If all goes well, you'll see him tomorrow." He left without another word.

Kara said, "Well, I should be off also."

Aster grumbled, "Since we are stuck here, at least take us with you."

Before Kara could protest, Calantha uncharacteristically chimed in. "Yes, it would be wonderful to see the Boscage School again. I will be joining as well. I cannot wait for Grovemother Lucinda to hear of my findings."

Kara lifted a large coin purse in her hand as she spoke. "I was hoping to have some alone time with my sister... but I suppose it doesn't hurt to have you all there. It's not like you don't already know my situation. Well, come on then." The crew grabbed their things.

"Janna once mentioned that the school was at the edge of the Snarled Forest on the South side of town," Kara added as they exited the Parched Root, treading in that direction.

Aster was already falling behind. "Wait up, will you? It's not easy to move around in this thing," he said, pointing to his brace. They slowed their pace as he limped along to catch up.

Before they reached the edge of town, trees appeared on the horizon. As they approached, Aster had to stop and gawk: It was the largest forest he had ever seen. Each trunk was as big as a house, the branches reaching high into the air. Underneath the largest tree, the grass and shrubs appeared to be intentionally cultivated. They were arranged in regular patterns of red and yellow flowers.

"That must be it. The Boscage School of Benia," Kara said, trudging forward.

Aster paused again, rubbing his leg while thinking about navigating the enormous roots. "We'd better not be going through the forest to get there. Otherwise, I think I'll wait for you here."

Calantha doubled back to help him forward. "No, we are very close now. The grounds around the school are well maintained and mostly flat. You would be remiss not to visit the place. Sometimes I dream about returning to the gardens here. It is quite beautiful, you know."

They followed a dirt path around the base of the largest tree, which took longer than Aster expected. The air was thick and smelled earthy. Aster saw many different types of moss and mushrooms growing just beyond the path. On the other side of the tree, the canopy of the forest opened up, letting the sunlight into a large clearing. Facing the center, each of the trees had a dirt path leading to a door in their trunks, the largest of which had windows carved into the wood itself that ran up the tree until they were out of sight among the branches. An old man was out watering flowers with a handful of students watching intently.

Kara looked both ways before leading the group into the trunk of the tree that they had just walked around.

As they were passing through the door, Chert stopped and ran his hand across the smooth bark. "Good wood," he said as he examined the tree and the structure that had been made from it.

Inside, a young woman sat behind a desk surrounded by staircases that twisted into the tree in all directions. In a squeaky voice, she addressed the crew. "Hello and welcome to the Boscage School. How can I assist you?"

Kara stepped forward. "Hello. My name is Kara Reeves. My younger sister Janna goes to school here. I was hoping that you could help us find her."

The woman nodded and began to rummage through a set of drawers behind her. After a moment, she pulled out a slip of paper, scanned it, then placed it back. "Her schedule shows that today is Janna's study period. Most of the students prefer to spend their self-guided time in the library. You are welcome to wait for her there. It is directly across the clearing from us," she said pointing straight out the door.

They thanked her and turned to leave.

"Please keep in mind, all guests must be off school grounds by nightfall for the safety of the students. We've been having incidents with a few of the locals, so we are quite strict about this right now."

After reassuring her that they would follow the rules, the crew went outside again.

Across the glade was the only true building in the

entire school. It was as if somebody had tried to widen the trunk of the tree. Supported by wood planks, it gave the impression of a potbelly pig: widest at the base and tapering off as it reached the top, where leaves stuck up like a feathery hat. Clear glass windows circled the tree, letting in as much light as was possible under the forest canopy.

Inside was even more awe-inspiring. Every wall was covered with bookshelves, filled to the brim with manuscripts, scrolls, and massive tomes. There were three floors that overlooked a sitting area with padded chairs.

After surveying the place, Kara said, "I don't see her. I guess we should just wait here." She led them to the chairs and took a seat, facing the front door.

Calantha was the only one who didn't join them. She bee-lined over to one of the shelves and started pouring through a particularly dusty tome, occasionally letting out a delighted squeak or a pensive, "I see. Very interesting."

An hour passed and the crew was becoming impatient. Aster had found a heroic fantasy story and brought it back to his chair. As he was scanning the pages, Kara jumped up. A young lady with fiery red hair curling down to her shoulders had walked by them, chatting with a plain looking older woman.

"Janna! Over here," Kara yelled out, breaking the silence and drawing everyone's attention.

The young lady looked annoyed at first, but her face lit up when she recognized who was calling to her. "Kara, what in Arathanon are you doing here?"

She rushed over to the center of the room, embracing her sister.

"It's been too long. But I never expected you to come see me in Tembour. You should've sent word that you were heading this way. Are these your crewmates?"

"Yes, this is Aster, Chert, and Tristram. Calantha is here too... somewhere."

"Hello, nice to meet you all." She stepped closer and faced Aster. "Has anyone ever told you that you have gorgeous hair?"

"Janna, cut it out." Kara cut in as Aster's cheeks flushed.

"What does it matter to you? We don't get many new faces around here. Besides, he isn't your type anyways."

Kara's face was next to turn red. "I wanted to see how your studies are coming along. Also, take this." Kara handed Janna the coin pouch she had been carrying. "This should be enough for another year. I'm not sure if I'll be able to send you any more after that."

"Why, what happened?"

Kara lowered her voice. "We're on the run from the law. Long story short, our captain betrayed us and somehow I'm the one in trouble."

Janna laughed. "I thought you hated pirates?"

Kara snapped back. "We aren't pirates. I'm just… temporarily without a job."

"Then how did you make it to Tembour in the first place?" Janna grinned smugly, leaning forward in her cushioned seat.

"We sailed here on the Blue Skies, of course."

"The Blue Skies, which is owned by the BTC, that you are not currently employed by? And you are wanted by the Council of Elders? That's textbook pirate behavior."

Kara scowled and crossed her arms. "Janna, even after all this time you still know how to get under my skin."

"Ah yes, about my studies," Janna announced. "I'm more than halfway through our program. The Collective is treating me well and I feel like I've learned pretty much all the Boscage School has to offer. Did you know that this course was originally intended for the king's advisors? It's hard to say exactly what comes after. I suppose I will run for Council. In any case, I've already completed the classes in history, economics, politics, science, and religion. I'm currently in the middle of botany lessons. Soon, I'll be done with all my lectures and can begin work on my independent project."

"Grand plans. I expect nothing less from my genius

sister." Kara smiled and rubbed her shoulder. "What's an independent project?"

"We get to choose a topic of our choice and spend two years researching it. After which we collect our notes and write a book on the subject." She pointed to the shelves around her. "As you can see, literature is fundamental to the Collective."

Aster added, "Writing must be easy with this massive amount of knowledge all in one spot."

Janna laughed. "I wouldn't say it's easy. And Grovemother Lucinda declared that all students must spend at least one year outside of Tembour during our research. She always says, 'Shut-ins can't grasp the nuances of the world, let alone write to it'. I have to say that I agree. Plus, I've been itching to see Arathanon after spending so much time hearing its stories."

Kara added, "I'm sure. You haven't really gone anywhere besides Tembour and or the farm. The world is nothing like what you'd expect."

Aster nodded enthusiastically.

The crew stayed and chatted with Janna for the rest of the afternoon. Calantha reappeared, but was so engrossed in the stack of books she had taken off the shelves that she rarely participated in the conversation.

When the shadows grew long inside the library, the group headed back to town. Janna made them promise to come visit her again before they left, especially Aster.

They found Peter waiting for them at the Parched Root. "Everything is set for us to visit him tomorrow," he said through a mouthful of wine.

Kara grabbed a chair next to him. "Good. Then we can relax for the rest of the evening." She flung her boots off and ordered a round of ale. Everyone had a pleasant night, drinking and chatting until they were too tired to go on.

The next day, they arrived at a pair of houses at the far edge of town. Modestly sized, but in top shape, as if they had been constructed yesterday. Peter knocked on the door three times, pausing for a moment and then twice more.

It opened a crack, just enough for one person to slip out, closing it behind them.

"Hello again, Joss. Is he ready to see us?" Peter asked.

The woman stood straight and cleared her throat. "Can they be trusted?" She thrust her pointed chin in the direction of the crew.

"Yes, I told you yesterday I trust them with my life."

"Swear it on... swear it on whatever god you worship these days." With one hand on the hilt of her sword, Josselyn stared Peter down.

"As particular as ever. I swear on the great Loctee that the men and women here today are trustworthy. There, satisfied?"

"Not really." She turned to the rest of them. "You are all bound by this oath. Never discuss what you see or hear inside this house for as long as you live. If word ever got out... it would cause chaos. And I would personally hunt you down in retribution."

Kara piped up. "Joss? As in Sir Josselyn Helisent? You look much healthier than you did in that cell."

"Very much so. Both in body and in mind. I owe both you and Peter a great debt for what you did for me back in New Portsmith. But we can talk more inside. Come now." She opened the door again and directed the crew into a parlor room filled with ornate cushioned chairs. A fruity, bitter smell greeted them as a servant came by offering tea.

Aster had never seen a teacup as intricately decorated as the one now warming his hands.

Moments later Josselyn stood, directing her attention to a man who entered the room. She cleared her throat loudly and Peter stood as well. The others followed suit.

"Good morning, your highness. Peter Keeton is here with some crew members to visit today."

Upon seeing Peter, the man's face lit up. He smiled through perfectly straight teeth, his blue eyes dazzling. His clothes were remarkably vibrant—reds and golds, brighter than Aster thought was possible for cloth. The two men embraced. "I never expected that we would see each other again so soon, but it's a pleasure as always, Peter."

"Likewise on both accounts. Happy to see that Joss found her way to you as well." Peter clapped the man on the shoulder as he was released.

"Yes, a blessing that you found her when you did. She nearly died of shock when she arrived. Between that and malnourishment, it took us hours to revive her."

Peter laughed heartily. "A warrior like Joss, fainting? Wish I'd been here to witness that."

"Peter, I cannot thank you enough," Josselyn said. "You gave my life purpose once more by freeing me and directing me here. You have no idea how lost I've felt over the last few years."

"It was the least I could do for an old comrade. I still owe you a thousandfold from back in the day. And you looked pretty pitiful in that cell. I barely recognized you!"

Aster grew impatient and cut into the conversation. "While catching up with old friends over tea is nice and all, why are we here? Who is this man? I don't see why this was more important than going straight to New Portsmith," he grumbled.

Peter sighed and said, "Aster this is—"

Josselyn cut him off. "Child. It would do you well to have some respect. You are in the presence of King Federyc Benia. You will refer to him as 'your highness' or 'your majesty'."

Federyc held up his hand and Josselyn fell silent. "Now Joss, I appreciate your devotion, but remember I'm a king no longer. In fact, I'm nobody important." He turned back to Peter. "In any case, what business do you and your friends have here today? I assume this is more than a social visit."

Kara crossed her arms and said, "Wait. I need an explanation. King Federyc is dead. He was assassinated nearly fifteen years ago during the People's Rebellion. Everyone knows this. Besides you are far too young to have been our king. So, I don't understand why you are claiming to be him."

Federyc turned to Peter again. "She's sharp and assertive. I like her." He gestured to the chairs. "Yes, yes. I will explain it all to you, friends of Peter. Have a seat as there is much to discuss. But first, Peter please introduce me to your crew. Especially this beautiful young lady." Federyc tilted his head towards Kara, revealing a thin, golden circlet hidden in his curly blond hair.

They all sat back and sipped their tea. The servant came back and brought a cup twice as large for Federyc and then disappeared into the back room again. He returned with milk and sugar cubes and placed them on the table.

Just as Federyc was reaching for the sugar, Peter stopped him. "Wait, I brought you something'." He pulled out two jars of honey and handed them over. "From Buckwheat Village. The best there is!"

Josselyn eyed the jars cautiously but said nothing as Federyc scooped out two globs of the amber liquid into his tea. "Thank you, you always know how to butter me up. Now where were we?"

"Right, first off, this is Kara Reeves, captain of the Blue Skies."

"And she's your captain too! Quite the upgrade from Whitlock," Federyc mused.

"The mouthy boy is Aster Rutherford. He's from Buckwheat Village. And this is Chert Penya from Strongfair. The lady to my left is Calantha Coronatus from... actually I don't know. Calantha, where do you call home?"

She shrank back, as if she hadn't expected to be a part of the conversation. "I have forsaken my home. Now I wander as I please."

Peter blinked twice. "Uh sure. Last we've got Tristram Ederyc. He has been sailing with us for just as long as Kara has. A New Portsmith native, like myself."

"What a motley crew!" Federyc laughed and sipped his

tea. "A pleasure to meet you all. Now that I know a bit about you, it is only right to share a bit about myself as well. I'm sure you are curious about why I am sitting in front of you and not rotting in a grave somewhere.

"Let me start by saying: I never wanted to be king. My older brother, Brannus, was the heir to Benia. I would watch him study, train, and learn etiquette every single day from sunrise to sunset. He never had time to explore in his youth or play with me. I was not envious of his responsibility.

"I still remember the day when father took Brannus out to sea. They were to visit each of Benia's trading partners for a bit of hands-on economics lessons. They made it all the way to Sumas, but something went wrong, and they never returned. The advisors looked for them for an entire year but never found any sign of the crew or the ship. So after they gave up, I, only fifteen at the time, was crowned king.

"Many people were upset by this. 'How can this child rule our kingdom?' A phrase repeated often in the streets. Everything that went wrong in the country was blamed on me. I took it in stride and laid low for three years. I doubled down on my studies and did everything in my power to be as good of a king as Brannus would have been. The unease never really faded. I believe it was fanned by a few who wanted power for themselves.

"Before long, rumors of revolution began to swirl. Many called for an end to the monarchy. And then the assassination attempts started. Thankfully, Peter kept me safe. It got to the point where he was by my side all the time. He even started to sleep in my bedroom to keep an eye on me.

"But the stress of it all began to get to me. Was the revolution a just cause? Why should a child rule this kingdom just because of his blood? Wouldn't it be best if the people themselves choose who governs?

"I drafted a transition plan and presented it to my advisors. A democratic Benia: I was convinced that was the best path forward for the country that I loved. Not everyone agreed. Emmeline was against it. She said that the only way to quell a revolution was with blood. Either us or them, probably a bit of both.

"After much soul searching, I decided to give them exactly that in the most peaceful way I could think of. There were only four of us in on the plot. It took us a month to find a corpse that was similar to me. We were lucky to find a street urchin about my height. He'd had a fatal run in with a pair of guards that had caught him stealing.

"It was Peter's idea to douse the body in acid to warp the face. He placed the corpse in my bed and then they smuggled me out of the city. The next morning, Peter rang the alarm bells. He convinced everyone that he had found me dead, clearly an assassination. The plan was a success. With no lawful heirs or claims to the throne, the Council was formed in the ashes. I've been keeping a low profile ever since."

The room was silent after he finished speaking as each of them contemplated what they'd just heard. The reality of Benia changed forever in Aster's mind.

"With that out of the way, Peter, what brings you here today?"

After taking a deep breath, Peter explained everything. From Aster joining the Blue Skies, to Whitlock's betrayal, to the chase in Munayallpa, to Baxter's attempt on Kara's life. Each of the crew added their own detail to the story as he spoke. And just as the sun reached its apex in the sky, the tale was concluded. "So Federyc, now that you've heard our tale, do you have any advice for keepin' out of the Council's eye? We are mostly worried about Kara, but I think more caution would be good for all of us."

Federyc considered it carefully. "Well, the beautiful lady is welcome to stay here with me... but I'm sure that's not what you meant." He raised an eyebrow and watched Kara, who didn't react, so he cleared his throat and continued. "Let's see. Keep your face covered. Avoid major cities and never give out your real name. Absolutely never trust a person that you don't already know." He finished his cup of tea and placed it down on the table with a sigh. With a solemn expression he looked at Kara. "But these actions bring with them a paranoia. You are far too young to have to experience such a life. Fear and loneliness that is unbearable at times. No, you should not follow the same path that I have. The only real solution lies with the government. If you are no longer a threat to the Council, they will not look for you."

"I'm not a threat to the Council," Kara protested. "They should be after Whitlock, not me. Why am I their target?"

Federyc's expression turned sour. "Their obsession with Whitlock concerns me. Do you think they know, Peter? You were supposed to keep an eye on that man."

Peter shifted uncomfortably, placing his cup down. "Yeah, I was. But he got away twice. There was no knowin' that he was plannin' to steal the gold and run. Now we've got our own problems and he's disappeared. But he's been true to his word."

Whitlock hardly matters anymore! Aster smacked the table, sloshing milk onto the carpet. "None of this has anything to do with finding Fletcher and getting... uh... that thing back."

Peter stood and pointed a finger at Aster. "I've had about enough of you today. Show a bit of respect for—"

Federyc raised his hand, stopping Peter in his tracks. "Aster, you've been fidgeting ever since you arrived. First New Portsmith and now Fletcher. Please tell us what's on your mind and why you can't seem to be patient enough for us to finish our conversation. Did this Fletcher fellow steal something of importance to you?"

Aster fell silent, looking at Kara for advice.

She shrugged and said, "Do as you wish. It was Fletcher who wanted to keep it quiet in the first place. Besides, we already have a whale of a secret between us now."

Aster hesitated then said, "He stole something very valuable to me and now he has probably already made it to New Portsmith. It's called the Odyllic Stone. We need it back to save Buckwheat Village."

Peter scratched his head, Tristram went pale, and Federyc's chiseled jaw dropped.

Aster went on. "Fletcher plans to deliver the stone to the Council in exchange for fortune and fame."

Federyc gestured to his servant, whispered a few words to the man, then waved him off. Turning to Aster, he said, "The will of the four gods must have brought you to me this day. I never expected that my family birthright would be discovered again. And during our generation, no less! I offer my support to your recovery efforts. But keep in mind, I no longer have any responsibility for the empire."

He knows more than he's letting on. Aster asked, "What do you know of the stone?"

"It's a herald of war and destruction. The tool my ancestors used in Benia's founding, warping Arathanon in the process. But history aside, what do I have that could assist you?" Federyc scratched his golden brow.

Peter answered him. "Information. Advice. A plan. Anything you're willing to give."

"Well, I do have a contact that is keeping tabs on the Council's activities. They may be able to provide us with some intelligence. Perhaps they can discover the storage location of the stone when it arrives? And in the meantime, I can offer you Josselyn's assistance in training."

Aster tilted his head. "Training for what?"

"You're on a path of blood. The stone will be carefully guarded and the Council won't give it up without a fight." Federyc pointed to Aster's scrawny arm. "And you don't appear to have faced many battles yourself. It isn't much, but it's all I have to offer at the moment. I hope it will be enough to keep you alive long enough to see your wish come true."

Josselyn bowed her head. "If that's your wish my lord. Aster, please meet me outside this house tomorrow. We'll begin our training at dawn. Peter, you should join us as well. I'm sure you've grown soft in your old age."

Federyc added, "And Kara, I can give you some one-on-one instructions for how to avoid attention. It will be weeks before we hear back from my contact so you all will have plenty of time to learn. Oh and Aster, in exchange for my assistance, there may be a time in the future where I will call upon you for a favor. I hope that you will be a man of honor on that day." He fixed his gaze on Aster with a sternness in his eyes.

Aster found himself nodding his acquiescence. "Do... do you want the stone afterwords?"

The former king glanced to an old portrait on the wall. "No. I made my choice already. I am learning to love the simple things in life. Having the Odyllic Stone... well I wouldn't be able to help myself meddling. No, you should keep it. Use it to make Arathanon a better place for everyone."

"I'll try... if we manage to get it back."

Federyc smiled in a way that made him look sad. "That's all I ask."

Peter stayed behind to chat with the former king while Josselyn escorted everyone else out, bidding them farewell for the day.

As they doubled back to the Blue Skies, Calantha caught Chert's attention and said, "It seems that we will be staying here in Tembour for a while. Chert, would you like to join me on a bit of an expedition since you and I have nothing better to do?"

"Sure," Chert replied.

Tristram grumbled under his breath, "What about me?"

Aster cut in, wincing with every step, "Tristram you should join us in training. I've heard that Joss is the best fighter in all of Benia."

"Don't lump me in the same barrel as you, Lantern. But I guess if Peter's doing it..."

The next morning, Chert and Calantha joined the others for breakfast, but bid them farewell as they stepped out of the inn. As they were eating, Calantha mentioned that they would be taking a few days to hike to an old shrine that she had discovered many years back. The rest of the crew wished them luck and hustled to reach Federyc's house before the sun had fully risen.

When they arrived, Josselyn was standing outside waiting for them. "You're late," she said, glancing upward.

"Sorry, we almost made it on time," Aster said, rubbing his tender leg as he watched Kara walk past them into the house.

Josselyn cleared her throat. "Now that you three are finally here, I will teach you how to fight properly. Lesson number one: Don't talk back to your commanding officer." She glared down her pointed nose at Aster—arms crossed. "Now, I don't just say this because *you* need to hear this. I say it because it is critical to the success of a mission or a battle. In combat, there is no time for you to second guess your commander. Strategic discussions are best held prior to fighting. Lesson number two: Before you can help others on the battlefield, you must be able to help yourself. More than anything, this means that you should be able to hold your own in one-on-one combat. Aster, this is what you will be spending most of your time on practicing."

She handed him a dull wooden sword. "Seeing that you have limited mobility at the moment, you will be focusing on your technique to start. Peter, why don't you take Tristram and exchange some blows while I show Aster the basics? This afternoon, we can swap partners so I can give you pointers."

She watched Aster flail about for a minute before guiding his arm with her hands. "To effectively wield a weapon, it must become an extension of your body. Feel its weight. Learn its motions. And develop the muscle to use it to its fullest."

Aster swung his sword over and over. Josselyn critiqued his form until he couldn't lift his arms.

Chert grumbled as he joined Calantha on the Northern side of the city. They passed under the thick canopy of the Snarled Forest. It grew darker with each step as the trees became thicker and closer together. It made Chert nervous. He was already feeling lost without the sun to guide him.

Calantha hummed to herself.

The forest and Calantha. He watched as she glided over roots and between branches. She was the most graceful person he'd ever met, but she was also the hardest to figure out. Quiet, like him, but she always seemed to be thinking a thousand things at one. Probably more if she could explain them.

He didn't think they were friends, necessarily, but they had a certain solidarity—both mostly ignored in group settings while the more assertive people took the spotlight.

Calantha cleared her throat. "I wanted you to join me on this little walk to have some time alone, away from the others. Our destination is rather trivial, to be honest, but it is a good excuse to discuss things in private."

Chert replied, "Sure. Talk about what?"

"I believe that you and I are the same. Kindred spirits, as they say. Although we were raised in separate worlds, our experiences have led us to the same place."

Chert grunted. He agreed only if he twisted the words a certain way.

"I believe that of all the people that I have met on this journey, you are the most likely to understand me. But before I say more, please could you tell me more about yourself?"

"Not much to say. Chert was born in Strongfair, and lived there. Father was treasure hunter. Left Chert behind to take care of brother and sister. Liked rocks so became mason. Wood nice too, though. Been adding wood into shop."

"No, that will not do at all. Maybe a better way to ask is, why are you the way you are? Why is Chert? I am interested in your motivation in life as well as your bloodline."

"Chert's motivation? Chert's blood? Huh?" He scratched his uneven dome of a head.

"Yes, yes. Why have you left your shop to join this variegated group that they call a crew? You mentioned looking for a chalice that was once possessed by your father, but why? You have that item now, yet you remain with us."

"Hmmm, Chert understands." He meekly rubbed his arm as he spoke. "Father left to explore world. Chert took care of family. After family has grown up, Chert lost purpose. Aster came with adventure and chance to learn more about father. Even with chalice, Chert still doesn't understand."

"Just as I expected. You are a lost soul, the same as me. A being without purpose in this mysterious world. Though, you seem to be seeking your past whereas I am running from mine." Her hands wove around in the air as she spoke, animating her words.

"Why?"

"That brings us to my primary reason for our discussion. You see, my family is aggressive and tribal. The best warriors in battle rule, and there is no place for science or logic. I fought against that mindset and was labeled a witch. I was only twelve when mother exiled me." Her voice strained and a lone tear fell down her cheek, but she pressed on. "When that winter came, I sheltered in the Boscage School of Benia."

Chert found it hard to swallow. His tongue was like gravel against his throat. *What a horrible thing to do to a child.*

"At first I hid in the shadows, careful to avoid any contact with the scholars there. Thankfully my clan knew enough of the Benian tongue that I could get by. One day I overheard a scholar describe the grand library to one of his students. I followed them and was stunned by the amount of knowledge that was rumored to be there. The tomes themselves were a mystery. I was unable to decipher how an object so small could contain such detail.

"By springtime, I created an identity for myself. Calantha—based on the word they used when describing their garden and Coronatus—an homage to my heritage. I managed to trick them into accepting me, though not completely.

"Grovemother Lucinda must have known that I was not everything I claimed to be. She took pity on me and allowed me to stay and provided me with tasks to do on school grounds to earn my keep. It was a struggle at first, learning to read and write, but once I mastered those, I began consuming the literature at an astounding rate. Before long, I was the top student in the school, surpassing most of the teachers.

"I continuously altered my appearance, iterating until it felt right. Looking back, I unknowingly risked it all, but because it coincided with the coming of age of my peers, I was rarely questioned. Finally, I settled on the form you see now—my true self.

"But once more I must digress before I get to my point. The tome that excited me the most in the entire library was called *The Birth of the Fourth Age*. A mundane history translated from the oldest book that remains, covered in dust from lack of interest. Grovemother said the content was suspect, but it was too exhilarating to ignore. I learned of how Charles Benia came to power. I learned of the Odyllic Stone. And most importantly, I found hints of my clan's origin. Though very limited in its knowledge of us, the literature seemed to imply that the beginning of our existence coincided with the end of the

Golden Age. The same is true for the Munayallpans.

"In any case, I reached the limit of what the Collective of Scholars could teach me and set off into the greater world to seek answers to my remaining questions. One day, I'll return to the Collective and pioneer a new field of research."

Chert bowed his head slightly and said, "Thank you for trusting Chert with this. But, why you say we are same?"

"There are two reasons. First, we are both seeking answers about our families and our pasts. Second, we are both bound by our heritage. To put it simply, I believe that the Manti Clan as well as the population of Munayallpa were created by the Odyllic Stone."

Chert stopped in his tracks. "Created? No. Chert was there for Jasper's birth. He came from mother's womb, same as in Benia."

"That is not quite what I meant."

Chert shook his head, confused.

"One of the scholars at the school, Gregory, has published over fifty works on botany and has been tracking the morphology of his beloved plants through the generations. Constantly interbreeding them and observing the new offspring. He has developed a method for predicting their traits based on the parent plants. Their essence, the core of their being, is blended and passed down somehow."

Calantha was elated, her thin lips stretched into the biggest grin that Chert had seen from her. "If you apply that theory, along with the power of the Odyllic Stone, to the history of our people, it all makes sense."

Whatever she was saying was clearly important to her, but Chert felt as if he was missing the point. "Sorry, Chert still confused."

"I shall show you. It is not very pronounced in your case, but it is quite obvious in mine. I wish there had been more literature around the Manti, but perhaps the lack of knowledge is what kept us alive for so long. Please remain calm."

Calantha took two steps back and faced Chert. The air shimmered in front of her as if they were back in the hot sands of the Kaleenmunda Desert. Then her shape began to change.

In her place stood a beast with elongated eyes and a pointed mouth. It was pale pink, fading into an off-white around her elongated abdomen. Four segmented legs gripped the leafy ground and two scythe-like claws were folded in front of its body with delicate hands underneath. Atop its head were a set of thin antennas.

The monster spoke. "This is who I was before I discovered my true self."

Zinnia Hollyhock,

The outside world continues to be a place of mystery. Never in a thousand years would you guess who we met in Tembour. Even now I cannot tell you, but next time we meet, I will.

We also got to meet Kara's sister, Janna. She's as striking as her sister. Strong-willed, passionate, and extremely smart, too. She came across as a bit of a know-it-all, but I'm sure that comes as part of a formal education. The Boscage School itself was a sight to behold, carved from the very trees that grew there. The library alone was worth the visit. It would take a lifetime to read all of its books!

Also, I'm being taught to wield a sword! They are much heavier than they appear. After my first lesson my arms were so sore that I could barely make a fist, even though I only used a wooden one. I feel like Pacari the Lionhearted, honing his skills and preparing for battle.

My thoughts keep drifting back to Lavender and my father lying sick in bed. Please check on them as often as you can.

Your friend,
Aster

9 DISCOVERY OF DRAKŌN

A cool breeze whistled across Patzu lake, blowing a crisp smell to the forest. The damp air was tolerable under the shade of the trees.

The steel short-sword impaled the hay dummy with a crunch. Aster stepped backwards gingerly, careful not to put too much weight on his leg. It had been a few days since he was able to walk around without the brace. Only at night, in bed, when his muscles started to relax, did his leg feel tender. But Aster remained cautious nonetheless.

"You've gotten good at that, Lantern," Tristram remarked, as he walked over, Peter at his side. Each of their shirts was stained with sweat and they panted from exertion.

"Yes, for only three weeks of practice, he's progressing well. Those knife lessons were a useful starting point," Josselyn said as she rose from her seat on a nearby stump.

Peter wiped his boots in the grass. "Let's take a break. I'm tired of beatin' on Tristram."

Joss watched as Aster finished his next round of thrusts. "Good. Stop for now, and drink some water. We need to discuss the next step in your training."

Aster wiped his brow and settled in the sand. He was happy to have a rest. *Joss really knows how to work you to the bone.*

"So Aster, now that you have the basic strokes down and you seem to be able to put more weight on your leg, I want you to prove your practical skills." Josselyn collected her weapons off the ground as she spoke. "There have been a few reports of hens missing from the farms near the forest's edge. There were sightings of a green wolf-like creature skulking around. It is most likely a lovine. The locals have been begging me to search for its lair. I want you to go into the forest and kill it."

Aster shook his head. "How would I do that?"

"I have tracked it to a ravine just beyond the southern path. I'm sure that's where the beast lives. Return with its head."

Peter grumbled. "Woah now Joss, you sure he's ready to go into the forest alone? He's barely recovered."

Josselyn glared at Peter. "Practicing techniques and friendly sparring will only take a person so far. What he needs now is experience."

Peter raised an eyebrow.

Josselyn heaved a sigh. "If you're so uncertain, I'll go with him." She paused to point at Aster. "But don't expect me to help you boy. I'll stay within earshot, that's it. If you howl in pain, perhaps I'll come find you."

"Uh... thanks," Aster said. "Though, I'd like to practice for a few more days before I go out."

"Suit yourself. There's no reason to rush. Besides, all of this training is helpful for me, too. Before you arrived, I'd been doing it alone."

Peter quipped back, "His majesty isn't much of a sparrin' partner, eh? He should be able to hold his own. After all I taught him the basics myself."

"I could never raise my sword against him," she conceded. "If he got hurt, even by accident, I wouldn't forgive myself."

"Joss, I never really understood. Why do you care about Federyc so much?" Aster asked. "I know he was your king, but even when we met you in that cell, before you knew that he was still alive, you said that your purpose in life was to avenge him. You used to be the Council's Elder of Defense, but now you're here. I just don't get it."

"It's a matter of honor," she replied, simply.

"Joss, what's the harm in tellin' him?" Peter asked as he turned to Aster. "The king took a huge risk on her. He gave her everythin' she's ever wanted. It was probably part of why he lost his crown."

Josselyn pinched the bridge of her nose. "Very well. I shall tell you." For the first time since they met, Aster saw her relax. Abandoning her rigid stance, Josselyn sat cross legged in the grass. "Where should I begin? I was always a good soldier."

Peter cut in. "You were the best soldier."

"As I was saying, I was a good soldier: I always followed orders and always completed my mission. The Marshal loved me. I was promoted through the ranks. The first time that I really felt accomplished was during a covert operation in El'tonne. This was back when we were at war. I lead a squad over the border and around the enemy troops, flanking them. In short, that maneuver proved to be decisive for that battle. And that battle proved decisive for the war.

"We won the independence of Munayallpa on that day. The territory was no longer claimed by the El'tonnians. After that, I was promoted to leader of the special forces. A modest team responsible for delicate and risky missions. Peter became my subordinate during that time."

"Things changed when Federyc was crowned king after his father failed to return from that foolish trip. Federyc was kind, but woefully inexperienced. I... did my best to make sure he understood the good and the bad of my missions. I advised him on tactics for managing the knights, when most of the other leaders were happy to leave Federyc in the dark."

"A year after the king's coronation, the commander of the King's Knights passed away in a hunting accident.

Federyc needed a new one and took a chance on me. He appointed the first ever female commander in spite of push-back from his advisors. I was clearly the most qualified for the position, but tradition held me back. Federyc disregarded this tradition, so I vowed to remain forever loyal to him."

Peter shook his head. "That's a weak way to put it. Benia never had a woman in charge of anythin' useful before Joss. In fact, if it wasn't for her, there's no way the people would've accepted Emmeline to be in the Council. And probably Kara wouldn't have gotten the chance to be captain. It may seem normal now, but Federyc really did somethin' special by appointing Joss as the commander."

Josselyn pursed her lips and nodded with a gloomy look before speaking again. "When he was assassinated, I blamed myself. I always wondered if his choice to have me lead the King's Knights was why the people rebelled. So, I joined forces with the new government, the Council, to continue carrying on the will of the king. There, I used my position to try and ferret out who had killed him.

"I never found out, but in my investigations, I fell from Emmeline's good graces. Last year she jailed me and used my name to further her own goals. That's when your crew rescued me. I thank the fires of Conflag that Peter had been there to tell me of Federyc's true fate. Today I feel more at ease that the king wasn't killed by my ambitions. I will serve him till my last breath."

Aster rubbed his tender leg. "That's not fair. You didn't do anything wrong."

"As you get older, you realize that nothing's fair. But that's enough about the past. It's time to get back to work," Josselyn said as she quickly wiped her eyes. "Aster, grab the wooden practice sword. I think you've had enough time with the dummy today. You and I will spar. Maybe today you will finally land a blow on me."

Chert sat beside the lake under the shade of a leaning cypress tree. Calantha had gone back to the Boscage library, but as Chert was tired of spending time among the books, he had wandered to the water's edge to be alone with his thoughts. A cool breeze blew across the lake causing him to rub the goosebumps on his arms. Cattails grew so tall that he could hardly see the symbol of Tembour sticking out over them.

Calantha's words were running through his mind again. Three weeks ago, when they had talked in the forest, he hadn't known how to react. But now that he had time to process what she said, he had a better sense of how he felt about it. She couldn't be right. Munayallpan folklore was older and more nuanced compared to myths of Benia. Sure, they had some legends of the past and a unique culture, but nothing like the stories from back home.

Though it was strange how much Munayallpa was reliant on Benia.

But were they really an artificial race? Something made by mortal hands and not of the Goddess Ochress? He wished he could discuss it with Beryl. He only knew pieces of the origins of the Munayallpan people from his father.

The stories said that Goddess Ochress long struggled to communicate with mortals. Even though she was the eldest god and the most deserving of reverence, she was frequently forgotten by the people of Arathanon. To correct this, she carved a race out of granite. In each person, she placed a diamond heart to grant them life.

They could hear the vibrations of the earth and could speak through music. But it wasn't enough. Like her, they struggled to communicate. It wasn't until a girl fell in love with one of the granite men did they find speech. Their child, Lithia, the first Munayallpan, was able to speak and became Ochress' first priestess.

Something about the concept of divine creation comforted Chert. He didn't like the idea that his friends and family had been created by the whims of some king. It was less sturdy, a notion made of mud. Dad would hate it too.

If Hugo ever came home, he'd ask. But it had been too long. The man had either met an unfortunate end or made a new life for himself somewhere else.

Another breeze crept under Chert's clothes. "Time to sit in sun," he remarked standing up from the root. His foot collided with the onyx chalice he had brought with him.

It bounced down the grassy slope and splashed into the lake.

Chert sprang into action. After years of searching for it, he would not lose his father's legacy in such a silly way. Luckily, it caught on a cluster of cattails in the shallows.

Chert fished the cup out of the water, grumbling as his feet sank into the muck. He steadied himself; his clothes now sopping wet.

Muddy water cascaded out of the holes in the chalice. Aster had a point; why would anyone create a cup that can't hold water? Was it merely for decoration? Was he thinking about things backwards?

He cleaned debris off of the rim with his shirt. Did someone, long since dead, really have a use for this thing? He turned it around in his hand.

Chert tried to put himself in the mind of a noble. What would be more pompous than a drink from an impossible cup? He brought the chalice to his mouth, as if to take a sip, pretending that it was filled with an expensive wine. As the rim touched his lips, the world went black.

Chert awoke, no longer feeling the air chilling his wet arms. He had a much better view of the lake now that the cattails were gone. Taking a moment to enjoy the sights, he studied the symbol of Tembour just above the twisted cypress trees. Fierce—like an animal on the hunt. It's a fine offering to God. Munayallpan craftsmen would be proud.

But something felt wrong. The birds had gone quiet and his legs weren't stuck in the mud.

He looked down and howled in shock. The lake was far below him. The reeds looked like a carpet of golden brushes, swaying gently.

It took him a while to compose himself. Still dreaming against the cypress, he concluded.

He looked towards the tree. A Munayallpan man was half-sunk into the mud at the water's edge. Luckily the man's bald head and right shoulder were above water. Chert's heart beat fast in his chest.

That was his body.

Was this the chalice's secret? What Dad had abandoned us for?

He wiggled his way forward, pushing against the thick air until he was beyond the vegetation. At least this was a good way to get a better perspective on things. A twinge of fear penetrated his mind. He had to get back.

As he struggled forward he watched his lumpy face sink. He'd drown.

Chert reached down and tried to prop up his head, to no avail. He couldn't move it. He couldn't feel the water either.

His body was tense. In a panic, he shoved the corpse. It didn't budge.

Then the world went black.

Chert's body screamed in pain, lungs filled with water. He was on the verge of fainting again. With his last bit of energy, he lifted himself out, throwing himself on the grass.

His head pounded as he gasped for air between coughing fits.

"Close," he said as he recovered his strength.

He needed to tell the others.

His teeth chattered as he sloshed back to the Parched Root, a change of clothes and some hot soup at the forefront of his mind.

Calantha was already there. "Ah, Chert," she said as

she noticed him. "Come look at this manuscript. I believe it holds a vital clue to the Awakening. If you look closely..."

Chert waited patiently for her to finish describing the tomes she had discovered that day. He could barely understand the nuances of her story. She kept repeating something about the Awakening. Chert was too distracted to pay close attention.

He'd finally found something useful. Something important. This time he'd be the one to contribute. While he valued his friendship with Calantha, she could be long winded.

Just as the sun set, Aster and the others walked in, joining them around the table.

Aster loudly interrupted Calantha's story, arguing with Kara. "You said that already, but what does it mean? Alone with him all day, what could he possibly be teaching you?"

Kara rolled her eyes. "Today, he was going over how to create a new identity for oneself. The importance of a common, ordinary name. Memorizing the details of who you are and where you are from. Can't be inconsistent with your story if you stay in the same town for long. Otherwise people may get suspicious."

"I suppose that makes sense, but you could at least come outside and say hello from time to time. You haven't done that once since we started our training."

"Ha!" Kara's laugh echoed through the room. "What, are you jealous?"

"No..." Aster frowned in silence. The crew all looked at Aster and he turned red.

Chert sighed. He finally could get a word in. "Chert found something." He pulled out the onyx chalice and placed it in the center of the table. "It's magic."

Aster jumped at the change of subject. "What do you mean, Chert? What does it do?"

"You become spirit by drinking," Chert answered, moving his hand to his mouth as if taking a sip of something.

"But it can't hold water. How can you drink from it?"

"Try." Chert moved the chalice towards Aster, who picked it up in his hands and examined it. "Drink," Chert said, gesturing to his lips once more.

Aster brought it to his mouth. As his lips touched the rim of the chalice, the world went black. Chert reached his arm out and steadied Aster's body as it went limp.

Kara gasped as the chalice crashed down onto the table, out of Aster's grip.

When Aster came to, he was floating a few feet above the table. The bustle of the inn was replaced with a distant hum. The discomfort in his leg had disappeared altogether. Nobody else seemed to notice his new position; they were more concerned with something below.

"Chert, is it some sort of levitation device? This is amazing!" Aster floated up to the ceiling and grabbed the chandelier. He was taken aback that it didn't move at his touch.

His attention quickly shifted, and he glided back towards the floor. "I bet I could get a great view of the city from outside!" He edged towards the door. Moving turned out to be more difficult than he expected. He had to push off of the table, but only made it halfway before slowing to a stop.

"I feel as if I'm back in Buckwheat Lake, swimming in the mountain water." He forced his hands outwards, kicking his feet. It was helping. He slowly made his way to the door, swimming through the air. However, when he pushed on its wooden planks, it didn't budge. "Oh well, I can always look outside later. Chert, you must tell me more about—" His jaw dropped. At the table, his body was still in Chert's arms.

Aster panicked. He swam over to his body and pushed against it to no avail. He grabbed at Chert, dove into his own body headfirst, and slammed his fist into the chalice. Nothing he did helped. And oddest of all, none of the crew was responding.

"Am.... am I dead?" Aster nerves began to get the better of him—his breathing quickened and the room spun. He closed his eyes to try and get himself to calm down.

A deep, gravelly voice replied, "No, you aren't dead. Though some consider this place to be worse than death."

Aster's eyes shot open and he searched, tracing the sound back to the table next to his—one that had been empty moments before. The owner of the voice was unlike anyone he had seen before. Closer to a cockatrice than a Benian, green scales covered its body, and a pointed chin punctuated its elongated snout. Two broad wings were folded on its back above a thick tail that flicked back and forth beside the chair. It wore a white robe that nearly touched the floor.

"You do understand me, right? It has been a long time since I've used this tongue," the beast asked. A set of pearly white fangs flashed as he spoke.

Aster froze, staring at the creature.

"The noble heron waits patiently for the fish to pass by. So too must I be patient for this opportunity."

Why does it look familiar? Aster rubbed his temple. "Yes, I understand. Who are you and what is this place?"

The creature's face twisted into a smile, if that was even possible with its pointed snout. "That is most excellent. My name is Quell'est, and we are currently in a plane of existence that I call the Null Realm."

That answer only generated more questions in Aster's head. He stumbled across his words as he asked everything that came to mind. "What are you? How did you get here? Why am I here? Why can't I seem to push anything? Why can't the others see me?"

"Many questions, all good ones. I will try and answer as many as I can. However, I don't know everything. And the best questions have no answer."

Aster remained silent, watching, so Quell'est continued. "I am of the Drakōn bloodline. We were an advanced society, though we have long since been removed from this world. Our homes contained mechanisms far beyond the simple tools you use today. We had harnessed the power of lightning. We fought the pull of the ground. There was nothing that we couldn't master. Even the secrets of the Odyllic Stone."

Aster perked up. "You know of the Odyllic Stone? Do you think it's capable of curing my village of quicksilver poisoning?"

"Quicksilver? Yes, that should be well within its power. But be aware that the stone isn't what you may think—"

Before Aster could respond, the world went black.

He opened his eyes and found himself back in the chair at the table, Chert's bulky arm keeping him upright. His head throbbed, scattering his thoughts.

"You good?" Chert asked as Aster looked at the spot Quell'est had been sitting. The table was empty; there was no sign the creature had ever been there.

"Yeah, for the most part. I've got a bad headache though." Aster said before recounting the full details of his experience to the group.

When he was done, Kara said, "Well it sounds like you've got confirmation of the stone's power. That's good."

Peter cut in. "Somethin' about that creature unnerves me. It ain't natural. What could it possibly be doin' there anyways?"

Aster replied, "I don't know. He didn't tell me before I came back. But the feeling of that place frightens me."

Chert had been frowning quietly. "But nothing about Chert's father?"

Aster patted his back and said, "No, Quell'est didn't mention him, but he seemed to know a bit about everything."

Chert grunted in disappointment.

"Why don't we just use it again?" Kara asked. "It's pretty quick."

"I don't think I could manage," Aster rubbed his temple.

Chert shook his head as well. The others scooted their chairs back slightly.

Kara laughed. "I guess there's no rush. Especially if it's that unpleasant."

Aster replied, "Yeah. I think a good night's sleep is all I need."

The crew chatted about their theories of magic and the creature until nobody had anything new to say. Then the conversation turned to talk of lighter things until it had gotten late. Each headed off to their rooms with smiles on their faces, knowing that they would have plenty more time to study the chalice the next day.

Aster was distracted. Twice during sparring he failed to move out of the way of Josselyn's blows. He kept replaying the events of last night over and over in his mind. *Quell'est was frightening, but there was more that I could learn from him. I could manage again so—*thwack. Aster doubled over in pain as the wooden sword smacked his chest.

"Not again." Josselyn stepped closer shaking her head "You don't seem to be taking our lessons seriously today."

"I know. I'm sorry." He rubbed the sore spot on his chest with his knuckles.

"Let's take a quick break. But after that, I need your focus."

"Sure."

Josselyn marched over to Peter and Tristram who were training nearby.

Aster found a shady spot under a nearby tree. He rested his head on the weathered trunk, slipping right back into his thoughts. *Quell'est named the Odyllic Stone unprovoked. He said that his people knew of its secrets. But how is that possible? Fletcher said that the stone had been missing since King Charles' reign ended. Did he lie about that, too? No, that doesn't make sense. The tomb we found was ancient. Also, Calantha had said the same thing. What are the Drakōn? He had said that they were removed from our world... which makes sense since Calantha had never heard of them.* Aster recognized the creature, but he couldn't put his finger on why.

"Let's continue," Josselyn commanded, helping Aster off the ground.

If I only have a few minutes in the Null Realm, then I'd better sort out my questions before I use the chalice again. He had no intention of staying there for very long. *I need to focus.* Aster picked the training sword up off the ground and thrust it at Josselyn, who deftly deflected the blow.

"For now, I won't attack back. Try to strike me anywhere."

He nodded and continued his attacks. He swung at her left side. Blocked. He swung at her head. Deflected. He thrust at her chest. Parried. He stepped back before rushing forward, feinting an overarm strike before sweeping her feet. Thankfully, the pain in his leg was mostly gone, so he could focus on the fight. She gracefully hopped over his wooden blade.

"Ugh. Why is this so hard?" Aster griped after missing for the fourth time.

"Well, that's simple," Josselyn chuckled. "Your eyes give your intentions away. On that last one, you were staring at my feet after you stepped back."

Aster grumbled to himself and raised his sword again. He took a few more swings which were avoided, as usual. Then he stared at Josselyn's feet as he brought his blade down from above.

She already had her sword held above her head to block it. "Better," she remarked. "Keep it up and once you get a bit faster you might actually touch me."

Aster kept at it for another hour. Josselyn had a couple

of close calls, but in the end she stopped every attack. Aster was both frustrated and exhausted. *One more try, then I'll need another break*, he thought to himself, considering the best way to fool the veteran fighter in front of him. He attacked her head, then chest, then thigh. She blocked them all, so Aster pulled his arm back to thrust it into her stomach, then he stopped.

Kara had walked into view wearing a dark blue ball gown. It had a low neckline and ruffles at its base.

Aster had never seen anything like it. *It's beautiful. Kara is beautiful in it.*

Josselyn turned around to see what Aster was looking at.

Seeing his chance, Aster finished his thrust and poked Josselyn in the side.

"Well done. With your jaw on the ground like that, I didn't expect you'd have the presence of mind to finish the job," Josselyn said as Kara approached, holding the hem off of the ground.

"Wow Kara, you look like a princess," Aster muttered, just loud enough for her to hear.

"No, you look like an idiot." Peter corrected, as he and Tristram joined them. "What are you doin' in that poofy waste of coin?"

"As a matter of fact, I think it's nice." Kara smoothed the fabric of her dress. "Federyc is letting me wear it during our discussions. He says I need to learn to be comfortable in something other than a tunic and pants— for disguise reasons. Not sure I believe him, but since I've always wanted to try one of these on, I couldn't miss my chance." She grinned as Peter scowled.

"As long as you aren't plannin' on bringing it on the Blue Skies. Though it would be funny to see you stumblin' around the ship with it on."

"Very funny, Peter. Surely Federyc wants it back before we leave."

"At the rate you're goin' at it, I'm wonderin' if he'll even let you leave. He seems to like you too much."

"I don't think I'll be staying here. Aster would be heartbroken." She winked playfully at him, causing him to turn away in embarrassment. "Besides, he isn't really my type. I'd consider it if he was still king."

Peter joined her in laughing at her own joke. After a bit more banter, Kara left them and headed back to the house and everyone got back to their training.

The day had arrived. Aster met Josselyn at the forest's edge just as the sun peeked over the lake. She handed him a sheathed metal blade, which he strapped to his waist. He rarely got to use the real sword during training.

Aster stretched his legs and bounced up and down, testing the limits of his barely-healed bone. It still ached when he put too much weight on it. He would have to be careful not to trip or land on it wrong. He couldn't afford to injure it again.

"Well, go on now." She pointed to the trees. "Hesitation has no place in combat. You've got to put it all aside and focus on the task at hand." Aster nodded and stepped forward into the shadows.

This place frightened him. It was nothing like the forests back home. The trees here were much larger and the air was thick, so full of moisture that Aster had difficulty breathing. Not only that, but the darkness here was daunting. The sun was high in the sky and yet the light didn't make it past the canopy leaves. It hadn't bothered him as much before, when he was with Kara and the others on the way to the Boscage School. But now that he was alone, everything seemed more dangerous.

Josselyn insisted on staying far enough behind that he couldn't see her. Her presence was comforting, but the task was his alone.

Aster trudged down the path until he could no longer see through the undergrowth. The ground was littered with mossy stones and fallen logs, covered in mushrooms. It was the time of year where the leaves were starting to fall off the trees. Bright yellows and reds floated down around him.

The sword strapped to Aster's belt made his gait irregular; he wasn't used to walking with a weapon. As he slowly pushed forward, creatures darted just outside his field of view. Occasionally there was rustling ahead of his path, but he never saw the source. There were birds somewhere high up above that called back and forth.

Josselyn said that he had to follow this path until he reached the ravine. She insisted that he would know when he had found the place. *How could I know a place I've never seen?* Afraid he'd miss it, he stopped at every stream and valley to examine it for the lovine den. Aside from a colony of harvest-men spiders he didn't see anything, so he moved further along the unkempt path.

He heard its cry before he saw the beast; a deep howl that silenced the other noises of the forest. Aster brushed aside the leaves of an oak sapling that had sprouted in the path, finally laying his eyes on the ravine.

On the ridge, opposite from Aster, was his quarry. Dark green vines wrapped around its torso and head, leaving holes for its glowing yellow eyes and a pointed snout. Its tail was likewise barely visible under the vegetation. As Aster approached the ravine, the beast looked up at him briefly before continuing on with its business. He was too far away to be a threat.

Aster scanned the area, searching for a way to the other side. The beast crouched down, disappearing briefly before returning to view. Around its paws pale white leaves littered the ground. *That must be its den,* Aster thought to himself as he maneuvered around the gap. Twice he stumbled, giving him an unwelcome view of the bottom of the ravine. It was too far down to scale and the mossy rocks looked slippery even at a distance. *I hope there's a bridge nearby.*

Time passed and Aster was no closer to finding a way across. Could he jump? No, his leg wouldn't allow it. If he landed wrong, he'd need even longer before it was fully healed. The gap was wide and he didn't want to think about missing the jump. Not wanting to forget where the creature was, Aster turned around. *Conflag, have mercy, I've got to go back.* Perhaps there was an easier path in the other direction.

When he made it back to the den, the lovine was gone. He was sure that this was the right place because of the patch of white surrounding a hole in the ground. *Oh, feathers! That's what's scattered about.* He grabbed the trunk of a young tree and leaned as far as he could to get a look to confirm his suspicions. *Joss did say that there had been chickens missing.*

Sure enough, they were feathers, not leaves. But there was something else as well. Rustling around the opening, two pups were playing. Tiny vine sprouts poked through their beige fur. They couldn't have been more than a month old, if they were anything like the puppies from Buckwheat.

His heart dropped as guilt interrupted his thoughts. *This intelligent creature is stealing chickens to feed its children. Why am I here to kill it, anyways? The villagers in Tembour have plenty of livestock and surely would make do without a hen or two.*

Besides, I'm only here to prove that I can defend myself with a sword. But that's already clear—I came to Tembour never having picked one up, and after more than a month of daily training, I can beat Tristram more often than not. And I'm able to keep Peter at bay for nearly ten minutes before he could land a single blow. That's evidence enough. He took a final look at the lovine den and then turned back to find the trail out of the forest.

Aster had just stepped back onto the trail when he saw Josselyn glowering as she leaned against a knotted trunk. He avoided her gaze, hoping that she hadn't followed him too closely. He didn't want to lie to her, but he didn't know what to say either.

As he walked past, Josselyn broke his silence. "You

didn't do it, did you?"

"No." Aster looked down at his feet.

Josselyn sneered at him. "Judging by your lack of sweat, blood, or dirt, I'd say that you didn't even try."

"No, I decided against it," Aster said, falling behind her stride.

"You shouldn't show sympathy for these monsters." Josselyn unsheathed her sword and swung it in front of herself. "You are probably too young to remember, but the lovine used to be a fearsome threat to Benian society. There were rumors that they would kill adult villagers who wandered alone at dusk."

"I can't say that I'd ever heard of them. Maybe Rowan Goodwin has seen one before."

"They're less common now. During the monarchy, we were ordered to hunt them down. I'm surprised there are any left."

"I just don't see the point in hurting it. I shouldn't have come into the forest in the first place. This is none of my business."

She drove the sword into the dirt path, stopping him in his tracks. "Aster you should give up on the Odyllic Stone."

Aster's mouth fell open. "Why? What makes you say that all of a sudden?"

"You lack resolve and you lack discipline. You are too inexperienced for the quest that you are on. It will lead you to nothing besides your own death. I recommend that you take Kara and disappear. I've seen the way you look at her and you'd be better off holding onto what you've already got. Fantasies of magical stones are best left to storybook heroes. A genuine and sympathetic leader is worth more than any trinket. And you've already found that."

"No. Everything that I care about is in Buckwheat. I need the stone to turn it back into a place that is safe for everyone."

"You don't know that for certain. Aster, listen. I've

wasted many years of my life on a fruitless mission only to find out that I was wrong about what actually happened. Thank the Divine Conflagration that I've gotten a second chance to protect Federyc. I'm going to use this time to its fullest. I recommend that you do, too. Perhaps instead of spending all of this time plodding across the country, you should be at home with your friends and family?"

"I already know what I need to do: Find Fletcher and take back the Odyllic Stone. I'll use it to cure my village and put things back in order. After that, I'll have plenty of time to be with them."

The familiar glint of light poked through the trees. They had made it back to the forest's edge.

"If you say so," Josselyn muttered under her breath as she stepped into the sunlight.

They had only taken a dozen steps when Kara approached them, out of breath. "Here you are! We need you both to come back to Federyc's house now. The messenger has returned, and he has some dreadful news. Hurry."

Kara led them back to the house where they found everyone gathered around the table. The servant looked exhausted, hands shaking as he held a cup of tea. She hadn't seen him since their first meeting in this room.

"Well, we're all here now. Get to it then," Peter said gruffly, pointing to the servant. He looked more irritated than usual.

"Calm down Peter, he gave me the full report before you arrived," Federyc urged. "I'll tell you what has happened."

"I don't like the sound of this," Kara muttered under her breath as she sat. *Federyc has been almost carefree since we got here, but now he looks shaken.*

Josselyn remained standing beside Federyc's ornate

chair.

"I suppose I should start with the most mundane item. Aster," he tilted his head toward the young man, "When we met, you were haranguing us about a man named Fletcher. Might you tell us his full name?"

"Fletcher Abberton."

"Yes, I expected it was the same man. Fletcher has been knighted by the Benian Council."

Josselyn's rigid stance broke as she gasped at Federyc's words.

"Good for him," Aster said sarcastically.

Federyc added, "It's unusual. He's the first person to be knighted since the Council was created. We had thought, perhaps, that they wished to do away with that particular distinction, but it appears that this is not the case."

Josselyn rocked back and forth waiting for Federyc to finish, before adding, "I can't believe those scoundrels did it. They swore up and down that no man was to be above another in this age and therefore titles were no longer needed. They stripped all of the knights of their names, save my own, and that was only because I was part of their beloved Council. Why would they go back on their word?"

"Fletcher offered them something nobody else could. The Odyllic Stone. And now he's getting what he wanted," Aster answered, flatly.

"He certainly did. I'm sure that kind of news will make it all the way to Jash. In any case, that leads me to my second piece of news," Federyc said, reining in the conversation again. "The Council is now in possession of the Odyllic Stone. Our contact has located it inside the vault at the base of the clock tower. Which, unfortunately, is the best-guarded spot in all of Benia."

"Peter and I have been inside at least four times," Kara said. "We would help unload the gold shipments inside the vault. It shouldn't be too hard to break in there and get it back."

Federyc shook his head. "I do not think it will be as easy as you expect. They have placed additional soldiers to guard the entrance and have stopped allowing the Trading Company members to drop off their valuables inside. Instead, Shaheed Iman personally oversees every deposit. And I am sure that he will be watching for you."

"We'll find a way to get it back." Aster stood, clutching the sword at his waist. "It doesn't matter if they've got guards. At least we know where it is."

"Sit down, Aster, and listen until I am finished." Federyc put his hand out and lowered it, directing Aster back into his chair. "Third, and most concerning of all, we have learned that in a few days, Benia will be declaring war."

"War? On who?" Peter grumbled and scratched his beard. "El'tonne has a few spices that are worth a fortune. They've got the red sand too, but that's still outlawed in Benia. Or is it Jash? They don't have many resources worth tradin' for, but they've been a thorn in our side for decades now."

"They plan to declare war on everyone," Federyc said with uncharacteristic meekness.

"What do you mean everyone?" Peter shot back.

"El'tonne, Malvez, and Jash. They plan to take their lands, pillage their resources, and subjugate their people. Munayallpa too, but they were offered a special arrangement. Munayallpa has been granted statehood under the condition that they forsake their goddess and donate their entire treasury to Benia. I do not understand the ramifications of this offer, but I suppose it has something to do with Shaheed's position on the Council. He was from Munayallpa before he emigrated here."

The room fell silent.

After several minutes, Peter grumbled, "You sure? It's suicide to anger the whole continent at once."

"I'm sure. And I think it has something to do with the Odyllic Stone. I don't know how, but they must think they can use its full potential. There is no other explanation for this rash behavior." Federyc sighed as he massaged his temple. "But these politics are no longer my responsibility. We should focus on the one thing we may actually be able to control. Now that we have the location of the stone, I believe you should steal it back. That may end up being beneficial to all of Arathanon."

Kara jumped in. "I know the clock tower well. We can come up with a plan to get inside the vault."

"Forget the vault," Peter cried out. "We don't even have a way into the city. They know our names and our faces. Taking the Blue Skies there is suicide. I'm sure Fletcher told them everything."

"I do have a solution for that particular issue," Federyc interjected. "You can take my ship, Moonlight. It has been seen in New Portsmith before. No one would think twice about it docking there. You would need to leave your own vessel here, but I'll have it looked after."

"Sure, that may get us to the docks, but what do we do once we're there? Wear cloaks to cover our faces and pray we aren't questioned? And what about the vault itself? It'll be guarded for sure. And no chance we can get past that monster of a lock. This whole idea is foolish. I think we just need to give up and find another current to follow." Peter set his jaw and crossed his arms.

"What about Vincient? You think he'd help us out?" Kara asked, ignoring Peter's last statement.

Peter stroked his goatee as he considered her question. "It's a toss-up. He's always been kind to us, but he could lose everythin' if he gets on the wrong side of the Council. It's more likely he turns us in."

Tristram, who had been listening silently the whole time, stood, drawing everyone's attention. "I have an idea," he said. "But first, I need to make an apology to all of you."

"What are you talking about?" Kara asked. "You haven't done anything wrong."

Tristram's voice wavered, and he looked down, avoiding eye contact with the others. "But I have. It's my fault we're in this situation in the first place. I didn't know it would turn out this way. I'm sorry."

Peter eyed him suspiciously. "You ain't makin' any sense."

Tristram frowned at his feet. "I've been making extra coin on the side as Shaheed Iman's personal informant. He wanted simple stuff at first. Like a summary of our latest delivery or how many crates and barrels we had carried in the hull. The requests stepped up after the incident with the missing gold. I had to sneak into Whitlock's quarters and search for clues. And I did find the missing gold, mind you. Whitlock had it stashed in the bottom of a chest with his personal belongings.

"After Aster boarded the ship in Buckwheat Village, I was on high alert. Whitlock was being suspicious, but after the incident with the pirates, I realized that my job was much more important than I had thought. When we arrived in New Portsmith, I told Shaheed everything. He wasn't surprised and confirmed my belief that Whitlock was a traitor. We planned to catch him in the act and arrest him. But Whitlock acted first. Stranding us in that cave, forcing us to follow him to Strongfair.

"If that was all, I would've felt justified. But after we recovered the Blue Skies and retreated back to the capital, I reported everything that happened to Shaheed. His reaction wasn't what I expected. He said that for the good of the country, we had to find the rogue captain at all costs. And to do so, we needed to imprison Kara, his co-conspirator. I didn't understand how he made the connection between Kara and Whitlock, but I trusted his judgment more than my own at that point. I turned Kara in —giving the soldiers her location at the Beached Whale."

Kara gasped and covered her mouth. *He sold me out.*

"When Peter returned to the city and proposed a jailbreak, I was shocked at your response. I left you all, sad and conflicted. It happened too quickly, and I couldn't find Shaheed to warn him of your plans, so I decided to follow you into the castle ruins myself. But, in time, I changed my mind.

"Learning that they didn't charge Kara of collusion when they arrested her. The assassination attempt by Baxter. The story of King Federyc. And now this business with the Odyllic Stone. I'm still not certain what I believe, but I don't think that what we are trying to do here is wrong.

"All that to say, Shaheed Iman still thinks that I'm his informant. If I were to tell him that you had already stolen the stone, he would rush down to the vault and examine it himself. That would give us a window for Calantha to slip inside. I've seen her sneak past an entire crew of pirates, if we distracted the guards, she could be in and out without them noticing."

A dozen emotions cascaded through Kara's mind as she listened to his story. *Tristram had almost gotten me killed.* She couldn't decide if she was more angry or embarrassed. But either way, she didn't trust his plan.

Peter stepped towards Tristram, knife in hand. "You're a traitor. Since Loctee won't drown you, I'll cut your throat myself."

"Wait!" Kara raised her hand, stopping Peter in his tracks. *More than ever, this is my chance.* The title of captain had felt ceremonial up to this point. *My next few words will set the tone for who I am as a leader and whether or not we will succeed.*

It weighed on her soul. What felt like hours of silence went by as she fought with herself. *What to do about the stone, about Tristram, about the war? If only Peter had taken my place as captain. He always knows what to do, even though he hates the attention that comes with taking charge. And his choice is obvious...*

We've got to take action before this information becomes irrelevant. Who knows what'll happen once the fighting starts.

"I've made up my mind," Kara said, summoning all of the authority she could in her voice. "First, we will forgive Tristram. To me, it seems he was unaware of what the results of his actions would be. I cannot say he was wrong to report our actions to Shaheed, nor blame him for my imprisonment. It would've most likely ended up that way regardless."

Peter grumbled under his breath, but sheathed his blade and sat back down.

"Second, we will help Aster take back the Odyllic Stone. Although it's a foolish journey, it's Aster's best chance to save his village. Just like how you all risked your lives to save me, we shall do our best to help him. I cannot think of a better plan than the one we have put together today, and since we don't have the luxury of waiting, that's how we'll go about it. We leave in the morning."

Aster smiled and clapped his hands together.

"Finally, all of this nonsense about kings and wars. That has nothing to do with us. Perhaps it's even a blessing in disguise. A country at war doesn't have time to be searching for an escaped prisoner. Especially one that has done no harm to Benia. Once we have saved Buckwheat, then we can decide where the Blue Skies will go from there. But that's a decision for another sea."

"Thank you." Tristram was on the verge of tears.

Aster nodded then side-eyed Tristram.

Peter didn't look pleased. "If that's your order..."

"Wise choices, Captain," Federyc said, uncrossing his legs to stand up. He held out his hand to Kara. "I wish you all the best of luck."

"Thank you for everything, Federyc," she replied, grasping his hand in her own.

Everyone said their goodbyes and left the former king's house. Josselyn joined them to hand over Moonlight and help prepare.

Kara's head was still swimming. She was exhausted, but she couldn't rest yet. *I need to visit Janna one more time before we leave Tembour.* With a brief explanation and a wave, she split from the rest and headed towards the forest and the Boscage School. *I'd better hurry, there's not much light left in the day*, she thought to herself as she picked up her pace.

She found Janna in the clearing at the center of the school. She was sitting cross-legged in a patch of grass under the evening sun with a book in hand. Kara settled beside her, drawing her attention away from reading. "Oh, hello Kara," she said, closing the book.

"Hey Janna, I wanted to see you one more time before we left. We are sailing back to New Portsmith in the morning."

"I'm honestly surprised that you stayed in Tembour as long as you did. You never really liked to be in one place for long."

"Me too. And I'm not sure when... or if I'll be back," Kara confessed.

"Are you doing something dangerous again?" Janna placed the book down, giving Kara her full attention.

"Yes."

"We'll then, I'll pray to Viridus for your safe return."

"Viridus? Really?" After what their family had been through, she was shocked at her sister's words. Her mother's words were forever etched into her brain, 'Gods have no place on a farm.'

"What if we were wrong? I'm following the grassy path in hopes to understand. That aside, does this dangerous stuff have anything to do with Aster?"

Kara was hurt by her sister's choice. Viridus betrayed their entire family and now Janna was trying to make amends. She had been young, but did she still remember? "Yeah, we are trying to save his village. It's a long story and I can't really tell you the details, but there isn't a better way."

"Why are you going so far to help him?" Janna asked. "Do you love him?"

"I... I don't know."

Janna laughed and shook her head. "I was just teasing. I thought you liked girls?"

Kara scowled. "Am I not allowed to like both? Look I

don't really have this figured out myself. He reminds me of a simpler life, like we had at home. Other times, he just frustrates me. But none of that matters. I'm helping him because he's my friend and he needs it."

"If you say so. Just make up your mind before I see you next," Janna said with a devious smirk. "Once I'm on my independent project and can travel around, he's mine if you don't take the initiative."

"You're a brat. Did you know that?" Kara shot back.

"Just a bit of sisterly love to help you make up your mind. But, seriously: Do be safe."

"I love you too, Janna. And don't forget to stop home before you go out adventuring. Mom and the others miss you."

"I will."

Kara hugged Janna earnestly before walking away under the darkening sky. As she crossed the forest into the open field, she quickened her pace.

Morning came as the crew was finishing off breakfast in the Parched Root. Aster savored the Tembourian game hen he was eating. *An unusual choice, but given the paltry meals that we eat at sea, I've got to make this breakfast count.* He sighed. *Especially since Pat is no longer with us.* A tap on the shoulder pulled Aster away from his melancholy.

A man, only a few years older than Aster stood behind him, trying to get his attention. "Are you Aster Rutherford?"

Cautiously, Aster replied, "I might be. Why do you ask?"

The man smiled in a disarming way and ruffled through his bag, pulling out a letter. "I'm glad I found you. Been looking for days, almost gave up. This is for you from a young lady named Zinnia Hollyhock." He handed Aster the letter before leaving the room.

How'd he find me? I guess we've been here for some time. Before he could open it, Kara gathered the crew and directed them out to the harbor. It was time to leave. He tucked the parchment into his bag for later.

The vessel called Moonlight was jet black with bright yellow sails. It had a very different feel than the Blue Skies. This ship was built for luxury, not cargo. There were ornate chairs, exotic rugs, and silver utensils.

Kara was shocked to find out that Federyc had arranged for his own crew to sail them to New Portsmith, leaving her without anything to do. She paced back and forth across a golden carpet below deck as they set off.

This is for the best, Aster thought. *We need this time to figure out how to take back the Odyllic Stone*. His mind drifted to Zinnia's letter, which he pulled out to read.

Aster Rutherford,

Lavender Goodwin passed a few nights ago. She had another episode that was too much for her body to handle. Rowan was furious, screaming at the doctor for hours. I think Malvin convinced him that there was nothing more that could be done, because he packed his bags and left after the funeral this morning. Gilroy said he was heading to Jash for vengeance.

I'm tired of feeling helpless and scared, so I finally did it. I left the village. I paid for passage on a fishing ship that was heading to the ocean. They are friendly, but one of them keeps telling me that my "eyes are beautiful, like small brown potatoes". It's making me uncomfortable. I'm anxious to arrive in New Portsmith and get away from these people.

My destination is Strongfair. I decided to visit your mother. As a priestess of Ochress, she must have some advice for our quicksilver problems.

The thought of leaving Benia frightens me, but I'm pushing forward. When I'm feeling overwhelmed, I read your letters and think of your courage.

I hope you are still in Tembour to receive this letter. If you end up in Munayallpa, come find me.

Your friend,
Zinnia

10 ZINNIA'S COURAGE

The sky here is too large, Zinnia thought to herself as she stepped onto the worn dock. On the fishing ship she could hide below deck, but now that she was on dry land she could see for miles. If not for the mountains to the east, she would've believed that Munayallpa was completely flat. She chewed her lip as the familiar feeling of dread crept into the corners of her mind.

"I should never have left Buckwheat," she whispered to herself as she forced her legs to move forward.

It's too late to go back, anyway. The fishing ship is gone, thankfully. Those men were immoral. If not for their captain, I probably wouldn't have made it here in one piece.

The trip cost her the only wealth she had ever known —the single gold coin from Fletcher. She flinched at the reminder of the Pelware Mines. The leathery wings of the cockatrice invaded her thoughts, filling her mind with a searing fear.

She clutched her arms. "Not here."

Her eyes darted around, looking for where she needed to go. For a dark corner to hide in. *No, I need to find Beryl.*

She crept forward between the earthen buildings,

toward the center of the city. *What would Aster do? Probably find somebody who looked honest and ask them for help.*

After what felt like a lifetime, she had made it to a stone water fountain, where she stopped to collect herself. The open air, the crowds, and the newness had attacked her senses leaving her exhausted.

She sat by the water's edge. The stone was hot from the afternoon sun. *What had Aster told me about his mom? She's a craftsman of some sort.* Zinnia had been so focused on getting to Strongfair that she hadn't given any thought to how difficult it would be to find someone in a foreign city.

Just beyond the fountain there were rows of stalls where merchants displayed sculptures, pottery, and other handcrafted trinkets.

She hopped off of the fountain. *I just need to ask someone,* she thought as she walked to the nearest stall. There was a vase there with a vibrant lapis lazuli flower painted onto the side.

Zinnia looked at the elderly Munayallpan merchant. "Hello. Do you know where I can find a woman named Beryl?"

The man peered at her but said nothing.

Zinnia asked again. "Beryl Rutherford. Do you know where I can find her?"

He still didn't speak, so she left, walking further down the pathway between the stalls looking for somebody more sociable.

She stopped to admire a set of tiles painted with lizards basking in the sun. *If only I had more coin. Dad would have loved an exotic item like this in his shop.* Out of the corner of her eye she saw the man from the first booth hobble towards her.

She jumped and backed away from the wares. *Is he following me?* Chills rippled down her spine. *This is bad, he must know that I'm not from around here. I'd better lose him.*

Zinnia darted down the nearest side-street, but the man pursued, so she ducked into a building with a quarry sign out front. Closing the door behind her, she let out a big sigh. *There's no way he would follow me inside.*

"Yanapa." A deep voice addressed Zinnia from behind. "Can I help you?"

Zinnia jumped again. She bit her lip as she slowly turned to face the speaker. It was a young man with dark skin, nearly bald save for a tuft of light brown hair on the top of his head, like a lone patch of grass desperately clinging to sheer stone.

"N... no. I'm just looking," Zinnia muttered, trying to end the conversation before it began.

"Looking? This is a stone cutter's shop. You don't look like you need any stone cutting." He stared at her with one scraggly eyebrow raised.

She was caught in her own lie and couldn't come up with any excuse to be there. "No, I'm not looking for any stone... at least not one you sell," she confessed, trying to judge the integrity of the man in front of her.

"Well, my name's Jasper. And you're welcome to stay here as long as you need," he added before returning to work on some papers behind the counter.

Zinnia was relieved. Jasper seemed completely uninterested in her, which meant that he wasn't dangerous to be around. Even if it was just the two of them alone in the shop.

She stepped away from the door and pretended to be interested in the different samples of stone laid out on the tables. There was one with shiny flecks scattered among the grays and backs that caught her attention.

Zinnia's mind was back on the old man who had chased her. Dread bubbled up inside her, like a spring. *Did I run away too soon? Maybe he was following to give directions? Why would an old man was try to rob me?* Her stomach knotted in embarrassment. She wished to never run into him again.

After a few minutes inside the store, Zinnia had

calmed down. Bored by the stones on the tables, she began to think about what to do next. *I need to find Beryl. Perhaps Jasper would know something? I should've been more polite to him. Oh well. I need to start being friendly now. Hopefully he won't be too put-off.* She stepped closer to his counter.

"Hello Jasper. My name is Zinnia Hollyhock."

He looked up, patiently waiting for her to continue.

"I was hoping that you could help me find somebody. A woman named Beryl Rutherford. Do you happen to know where she could be?"

"Again?" Jasper scratched his head, just under the hairline. "Yes, I know."

"Oh, that's wonderful. Where can I find her?" Zinnia was thrilled to have found someone who knew her so quickly.

"But why do you look for Beryl?"

"It's a long story. To put simply, she's the mother of a friend of mine."

Jasper squinted for a second, then his face lit up. "You must be a friend of Aster Rutherford! Have you met my brother Chert?"

"I didn't realize he had a brother! He didn't say much about himself." Zinnia smiled. She was thankful for the connection in this foreign land. Even though she had not spent much time with Chert, she had found him to be a kind man and expected Jasper to be as well.

Jasper laughed, grabbing his belly as it poked out of his tunic. "That sounds like Chert. Munayallpans are known for being brief when speaking. Chert more than most."

"So you'll help me?" Zinnia asked.

"Yes, yes. Let me show you around Strongfair and the Artisan's Guild. Beryl will be there." Jasper scooped some papers into his hand and led Zinnia out the front door.

"Aren't you going to lock up? Wouldn't want anything to go missing."

"There's no theft here. Amasu is Ochress' second

tenet.”

“Amasu?”

“It means don’t steal. We use the tenets as a greeting in Munayallpa to remind ourselves of how to be moral in life.”

Zinnia clapped her hands together. “I wish we had something like that in Benia. Dad’s always diligent about locking our store. And constantly reminds me to ‘watch for sticky fingers’ from patrons.”

Jasper’s house was fairly close by. A modest sandstone hut with wooden beams holding the roof. What stood out to Zinnia was the intricately carved pattern crisscrossing around the windows and doors. None of the other houses she had seen were as well decorated.

Now that Zinnia’s adrenaline had run out, she was starting to look forward to sleeping in a warm bed again. *That's one thing I'll never understand: How Kara can be comfortable sleeping on a ship.* Zinnia had hated every minute of it.

Jasper noticed her drooping eyes and said, “You should stay here for the night; we’ve got a spare bedroom. We can visit Beryl in the morning.”

To Zinnia, this sounded better than trying to find an inn. Just the fact that Jasper was Chert’s brother made her trust him more than anyone else in town, except maybe Beryl herself.

As soon as Jasper showed her to the empty room, she laid on the bed and fell asleep, without bothering to take her shoes off.

Morning came and Zinnia rolled around in bed avoiding the sunlight peeking through the window. *I wish I was home in my own bed with dark curtains that block out the light, sleeping as late as I please. Why did I come here in the first place? What if Beryl can't help? What if she doesn't want to? After all, she had abandoned Aster.*

How am I even going to get home? I don't have a single coin left. She pulled the blanket over her face and fell back asleep.

Knocking woke her up again.

"Hello, Zinnia. It's the afternoon already. We should leave now," Jasper said from the other side of her door.

"I... I don't want to go anymore," Zinnia replied from under the sheets. She felt drained. *Is it really that late in the day? How could I feel so tired if I slept that long?* She wasn't ready to talk with Beryl. *Perhaps tomorrow.*

"I made you food."

Zinnia was on the verge of declining again when the smell reached her. The smoky, meaty scent made her stomach growl. *Perhaps I should get out of bed. I haven't eaten a decent meal since leaving Buckwheat, and nothing at all in Strongfair. It would be rude not to, anyways.*

"Alright, I'll be out in a minute," Zinnia called, hastily jumping out of bed to grab a fresh pair of pants and tunic. She joined Jasper at the table in the central room.

A younger woman joined them. She had short black hair that poked straight up out of her head. Her facial features were sharp, as if carved of stone.

"Yanapa Zinnia, this is my sister Sienna."

Zinnia froze. She wasn't expecting to meet someone new. Her father's etiquette training kicked in before the silence became awkward. "Hello Sienna. Nice to meet you." She paused again, not sure what to say next. All that came to mind was how pronounced Sienna's nose was. *Is that unkind to mention? I shouldn't.*

Jasper interrupted her thoughts. "Zinnia came here to talk with Beryl Rutherford. She is from the village in Benia that Chert went to help."

"Amasu," Sienna said before lifting her food above her head. "T'Och!" Then she brought it down and started eating.

Jasper laughed. "Don't mind her, she takes after Chert. Please have some." He handed her a bowl of thick red sauce. There were chucks of ground meat along with beans and several other things Zinnia couldn't identify. It smelled earthy and pungent and made her mouth water. She brought a spoon of the warm liquid to her mouth and tasted it. Her lips tingled as she swallowed. It was hotter than she expected, but delicious. She ate three more spoonfuls and instead of cooling down, the liquid seemed to heat up in her mouth. By the time she had scarfed it down, her nose was runny, and beads of sweat appeared on her brow.

"What kind of spiced soup did I just eat?" Zinnia asked after wiping her face.

"It is chili. The hotness comes from the picreete peppers. They grow all over Munayallpa. Have you never tasted one before?"

"No. Back in Buckwheat, we try not to eat anything that can make you cry," Zinnia replied, wryly. "But I did like it. Thanks for sharing your meal with me."

"You're welcome," Jasper replied, clearing her bowl.

"I was curious: You seem to have a great life here. Why did Chert leave all of this behind?" Zinnia asked, pointing to the house around her.

"Two reasons. Our mother became one with the earth when we were still young. Father was never home, always some place foreign. I think Chert is still looking for answers. But there's also part of him that yearns for the adventures he missed out on while he raised us."

Sienna nodded in agreement. "Chert having fun now."

"I suppose I would want to see the world too," said Zinnia.

Jasper looked at her confused. "Isn't that what you are doing right now?"

"I suppose I am... in a way," Zinnia mused. "What about you, Jasper? It's rude of me to ask so many questions about Chert when I don't know anything about you."

Jasper laughed. "Bonds we have are always easier than bonds we don't. I'm managing the family stone cutter's shop in Chert's absence. And I take care of Sienna."

His sister glared at him.

"Don't have time for much else. Before that I was a spear-man for the Munayallpan army," Jasper said as he cleared the table. "My service was completed last spring. You see, in Munayallpa each citizen is required to serve their country for two years in times of peace. More if there is war." Jasper frowned as he continued. "I hated combat training. Many of the others would rant about their chance to poke holes in people. To see them bleed out. Barbaric." He lifted his hands in front of his face. "These hands are for building, not destroying."

"But you're done now, right? You don't have to go back again," Zinnia added, trying to cheer him up.

"I hope so," Jasper replied. His frown lines betrayed his concern as he changed the subject. "We need to get moving now. The artisan's guildhall isn't too far from here, but we wouldn't want to miss Beryl."

Zinnia hesitated, but didn't want to seem ungrateful to her host, so she didn't object.

They waved goodbye to Sienna before Jasper led them down the earthen streets. He paused twice to say hello to passersby.

Each turn made caused Zinnia more and more anxious; she was enjoying their walk, but dreading what came next.

"Jasper, I wanted to know: Why was your father never home?" Zinnia asked as they passed by the market stalls.

"Our father, Slate, was an archaeologist. He used to travel all over the world looking for ruins of ancient civilizations and their artifacts. When he found something interesting, he would set camp there for months, scouring the area, trying to uncover all the secrets he could before somebody else did."

"What happened to him?"

Jasper shrugged. "After a particularly long expedition, he came home with an onyx-colored chalice. He claimed that it was the discovery of a lifetime and that he'd be the one to figure out its secret. But something happened when he showed it to his employer. He rushed back home, grabbed his camping equipment, and we never saw him again. People came to the house looking for him, but we didn't know where he had gone.

"I remember Chert shouting angrily, but I don't remember what he said. Whatever it was, they left us alone. After that, Chert changed. He was quieter and looked after us more. He also took an apprenticeship with one of the local stonemasons. Looking back, father must've told him something about what was going on. Not Sienna or me. We were too young."

Tears stung Zinnia's eyes as she listened. She had more respect for stoic Chert after hearing that. "It sounds like Chert is a wonderful brother." It was the only upbeat thing she could think to say.

"Yes, he is. We owe him so much. That's why I'm happy to look after his shop while he's away on his adventure. He deserves it," Jasper replied, smiling. "But enough of that. We're here now. This is the artisan's guildhall. Beryl has a room in the back."

Zinnia looked up and saw the flat roof of the building in front of her. It was the same worn sandstone as all the other buildings, but larger.

She stepped inside the door and into the trading floor. Merchants and artisans packed the room. In every direction there was a deal being made and coin being exchanged. The stalls beside the fountain were nothing compared to what was here. This was the true heart of Strongfair.

Jasper held Zinnia's arm as he pushed through the crowd. He nodded to a few people who shouted his name as he passed. Zinnia was overwhelmed by it all. She bit her lip, closed her eyes, and allowed herself to be dragged forward.

Jasper stopped. "We're here." His brawny arm pulled a beaded curtain aside, pulling Zinnia into a back room.

A woman sat cross-legged on her bed among half-finished jewelry scattered across the blanket. Zinnia cowered behind Jasper in the cramped space.

"Kapchi Jasper. Good to see you again," she said as they entered. "What can I help you with today?"

"Kanpas Beryl. I don't need anything myself. My friend here, Zinnia Hollyhock, was hoping to speak to you." He prodded Zinnia forward.

Zinnia stood silently next to the workbench, words suddenly out of reach. She could only think of how foolish she was. *A girl from a small village traveling to a foreign country, to ask questions of a person she's never met, about a mythical object she doesn't understand.* Zinnia shoved her hands into her pockets and took a deep breath to help calm her nerves.

Beryl smiled compassionately. "Zinnia Hollyhock. I feel like I've known you for many years now. Ever since Aster could write, he would gush about you in his letters. From the bottom of my heart, I thank you for being such a good friend to my son. Why have you traveled such a long way to see me?"

Zinnia blushed at the kind words. "I... I was hoping that you could help us."

"What can I assist with?" Beryl asked, setting aside the jewelry and giving Zinnia her full attention.

Zinnia's thoughts were cluttered. "Buckwheat Village is sick."

"Yes, Aster mentioned that when he visited."

"And Dr. Malvin has told us it is caused by quicksilver poisoning."

"Hmmm. I see." Beryl's smile briefly dropped at the news.

"And I thought the Odyllic Stone could help cure them because it saved the miners."

Beryl furrowed her eyebrows. "Please continue."

"But Fletcher stole the stone. Aster and the others went after him."

"I see. And your question for me is?"

"Do you know about the Odyllic Stone?" Zinnia asked, feeling more confident as the conversation progressed.

"I know some of the legends, yes."

"Is it possible for the Odyllic Stone to cure Buckwheat Village?"

"In our stories, the stone birthed the four gods we worship to this day. And you're sure that you've discovered the real thing?" Beryl asked, folding her hands in her lap.

"I think so. It caused a field of flowers to bloom in the desert around us, it revived some miners that turned to stone, and Aster said that it caused a statue to come to life."

"Yes, those are miracles beyond anything I have witnessed before. If what you say is true, then I don't see why not. But you said that Aster and his friends are trying to get it back?"

"I was hoping there was another way. Do you know of anything? Aster told me that you are a priestess of the goddess of minerals. Quicksilver is one of those minerals, right?"

Beryl looked thoughtful for a minute and then said, "What you say is true, but I know of no remedies to help. I could guide you to find the answer yourself, but... first you must find your center." She glanced over to Jasper, one bushy eyebrow raised. "Alone. Everyone's path is different. I cannot take you there."

"I need to do something! That's why I'm here." Zinnia tried to keep desperation out of her voice.

"Though if you'd like, I can arrange for a ship to take you back home instead. The choice is yours."

Feeling optimistic and bold, Zinnia said, "As much as I'd like to, I can't go home yet. So, please help me find answers."

Beryl looked up at Jasper again. "If you don't mind, could you leave us for a moment?"

"Not at all," Jasper replied, bowing respectfully as he ducked under the curtain and out of the room.

"Zinnia, to the east of the city there is a mountain range. Atop the third peak, facing the ocean, there is a lone mesquite tree. Behind it there is a cave. I want you to meditate inside of it. Close your eyes and clear your mind of thoughts. Focus on your senses in the present. Don't analyze, just feel."

Zinnia bit her lip. "I don't know. What if I get lost?"

"I'll take you to the path that runs past that mountain. You only need to split off the path once you see the tree. Oh, but you'll need to be sure and avoid the boulder beetles. Do not linger under the rocky cliffs, or they'll crush you."

"Are there bears?" Zinnia asked, voice trembling.

Beryl looked her in the eyes. "Bears are the least of your worries. Find your center."

Eyes wide, Zinnia nodded.

"Meet me here tomorrow at sunrise." Beryl picked up the bracelet in her lap and began to examine it again. "Oh, and one more thing Zinnia. How is Hugo doing? Last I heard, he was bedridden."

"He isn't doing very well. Doctor Malvin says he's in the late stages of his illness. He... he won't last till spring."

Beryl frowned and her eyes glassed over. "That's too bad. I wish I was able to see him one more time."

The curtain moved aside and Jasper reentered. "You done in here?"

Beryl replied, "Yes. See you tomorrow, Zinnia." She kept her eyes down and focused on the jewelry in her hands.

Jasper led Zinnia back outside.

"Well," he said looking up at the sun, "We've got plenty of time left in the day. How about I show you around the city?"

"Sure," Zinnia replied absentmindedly. She was still hung up on the discussion with Beryl. *I was too careless talking about Hugo's condition. And I don't like the idea of this trek through the mountains. What if I came face-to-face with a boulder beetle? I might die on the spot.*

He took her past the market and down to the docks.

"I'm sure you've seen this already, but you probably don't know its importance," Jasper said, pointing to the water fountain that greeted travelers to the city. "The faces on it represent the citizens of Strongfair on the night they founded this city." Zinnia looked at the happy faces carved into the fountain's base.

"They say that our ancestors wandered the land for years before settling down here," Jasper added. "Finally, they found this spot, more importantly the fresh water under this well, and decided to establish a city. Even now, this fountain provides clean water to all of the citizens of Strongfair."

"It's a beautiful place," Zinnia remarked, glancing towards the mountain-filled skyline.

Jasper nodded, then led her over the sandstone path to the northernmost part of the city. At the end of the path, was a sizable dome. The shape and bright white color made it stand out from the houses in the area. "That's the mogul," Jasper said as they approached.

"What does that mean?" Zinnia asked, scratching her head through her short hair.

"How to explain?" Jasper paused a minute before saying, "The Mogul is the leader of Munayallpa. You can think of him as our king. His house is also called mogul and it is where all of the government business happens. There is also a special room inside. Come I'll show you." Jasper grabbed Zinnia's hand and beamed as he guided her closer.

Before they made it to the door at the base of the building, the air began to rumble. Zinnia stumbled, leaning her weight on Jasper as the ground swayed underneath her. A rhythmic rattling and swishing sound followed. To their right a crowd had formed around the source of the sounds.

"Ah good timing," Jasper exclaimed as he jerked Zinnia toward the crowd. "They are practicing for the festival." He pushed through the crowd until they could see a dozen people holding strange objects and dancing to the sound. At the very center, a man pounded at a drum with a long wooden stick with a ball at the end. The others held smaller drums and spheres that looked like they were covered in beaded fishnets. The beating of the drums gave a pleasant tune while the spheres rattled.

It's like the pattering of rain on exposed stone. "This is wonderful," she told Jasper as they listened to the performers finish. "When is your festival?"

He smiled. "Come." And he led her back to the mogul. There were two guards at the door, each holding a spear. As Jasper approached, he waved at them. "Kapchi."

"Kanpas," they replied, stepping aside to let him enter.

Zinnia saw many rooms to each side of them, but Jasper kept moving to the building's center. He pulled her into a cylindrical room decorated with four different types of stone on the floor and the walls. At the top were two triangular shaped cuts in the dome for sunbeams.

"This is our festival," Jasper said, pointing to a thin band of sapphire that separated one sheet of stone from the next. A beam of light was nearly touching it.

Jasper pointed up at the ceiling then back at the sapphire. "When the sun hits the sapphire, it is the winter equinox. That is time for the Karrath Festival to honor mother Ochress." He stepped to the other side of the room and gestured to a similar band of fire opal in the wall in the shadows. "That is for the summer equinox. Our festival on that day is where we make sacrifices to appease our god for the year ahead."

"Sacrifices?" Zinnia gulped, visions of dead Munayallpans souring her stomach.

Jasper let out a full-bellied laugh when he saw the look on her face. "We're not barbarians! Ochress receives our finest jewelry, pottery, and sculptures. Those are our sacrifices. In Munayallpa, we take the gifts from our god and give them back more beautiful than before."

Zinnia sighed, embarrassed at her own thoughts.

Jasper showed her more highlights of the city before it got dark. Then they headed back to Jasper's house. After a quick meal involving a yellow bread, Zinnia went to bed early, nervous about the task that lay ahead.

Morning came and Zinnia walked to the guild hall. Jasper had dropped her off to meet with the owner of the Pukyuwasi Inn, who would be potentially making a big purchase at his shop.

Beryl met Zinnia outside the guild hall. Between yawns, Beryl led her outside of the city and towards the mountains. Just as the ground started to slope upward, they stopped.

"Here's the path," Beryl gestured to a trail with compacted dirt and no vegetation. "You'll be fine," she added after noticing Zinnia fidgeting. "This area is mostly safe. Your trip across the Sea of Loctee was more dangerous than this will be."

"I... I don't know." Tears welled up in Zinnia's eyes. "I don't think I can do this. I never go alone. Not since mom..."

Beryl embraced Zinnia. "You have every right to be afraid. When I was your age, I was lost as well. Not in quite the same way, but I know how you feel." She let go and smiled as Zinnia wiped tears out of her eyes. "You're stronger than you think you are. Very few village girls have found courage to leave their homes and visit countries unknown."

"I've already come all this way. I can't give up now," Zinnia added, feeling a bit better. She took a deep breath and straightened her clothes before trudging forward.

"Remember: When you get to the cave, you must focus on your senses," Beryl called after her.

Zinnia waved her hand in the air without looking back. *I need to focus on putting one foot in front of the other for now, I'll worry about the cave later.*

The mountains reminded her of home, where she would go on walks with Aster near the Pelware Mines. There were fewer trees in Munayallpa, and none of them were evergreen like back home.

Zinnia pushed further, and as she passed the base of

the first mountain, the crisp sea breeze rippled her clothes. It was a welcome feeling. Strongfair itself was hot and humid. It was so different from the cool autumn weather of Buckwheat that she was perpetually uncomfortable. Almost like Munayallpa didn't have winter.

Beryl was right about it being easy to follow, she thought to herself as she passed the second peak. There was only one spot where Zinnia was uncertain which way to go, but after backtracking a few paces, she figured out that she had been tricked by a dry riverbed and quickly got back on track.

The environment changed after that: The greenery all but disappeared, replaced by loose rocks. She was now far up the mountain. Looking back, Zinnia could just make out a few Strongfair houses below, far off in the distance. *I must be close now. Perhaps I've been overthinking this whole thing.*

As she approached a dirt overhang, Zinnia trembled slightly. *Something's wrong.*

Then she saw it. There was a precariously placed boulder a bit farther up the slope from where she stood. It wouldn't have bothered her if she hadn't seen the spindly legs holding the stone back.

A boulder beetle? Zinnia's heart began to race. She could feel the blood pounding inside her ears. With every beat the beetle's form seemed larger and more terrifying. The spots on its shell darkened as if to threaten her.

She held her breath, praying for it to leave her be. Everything slowed down. She was an observer outside her body. Watching. Waiting. Even the rocks at her feet were changing shape with every heartbeat. *It's happening again.*

Memories of the cockatrice flooded back into her mind. The fleshy red comb on its head and the serpent-like tail menacing her from the past.

Memories of her mother's death resurfaced.

Back in Buckwheat Village, Rowan had given her a bit of chamomile to calm her nerves. It wouldn't help her now. *How do Aster and Kara manage these feelings? They jump into danger so easily.*

The beetle quivered again, snapping Zinnia's attention back to the present. This beast was not nearly as intimidating as a cockatrice. Under its dull gray carapace, Zinnia could see six legs. Two were propped up on the rock it was hiding behind and the other four were planted on the ground. Its round head almost pressed against the soil, its antenna waving back and forth in the breeze.

Zinnia stood there, frozen.

The beetle didn't move. It was waiting for something.

Zinnia took a deep breath. *Now's not the time to dwell on monsters. I need to find the cave that Beryl told me about. There's no turning back.*

She took a shaky step forward, then another. *Keep moving*, she thought to herself as she crossed underneath the monster.

With the next step, loose soil cascaded down upon her, dirtying her short brown hair. Her reflexes kicked in and Zinnia dove forward, scraping her arms on the jagged path.

The boulder crashed down, splintering as it hit the path where she had been standing moments before.

She looked up at the boulder beetle, which was peering over the edge, investigating her. Zinnia froze as she watched its antenna sway back and forth. *Searching for the scent of fresh blood?*

The beetle turned, as if sensing that its trap was unsuccessful, and crawled further up the mountain, examining another boulder on the way.

Zinnia was more angry than scared at this point. *Beryl had warned me about the beetle's behavior, so why did I let myself almost be crushed? I'm so stupid! I was too scared to think properly.* As she rubbed her scuffed up arms, a pale orange twinkle caught her eye.

Embedded into a fractured chunk of the boulder was a crystal, shining in the sunlight. Zinnia slid back down the path for a closer look. One side of the gem was crystal clear with an orange glow in the light. The rest of the stone was opaque and dirty. She tried to pull it loose from the surrounding rock. It shifted, but was still stuck inside. She grabbed another stone from nearby and slammed it against the boulder until it split, freeing the fist-sized gem.

Zinnia pocketed it; *a reminder to overcome my fears.* More soil sprinkled down from above. *I'd better keep moving before that beast returns.*

She brushed herself off as she stood and continued up the path.

A lone tree sat between the sharp cliffs; Zinnia spotted the place that Beryl had described to her. She struggled to navigate up the slope. Using the stones as grips, she climbed to the entrance of the cave. The view was beautiful from here: She could make out the sea's blue hue where it met the sky in the distance. Zinnia took a deep breath of crisp mountain air and then ducked into the cave entrance.

It was dark. Judging by the echoes of her footsteps, she was in a large chamber.

Zinnia bit her lip as she tried to remain calm during the agonizingly long time it took for her eyes to adjust to the darkness. Eventually, she was able to make out the outlines of the room and the glint of gemstones embedded in the walls.

The cavern was round with a drop at the very back that seemed to expand deep into the earth. *Better not get too close.*

She inched to the center of the chamber, settling cross-legged on the cool floor. She felt calmer now that she couldn't trip and fall over the edge.

Alright, I need to meditate here. What was it that Beryl had said? Clear my mind of thoughts, focus on the senses. Ha! Easier said than done. Zinnia closed her eyes and listened to the noises of the cave.

She felt a light breeze on her neck coming from the entrance. Her thoughts drifted to the boulder beetle from before. *It wasn't actually that frightening, was it? They move slowly and keep their distance. Nothing like a cockatrice, where just being near it could get a person killed. Are there other monsters like the cockatrice in the corners of the world?*

She smacked her thigh. *Stop it Zinnia, you're not supposed to be thinking right now.*

She took a breath and listened to a drip of water echo off the walls from somewhere deeper. Drip, drip, drip. *If there were other monsters, a hidden cave like this one is surely where they would live.*

A chill ran through her body and goosebumps sprouted on her arms and legs.

Zinnia snapped her head back and forth trying to hear for predatory movement. She opened one eye and glanced back toward the cave entrance, making sure she knew where it was in case she needed a quick escape.

Nothing changed, so she settled down again.

The ground vibrated ever so slightly, almost melodically in sync with the breeze. *I bet Kara isn't afraid of anything. She could probably sit in this cave alone for days. Kara has everything. She's strong and accomplished. I've never heard of a captain as young as she is. Beyond that, she's beautiful! It isn't fair. The way her auburn braid seems to glow in the sunlight.*

Zinnia ran her finger through her short brown hair. *Maybe I should grow it out and braid it too? No. My hair isn't the right shape for that. It's too flat to fill a braid as well as Kara's hair does. Ah, I did it again!* She squeezed her arms together. *I'm not supposed to be thinking about anything, just listening.*

She took a deep breath and held it. The dripping water echoed off the walls. *What type of monster would live in a cave like this? It must have three sets of ears and a huge nose. And would be covered in slime that would let it squeeze through tight passages. Slime that would sound like dripping water when it fell.* She let go of her breath with a shudder. *Stop it Zinnia!*

No, this would be the perfect bear den. Her eyes

flicked open, darting hopelessly against the blackness. *No, anything but that.* Her mind fixated on it despite her protests.

The bear materialized. The same bear that was always there, lurking in the corners of her mind. Dark brown and as big as a cow, it lumbered towards her. She was picking berries in the woods, like she always did. Something Dad always praised her for. "Good for canning," he would say when she returned with pockets full. *Danger.*

But mom was there, too. She waved from the next bush over. Her bucket was already halfway filled. Zinnia drooled at the thought of the blueberry jam they would make for the winter. Her mom was still waving, more frantic this time. The bear grazed a few bushes over. *Run.*

Her mom grabbed her hand and pulled her away. Zinnia reached for another handful of deep purple berries. *Fool.*

The brown bear had two cute cubs with it—their bellies fat. A good thing, with winter coming. Her mother screamed and pulled her so hard that she thought her arm would break. Tears poured down her mother's face as they ran, but the bear was faster. Zinnia tumbled to the ground and her mother threw herself on top. The bear huffed and growled as it dragged its rancid claws across them. *Too late...*

She came to in a pool of blood, her mother's body shredded above her. She crawled out, like she always did, and saw her mother's white spine poking out of the crimson gore. She wouldn't have even recognized her except for the tangled wisps of dark brown hair that they shared. *Your fault.*

She pinched her leg to clear her head. *Breathe, breathe, breathe.* Her heart raced, and tears streamed down her cheeks. *No, that was a decade ago. I've got to focus on the present. The people that are here today. For Aster. For Buckwheat.* She returned to the blackness once again.

Whoosh, the cave breeze passed her by again. Its

rhythm was distinct; there was a pattern to this place. She strained to focus on her senses. The cave was talking to her, trying to tell her something. The pattern meant something.

The breeze passed by in sets of three, with the third one almost a hiss. *Per... si... st.* Zinnia opened her eyes and looked around to see if anyone was there. Nothing but the breeze. She stood and for the first time since she entered the cave, spoke. "Persist? But I don't even know how. I can barely handle my own thoughts..." she trailed off meekly. It was probably all in her head. *Maybe I should take a break outside before trying to meditate again?*

When she stepped towards the entrance, she noticed it. The cave was silent now. No dripping, no breeze, and no rumbling. It was eerie how different she felt compared to moments ago. Her skin prickled and her hair stood on end. *Something's here.*

Zinnia's heart raced at the movement in her pocket. The gemstone that she found earlier was pulling on her pant leg. She looked down just as it popped out of her pocket and glided upward in the air in front of her. "Persist," the cave spoke, more clearly than before, and the gem glowed a brilliant orange light before gently floating down. Zinnia reached her hand out and the gem fell into it, no longer glowing.

This must be what Beryl wanted me to see. She stood still until her arms grew tired. *I don't really understand what happened. Maybe Beryl can explain?* She sat back down for a little while before deciding that there was nothing more for her.

She walked out of the cave into the sunlight. As her eyes adjusted to the dazzling midday sun she was again reminded of her visit to the Pelware Mines. She tightened her grip on the gemstone in her hand and pushed her anxiety aside. "I should get back to Strongfair," she said out loud. It helped to break the spell of fear as she maneuvered back down the slope.

Zinnia made it back to the guildhall before it got dark. The nights in Munayallpa were pleasant; the heat from the afternoon had soaked into the stones and radiate back to keep the chill of night at bay. *This time of year, Buckwheat would be finishing the final preparations for winter. In Munayallpa they barely seem concerned by the changing of the seasons.*

Zinnia found Beryl in the back room, where they had first met. "I did as you asked and meditated inside the cave." She went on to describe what happened.

"Very interesting. May I see the gemstone?" Beryl asked, holding out her cupped hands.

She placed the round, opaque stone into Beryl's calloused hands.

"With your permission, I'd like to examine and shape this." Beryl looked at Zinnia expectantly.

Zinnia nodded, to which Beryl sprung over to her work bench and started to tinker with the stone. Zinnia watched in awe as she pulled out tool after tool to examine, clean, and shape the gem.

"What is it? What happened to me in that cave?" Zinnia asked as Beryl worked.

"The stone appears to be a golden-brown hue of topaz. Somewhat common in these parts. Topaz is one of the hardest materials we know of. However, it's weak along the axial plane. This means that it has a tendency to break if it is hit or dropped from a specific direction. But this particular gem possesses an unnatural strength along all of its planes."

"I don't understand," Zinnia replied sheepishly.

"Here." Beryl grunted as she reached her hand into a bag that was sitting on the floor under her desk. She pulled out a similar looking yellow stone and placed it on the table. "This yellow topaz is the same material as yours." She grabbed a hammer and smacked the rock repeatedly. Slivers of gemstone fell away until there was nothing left of the original stone.

Zinnia's eyes were wide open at the destruction of the

gemstone.

"Don't worry. It was cloudy—not fit for Ochress. Now look at yours." She pulled Zinnia's stone closer and hit it in the same way. Pieces of gray rock and dirt flew off, but the gemstone itself remained intact. "I've never seen topaz behave this way before," Beryl concluded, turning back to face Zinnia.

"What does it mean?" Zinnia asked, trying her best to follow along with Beryl's logic. It was clear that Beryl had spent her life examining and shaping stones, but to Zinnia it was like a foreign language.

"I believe that Ochress has blessed your Topaz. Infused it with the strength to persist. She has chosen you to be her champion, Zinnia."

"Me? Why me? I'm nobody. An outsider. I don't... didn't believe in Ochress before coming to Munayallpa."

"I'm not entirely certain, but if what you said about the cave is true, then you are the first Benian to have heard Ochress' voice. For a moment, you touched the edge—the interface between the known and what cannot ever be discovered." Beryl's eyes were trained on her, deadly serious.

"Now I'm questioning if that's what I heard. It could've been my imagination..." Zinnia looked away, at her stone sitting on the workbench. She couldn't hold that steely gaze any longer.

"I have been meditating in that cave for nearly twenty years now and I have not once heard what you described. In fact, before Aster came here, I hadn't witnessed any changes in that cave. No response to my presence. Nothing." Beryl sighed and closed her eyes. "And now twice Ochress has responded and sent us a message. This is no coincidence. I... I would like some time to work and think. Zinnia, would you please come back tomorrow? I'll return your topaz then."

Ochress' champion. But why? I'm just here to help Aster... and Buckwheat. "Why me and not somebody important like you?"

Beryl placed her hammer gingerly beside the topaz. "Have you heard the story of Lithia, the first priestess?"

Zinnia shook her head.

"Well, many Munayallpans believe that she was special because of her heritage. But I think they've got it backwards. She was special for her ability to listen. The stories say that she put aside her desires, her preconceptions, her expectations, her plans, and even her fears until she was one with her surroundings, experiencing the present and nothing else. Only then was she able to hear Ochress' voice."

"If you know all this, then why can't you hear her too?"

Beryl let out a weak laugh. "Because I cannot let go of my regret. For what was and what could have been. And I cannot let go of my expectations. Expectations that would validate my choice to stay here…"

"What about Aster? He's the son of Ochress' priestess. He's half Munayallpan! He's twice as brave and much stronger than me."

Beryl placed a hand on Zinnia's arm. "Would you be able to truly listen to what stole your mother away from you?"

Zinnia's heart skipped a beat. *How'd she know about mom? No, she's speaking about Aster. It's true. Growing up, more than anything else, Aster talked about Beryl. And no matter our theory, whatever kept her from Buckwheat Village was pure evil.* "I see."

"But it seems you were able to put aside those things, if only for a moment, and truly listen. But enough about that. I'm sure you're hungry. Why don't you head back to the Penya house and have some dinner?" She wrapped an arm around Zinnia's back and guided her to the door of the guildhall. "Please come back tomorrow."

As Zinnia ambled through the earthy streets back to Jasper's house, her mind was awash with the emotions of the day. She had done something truly amazing today. For the first time since she left Buckwheat Village, she felt triumphant and excited. She had managed to push beyond her fears even when they seemed too much to bear. *Perhaps it isn't so hard after all*, Zinnia thought to herself as she pushed open the door to join the others for dinner.

As she entered the room, she saw Jasper slumped over the table, head in his hand. Sienna stood behind him, rubbing his back, gently.

"Is everything alright?" Zinnia asked.

Sienna replied, "No," as she continued to console Jasper.

"What happened?" Zinnia sat down and saw teardrops fall to the table from underneath Jasper's calloused hands. He blew his nose into his sleeve, wiped his eyes and looked at Zinnia with reddened eyes.

In a hoarse voice he said, "Peace is over. We going to war."

"I don't understand." Zinnia tried to piece together her thoughts. "Who would want to go to war with Munayallpa?"

Sienna glared at her. "Benia does."

"Benia has given Munayallpa unfair choice. If we renounce Ochress, we granted statehood in Benia. Otherwise, we considered an enemy of the state. They will send army to take our land." Jasper's voice deepened. "Some choice! Ochress the center of our lives. She the reason we build our houses out of stone. Munayallpans were created to worship her. Mogul never allow this. I won't allow this! Ancestors foolish to make peace with Benia. We should never have given them the golden bell." He stood and slammed his palm down on the table, causing Zinnia to jump.

Sienna smacked him on the head and scowled, motioning to Zinnia.

"You're right, sis. Before I must rejoin the army, I should take you back home, Zinnia. Munayallpa will no longer be a safe place for you."

"But what about Beryl?" Zinnia asked, voice quivering.

"I'll hear from the army any day now. We'd best leave as soon as we can. First thing tomorrow would be best. We can stop by Beryl's before we go." He moved to leave the room before stopping to say one more thing. "Excuse me, but I need to pack. Rest up. We will need to move quickly." Sienna let out a satisfied grunt before leaving Zinnia alone at the table.

Bags in hand, Zinnia and Jasper arrived at the guildhall just after sunrise. Most of the artisans were still sleeping. Only a handful had begun their work for the day.

Zinnia led the way to the curtain in the back to find Beryl slumped over, once again sitting cross-legged in bed. She snored lightly, fast asleep. Zinnia recognized the orange gem that had fallen out of Beryl's grip and lay beside her left foot. It was her topaz, already shaped and polished.

Zinnia didn't want to disturb Beryl, so she carefully stepped forward, avoiding a pile of tools on the floor, and picked up the gem.

It glittered even in the dim light of the room and now carried the shape of an arrowhead, though much larger than any Zinnia had seen before. She backed up as she examined it. *I'll have to be careful carrying this around now, it is rather sharp.* She gingerly fingered the edges then cupped the weight of it in her palm.

Beryl's left eye opened. "It took me all night to shape that. I tried to create a pendant for you, but the topaz had a mind of its own. As if that is the only shape that it could be. And who am I to question the will of Ochress?"

"Thank you," Zinnia replied, half expecting Beryl to nod off immediately. "I have to leave Munayallpa now. Jasper is taking me back to New Portsmith before the fighting begins."

"That is for the best. I wish you luck with your village," Beryl replied. "Oh, and take that letter off my desk. It arrived for you yesterday, from Aster." Zinnia grabbed it and stuffed it into her pocket.

Jasper motioned to the door. Beryl closed her eyes again.

Zinnia whispered, "Thank you for everything, Beryl," one more time before she left.

Without any breaks to catch their breath, Jasper and Zinnia passed through the northeastern gate of the city, the shortest path to New Portsmith. The ground outside was littered with tree stumps as far as she could see.

Jasper said, "Greenwood Forest is where the city gets all of its lumber. As you can tell, we've harvested all we can. There have been talks of replanting, but Mogul is opposed for some reason."

They followed the path as it slowly elevated until they had a view of the ocean on their left. Zinnia could see four boats sailing back and forth in the Bay of Strongfair. In front of them, trees with foliage, bark, and shade grew instead of stumps.

Once they had gone too far to see Strongfair, Jasper relaxed. He began to chat with Zinnia about Buckwheat Village, her family, and other things. "What was that gem that Beryl gave you?" He asked after a while.

Zinnia pulled it out of her pocket to show him. She had wrapped it in cloth to stop it from poking into her leg. "It's topaz. Beryl says it has been blessed by Ochress."

"Topaz? Munayallpans have a saying: A touch of topaz can transfer tranquility."

"Well, that's a nice thought. Though I don't see anything tranquil about a weapon." She said, holding the oversized arrowhead in the air.

"It almost reminds me of my spear tip." Jasper said as he pulled his spear from the strap around his chest. "Let me show you a few tricks with a spear. You could practice swinging it while we walk."

"I don't want that." Zinnia scowled.

Jasper lowered the base to the ground. "Few of us do, but knowing how to defend yourself is important.

Especially with Arathanon in the state it is.

I guess it couldn't hurt to try it out. She pictured Kara fighting pirates aboard the Blue Skies and smiled. *I could learn to be a warrior.* She held out a hand to Jasper.

As he handed Zinnia the spear, a man approached them. He stumbled repeatedly, picking himself back up before taking another dozen steps and falling again. His tanned leather shirt was speckled with blood.

Zinnia didn't recognize the man's clothes, which were adorned with tiny beads around the chest and arms. *He's not from around here.*

Jasper rushed over to help him remain steady. "Yanapa stranger, are you alright?" He asked, holding him up from underneath his arm.

The man was panting and drenched with sweat. His curled mustache was plastered with twigs and dirt.

"No," he said in a thick accent, catching his breath. "They are going to kill us all. Nobody will be able to stop them."

"Stop who?" Jasper asked.

Zinnia shivered. *There's terror in this man's voice. Whatever happened shook him to his core.*

"Benia."

"Benia?"

"Yes. Our army—five hundred of Malvez' best warriors, marched into Benia to squash the Council's latest aggression. We spotted them just at the outskirts of Tanalba Fields. We expected to find Benia's forces, but it was just a few dozen people. I was in the parley team. Emmeline Dolloway was there with a few soldiers. It was suicidal for her to be there, or so we thought. We couldn't be more wrong.

"She asked us to surrender to Benia. She said it was the best way to keep our lives. I laughed. It seemed so ridiculous that the entire nation of Malvez would be beaten by no more than thirty men.

"We declined and prepared to fight once again among the white flowers. Just as we began our charge, the ground below the troops on the left flank opened up, revealing a pool of molten rock. They all died instantly. I was part of the frontal assault. Living bones climbed out of the ground under our feet and began to tear at our horses and bite our men. Every time they were felled, they got back up and continued to fight. It was horrifying.

"Our only option was to retreat. But even that was meaningless. We hadn't made it far before a giant bird descended from the sky above us. The wind howled, pushing us backwards and lightning rained down with every flap of its wings. I was lucky. I tripped into a crevice, hiding me from the slaughter. I only wish to travel back to Malvez and report what happened. To warn the world of the terrible powers of Benia."

Zinnia Hollyhock,

I hope this letter finds you safe in Strongfair. I'm shocked and saddened to hear about Lavender. She was a kind girl and a good friend. We will cure Buckwheat in her memory.

I hope you find what you are looking for in Munayallpa. To be honest, I was so preoccupied with meeting my mother there and the thing with Whitlock that I don't think I saw much of the city.

I'm proud that you overcame your fears and left the village. It was something I wasn't sure that you could do.

We are on our way to New Portsmith to take back the stone. I think this is the most dangerous thing I will ever do. I'm confident in my skill with a sword, but I'm not sure that I want to use it. Stories of heroes always seem to leave out how much fighting weighs on your soul. They wanted me to kill a monster called a lovine, but when I came face to face with it, I couldn't do it. I cannot even imagine killing a person.

May the Divine Conflagration watch over us both.

Your friend,
Aster

11 BREACHING THE VAULT

Moonlight rocked back and forth on the waves as she inched closer to New Portsmith. The crew milled about inside, making final preparations for the days to come. A cold ocean breeze whistled through the boards of the ship; winter was fast approaching.

Aster pulled his blanket closer as he rested on a plush, regal looking chair. Calantha was writing intently at the dining table, notes scattered about. One by one, she picked up a page and transcribed a few lines of text.

The others were up on deck; Aster could hear them arguing, but not enough to make out what they were saying. His own thoughts were of simpler things: Gilroy's pleased grin as he let Aster sample his latest batch of honey, exploring the forests of Buckwheat with Zinnia, helping his father transcribe letters from far off places about trade, taxes, or village politics.

Just a little bit further. Aster told himself. *We'll be back in Buckwheat before the first snow. Father will be cured, and he can lecture me of the dangers of the outside world until he's blue in the face. My biggest concern will be finishing my postman duties quickly enough to reread my favorite stories by the lake.*

Kara marched through the door, interrupting his

thoughts. "We can't be more than a day away from New Portsmith now." She ushered the rest of the crew into the main sitting quarters.

Peter and Tristram filed into the room behind Chert. The three of them were in the middle of a heated debate about playing another round of coin drop.

Aster stood to join them. Calantha didn't even look up as the group sat around her table.

Kara gave them a stern glare to get them to quiet down. When the only sounds were a whistling of wind through the sails and the occasional splash from below, she took a deep breath to start speaking.

But before she could get a word out, Calantha exclaimed, "I have done it!"

This drew everyone's attention.

"I have completed my latest work. A treatise on the sexual dimorphism of the cockatrice."

Startled, Kara bent over the table to look at the papers. "What does this have to do with taking back the Odyllic Stone?"

"Oh, it is unrelated. However, I believe the contents of this text will revolutionize the Benian understanding of monsters. Please have a look," she said, pushing a stack of paper into Aster's hand. "Though it is a shame that I did not have more time to study them in the Kaleenmunda Desert. That will have to wait for the following publication." She stared at Aster, making small circles with her hand until he began to read the first page aloud.

A Treatise on Sexual Dimorphism of the Cockatrice Family

Due to the scarce interactions with the monster commonly called the cockatrice, little is known about their life cycle. The deadly powers the creature wield typically prohibits such study. This work seeks to describe the life cycle of the cockatrice, from its development as a clutch of eggs to the connection with the monsters known as basilisks. Morphology, behavior, and reproductive cycle are explored as evidence for the claim that the cockatrice and the basilisk are sexually dimorphic members of the same species.

"Well, I guess that makes sense. We did see the basilisks with their eggs and the cockatrice seemed to be protecting them," Aster remarked, placing the paper back on the desk.

Kara cleared her throat, brow furrowed at Calantha. "We need to be spending our time on something more immediately important. First, Aster, can you use the onyx chalice and try to find out some more information about the Odyllic Stone? After that, I'd like to review our plans for New Portsmith."

"I'm not sure I want to use the chalice again. That place was unnatural," Aster said as stared at the filigree cup. "It feels like you aren't part of reality."

Kara tapped her fingers on the table while she thought. "But Quell'est knows many things. It would be a shame not to ask him more. What if we learn something that could help us take the stone back?"

Chert reached out and grasped the chalice in his hand. "Chert will go. He may know of father."

Kara smiled with thanks while Aster averted his eyes.

The Munayallpan looked warily at the chalice before bringing it to his lips. The world went black.

Chert opened his eyes in the Null Realm. The splashing waves were silent, and the cold breeze was gone. Like before, he floated just above the others, drifting towards the back of the ship. The green scaly being that Aster had described sat sideways on the ship's rear wall, his thick legs dangling through the door frame.

"Quell'est?" Chert asked.

"Yes, that is who I am. May I ask your name, Munayallpan?" Quell'est replied, his voice deep and guttural.

"Chert Penya. Have questions for you," he said,

kicking off the closest chair and floating in Quell'est's direction. He pushed too hard and ended up bouncing off the wall and careening around the room.

"We all have questions. Some with answers and some without. However, I shall do my best to resolve yours."

"Do you know Slate Penya?" Chert asked, once more attempting to direct his body to Quell'est. He got the speed right but missed grabbing the door frame. Feeling clumsy, he resigned himself to drifting around the room while keeping his head turned to Quell'est.

"I cannot say that I know of someone by that name. Though, perhaps you can provide me with more information. If you couldn't tell, we are cut off from reality in this place. I can merely see the shapes of the world, so many details can scuttle by unnoticed."

"Slate found chalice before we did."

"A glitter of gold hidden in your babbling brook! He must've been the burly Munayallpan man. I had such high hopes for him, but that's neither here nor there."

"Tell me what you know!" Chert was unable to rein in his excitement.

"I first saw him leaving the city of Paraduciel. We don't often get visitors there, so I was immediately interested. He seemed overjoyed at what he had found within our relic sanctuary, so I surmised that he possessed the Null Chalice. It was the last item of any value that had remained within our once-great city. I ended up following him all the way back to Munayallpa. He stayed there for some time before returning the chalice to its chamber in Paraduciel. I felt as if the wind had disappeared from under my wings, leaving me drifting aimlessly once more." The edges of Quell'est's scaly mouth curled downward.

"Did you talk with Slate?"

Quell'est narrowed his eyes and shook his long snout. "No, he never ascertained the purpose of the Null Chalice, therefore we didn't get the chance to speak."

"Where is he now?" Chert asked, his hope fading.

"When he returned the chalice, I took the opportunity to enter the relic sanctuary and remain there. I cannot say where he traveled after that."

Crestfallen, Chert grunted and crossed his arms. He had already suspected that was what had happened based on where he and Aster had found the chalice. Nothing Quell'est had said gave any hint of his father's purpose or whereabouts.

"He wasn't alone. There were two men with him. As I'm sure you are aware, one cannot enter the relic sanctuary unaccompanied."

Chert wondered who the others could have been. Taking his eyes off Quell'est, he let his body drift around the room. As he harmlessly floated into Aster he was reminded of the primary reason he was here. "Other thing. What is Odyllic Stone?"

"It is... an anomaly. Something that should not exist but, at the same time, must exist. My people have had many philosophical discussions on this very topic. It appears to have a will of its own. Granting the wishes of those who hold it close, defying the rules of nature that the rest of us must follow... Chert, you should bring the stone here, so I can examine it closer. I shall ascertain the answers you seek."

"We don't have stone now." Chert said, as he floated upside down, no longer able to see his new acquaintance.

"I see. Well, that's too bad. If it has indeed been discovered again, it would be a shame not to learn all of its secrets. If you happen upon it again, bring—"

Quell'est's gravelly voice faded as Chert blacked out, returning to his body on the chair. His ears rang and his head spun as the others pelted him with questions. Chert took his time, but eventually repeated his conversation to the crew.

"That's too bad," Aster said after Chert finished. "I'd hoped he would have a lead on your father."

Kara cut in. "He did say something useful though. Your father wasn't alone. Do you have any idea who he could have been traveling with? If we could find them, they may know more."

"No," Chert replied. "Slate like Chert. Not talkative."

Calantha perked up at Chert's words. She lifted her eyes from her papers for the first time all day. "Sorry Chert, but could you repeat your father's name once more? I had a faint notion that I have seen that name before somewhere."

"Slate Penya is Chert's father."

"Slate Penya. Slate Penya. Why is it familiar? Oh! That must be it!" Calantha pulled a blank page of paper from her tallest stack and began to write fervently.

All eyes were on Calantha. She kept writing, oblivious to the others.

Finally, Kara cleared her throat and said, "Calantha? Where did you hear Slate's name before?"

"I am preoccupied at the moment," Calantha replied in her usual airy voice.

Chert couldn't help but smile. She always had such an intense focus when she'd figured something out. It was charming.

Aster waited for a while; his raised eyebrow settled into a glare as Calantha's slender fingers flicked across the page. "Quell'est called the Odyllic Stone an anomaly. And he said it could grant a person's wishes. I'd say that we already had that figured out."

"Yes, which is why we must get it back as soon as we can," Kara added. "I don't trust the Council. The faster we can take it back, the better." Kara sighed and brushed a stray auburn lock off of her face. "Let's go over the plan one more time.

"Once we arrive in New Portsmith, we'll enter the city in pairs. Make sure to keep your hoods up so you aren't recognized. We have to gather a bit of information, some food, and contact Vincient to set our plans in motion. Once everyone has done what's needed, we will meet up at Calantha's tower, east of town.

"Aster, you and Tristram are in charge of contacting

Vincient. Go to the Cathedral of Conflag and meet with our informant. She will be able to get in touch with him. Tell him to meet us outside the vault in the afternoon after the bell tolls twice. Remember to say that we found Whitlock's stolen gold and there was a big misunderstanding with the Council. After they get the gold back, our names will be cleared, and things will go back to normal. If he agrees to help, have him light a candle on the fourth floor of the clock tower after dark."

Tristram rolled his eyes. "Are you sure that you don't want me to get Shaheed to open the vault for us? And they'll figure out pretty quick that we don't have the gold."

"I've thought it over and it's too risky. We don't want the Council to know that we're in New Portsmith if we can help it—at least not 'till we have already set sail. Besides, that can be our spare oar in case Calantha gets trapped inside the vault."

Tristram muttered under his breath. "Fine, but I think you've got too much faith in Vincient."

"If he refuses to help us, we can do it your way. I just think your position is too valuable to waste. I'm sure Vincient will buy our story. He's a good man. After all, he helped us chase down Whitlock in the first place. He must've been just as confused as we were when I was arrested."

Tristram didn't press the topic, forming his lips into a thin line as if locking further arguments behind them.

"The second group is Peter and Chert. You guys need to buy rope and climbing gear. Enough for three to scale the clock tower."

Peter shook his head. "There's no way that I'm goin' to climb all the way to the top of the tower. It'll take too long; we'll be spotted."

Kara grabbed the bridge of her nose and sighed. "See, this is exactly why I'm repeating the plan once more. You aren't climbing to the top. You only need to make it up to the second-floor window and find your way to the stairs.

All the guards are on the ground floor making sure nobody gets through. There's no reason to have a watch further up. It's not like there's anything valuable up there anyway. But you'll need to find the bell-ringer first and tie him up so he doesn't interfere. He'll be a young boy, so please don't kill him."

Peter just shrugged and started to play with his knife, so Kara continued. "Calantha and I are the last group. We will stop at the market to buy some food. If everything goes well, Vincient will contact us tonight. But if not, the extra food will keep us from needing to re-enter New Portsmith and risk getting caught."

Peter asked, "And what about the heist itself?"

"As for the *retrieval*." Kara emphasized the word. "Tomorrow, we'll meet at the clock tower. Peter, you Tristram, and Chert will climb the outside and enter through the second-floor window," she paused to glare at Peter, "And get to the bell at the top. Fifteen minutes after two, you need to ring it as many times as you can."

Aster cut in. "I get that it'll make a commotion, but why are you so certain that this won't just draw all the guards to us?"

Peter replied, "In New Portsmith we use the bell not only for keepin' time, but also as an emergency signal. When it rings continuously like that, it's a warnin'."

Kara added. "Exactly. All of the common folk will hide in their houses and barricade the doors. Even better, all of the soldiers will rush to the barracks and the guards will stick by their stations. They'll be gathering to receive orders from their commanders, ready to defend the city walls.

"We'll still have to deal with the men at the vault, but nobody else should bother us. At least not for a while. If we time things right, the bell will ring right after the vault door is opened, giving Calantha the chance to sneak in unnoticed. Aster and I will distract Vincient long enough for Calantha to get back out with the Odyllic Stone. At that point it won't matter that we don't actually have the gold, we will just book it out of there. The guards won't be able to chase us far with their heavy armor, so as long as we surprise them, it'll work out."

Peter shook his head. "There's no need for three of us to ring a bell. I'll stick with you, Kara, in case any fightin' breaks out."

"No," Kara snapped before changing her mind "Actually, that does make sense. Only Tristram and Chert will ring the bell, everyone else comes with me." Kara looked around the table and set her gaze on Calantha, who had not looked up during the entire conversation. "So, is everyone clear on the plan, now? Calantha?" Kara gestured to Calantha, who had finished writing, but was once more poring over her pile of papers.

"Yes, I'm fully aware of the role I am to play in your heist," she responded.

Kara clenched her teeth. "And you're sure you can get in?"

"Assuredly so. As long as they are not specifically looking for me, they will not notice a thing. Though, do not expect me to fight. I detest such brutish behavior." Calantha tapped her quill hard for emphasis.

"All you have to do is sneak in," Kara concluded with a smile. "Everyone should go to bed early tonight. The next few days will be busy."

After they finished talking, Peter and Tristram pulled Chert away from the table in their third attempt to have him join a game of coin-drop.

"C'mon what have you got to lose?" Tristram asked, egging him on. "It'll help you relax before our big day."

"Fine," Chert replied, grumpily. Everything about this plan made him nervous. There were too many uncertainties, but he couldn't think of anything better to suggest so he kept his doubts to himself.

Aster was just about to join them when Kara called

him back. "Hey Aster, can we talk for a minute?"

"Sure." Aster followed her into the captain's quarters.

"I want to be honest with you, Aster. I'm nervous about this whole thing."

"But it's a good plan!" Aster protested.

"Please let me finish. Yes, it's a good plan, but it's still dangerous. I wish Pat was still here. He always kept my feet on solid ground..." She trailed off. "But anyways, Aster, what I wanted to say was keep yourself safe. I feel responsible for you and wouldn't forgive myself if you got hurt... or worse..."

"Don't worry about me. I'll be happy as long as we can cure Buckwheat Village."

Kara frowned. "I don't think you're understanding what I'm trying to say."

"I can't consider that. I'm afraid I'll lose my nerve. Besides, there's no safer place than with you and Peter."

"We won't always be around," Kara massaged her temples. "You'd better get some sleep. We'll arrive soon." She gestured to the door and pulled out her notebook. Aster left, less confident than he had been before their talk.

It was raining when Moonlight docked on the long pier in New Portsmith. The cold permeated through their cloaks and the air smelled of petrichor. Kara thanked Federyc's men for the ride and promised that they wouldn't be staying more than three days.

"Well, at least nobody will be milling about on a day like this. Less chance someone will recognize our faces," Kara said with a smile as she rejoined the others on deck.

Peter grumbled and pulled his cloak tight. "Calantha's tower had better have a fireplace."

"Oh no. There are no flames near my plants. The soot is not good for their leaves," Calantha responded, peering towards the city.

Peter swore under his breath, but Kara interrupted before he could say more. "Everyone, time to head out. Good luck." She darted out into the rain and down the boardwalk. Calantha followed a few paces behind.

Tristram cleared his throat. "You know, there's one thing that's good about the Cathedral of Conflag... they've got a roaring fire inside. C'mon, Lantern." He winked at Peter as they stepped off the boat, barely dodging Peter's boot.

"Let's go too, Chert. The sooner we're done with this, the sooner I get to warm back up." Peter trudged down the pier and into the city with Chert trailing behind.

The bell tolled ten times as Aster and Tristram caught sight of the red stained glass of the cathedral. Remembering his encounter last time, Aster paused to tuck his pendant into his tunic. *Won't give them any reason to turn me away this time.* They ducked under the stone archway. Water cascaded out of the gargoyle's mouths and splashed on the ground around them.

Inside was as cozy as Tristram had predicted. The holy fire at the center of the room was surrounded by novices and townsfolk. It was more crowded today than the last time Aster had visited.

Tristram hurried over to the fire and sat with his back to it to dry off, leaving Aster to search for Martha.

He paced around the room, but didn't see anybody he recognized. *I hope she isn't away today,* he thought, before turning into an alcove to his right. Someone in burgundy robes was lighting prayer candles at the far end. Aster walked up and noticed familiar golden locks.

"Martha, good to see you. How have you been?" Aster asked, glad to have found her.

"Hello, true believer," she replied after turning around. "The Divine Conflagration's presence is burning brighter than ever before. We are truly blessed to live in these times." Martha lit two more candles, then closed her eyes in prayer. When she opened them again she said, "You never did tell me your name."

Aster blushed. "Oh, right... sorry. My name is Aster Rutherford. And... Thanks for helping me out last time."

"Good deeds bring a person closer to Conflag's

warmth. So Aster, is there something else that I can help you with?" She tucked the long stick under her arm and turned to face him directly.

"Do you know Vincient Harlow? He's the BTC master of shipping. I need you to give him a message." Aster pulled out a rolled-up piece of paper and handed it to her.

"I will do this for you Aster, but in exchange, please do something for me."

"Huh? Oh I... uh sure. What?"

"Come join me to witness the miracle."

Aster shifted his eyes to the door.

Martha added, "Don't worry. It's starting soon. They don't take long." She lit a final candle then grabbed his hand and led him outside.

Tristram followed hesitantly, glaring at the sky.

"It's raining pitchforks today," Martha said as she pulled a burgundy hood over her golden hair. She pointed to a platform near the side of the cathedral. A large crowd had already gathered. "There. Archbishop Nicholas will be speaking soon. Hurry." Martha dragged Aster out from under the stone arches and into the crowd.

Tristram let out a groan from behind them and didn't follow.

As they pushed to the front, Aster saw the archbishop on stage alongside two other priests. He took a few steps forward and caught a glimpse of Fletcher, who was lingering to the side of the stage. *I can't let myself be recognized.* "Here is fine, Martha," Aster said as he put his hood up and ducked behind two large men.

"But you won't be able to see the miracle," Martha protested.

"I can see fine from—" But before Aster could finish, Archbishop Nicholas cleared his throat, silencing the crowd.

"Citizens of Benia, long have we been blessed by the Divine Conflagration. Since the early days of the kingdom, God has looked upon us with favor. But now he acts to directly improve our lives. Now that New

Portsmith is perfected he showers us with his love. He tells me that Benia is mandated to rule over every corner of Arathanon. Now witness the miracle of Conflag!"

Fletcher hunched down, digging into his bag and pulled out a round object covered in brown cloth. Blue light spilled out from the side folds.

Nicholas held his hands up in the air, closed his eyes and yelled, "Conflag, give us a sign that I speak your will!" Aster's pendant danced under his shirt as he watched.

Thunder clapped.

The crowd gasped.

Clouds above the cathedral swirled as if caught in a whirlpool. Faster and faster, they spun until a spout formed, which twisted and snaked its way to the ground directly in front of the stage. The wind howled and the rain fell sideways, pelting the commoners. Several screamed and ran, but most were transfixed by the miracle.

Then, as quickly as it had begun, the vortex disappeared, taking the clouds along with it.

Aster blinked as the midday sun beat down upon them. There was no sign of the rainstorm that had been there moments before.

Martha dropped to her knees and cried out. "The will of Conflag. We are but humble servants before your everlasting might!"

A dozen more dropped to their knees, with similar prayers. Aster joined them on the ground to prevent himself from standing out.

Nicholas spoke once more. "As you can see, Conflag compels us to bring his holy light to all of Arathanon. Now go. Spread the word to everyone you know." Then he gave a single nod in Fletcher's direction who disappeared behind a nearby building while the priests conferred blessings on those closest to the stage.

With the miracle completed, the crowd dispersed leaving space around them. Martha was still on the ground, muttering prayers.

Aster put his hand on her shoulder.

She looked up at him. Tears welled in her eyes. "I'm happy that we could share the miracle together, Aster. I hope that it has dispelled any doubt in your heart. Now you know that our faith is true, and our mission is just."

"I guess so..." Aster replied, still in shock.

Tristram joined them once more. "Lantern, it's time to go." He gestured to the east.

"Yes it is. Martha, don't forget the note. And... thank you for sharing this with me."

They left Martha kneeling in a puddle with her hands up to the sky. All around them, people were gossiping about what they had just witnessed and what it meant.

Chert followed Peter out of the busy shop where they had found rope and iron hooks without trouble. The shop was nice enough, but things in New Portsmith lacked character. Even his stone-cutter shop, plain compared to others in Strongfair, had a presence. It was the emotion of the artwork. Or the earthen walls. Probably both.

"Glad the rain let up," Peter said as he adjusted the rope on his shoulder. "Let's give the clock tower a wide berth and stick to the outskirts of town."

Chert nodded and looked up at its peak. "You know bell is gift from Munayallpa? K'en'amiguh is Munayallpan name for it. Chert sad about what happening in Benia."

"Me, too. Everthin' that happened to the king was supposed to keep conflict away from Benia. But it seems like it wasn't good enough. Let's get back to Calantha's tower. I'm gettin' nervous about spendin' so much time in public."

Chert followed Peter down the back alleys until they reached the cliffs by the sea. Then the two of them marched through the city's residential quarters. The streets reeked of rotting fish as the sun had begun to warm them. They twisted and turned reaching the eastern gate of New Portsmith. The guards were chatting, barely paying attention to the two men with rope.

The pair arrived at Calantha's tower to find that everyone else was already there. A fire was burning on the floor inside a makeshift circle of stones against one of the windows. Peter hurried to it and warmed his hands.

Calantha and Kara had prepared a small feast of fish chowder, grilled red snapper, and a medley of vegetables.

Chert smiled. He liked it here. Aster's situation aside, things were good. Everyone was looking out for each other. They acted more like a family than a crew of sailors.

He watched Calantha lean over the fire, stirring the chowder. Whenever she got too close the the flame and the heat twisted the air, he got a glimpse of her pink carapace peaking through.

She was something special. After all the trauma she'd endured, she still viewed the world with childlike wonder. Anything she learned was an important discovery and she marveled at the mundane details.

Chert could barely remember when he'd stopped thinking like that. Before his father had left. Before he had to be responsible.

They milled about after they had finished their meal, keeping an eye out the window that faced the clock tower.

Chert sat on the stairs, lost in thought. He felt a touch on his shoulder. It was Calantha, finger on her lips. She slid her hand down into his and lead him up the spiral staircase, to the top floor.

Halfway up, thick green vines enveloped the walls, concealing the stonework beneath a thick blanket of leaves. The roof was missing and the walls had broken off in jagged pieces but the vines seemed to heal the broken stone, smoothing and completing the structure.

Calantha laid down in the foliage and gestured at the stars in the sky. "Come join me. I am not skilled in astronomy, but I do enjoy looking at the constellations. When I was little, I climbed to the tops of our trees to look at them. It was my escape."

Chert sat beside her and looked up. "In Munayallpa, they say stars are sapphires. Ochress's gift to Loctee to help him find way home."

She laughed. "Of course your people would say stars are gemstones. It's poetic."

Chert shivered as the ocean breeze whistled around the stonework. Calantha was nestled in the vines. "What your people say about stars?"

"That they are not worth paying attention to. Anything that does not impact one's day to day life is disregarded back home." Calantha sighed and rolled over to look at Chert. "No matter how I tried to convince them, they always failed to see the truth behind the simple things. They act hastily because they cannot think about a cause separated by time from its effect."

Chert brushed aside a leaf that had been tickling his leg. "Munayallpans have opposite problem. We think long. But don't act. Chert fights this weakness daily."

"You do a wonderful job. I would never have guessed that you consider yourself slow to action. To me, you seem so rational with your actions and words. It is refreshing. The others can be rash."

"Thank you," he replied, taking another look at the night sky. He savored the moment. "You should tell others."

"Tell the others what?" Calantha asked, scooting closer to Chert.

"Your true self."

Calantha stopped. "I am not sure that is a good idea. People are always fearful of things that look different. You have seen how the others talk about the cockatrice and lovine. They are monsters and must be slain. Sometimes I feel more akin to those monsters than I do to the Benians."

"Benians can be cruel. But crew not bad... Chert thinks. Knowing could help plan."

"They will be frightened. Besides, I am happy with how things are now. It would be a shame if—"

"Calantha. Chert." Aster called out as he bounded up the stairs onto their landing. "The clock tower is lit! It happens tomorrow! Kara needs you, Chert."

Chert got to his feet, looking back to see Calantha pouting in the dim light. He almost sat back down, but decided against it. The others needed him. The plan had to go smoothly for everyone's sake.

He followed Aster back downstairs, leaving Calantha alone under the stars.

Sleep didn't come easy to the crew that night. By the time sunlight peeked over the horizon, Kara had been awake for hours and already prepared breakfast. Peter left the tower early to scout. Chert and Tristram went next, carrying a wooden crate filled with climbing supplies. They wanted to bring it by the docks first to seem less suspicious at the clock tower.

When the day had gotten late enough and their patience had worn thin, the rest of the crew ventured into the city.

Aster, Calantha, and Kara arrived early. They waited underneath the clock tower, beside the curved ramp leading to the vault. Calantha stood against the wall, inside the shadows while Kara was staring at each entrance, flinching at every passerby.

Aster sat on the ground, nursing an uneasy feeling that he couldn't place a finger on. He gripped his pendant tightly as he thought about Buckwheat. *Just a little bit longer, and the village will be cured.* They were waiting for the bell to ring twice, the signal to start their plan. Peter joined them shortly after, with nothing unusual to report.

BONG... BONG. Vincient walked in as the chime faded, his crimson hat rustling in the breeze. "Kara, I'm not sure what you were thinking, calling me here today. You shouldn't have come back to New Portsmith."

"Come on, Vincient. You know exactly what happened with Whitlock. Do you really think that I'm guilty?" Kara scowled.

"Unfortunately, what I think doesn't matter," he said tersely, looking from Peter to Aster. "The Blue Skies was the pride and joy of the BTC. I'm sad it's no longer so. You wouldn't be willing to give her back, would you?"

"Afraid not," Peter replied as he stepped over to the chest that they had brought.

"A shame. Perhaps you can let me look upon her once more? Is she docked somewhere nearby?" Vincient stroked the feather in his crimson hat while the others stared back in silence. Finally, he said, "Well, show me the gold."

Peter bent down and picked up an ornate chest. "Here's what Whitlock stole. See? We ain't bad guys."

"Open it," Vincient commanded.

Kara stepped between the two men. "We will once we're safely inside the vault."

"So be it. Let's just get this over with." Vincient made a wide gesture for them to go down the dirt ramp.

Aster grabbed one handle of the chest from Peter and they both descended with Kara and Vincient following behind.

Aster caught glances of Calantha darting from shadow to shadow. If he hadn't known she was there, he doubted he would have noticed anything.

As they reached the enormous steel door at the bottom, they saw two guards with full plate armor in front.

Everything is going smoothly, Aster thought to himself as Vincient greeted the men. The slightly larger guard stepped closer and asked, "Is this the shipment from Buckwheat that we were expecting?"

"Yes, unfortunately it is." As soon as the words left Vincient's mouth, one guard grabbed Kara's arm. The other pulled out his sword and pointed it at Peter.

"Just so you know, Archbishop Nicholas read your note before it had reached my hands. It was his idea to go along with your plan in the hopes of trapping you down here along with that gold. As for myself, I had hoped you wouldn't try something so foolish. Kara, they are willing to do anything to catch you and finish your sentence."

Two more guards with swords raised, clanked down the ramp, trapping them in front of the vault.

Kara's eyes widened. She drew her knife.

Then the great clock bell rang. *BONG... BONG... BONG.*

The soldiers' eyes darted up instinctively.

Kara yanked her arm away and dashed up the ramp, dodging the soldiers' swords as she went.

They ran after her as the bell kept chiming.

Moments later, Kara screamed.

"Loctee drown us." Peter sighed as he heaved the chest out of Aster's hand and into the soldier next to him, causing the man to topple over. Peter sprinted after Kara and yelled out. "Pull the lever on the right, then spin the wheel on the left. Good luck." Then he was gone, leaving Aster alone with Vincient and the two soldiers.

"Take care of him," Vincient pointed towards Aster as he trudged up the ramp after Kara and Peter. "They'll have my head if the other two get away."

Aster drew his sword as the soldiers circled around him, waiting for an opening to strike. *This isn't good. Maybe I could fight off a single soldier, but not two.* He hadn't expected to face experienced fighters tonight, especially not alone. Aster gripped the hilt tightly as he examined their plate armor.

How in Conflag's warmth am I supposed to cut through that metal? Think! Aster racked his brain.

It was too late though, the first soldier stepped in, swinging his sword.

Aster's body moved reflexively, jumping backwards to avoid the blade. He crashed into the armor of the second soldier, who wrapped his arms around Aster, holding him in place. *It's all over. I'll never save Buckwheat Village. My father will not live to see another summer and all of my crewmates will be hanged.*

Another loud crash sent Aster sprawling to the floor. His pendant slid out of his shirt and settled on the stone. Aster scrambled to pick his sword back up as he watched a beast with elongated eyes and a pointed mouth slash at the man with scythe-like claws.

"Calantha, is that you?" Aster asked, as he tucked the symbol of Ochress back under his clothes.

"No time to explain. I cannot pierce this armor, so you need to take care of the other one and open the vault." Calantha's airy voice coming from the monster felt unnatural.

Aster stood to face the last soldier who was fixated on Calantha's appearance. The bells still echoed through the passageway.

Bells? Aster had an idea. He lunged at the man, slamming the sword into his chest. Aster's hands erupted in pain as the vibration rippled into his arms.

The soldier seemed unfazed, his armor only slightly dented. He turned his attention back to Aster and returned the blow.

Aster pulled his sword in time to deflect it. *Good thing I had practiced with Joss so much. She's a much better swordsman.* They traded blows. Aster dodged or deflected each one, but he was reaching his limit: Aster could feel himself slowing down, exhausted from swinging the heavy blade.

Calantha had managed to pin the other soldier down on the ground. He struggled against her weight, grabbing for his sword that lay in the dirt next to him.

Aster took a step back and lifted his weapon above his right shoulder, staring at the soldier's feet. The man looked down. Aster brought the sword down into his helmet, which dented with another clang.

It was enough: The man crumpled to the ground as Aster's arms shook with pain again.

Without pausing, Aster strode over to the steel door, turned a knob and then cranked the wheel until it slowly opened. He looked back at Calantha's horrific form as another set of guards dashed down the dirt ramp towards them.

She said, "Go. I'll keep them here."

Aster stepped through the doorway, which quickly shut behind him.

He was stunned by the wealth in the room. Piles of gold, silver, and gems covered the floor. Glass display cases with priceless relics. The air was stuffy and carried a faint metallic odor.

Aster's eyes darted across the piles, looking for anything that glowed or resembled the brown cloth he had seen yesterday. Nothing. None of the displays contained the Odyllic Stone, either.

Aster stepped into the center of the room, peeking around stacks of gold bars tall enough to reach the ceiling. *Where is it?*

"What you're looking for isn't here," a voice spoke from the corner behind him.

Aster whirled around. He lifted his sword pointing it towards the sound. "Who's there?"

"It's me." Fletcher stepped out from behind a stone pillar. His left hand was clutching something, awkwardly held in front of his body. "We thought you may be trying something, so we moved the Odyllic Stone."

"I... well..." Aster stumbled across his words. The feeling of unease was back. Aster pressed his hand against his shirt and touched his pendant. It pulled against him weakly, much weaker than when he was near the Odyllic Stone before. *I should've known it wasn't here!* Aster clenched his teeth and berated himself for missing the obvious.

"No need for excuses. You're trapped. You know, Aster, I thought you were smarter than this. But you never learned."

"What are you talking about, Fletcher?" Aster asked as

he moved to place a pile of gold coins between them.

"You're too green. An idealist. Stuck in your head about the way things should be. But the world doesn't fit into your box. And yet you can't see that. People don't give a shit about what is 'right' and what is 'wrong'. It holds no value when everyone is just selfish in the end."

"I'm not selfish. Everything I do is for Buckwheat Village."

"Isn't it? Come on, Aster. You and I both know that your father is sick. How can you say that your quest isn't selfish, when you have the most to gain?" Fletcher beckoned him closer with his right hand.

"That's not true! I would be here for the village regardless."

"Are you sure? There's no point in speculation. You're done now."

Aster brought his sword down into the coins at his feet, which bounced across the room. "Is that why you stole the Odyllic Stone from us? I hope you got what you wanted." Aster's voice filled with venom as he spoke the man's new title. "*Sir* Fletcher."

"Oh, I did. They were very generous. I'm the first knight appointed by the Council. They've given me more gold than I know what to do with. And best of all, I'm the Council's consultant for matters related to the Odyllic Stone." Fletcher smiled a toothy grin. "But no, I didn't take the stone from you because of that. I was happy enough to let you play around with it. But you messed everything up. It's your own fault." The burly man pushed closer, trying to get around the pile of coins, but Aster kept the distance between them.

"My fault? I didn't force you to take the stone from me!" Aster snapped back, already tired of this conversation.

"I told you so many times to keep it a secret! And what do you do? You went and cured those miners."

"It was the right thing to do!"

Fletcher let out a laugh and shook his head. "Since you

can't grasp it for yourself, let me spell it out. Each of those miners had families. Families that thought their beloved ones had died. When they suddenly come back home, that's big news. It spread like wildfire. Did you know that Hannes sent me a messenger that very night telling me what happened? He sent one to Jash, too." Fletcher laughed at Aster's puzzled look. "Oh, are you confused by that? Hannes is a Jashian spy."

"I don't believe you, Fletcher. You've lied to me before."

"Aster, I couldn't be more sincere. What would I have to gain from lying to you about this? I hope you're starting to understand what I mean when I tell you that you are green—a sprout in fresh soil. You can't just trust people. You must look at their motives."

"It's not like you understand the Council's motives." Aster shot back. He was trembling in anger—knuckles white on the hilt of his sword.

"The Council wanted the Odyllic Stone more than anything else. I gave it to them. I think that's pretty clear." Fletcher wore a smug smile, confident as if he'd practiced this exact conversation.

"Did you ever ask yourself why they wanted the stone? And you are fine with all this talk about war? How does that help you?"

"Emme has some grand plan for unification of Arathanon, but that's none of my business," Fletcher stepped closer. "I don't care much for politics."

"Don't you? I've seen you help them with these 'miracles'. Using the Odyllic Stone as a perverse justification for war!"

"There's no harm in a few party tricks." Fletcher waved his left hand which was still balled.

"And if they plan to use it as a weapon?"

"Aster, I'm not interested in hypotheticals right now." Fletcher's focus shifted from Aster to the object concealed in his hand.

"Fletcher, we're friends, right? Just let me out. Open

the door and we can figure this out."

"Sorry Aster, I don't think so. Emmeline gave us permission to kill you." Fletcher lifted his fist up in the air menacingly.

Aster glanced at the vault door. It was still bolted shut.

"But I don't think that's necessary." he smirked, lowering his hand. "I've told her that we need you for something. If you cooperate, maybe she will let you be my apprentice."

"I... I'm not sure," Aster replied, taking a step back and raising his sword.

"I don't need an answer now. Regardless, you're going to sit in a cell for a while. When I stop by, we can talk more."

Excitedly, Fletcher opened his palm and a small brown mushroom fell onto the floor. The moment it touched stone, its cap elongated and sprouted until there were so many strands sticking up into the air that it could pass for hair. Underneath, discolorations darkened and bulged out into a field of black eyes. Its cream-colored stripe split into four, with two spindly legs below a pair of bulbous arms. Aster witnessed the birth of a living creature as tall as his chest which was now standing in front of him.

"A gift from the Council, and a demonstration of the Odyllic Stone's power." Fletcher proclaimed before turning to the creature and saying, "Your name is Buna and you will obey my every command." It tilted its head slightly, with many eyes fixed on Fletcher. A fine dust sprinkled on the floor from its caps. "Buna, restrain my friend Aster. I don't think he'll let me get close with that sword."

The moment the words left Fletcher's mouth, the creature advanced on Aster. With each stride, its footing became more firm and graceful.

Aster swung for its neck, but his sword got lodged in its spongy stem, unable to cut all the way through.

Buna ignored the blow and wrapped its arms and legs around Aster. He tried to pull out his blade for another strike, but couldn't. He tumbled to the ground, unable to free his arms. Escape was impossible.

Grovemother Lucinda,

Please forgive my irregular correspondence. I recently visited the Boscage School and was disappointed to find that you were away. I am sure that you are busy with your campaign to become the Elder of Religion. Surely the citizens of Benia will appreciate your passionate beliefs and deep knowledge of history.

I am writing to you because I have a special request. Could you find the journal of a man named Slate Penya? I believe that I ran across it on the second floor of the library in the archaeology section. It was a small set of notes bound with twine. Could you send me a transcription of the contents? I will be in New Portsmith for the foreseeable future, so you can have it delivered to the usual place there.

As for the proposal that we discussed last time; I have given it much thought and will accept it under one condition. I need the flexibility to continue my current line of research. I have made an important breakthrough and believe that I am on the verge of discovering an entirely new field of study. I will spare you the details now, but know that I may need to travel away from the school from time to time.

I hope to hear back from you soon.

Sincerely,
Calantha Coronatus

12 DESPERATION

Peter burst through the door of Calantha's tower. "Drown this whole city. The only thing I found was talk of the election or miracles. Nobody witnessed our commotion from earlier." He slid into a chair and rubbed his temples. "As far as we know, he could still be stuck in the vault. Or worse..."

"I guess that means our plan worked. So, nobody saw Aster leave the clock tower?" Kara asked, turning away from the window she had been staring out of.

"Nope. I also found out that the new Elder of Defense is officially that lunatic Baxter. 'Course the other grandstanders stayed the same. Otherwise, nothin' useful at all. How 'bout you, Tristram?"

"Well, it coulda gone worse." Tristram ruffled his blonde hair, nervously.

"What current snagged you this time? Must not be too bad since you're here."

"I met with Shaheed and gave him the fake story, like we planned. That we had just arrived and that our plan was spontaneous, so I didn't tell him ahead of time. All in all he wasn't happy, but I think he bought it. He seemed much more interested in what we had been doing in Tembour. It caught me off guard, but I told him we were visiting one of my cousins. I tried to ask about Aster, but he just kept peppering me with questions."

Kara crossed her arms. "That isn't good. It sounds like he was trying to catch you in a lie."

"I thought so, too, so I made an excuse to leave. That's the strangest part—he mentioned one last thing and then let me go." Mimicking Shaheed's accent he said, "The best trade routes go both ways, Tristram."

"What did he mean by that?" Kara shook her head. "In any case, I'm glad you aren't rotting in a cell somewhere."

"So, what do we do now?" Peter asked. Everyone turned to Kara.

"I don't know... first we should find out where Aster is."

Aster awoke in a musty dungeon, his clothes replaced with rags. He rubbed his aching back: The night on the stone floor had been unpleasant. There was a bit of straw in the corner for a bed, but it was neither warm nor comfortable. He pressed his face against the bars of his cell and saw a beam of light shining on the stairs from a crack somewhere above. *It must be day again, though the guard is still nodding off at the table.*

The other cells around him were empty. *I hope that means everyone else is safe. I should've noticed something was off. I should've remembered my pendant.*

Footsteps woke the guard up. He jumped to his feet and stood at attention just as Fletcher walked into the room. "Sir Abberton! I didn't expect you. You should've sent word that you'd be coming."

"At ease, Vernon. I just wanted a word with our prisoner. Could you step outside for a bit? I'll come find you when I'm finished." The soldier looked uneasy, but replied, "Yes, sir," and scrambled to exit the room.

Fletcher pulled the table closer to Aster's cell. Onto it he dumped out the contents of a messenger bag. Aster flinched as odds and ends crashed onto the wood. "Your possessions." Fletcher smirked as Aster's ink bottle began to leak out onto the table, staining the wood black.

"And?" Aster asked, eyeing his belongings.

"And I'm here to offer them back to you. Not the sword, though... I'm sure you understand why." Fletcher righted the ink bottle and rescued the wax seal stamp from the puddle's encroach. He turned it over in his hand and said, "B for Buckwheat, I suppose? A nicely crafted reminder of home. You want it back, yes?"

Is he trying to win me over? Aster slowly nodded.

Fletcher tossed the stamp through the bars and into Aster's hands. "Keep it safe," Fletcher said as he grabbed the next item off the table. "And what's this?" he held up the black pendant.

Aster stiffened when he felt the stone sway to one side. *The symbol of my failure. Would Fletcher notice? No, he can't, I can't let him. It's the only thing left that could give me an edge. My last chance.*

Fletcher kept talking, his eyes fixed on the jewelry. "The symbol of Ochress? I would never have guessed that anyone from Buckwheat would stray from Conflag's fiery gaze."

"It's a gift from my mother. She's Munayallpan."

"Your mother is Munayallpan? Aster Rutherford, you are starting to make sense to me. I should've guessed it from your... complexion."

"Can I have it back now?" Aster asked, focused on each pendulum swing. Luckily, Fletcher's fidgeting obscured any noticeable movement of the pendant. *The Odyllic Stone must be far away from here. Outside of the city or farther.*

"First, answer me." Fletcher flicked the chain up and grabbed it in a fist. "Have you considered my proposal?"

"To be your apprentice?"

"Yes."

Aster just scowled in silence, so Fletcher added, "I'm sure you'd rather not rot in this cell."

"I don't get it." Aster shot back. "You made such a big deal about motives. But what do you get out of this deal? You already have everything you could want. Worst case, the Council could find their knight a different apprentice."

Fletcher grinned and tossed the pendant to Aster. "Good. I knew you'd ask eventually." He leaned back and glanced towards the entry, then lowered his voice. "First off, I'm starting to distrust Emmeline. I can't put my finger on why, but she's been getting bolder with the stone and I don't think she needs my assistance any longer. Twice now, I've sworn one of her assistants was following me. In any case, I don't think I could trust someone unfamiliar."

Returning to his boastful volume, Fletcher continued, "Second, I'm not happy with my fame so far. Yes, I'm recognized on the city streets as a knight. But nobody is talking about my accomplishment. The Council covered up the existence of the Odyllic Stone, so the weight of my discovery was never made public. Instead of being seen as the legendary treasure hunter that I am, people see me as the Council's favorite. It's beginning to wear on me."

Fletcher scooped the rest of the items from off the table and placed them back into Aster's messenger bag. He reached through the bars and handed it to Aster, who grabbed it and inspected the contents before dropping the honeycomb die inside.

"Appreciate it, Fletch. But how could I help you with that?"

"Well, I can't just announce that I found the Odyllic Stone. Either nobody would believe me or the Council would put a knife in my back. But there is another treasure that I could *discover.*"

Aster raised his eyebrow.

"The onyx chalice that you found in that ruined city. If you can get it for me, then I will surely be renowned!"

Aster tried to keep his surprise off his face lest he let Fletcher think he was interested. "Is it famous? I'd never heard of it before Chert's description."

"Not as much as the Odyllic Stone, but yes. Back home, the Collective would read stories of heroes, legends, and histories. It was part of our yearly celebration for Viridus's bloom. When those wise old scholars would speak of the onyx chalice, they would always describe it as a principal factor in the Great Calamity."

"But Chert needs it to find his father." Aster fiddled with the clasp on his bag, considering the offer.

"The Munayallpan man? Is his father's name Slate, perhaps?"

Aster blinked, trying to decide how Fletcher would know that. "Yes, it is."

"Slate is dead. Bring me the chalice and I'll be happy to tell you and your Munayallpan friend everything I know about him." The wrinkles around Fletcher's eyes deepened as the smug expression tilted the corner of his mouth upward.

"Why can't you just make a new artifact? You've got the Odyllic Stone now, right?"

"It's not that simple. I've experimented with it a bit—that's where the Buna come from." Fletcher pulled a small mushroom out of his pocket and held it for Aster to see. "But the stone isn't as predictable as I first thought. Besides, even if I did create something new, it'll never capture the hearts of the people quite like an object of legend. Still you've given me something to consider."

"And if I bring you the chalice, what happens to Buckwheat Village?"

"I'll see what I can arrange with Emmeline. She should agree to it as long as I accompany you."

Aster nodded slowly. *Maybe Chert will understand. Especially if what he says is true.*

Fletcher flashed another smile and then left with a wave. "I'll be back soon."

The midday sun gently illuminated Calantha's tower as

the crew sat around, racking their brains for a plan. Kara stood. "I think we should make an offering to Loctee."

Peter raised an eyebrow. "Never expected to hear you say that. Heck, with Whitlock and Pat gone, I figure we'd never do that nonsense again."

"I don't know. Anything could help."

"But I'm sure we'll need the gold later. You ain't got much left." Peter shook his mostly empty coin purse.

"I'll offer it all if I have to. Sacrifices to our god adrift."

Tristram put his hand on her shoulder. "I think that's supposed to mean lost at sea, not that we can't find someone in the city."

"That's not what Pat used to say..." Kara trailed off as she opened the door and stepped outside.

"Wait. I'll come, too," Tristram called out as he rushed after her.

Calantha glanced at Chert. "I would be remiss if I did not participate as well. I have never heard of this ritual before." She stood and Chert followed.

"Alright, alright. I'll come, too. It's just depressin' is all." Peter shoved his hands into his pockets and reluctantly joined them outside.

Kara led them to the cliffs that overlooked the sea, a bag of coins in her hand. She pulled the drawstring open and took out a single gold coin. When the others caught up, she handed each of them a coin as well. Her bag was empty by the time she made it to Peter, who grumbled under his breath and pulled out a coin of his own.

Kara stepped to the very edge and closed her eyes to pray. She spoke the words that she had been rehearsing in her mind.

Wanderer Loctee,
sovereign of vitality,
dweller of the vast sea,
in the language of currents and swells,
we ask for your guidance.
Show us the path forward,

so that we may return to where we should be.

She squeezed the coin in her hand. *Help me find Aster.* She threw it into the ocean, watching as it splashed under the surf. The others followed suit, tossing their own coins.

I took him away from Buckwheat Village. No matter what, I'll bring him back.

As Kara made the offering, her heart swelled with hope for divine guidance.

As she walked back, she felt only emptiness.

Peter caught up with her and placed his hand on her back. "You know, I've given it a lot of thought—about Loctee that is. I reckon he's no more lost than the rest of us. If anything, he's showin' us that it's okay not to know where you're headin', as long as you keep moving forward."

Kara frowned. *It's not like Peter to spout religious theories—especially when we need a real plan. I guess we really are all out of ideas.*

Chert lingered as the others returned to the tower. He sat down in the short grassy field and pulled the onyx chalice out of his pocket. He wasn't sure if he would learn anything useful, but it was worth a try.

Calantha paused to watch as Chert brought the cup to his lips and collapsed to the ground.

Chert woke up once more in the Null Realm. The crashing waves were no longer audible to him in this strange place. Quell'est was floating near the cliff's edge. When he noticed Chert, his face lit up.

"Fortune smiles upon me today. Chert, you're in time to help me with my latest dilemma."

Chert flapped his arms until he was drifting in Quell'est's direction. "How?" he asked when he had gotten close.

"I wanted to know more about that ritual you just performed. Half of me thinks it's a cleansing ceremony. A way to ward off evil spirits and bad luck. The other half of me thinks it was a divine invocation—beseeching a god, Loctee makes the most sense, for favor."

"Second one."

"The world these days is different, and yet so similar to the one we left all those years ago."

"What happened?"

"It's a magnificent tale, but I suppose you couldn't listen patiently even if you wanted to." Quell'est took a deep breath, while Chert stared blankly at him.

"I'll be quick," Quell'est added with a toothy smile.

"It all started with Charles Benia, just a boy at the time. I used to fly down from Paraduciel and we would debate various topics. He had an extraordinary mind—it matched the best of the Drakōn.

"You see. I was already famous by then. My peers were either too intimidated or too starstruck to have any healthy debate. But not this child. So, he became my closest friend.

"One day, we gained access to the Odyllic Stone. I shan't go into it now, but suffice to say it was a philosopher's dream. We used it to answer every question that we could come up with about the world. From nature, to government, to minerals and even the stars. We learned more than we had ever imagined was possible.

"The topic we got stuck on was that of moral responsibility. Should a more intelligent and capable person or race step in to assist those who struggle with simpler problems? My argument was no; it would deprive one of learning and could weaken their survival instincts. And more importantly, it distracts from progress. Charles didn't agree. He thought the opposite: He felt that it was the responsibility of the powerful to protect the weak.

"Charles created the onyx chalice as a tongue-in-cheek way to fuel his argument. 'The purest way to remain impartial would be to observe from a place where you couldn't interfere,' he used to say to me.

"That's how our competition was born. Each of us

started with a village of similar size and technology. I observed from a distance, using the chalice to discreetly get a closer look. Charles lived in his village, making them tools and teaching them things they never would have learned otherwise.

"But, we soon found out that our experiment was flawed. First, Charles' village became utterly dependent on him. I hadn't envisioned that he would come to lead these people in such an explicit manner. He should have only provided occasional help or guidance. Secondly, I failed to illustrate the benefit to the people that remained isolated. In my case, the Drakōn people were out of harm's way and had no burden of mentorship. But I should've given them the knowledge that we were graciously allowing them to develop in this way.

"So, to settle our debate once and for all, we needed a new experiment. In the end, the Drakōn used the Odyllic Stone to take ourselves out of the world for a time. We were transported here to the Null Realm and Charles remained behind. It was the end of an era—a suspension of the Golden Age of Drakōn.

"Now, I'm sure your histories overflow with descriptions of King Charles; however, he isn't—"

The world went black, and Chert woke up in the soft grass. His skin was icy, even though someone had wrapped a blanket around him for warmth. He shivered and walked back to the tower as waves crashed into the cliffs below.

Emmeline Dolloway stormed down the dungeon steps with Fletcher following close behind. Once more the guard jumped to his feet. Before he could say a word, Emmeline pointed to him and commanded, "out," with such force that Fletcher jumped, and Vernon scurried off with a look of fear.

She stopped in front of Aster's cell and asked, "Is this

the boy?"

Fletcher meekly replied, "Yes, this is Aster Rutherford."

"His name's not important," she snapped, causing Fletcher to shrink back She turned to address Aster directly. "Boy, you are from Buckwheat Village, correct?"

"Yeah... we've met before." Aster glared at her, remembering their last interaction.

"You can't really expect me to remember every beggar that finds their way into the Council's chamber? So, you helped Fletcher obtain the Odyllic Stone?"

Aster said nothing.

Her scowl deepened and her face began to turn red.

Fletcher responded, "That's right, Emmeline. He was with me when we discovered it. We were both in Charles's burial chamber together."

She smiled and her voice softened. "Good, good. Fletcher tells me that you want to borrow the power of the Odyllic Stone to save your village. I shall grant you permission to do this... if you answer a few questions for me." Her smile was beatific, but didn't reach her eyes.

Aster perked up. *Fletcher kept his word.*

Her eyes tracked him closely and her voice was oozed with honey. "You have been traveling on a ship with Kara Reeves and Peter Keeton, correct?"

"Yes." Aster didn't dare look away from her piercing gaze.

"And you assisted in breaking Kara, along with another prisoner, out of these cells?" She gestured to the room.

Aster hesitated and then said, "I did."

"And some time after that, you traveled to Tembour, did you not?"

"Yes, we went there." Aster could feel the tension creeping up his spine, unsure of where this was leading.

"And while you were in Tembour, you had discussions with Federyc Benia, the former king?"

Aster froze and Fletcher's jaw dropped. Aster stuttered.

"I... I.. why would you ask that, isn't he dead?" His stutter probably gave it away, but he did his best to hide his surprise.

"It's alright," she replied in a soothing tone. "I'm an old friend of his. An advisor from before he could even walk. Just answer this one last question and you can be on your way back home to cure your village. I'll even pardon your friends for their crimes. Did you speak with Federyc Benia?"

Fletcher took a step back so that he was out of Emmeline's sight. With eyes wide, he shook his head side to side.

"How did you know?" Aster asked after a second.

Fletcher gasped.

Emmeline's face lit up in a toothy grin. "I received reports of Wilbur Whitlock showing up there, then Josselyn Helisent, and finally Peter Keeton. I had my suspicions about one ship in particular, Moonlight, which is now sitting in our harbor once again.

"It's too big of a coincidence. The only explanation is that it is Federyc's ship and he loaned it to his former bodyguard, Peter." She folded her hands together and turned to leave. "After all this time, I never suspected he remained in Benia. Baxter will be pleased. It's taken him far too long to finish my little assignment."

She briskly walked out of the room. One last command echoed from the stairs. "Execute the boy at sunrise. He isn't needed any longer."

Aster was shocked. He dropped to the ground and put his hands around his legs, rocking back and forth. *What just happened? That wasn't how that was supposed to go at all.*

Fletcher crouched down and placed his hand through the bars and onto Aster's shoulder. "I didn't know. I'm sorry, Aster." He stood back up, walked towards the door, and then stopped. "By the sprouts of Viridus's footsteps, Aster. Motivations. I told you so many times now, but you never understood it. You should've just lied to her." He shook his head as he left the room. "Federyc Benia still alive... who would've thought."

The room spun as Aster's tears sprinkled the stone floor. *I'm worthless. It shouldn't have been so hard. I just wanted to save Buckwheat Village. What was so wrong about that? I wish I'd never left. I wish I hadn't delivered that letter for Fletcher.* Aster grabbed a handful of hay. *Fletcher. Conflag burn him. He got me into this mess.* He slammed his hand into one of the metal bars, scattering the hay outside his cell. His palm screamed from the impact, but Aster beat the bar over and over again.

"LET ME OUT," he screamed, but there was nobody there. Once more, he smacked the metal bar, his hand bright red and pulsing with pain.

It was too much for him, so he cradled it in his shirt. "Please somebody help me..." He held his messenger bag to his chest as if it would protect him.

"That's enough waiting around," Kara announced, standing up. "I'm going into the city."

Peter raised an eyebrow. "That a good idea?"

"No, but it's better than sitting around here." She grabbed her bow off the table.

"Just don't do anything too reckless. They're looking for you more than the rest of us."

"I know. I'll keep out of sight," Kara sighed as she walked out of the tower. She had no idea where to start. *Maybe I could peek around the vault and see if the guards are acting strange?*

Lost in thought, Kara wandered down the dirt path until she was at the city's eastern gate. She pulled her hood over her head in preparation for passing the guards. A young woman with bright red hair was ahead, in the midst of an interrogation.

"You sure that you ain't named Kara?" the taller guard asked the woman, accusingly pushing his finger towards her face.

"For the last time, my name's Mildred," she sighed and held out a woven basket. "I've been picking mushrooms in the forest."

The shorter guard held up a wanted poster and eyed her carefully. His helmet sat low on his face, almost covering his eyes. The man's voice was nasal and high pitched. "I dunno. This looks a lot like you. Freckles and everything. What do you think, Daniel?"

"I think we'd better take her to the barracks to be safe. Captain Elad's seen Kara in person. Besides, he'd have our heads if we let the real one go."

"Well, you mind if I take her in? If it's really her, I could use the recognition. Nobody round here looks twice at a newbie like me. And even us soldiers get a share of the reward."

"Sure, whatever. Just make sure that we both get credit for it."

"Thanks Daniel," he said before tying the young lady's hands behind her back. "Alright, come on," he commanded as he pulled her past the gates.

This is my chance, Kara thought to herself as she watched the guard pass out of sight. *They've got to know something about Aster's location at the barracks.*

"Oi, you coming or not?" The remaining guard, Daniel, waved Kara over.

She froze. *Think of a plan, think of a plan. He'll recognize you for sure.* In a deep grunting voice, she said, "Actually, I don't need to go through yet."

"Shit, that don't make sense." Daniel stepped forward brandishing his sword. "Come here. I'll inspect you now and then you can go."

Kara turned around and started to walk away.

"Halt!" Daniel began to run towards her, his armor clinking with each step.

Her palms started to sweat. *I could probably outrun him. But I don't want guards to show up at Calantha's tower if I return. Wait...* Kara stopped and turned to face the guard. He was breathing heavily as he got close. When he was three paces away, Kara sprinted around him and through the gate.

"Halt! Halt! Conflag have mercy." His shouts faded behind the city walls. There was no way he would catch up with her at this pace.

A few townsfolk glanced at her awkwardly, but she kept running, hood pulled as far forward as she could manage. This city had once been the biggest inspiration in her life. Back home, she used to dream about visiting the shops and watching the boats dock, unloading people and trinkets from far off places. And when she had first arrived in New Portsmith, it exceeded her expectations. It was everything that Wildflower Farms wasn't. But today the streets smelled worse than the pig-pens and the gates felt like a cage around her.

She was far down the main street before she spotted the other guard with the redheaded woman, Mildred. *This is my chance. If I turn her in, maybe I'll find a clue at the barracks.*

"Soldier!" Kara called out in the same gruff voice she had used earlier, causing the man to stop and look at her.

"What do you want? Can't you see I'm busy?"

"Sorry, Daniel asked me to deliver a message. Said it was urgent," she lied.

"Unbelievable! I bet he's looking for a bigger cut of the reward. Well? Spit it out."

Kara gestured to an alleyway. "Can't say in front of the prisoner."

He pointed menacingly at Mildred and said, "Don't move or you'll get the gallows." Her eyes filled with panic and she nodded violently. He followed Kara a few steps into the deserted alley. "Out with it."

"Daniel said that he changed his mind. He wants all the coin but you can take all the credit for finding her."

"Conflag have mercy. Why's Daniel always got to put the cart before the horse? Heck we don't even know if she's the real deal."

"He says that's his final offer and that if you have any complaints you should just bring it up with him directly." She discreetly slid her knife out, holding it behind her back. *Please go!*

The guard crossed both arms and stared at the sky. "That idiot. I can't just go back and argue with him."

"I can keep an eye on Kara, if you'd like?" She said, twisting her voice to make it sound as sincere as possible, while keeping it low pitch.

"No… no. I'll turn her in and deal with that blockhead after. Why don't you…"

Kara spun on her heel and slammed her dagger into the man's exposed neck. "Sorry," she muttered as he collapsed to the ground. As fast as she could, she yanked off his helmet and did her best to remove his armor without getting blood on it.

As the guard's life faded, she donned his plate mail, then wrapped him in her cloak. *I guess he kinda looks like a beggar... if it wasn't for all the blood. Don't think about it. Got to hurry.* She leaned down one more time to grab some dirt and smear it over the visible parts of her face. *This will have to do.*

Kara rejoined the main street in full armor. As she awkwardly marched forward, the over-sized plate mail bounced on her shoulders. Nonetheless, she grabbed the rope that tied Mildred's hands and said, "Move," in the best nasal impression she could muster.

Without a word, the woman walked forward.

He's my responsibility. I must find him, Kara thought to herself as they made their way through the streets.

The barracks were impossible to miss: The first stone structure before the city center. Guards were streaming in and out. Two ironclad men stopped her at the door. Kara's heart raced as she spoke, trying to recreate the nasal voice once more.

"We caught her at the eastern gate. Think it might be Kara Reeves. Want Captain Elad to give her a look to confirm."

"You must be new. You're as stiff as a plank," the man teased. "I don't think you got the right one. They say Kara is a fierce warrior, but pretty enough to lift your sail, if you know what I mean."

Kara turned red and Mildred nodded in agreement.

"Calm down there, recruit. No way your ugly mug would catch Kara's eye anyways." The second man howled with laughter and smacked his thigh with a loud clank. "Ha! Well, take her to the last cell on the left. The captain's in his office."

Kara bobbed her head and went inside. *I'll have to thank Federyc for those lessons. He was right, the best disguise is half confidence. Peoples' minds fill in the details for you.*

She walked down the row of cells, checking the occupant in each. Aster wasn't in any of them. After she directed Mildred into the last one, another soldier locked the cell behind her. *Now which room is the captain's?*

Kara surveyed the entryway. There were a few doors on the second floor that she could see; shouts echoed out of the center room. *If it's anything like a ship, that's where the captain would be.* She climbed the stairs and waited patiently outside the door.

"...I've had it up to here with all this talk of war and miracles! My answer is no."

"But this request is from Emmeline herself. You can't just tell her no," the second man said, his voice quivering.

"Unbelievable. We are guards. We are supposed to defend New Portsmith. How can we do that if half my men are on the battlefield? And if those miracles are actually real, then what does she need us for anyways?"

"But they'll only be a short march north of here. Besides, like I said, we have no choice."

"Conflag burn it all. Fine. But I have a bad feeling about this."

"Thank you. I'll let her know that the guards will join her tomorrow," the man said as he walked out the door and past Kara. When he was gone, she ducked inside. The room was cramped with spare armor scattered in one corner. Light from one of the windows illuminated a bookshelf filled with war stratagems. A middle-aged man in a red uniform sat behind a desk strewn with papers. He sat with his head in his hands.

"Captain Elad?" Kara grumbled, making her voice as low pitched as she could manage.

"What is it?" Elad started directly at her face, one brow raised.

"Got a possible Kara Reeves in the corner cell. Could you check her?"

"I hope you got her. I'd like to pay her back for that runaround yesterday. But if it's another boy, I swear I'll move you to night shifts."

He stood up from the desk. "Wait here."

He walked with a slight limp over to her and stopped. "What was your name again? I don't recognize you."

"Keith... Keith Ryaburn. I was at the eastern gate with Daniel."

"I see. You must be one of the newbies. For your sake, I hope you found the real Kara. There's a sizable bounty on her head now." He hobbled out of the room.

As soon as he turned the corner, she rifled over the pages on his desk. They were mostly lists of names and locations. Nothing meaningful to her. But she found one that caught her attention.

Request: Three guards for the special prisoner at the castle dungeon. Followed by an angrily scribbled *again?* Kara put the note back down just in time to see Captain Elad walk back through the door.

"Well, that wasn't Kara, but she did look like the sketch. Can't fault you for that. Now, hurry back to your post." He shuffled back behind his desk and collapsed into his chair.

Kara gave an awkward salute and left, wasting no time, marching straight down the stairs, and back outside. Her heart was thumping so hard it might jump out of her chest. Her jaw was sore: She'd been clenching it the entire conversation.

She strode all the way back to the eastern gate, when her stomach dropped at the sight of the guard, Daniel.

He spotted her instantly and called out, "Well, was it Kara?"

Assuming her false identity once more, she replied, "Yeah. Captain says to see him immediately for your reward." Daniel smiled wide and practically skipped past her on his way to the barracks. "See, I told you," he called out as he passed. "I think I'll buy a whole hog for dinner tonight!"

After having cleared her last obstacle, Kara was elated at the sight of Calantha's tower.

Peter didn't believe her story. By the end of her tale, he was muttering to himself, "Loctee's luck?"

As Kara removed her borrowed armor, Tristram spoke up. "So, it sounds like we need to check two places: the battlefield and the castle dungeon. For the Odyllic Stone and for Aster."

Calantha lingered nervously behind Chert. They whispered back and forth until Chert marched forward, leaned on the table, and said, "Tell them. It could help Aster."

Calantha grimaced, running her slender hands down her milky gown. "Before we go, I need to show you all something."

"Did you find some useful information?" Kara asked as she wiped the mixture of dirt and sweat from her face.

"I... I have not been entirely honest with you. Chert was concerned that I would hinder our mission if this knowledge would come to light at an inopportune time. I am not of Benian nor of Munayallpan descent. I am Manti."

The air shimmered around Calantha as her human form faded away. Instead of the delicate looking woman that they had grown used to, a pale pink insectoid with elongated eyes and a pointed mouth awkwardly bowed before them. Her two scythe-like claws nearly touched the ground as they swept apart. Four antennae bounced back and forth as she lowered her head.

Kara jumped in surprise and Tristram gasped.

Peter shook his head and said, "I knew there was somethin' off about you. I didn't expect that you were actually that monster we saw in Buckwheat."

"This is who I was before I discovered my true self. I prefer not to fight; however, I will do what I can to help. Please use this in your plans as you see fit. Chert has convinced me that you are worthy of my trust and that it may be useful to incorporate in your strategy."

Tristram shook his head. "I'll never look at you the same way... or sleep at night."

Kara stepped on his foot and talked over his cry of pain. "Thank you for trusting us with your true form. It may help us out, as a shock if nothing else."

"This is a minor part of me. You already know my true form well." Calantha brought her scythes up and the air shimmered once more. The woman they knew stood before them once again. Her pale skin and elegant face was back, but now she wore a floor-length moss colored dress with an amber brooch in the shape of a beetle.

"Of course," Kara added.

Peter scratched his head. "So you can make yourself look like other things?"

"Yes," Calantha replied, sitting down.

"Could you make yourself look like an army?"

"No, I am limited to my person."

"What about a commander? Could give orders to open the vault."

"I am afraid that is impossible. My illusion only alters my look. And I require careful movements to do so. Perhaps if I was allowed to study a person for several weeks, I could make a passable impression. But even then, I cannot replicate their voice."

Peter nodded. "What about a lowly soldier? The uniform would be pretty much all that mattered. Could stab a few guards in the back before they suspected it."

Calantha folded her arms. "I would appreciate it if you refrained from using my ability for violence."

"Right… Sorry."

"So you're a bug?" Tristram asked. "That means you've got green guts and no bones, right?"

"Technically I am protected by an exoskeleton and my blood contains high concentrations of biliverdin, which makes it look green."

"Creepy." Tristram shivered.

Kara, Peter, Tristram, Chert, and Calantha wandered around the forest until they found what they were looking for. The hill with a small cave at its base—the tunnel they had used to free Kara.

"Come on," Kara said impatiently as she ducked her head under the support beam. Tristram went second, but before Chert could follow, Kara let out an exacerbated wail.

Peter dashed forward, pulling out his knife.

"No, it's fine, Peter." Tristram stuck his head out. "Looks like somebody sealed it up. Probably after our last jailbreak."

Kara swore under her breath as she backed out of the tunnel.

"So much for a quick in and out," Peter remarked as he sheathed his knife. "What now?"

Kara paced back and forth. "It's a gamble, but I think we need to split up. Peter and Tristram will go to the front lines. Calantha, Chert, and I will rescue Aster."

"Why?" Tristram asked. "If you have to fight through the prison guards, you'll need everybody."

"But what about the Odyllic Stone? I promised Aster we would help him. And it's just north of here. Who knows when we'll find it again?"

"It'll be a battlefield. We shouldn't go there without preparation." Tristram's eyes darted from Kara to Peter and back again.

Kara stopped. "Don't get seen. Don't join the fight. We just need to know if the stone is there or not."

"I dunno. Sounds dangerous. Peter, what do you think?"

"Captain's got a point. I say we go with her plan. C'mon, Tristram. Unless you're scared?"

Tristram scowled and marched forward.

Peter chuckled and took off after him.

Kara hesitated. *Is this the right choice? It doesn't matter, we've got to act.*

She headed toward the castle ruins with Calantha and Chert close behind. They passed by a small creek that was beginning to freeze over, ice crystals forming in the eddies. Calantha pulled her cloak tighter around her dress, shivering in the cold.

The trees broke near an old retaining wall that surrounded the castle. The three companions ducked behind it and surveyed the clearing. The afternoon sun stretched out the shadows, giving them ample places to hide. Two guards stood in front of the main entrance. The archway was halfway collapsed, but still stood tall.

Kara sighed. "It's too far and too open for us to surprise them. We could try going around but, who knows if there are more inside?" Kara stood. "I'll scout around."

"Wait," Chert grunted, holding Kara back. "Chert has idea." He pulled out the onyx chalice and lifted it in front of Kara.

"We don't have time for that," Kara waved his hand away and peered over the wall once more. "Besides, if the station guards are here, then that must mean somebody is in the dungeon."

Chert grunted once more. "Chalice will let you see and not be seen."

Calantha perked up. "You are a genius! We have been pigeonholing the chalice as a tool to collect information from Quell'est. However, as Chert points out, it also allows one to observe the world, unseen. If we are looking to determine if Aster is imprisoned here, perhaps we should utilize this secondary application."

"I keep underestimating you, Chert. It won't happen again." Kara took the chalice and placed it against her lips. Her body fell to the ground as her mind went black. Moments later, she was floating above the group, no longer one with her body.

"Hello, and who might you be?" The gruff voice of Quell'est greeted her.

"Kara. I don't have time to chat." She oriented herself to the isolated feeling of the Null Realm, kicking her legs and pushing her arms to the sides, propelling herself towards the guards at the stairs.

"It is like swimming," she said as she picked up speed.

"Perhaps that is true. I would argue it is more akin to flying, but I don't suppose that you've experienced that sensation." Quell'est extended his scaly wings as he said this and with a single flap, sped past Kara.

He turned back and watched as she slowly caught up to him. "And where are you going with such tenacity? I hope the others have informed you about the time limit for which you can stay in this place," he added.

"I need to know if Aster is down there." She pointed to the stairs with one hand, while still kicking herself forward.

Quell'est laughed. "Clever. I see you have learned a new trick, but you won't make it there at this rate." He wrapped his arms around Kara, poking her sides with his massive talons. "Your struggle has entertained me, so I'll assist this time." And with another beat of his wings, he propelled them forward, over the unsuspecting guards and into the ruined stairwell.

The way down was too cramped for Quell'est to extend his wings out all the way, but he still managed to reach the bottom without incident.

After being let go, Kara kicked against the stairs and into the next room. She knew it well, from when she had been imprisoned here herself. The lone guard was half-asleep at the table.

"Aster," she cried out when she found him huddled in the corner of his cell. He looked miserable. His face was drained of color and his eyes were red and puffy. "Aster, I'm here. I'll save you." Kara swam over to the cell and tried to reach through the bars.

"You cannot interact. It's impossible," Quell'est said as he watched her.

As Kara turned, the world went black once more. She opened her eyes, back in her body, propped against the wall.

Her head pounded as she spoke. "He's here." She got to her feet, disoriented. "You two should go back and help Peter. I'll free Aster."

Chert cocked his head and Calantha asked, "You sure? There are guards."

"Yeah. I saw where they all were. I'll sneak past them without problem."

"If you say so," Calantha replied airily.

Chert grunted in disapproval.

"Do not make that face at me. Your captain has made up her mind. Come on." She walked towards the forest.

Chert twisted back to Kara. "Stay safe." Kara handed him his chalice back and waved goodbye. He hustled after Calantha, leaving Kara alone beside the ruined castle.

Kara wasted no time circling around the ruins until she was out of sight at the rear of the ravaged castle. The back wall was remarkably intact, but there were still stones missing. Kara removed her bow and quiver, slipped them into the hole and then squeezed herself through.

Now to find the stairwell again. She grabbed her gear and snuck towards the front entrance.

As she rounded the corner, she could hear the guards talking just beyond the wall. They were protecting the stairs from intruders outside the doorway. *They won't expect someone to come from within.*

She paused next to the stairwell and listened, waiting for the right moment. In the middle of a heated argument between the guards about a bet gone wrong, Kara descended the stairs.

At the bottom, she could make out the last guard nodding off with his helmet sitting on the table. *How can I get Aster out without him alerting the others? And the key! Ugh... I don't have time for this.*

She drew her bow and held her breath, watching his head bob. Her fingers opened and an arrow whistled through the air into the guard's skull. He was dead before his face touched the table. She crossed the room to search his pockets, pulling out a hefty iron key.

Kara unlocked the heavy door to Aster's cell. The sound caused Aster to sob loudly and pull himself further into the corner.

"It's me. Let's get out of here." Kara placed her hand on his short black hair.

He perked up at her touch. "Kara? How'd you find me? They... they were about to execute me!"

"Calm down." She put a finger to her lips and gave him a stern look. "It was a little bit of luck. I don't think I could've done it without your help."

Aster rubbed his eyes with his sleeve. "What do you mean?"

"I found a note that gave me the clue to look here. If you hadn't taught me to read, I wouldn't have known. I've been looking through the notebook you gave me, practicing on my own too."

He stood and embraced her. "I... I was so scared, Kara."

"It alright now, Aster." She kissed him on the forehead and his face reddened. "We can't linger, though. We need to hurry back to Peter. The others are on the battlefield just north of here searching for the Odyllic Stone."

She headed towards the stairs.

Aster grabbed his bag from the cell and followed. As he passed the body of the guard, he frowned and said, "You killed him?"

"Didn't have a choice. Now hush." They crept up until

they were in the sunlight again. The guards were still arguing, so Aster and Kara slipped out through the hole in the stone wall without notice.

Kara marched northward towards the forest but Aster grabbed her hand and pulled her back. "No, this is wrong." He pulled the pendant out from under his tunic and held it up. "It's pulling me to the city. We need to go there."

"But Peter is this way." She protested, confused by his argument.

"I never really understood this thing until we broke into the vault. It reacts to the Odyllic Stone. Somehow sensing where it is, pulling towards it."

"So it's not there. Not on the battlefield?"

"No."

Kara nodded and let Aster lead her.

Through the winding streets, they ran. Kara kept her head down, covering her face with one hand. Aster had thrown caution to the wind, his hood fluttering behind him. A few townsfolk stopped to stare at them, but mostly they were too busy with their own lives to care.

Aster stopped at the base of the golden clock tower. "It's there," Aster said as he pointed straight up with a trembling finger.

"Are you sure? Not the vault?"

"I'm sure." He walked around and entered the ground floor. It was empty. Not even the clerk, Olivia, was around. "Lucky."

Aster dashed towards the staircase at the rear of the room, with Kara hot on his heels.

Hugo Rutherford,

Dad, you were right. The world is too confusing and too dangerous. I feel as if everything is working against me. I couldn't do it. I failed.

The story of my name keeps popping up in my mind. When you found mom was pregnant, you ordered bright purple flowers with golden florets from Malvez. She loved them so much but was devastated when they wilted in the heat of Strongfair a few days later.

Just like the asters I was named after: I couldn't survive outside home for long.

I don't think I'll get to see you again. Thank you for all you've done for me. I hope Dr. Malvin will keep you comfortable until the end.

Love,
Aster Rutherford

13 BENEATH THE BELL

Aster dashed up the narrow staircase, Kara's footsteps keeping time with his. As he made his way to the top, his pendant danced beneath his shirt, a welcome distraction from the burning in his thighs. His recently healed leg twinged in pain, but he pushed through, eager for it all to be over. *The Odyllic Stone is here. We'll save Buckwheat Village. That's all that matters.*

"Slow down, Aster," Kara called out from behind. As they stopped to catch their breath, the golden bell peeked through the belfry floor.

Kara lowered her voice to a whisper. "We need to be careful. We don't know what's waiting for us up there, so let me go first."

Aster nodded. He was glad for Kara's bravery. She always had a handle on tricky situations.

These stairs were extremely narrow, not designed for multiple people. Kara gestured to the wall. Aster pressed himself against it to let her pass. As she brushed past him she left behind a sweet, nutty floral scent that made Aster's head spin.

"You smell beautiful," Aster muttered.

Kara flushed and grabbed her braid. "Calantha gave me some rose oil yesterday. I thought it was too much at first, but it's grown on me."

"I like it..." His heart was racing even harder than before. "Kara, after this is all over, you should come stay in Buckwheat with me. It's not like you can keep working for the BTC."

"I... I don't know. Buckwheat is a nice place, but it just isn't enough for me. My home's the sea. There's so much adventure. So many exotic places to visit."

She leaned against the wall and stared into her open hands. "Whenever I think about home, I'm glad I left. Life in a small town is suffocating."

Aster frowned.

"But you can sail with me! I could show you the red sands of Zeffarii. Or, I've never been there, but I've heard wild tales of the dueling cities of Sumas and Norcape. And who knows what else is out there?"

But before Aster could reply, Fletcher spoke from somewhere above. "Alright, I've had enough of listening to you lovebirds. Come up and tell me how you found me."

Tristram and Peter broke through the tree line towards the noise they'd been following. The scene was chaos: A thousand men in heavy fur coats were locked in combat with a skeletal host.

Jeering at the spectacle, Emmeline Dolloway sat atop a stage of sorts, raining orders down from behind a wall of living skeletons who fiercely guarded her hill—not that anyone could get past the ghastly army in the field. She wore a long dress that seemed unsuitable for combat.

Tristram could barely make out the smirk on her face. She was in complete control of the battle.

The Jashian men dodged and wove, brandishing poles with barbed tips. While clearly more skilled than the reanimated bones, they were unable to break through the enemy lines.

The unblinking army simply waited—picking off any soldier who found themselves alone. One by one a soldier would trip or dawdle or brake formation and the skeletons would swarm, piling on top until their bones were stained red.

Tristram never much liked Jashians, but he felt sorry for them now. "What in Loctee's dark blue sea is going on here?" He croaked, ducking behind a boulder to avoid being seen.

"It's war... plain and simple," Peter replied, joining him. "Though not the kind I've ever seen before."

"Are these the miracles that the townsfolk have been raving about? It seems more of a divine tragedy to me. Death should be the end of man's struggle." Tristram plucked a hair from his mustache.

"Aye, even those Jashian cold-bloods don't deserve this." Peter's eye was drawn to the fluttering flags on the hilltop. "That's where they've gotta be keeping the Odyllic Stone."

"I ain't going there!" Tristram counted four people next to Emmeline, including Baxter Meyer. "I'd rather be stuck in the doldrums without food."

"Don't be like that. I've an idea." Peter walked his fingers in the air. "The Elder of Tradition and the Elder of Defense without guard, waging war. Arrogant pricks." He doubled back to the forest line and skirted the edge of the battlefield, flanking the hill.

Tristram followed reluctantly, swearing under his breath. The hill sloped gradually, giving them no cover to hide behind. "How do you know it's there and not back in the vault?"

"I don't."

The skeletons edged towards them as they approached. Bones squeaking as they moved, occasionally popping in and out of place.

Peter marched up to the circle.

"Wait." Tristram pulled out his knife a few paces behind. "I don't normally question you, of all people, but this is madness."

Peter jumped back out of the way as the nearest skeleton swatted at him. "Even if it's not here, if I can take Baxter out. I'll be doing Arathanon a service."

Tristram sighed when the skeleton didn't follow up, simply remaining alongside the others in formation. "Can you actually beat him?"

"Maybe." Peter moved back and forth, trying to find a way around without provoking the creature. After three attempts, he gave up on getting past.

"Maybe? Maybe I should've been a banker, but no… I wanted to see beaches… idiot," Tristram muttered to himself.

"Baxter! Baxter come and fight me, you coward," Peter cried out. "You've got the backbone of a jellyfish and the yellow belly of a perch! You're as unwanted as jetsam and have the stink of sargassum!"

Baxter's head swiveled and his face lit up. "What a pleasant surprise."

He parted the circle of skeletons, walking down the hill towards them. "I was just thinking to myself that today couldn't possibly get any better. But I was wrong."

"I challenge you to a duel." Peter's voice shook with anger. "If I win, you give us the Odyllic Stone."

"Not a chance. Though I was growing bored from all this waiting around. Emme has the ridiculous idea not to allow any Benian to fight in this war, so now I'm a glorified standard bearer."

"So?"

"You're no citizen of Jash, so you're unrelated to the war. I can follow orders and have a bit of fun at the same time. Besides, I owe you for that humiliation in Buckwheat Village." Baxter pulled out his curved blade. "Don't interfere," he commanded the undead wall. "You neither." he pointed at Tristram.

Tristram let out his breath. *At least he's got a fair fight.*

Aster and Kara climbed the last few steps up to the belfry. The golden bell at its center was enormous, towering over them like a cavernous mountain. The stonework was exquisite; a gift from people long since passed. Fletcher sat alone at the far edge.

Good, Aster thought, relaxing the tension in his body. *Fletcher is no fighter. If the Odyllic Stone is here, it's ours for the taking.*

Through the stone arches, Aster could see the entire city and then some. It sprawled out below them with cobbled streets winding in every direction.

To the east, Calantha's tower, a union of stone and plant, was framed against the deep blue ocean. Looking down, Aster saw the townsfolk darting back and forth like minnows in a stream.

His leg throbbed and he shrank away from the edge. "I've never been this high up before... it's unnerving."

Kara laughed but kept her eyes on Fletcher. "The crow's nest on Blue Skies is worse. At least here you don't have to worry about the ocean swell." She pulled the bow off her back and aimed it at the man.

"It's beautiful up here," Fletcher said from the opposite edge, legs dangling over the city. "I had always wanted to see the top of the clock tower, but they don't let normal people up here. After I was knighted, places like this were no longer off limits. It's my new favorite spot to sit and think. How did you find me?"

Aster instinctively grabbed his pendant, which pulled towards Fletcher. "It doesn't matter. Give us the stone."

"You know I can't do that. I wish you had seen through Emmeline's intentions. I told you not to trust her. If only you'd just lied..." Fletcher pulled his cloth bag closer and wrapped its strap around his shoulder: Faint blue light leaked out from the seams.

Kara cut in, "You don't get it, Fletcher. We don't have

time. People are dying."

"I understand, but I still can't hand this to you. They'll send Baxter after me... or worse."

"Coward!" Aster was tired of Fletcher's excuses and half-truths, so he drew his sword. "We'll take it from you, then."

Fetcher sighed and lifted himself off the floor. "It wasn't supposed to come to this." His hand slipped into his pocket, and he pulled out three brown mushrooms, just as he had inside the vault.

As they fell from his hand, each morphed into a creature with two spindly legs, a pair of bulbous arms, and tufts of mushroom hair.

"Bunas, kill them." Fletcher's voice wavered as he commanded the monsters.

In a flash, Kara drew her bow and fired two arrows into the head of the closest monster.

It moved forward, unaffected by the injury.

Aster dashed at one, cutting through its spindly leg. The creature fell sideways, and flailed on the ground, struggling to raise its bulbous body.

"Their legs. Even my sword couldn't do much last time." Aster said as he jumped away from the buna's reach.

Kara exchanged her bow for the knife that was sheathed on the side of her belt. She glowered at the meager blade, then charged the closest mushroom monster.

It was nimble, pivoting sideways as she thrust her knife forward. The sprouts on its head bounced with every movement.

Again Kara attacked, aiming to topple the top-heavy creature. But once more it twisted out of the way at the last second. She glanced at Aster on the other side of the bell. Even with his longer reach, he was experiencing the same difficulties.

Kara had only taken her eyes off the buna for a second, but when she looked back, the creature was mid-swing, its arm aimed directly at her head. She dove forward, ducking just below the lip of the bell.

Two steps forward and the creature was beside her again, its arm raised for another attack. As it swung, Kara ducked and slid her knife across its leg. The buna lost its balance and collided with the bell, causing a single deafening chime.

Kara grabbed her ears and backed up to the ledge.

The buna regained its balance. A portion of the flesh on its leg was peeled back: The spongy inside was yellow at first, but quickly turned a purplish-blue. It rushed her again, but this time Kara was ready.

The creature was mid strike when Kara threw her full weight into its legs. Its bulbous body continued forward, while it kicked at her chest, toppling off the ledge.

It burst in a cloud of dust on the streets of New Portsmith.

Aster was locked in combat with the last buna. Fletcher stood a few paces back, shaking his head as Aster danced back and forth to dodge the sentient mushroom.

Kara crept towards Fletcher, careful to flank him while his attention was focused on the fight.

Aster was barely able to keep up with the creature. His arms burned from the weight of the sword and his legs still ached from climbing the tower stairs. Yet he persisted while Fletcher stood in the back, rubbing his temples. It was overwhelming. Rage welled up inside Aster, but he didn't have the energy for reproach.

I need a moment. Aster dashed for the bell. Buna's massive limb smashed into it as he ducked underneath. *BONG.* The sound vibrated through his skull. He dropped his sword, letting both hands cover his ears. *BONG... BONG.*

The creature was too large to fit under, so it was striking the bell instead.

BONG... BONG... BONG. Even with the cacophony, Aster was able to take a few deep breaths and calm down.

BONG. The bell sounded once more. As the noise

cleared the air, Aster picked his sword up and inched closer to the creature, careful to remain below the swinging bell. *BONG... BONG.* With all his might, Aster swept the blade low, cutting straight through the monster's spindly legs.

Buna collapsed against the bell which let out a final, imperfect *CLANG.*

Aster's ears were ringing, but thanks to his pendant, he knew exactly where Fletcher was. He ducked beneath the lip to see Fletcher dueling Kara.

He used an ice axe to deflect Kara's knife. She was gracefully maneuvering around, but the long, curved spikes of the axe were difficult for her to parry. Fletcher's other hand was white, firmly clasped around the strap of the cloth bag, which let out flashes of blue when he moved.

"Enough," Aster cried out, but neither of them looked at him. The noise of the bell had made it so Aster could barely hear his own voice: There was no chance they could hear him.

Fletcher raised his ice axe and brought it hurtling down into Kara's knife, which snapped out of her grip and spun off the ledge. She jumped back, nursing her bruised fingers before pulling her bow out. Drawing it back, she circled Fletcher, an arrow poised to fly.

Aster had gotten close enough to Fletcher for him to notice. The three stood still for a minute, catching their breaths, tense with anticipation. The air buzzed with aftereffects of the bell.

Fletcher was the first to act. He closed his eyes, muttering something inaudible under his breath. Then he dropped his pick to raise his bag into the air. The light flashed once, piercing through the cloth.

Kara reacted instinctively, sending three arrows. Miss —just high. Hit—but only a scratched leg. Hit—the last one embedded in his left arm.

Fletcher kneeled, nursing his wounds. He gingerly lifted the bag off his shoulder while scowling at the pair of them. "Back off! Don't make me use the stone."

"You can't. Otherwise, you would've used it already."

"Clueless as always. You're right that I'm not able to just wish you dead. The Odyllic Stone is a thing that creates. It doesn't destroy. But it takes time for its powers to return. I'd rather not waste that on you if I can help it."

Aster closed in on Fletcher. "Last chance. Do the right thing for once." He held out one hand for the stone, but his sword was ready in the other. *Josselyn's wrong. A firm strike and it's over.* The sword trembled in his hand.

Fletcher begrudgingly reached into his bag. With a wince, he pulled out the Odyllic Stone: the object of Aster's obsession, the panacea for Buckwheat Village.

It looked different from how Aster remembered. Inside the sphere, the miniature grassy world was gone. Instead, a vibrant blue color blanketed the surface, patterned with black stripes.

As he reached for it, Fletcher pulled back.

"Give it to me!"

Fletcher's eyes flicked to the side. "No."

Kara yelped, causing Aster to turn his head.

The remaining buna had crawled over to Kara and ensnared her leg in its lengthy hair. Each mushroom on its body contracted, letting out an amber cloud that enshrouded Kara. She began coughing and sneezing until her face was red and her eyes were dripping wet, finally collapsing to the ground.

A trunk-like arm smashed into Aster, sending him spinning into the bell. His lip split as his face collided with the metal.

He dropped his sword, which clattered to the ground near Fletcher's feet.

The creature struck again, sending Aster into the side of the bell with a metallic gong.

He had nothing left. No weapon and no energy.

Fletcher reached down and lifted Aster's sword off the ground. He had already tucked the Odyllic Stone back into his bag as he shooed the buna away.

"I'm sad we couldn't work something out, Aster. But you've proven yourself too naive to listen to reason. Too stubborn to adapt your views. And, as just demonstrated, lacking in resolve." Fletcher was solemn and resigned.

Aster's face grew hot, tears stung his eyes, and he could feel a painful throbbing from both places he'd struck the bell. "At least I'm trying to do the right thing. I just want to help Buckwheat Village. I'm a hundred times better than you." He spit blood at Fletcher's feet. "Can't you see all the harm you've caused for the sake of pride? You're a phony knight. You'll never be as famous as Ian Pelware."

"Stop comparing me to that hack! You have no idea what he was like." Fletcher growled as he lifted the sword. "Besides, nobody gives a shit about your backwater town. Being the *Hero of Buckwheat* is meaningless. The only reason your town is on the map to begin with is because of *my* gold mine."

"Then why isn't it called the Abberton mine?"

"You should've killed me when you had the chance... Goodbye Aster." He brought it down with deadly force.

Aster weakly lifted his arm to block it, protecting his head. He felt the cold breeze as the blade sliced his flesh below his right shoulder. It stopped with a popping noise as it severed the bone. The world stood still as Aster looked in horror at what had happened.

His arm fell limp as Fletcher yanked the sword back; it was hanging by one sinew that remained. Then all at once the searing pain hit him. Blood was everywhere. With every beat of his heart, his thoughts slipped further from his grasp.

Fletcher raised the blade once more.

Aster could hear someone screaming. *Is that Fletcher? Is this the end?*

His final thought was a memory of Buckwheat Village. It was the day he first felt like he belonged. He ran home and raved to his father about the first friend he had made. Somebody that didn't seem to care that he was different.

Zinnia's face appeared in the haze before everything went dark.

Tristram paced back and forth as Peter attacked, hoping it would wipe the smirk off Baxter's smug face.

Peter thrust his knife towards Baxter's stomach, missing as the man stepped back.

"You really should've brought a proper sword. It's not like you'll get lucky like last time," Baxter taunted.

"At least I don't go around havin' people call me the 'Dread Scorpion'. Is it supposed to be intimidatin' or impressive? Sounds moronic to me."

Baxter's smile dropped; his blade struck the ground, barely missing Peter. He lifted it and swung once more. Peter blocked the sword with his knife, using both hands to maintain his grip.

Tristram paced back and forth. *I've got to help, but in a way Baxter won't notice. One false move and he'll call over the skeletons, an even bigger problem.*

After side-stepping another blow, Peter slid his knife across Baxter's arm, making a shallow cut.

"Bravo! You really are a formidable fighter. But that makes it all the sweeter for me to end you," Baxter took a deep breath and threw out a flurry of attacks.

Peter dodged and parried until Baxter's fist collided with his head, sending him tumbling to the ground.

The Dread Scorpion kept his distance as Peter scrambled to his feet. "I've been dreaming about you, Peter. Ever since Buckwheat. It's my destiny to snuff you out."

Peter was panting heavily. He ran forward and rolled underneath Baxter's horizontal swing, plunging his knife into his foe's thigh.

Baxter stumbled back and pulled out the blade, tossing it to the side. Blood dripped down his pant leg. "By the fires of Conflag, that was a nice move. But now you've got no weapon."

He took a vial of pale-yellow liquid out from his pocket and began to dab it on his sword. "I usually save this for assassinations, but I'll give you a taste of what the Dread Scorpion can do, since you're interested."

Our only chance. Tristram tossed his knife to Peter.

Peter caught it out of the air and dashed to Baxter. His thrust collided with the side of Baxter's sword, missing its target, but the vial slipped, spilling onto the grass.

"Come on, that stuff ain't cheap. Do you know how many scorpions you've got to milk to get that? A lot!" Baxter grumbled as he reached down to salvage what he could, clearly unconcerned with being cut.

Peter jumped back, grinning as he lifted his own knife off the ground. With one blade in each hand, he rushed Baxter again, slicing anything he could reach. Blood splattered as Baxter retreated, poorly shielding himself with his sword.

"We found him, Peter," Baxter cried out in desperation. "Federyc's alive and living in Tembour."

Peter slowed. "What're you talkin' about?"

Blood dripped down Baxter's temple. His body was in shreds. The cuts were mostly shallow, but his pant leg was drenched red. It wouldn't be long before he'd lost too much blood.

"Emmeline had been on his trail for a while. But your idiot friend, Aster, cracked in prison. He gave Federyc up. Do you know how good it feels to get a second chance? A do-over for your biggest regret. I'm elated!" Baxter smiled, blood trailing down into the corner of his lips.

"Not if I kill you first," Peter hissed through clenched teeth. He continued his assault—slashing across Baxter's cheek, tearing his shirt, until finally sliding a knife into the giddy man's chest.

But Baxter had lifted his sword in time, piercing Peter's thigh at the same time.

Peter fell to the ground and rolled down the hill, back towards Tristram.

Baxter dropped to his knees and cried out, "Kill them!" Six skeletons dashed after Peter. "And take me to Emmeline."

At Baxter's command, two more dragged him inside the circle.

Tristram watched Baxter disappear behind the wall of bone, then turned to help his wounded friend. *Shit.*

Zinnia screamed again, horrified at the sight of Aster's bloodied body beneath the golden bell.

She had arrived with Jasper the night before. There were strange rumors flying around the city about gods and miracles which made her uneasy.

Jasper had left to investigate the movements of Benia's army while Zinnia had gone to explore. She had always wanted to see the golden clock tower up close, especially after Aster had raved about its sky-high bell. So she grabbed her newly constructed spear—carved from a fallen branch, her topaz arrowhead as the tip—and made her way to the tower.

The weapon was just starting to felt comfortable in her hands. Jasper had shown her every technique while they traveled and had her work harder than she'd ever worked before, but it paid off. At the very least, she'd felt confident.

Zinnia had wandered down the cobblestone streets, stopping at a dozen shop windows to stare inside. The Buckwheat General Store didn't have half of what was for sale here. What stuck out to her the most was the smell. She hadn't expected that the city would have a putrid, rotten quality that assaulted her nose from time to time. It made her stomach turn whenever she got a whiff of it.

When Zinnia had gotten close to the clock tower, she sensed something was wrong. The bell at the top was chiming erratically. Nothing like the grand sound that she had heard before. Suddenly, a creature had careened down, slamming into the nearby pavement, clouding the air yellow.

Zinnia had shrieked.

After letting her heart settle, curiosity had gotten the best of her. She had prodded it with the spear, feeling its springy flesh. A dark hat with gills sat on one end while the other had spindly limbs.

It was alive! She had backed away. The thought had given her chills.

She had looked up the stonework but thought better of it and ducked for cover inside the tower. Nobody was within the reception area. It had been surprisingly deserted.

She had followed the chiming bell up the staircase. Curiosity leading her, she had bounded the stairs two at a time, until her legs ached. Reaching the top, she made out a pair of familiar voices.

She stepped onto the platform under the golden bell as Fetcher cut through Aster's arm.

Tears fell from her eyes as she looked Aster's body, limp on the ground. His arm dangled to the side, bone jutting out. The pool of blood around him began to flow down the cracks in the floor and drip onto the staircase below. Kara was entangled with another monster.

Fear and regret clouded her mind, pushing out everything else. For Zinnia, time had stopped. She looked at Aster, then Kara, then Fletcher. A flash of her past. Aster on the ground, cockatrice poised threateningly over his body. *Do something! He's dying.*

"What're you doing here?" Fletcher asked as he pulled the bloody sword out of Aster.

Zinnia's body moved on its own. Spear held forward, she dashed at the mushroom creature. It stumbled on its damaged leg as it was run through. Zinnia threw her full weight sideways, extracting the spear at the same time, causing the creature to roll over the ledge, joining its kin on the street below.

Zinnia turned her topaz spear-tip to Fletcher, but he

was ready.

Zinnia charged; Fletcher parried. Zinnia spun on her heel and the tip barely missed Fletcher's stomach as he jumped to the side.

Fletcher hacked at her, but couldn't land a blow with her superior reach. He stepped back, dodging the spear over and over until he was at the edge of the platform.

Zinnia's teeth clenched. She thrust the spear at Fletcher once more.

With nowhere to go and no way to attack, Fletcher hurled the sword at Zinnia. It wobbled, going wide, and clattered across the floor. It was enough to distract Zinnia: Her spear struck the stone at Fletcher's feet.

He stomped on the pole with his full weight, splintering the wood and sending the topaz tip bouncing towards the bell.

Zinnia was dismayed by the splintered spear in her hands. She glanced at Aster. He was unnaturally pale, gasping in uneven, shallow breaths. *I have to help him.*

"Enough of this," Fletcher growled, seizing the chance to pull out the Odyllic Stone, letting the cloth sack fall to his feet. He lifted the orb into the air and closed his eyes.

"No!" The command came from Zinnia's lips. She hurled the broken spear at Fletcher. It wobbled through the air before colliding with Fletcher's fingers. He pulled back in pain and the Odyllic Stone fell to the ground with a melodic crunch. It rolled towards Zinnia, fracture lines visible along its surface.

Fletcher's eyes snapped to the orb as it bounced away.

Zinnia dove for it. Her thoughts were scattered, but her hands found the cracked surface of the Odyllic Stone. Fear, sorrow, rage, pain, anxiety all came out at once. *I have to do something.*

She closed her eyes and spoke every thought that came to her, stumbling across her words. "Don't let Aster die here. Please fix Buckwheat Village. Our friends and family there don't deserve to be sick." She sobbed as she looked over to Kara who was still struggling to free herself. "Gods help us. Why has this object brought only pain? Created monsters? It should be a gift, not a curse. No one person should be able to use these terrible powers." She glared at Fletcher before continuing. "It shouldn't be used to kill, to destroy. I wish the Odyllic Stone just disappeared so no one could own it."

Blue light blinded Zinnia and a sizzling pain erupted from her arm. Two other muffled screams filled the air which began to reek of burning flesh. Zinnia rolled to the side, dropping the stone to grab her arm just below the shoulder. The feeling lasted for what felt like a lifetime, overpowering everything else. And then it was gone. Fletcher was on the ground, seeming to have experienced the same sensation.

That's when she saw it. The Odyllic Stone was split in two. Next to it was an enormous blue butterfly, drying its wings out in the breeze. Its black markings resembled two large eyes, peering into Zinnia's soul. The remnants of the stone looked paper thin—an empty shell that had been spent.

Aster groaned. *A good sign, since he'd been unconscious moments before.*

Fletcher got to his feet, examining the vestiges of his obsession. He tried to pick it up, but it crumbled through his fingers. "What did you do?" he hissed.

"I... I don't know," Zinnia said sheepishly. She was exhausted now, and she could barely recall the words she had spoken. "I just didn't want you to have it."

The air around them swirled. The butterfly flapped its wings, lifting itself into the air and coating everything with a glittery cobalt dust. It hovered for a second, before flying through the golden bell at the center of the room. The metal evaporated at the touch of this creature. With every beat of its massive wings, dust swirled through the air and landed on the floor like drifts of snow in a winter storm.

Fletcher and Zinnia stared, mouths agape as the butterfly fluttered around. Cobalt dust rained down on the city, as it flitted over New Portsmith. It flapped its wings twice more before disappearing over the horizon.

Tristram danced around Peter, striking the skeletons with his dagger. It wasn't injuring them, but it was keeping them at bay. *Think happy thoughts. Of busty ladies and warm beachfront houses.*

Peter was lying on the ground, both his hands pressed against his thigh to stem the bleeding. The cut was deep.

The skeletons attacked again, biting Tristram with their ivory teeth and clawing at him with their decrepit fingers. Just as he pushed one back, the next grabbed him from behind. There were too many for one man to handle. "Loctee guide me. Loctee guide me. Loctee guide me," Tristram muttered over and over as he was overwhelmed with the creatures.

He kicked the closest one, only to find his knife arm ensnared in the clutches of another. Pain shot out from his shoulder as teeth tore through his skin. Tristram spun, freeing himself, but his knife hit bone and fell from his grip.

I can manage this. Just need to get him to the tree line. Tristram whipped his arm around, knocking two monsters back.

A crackling screech from above set every hair on Tristram's body on end. *Gotta go... now!* He lifted Peter on his shoulder as delicately as he could manage and struggled forward.

Thunder rumbled across the clear sky. An enormous black bird hovered well above the tallest tree. Rain clouds formed with every beat of its feathery wings until they blotted out the sun. Then the closest tree to Tristram exploded as a bolt of lightning struck its canopy. Leaves scattered to the ground as the now-hollow trunk popped, hissing as it burned.

The skeletons caught up to him, grabbing his legs and

biting his sides. He was out of options and out of ideas.

As a last resort, Tristram threw himself over Peter to shield him. His friend's body was hot—too hot. Baxter's poison was starting to take effect.

Peter groaned in pain and vomited to the side.

Dried-out bones clawed Tristram's back leaving it scratched and bruised.

With a clatter, the creature that had climbed onto his back was gone. He peaked out under his arm and saw Chert slamming the nearest skeleton into the ground, shattering its skull.

Calantha was there, too. A giant mantis once more, flinging two more away from the dog-pile and freeing Tristram. A wall of vines burst from the ground, separating them from the hill.

"Come," Chert said as he gingerly lifted Peter off the ground. The four of them sprinted back into the woods.

The skeletons followed but couldn't get close with Calantha protecting their rear. Lightning tore the ground around them and more trees exploded, but deeper in, the forest was too dense to see the sky.

When they had gotten far enough from the skeletons, Calantha pulled them behind a muddy outcropping by a stream. There they waited until the clattering of bone faded.

"Look what you've done!" Fletcher screamed at Zinnia. The Odyllic Stone lay in pieces, like a glass jar fallen off the shelf of Buckwheat General Store.

He gripped his trembling hand in a fist and shook it menacingly at her. "Decades of my work, gone in seconds. How could you?" The dust that was covering his body glowed, then vanished. The arrow that was stuck in his arm grew as if it was a branch of a tree. Fletcher yanked the leafy stick from his arm with a wince and pointed it at Zinnia. The arrowhead and newly elongated shaft, now a makeshift staff.

Fearing for her life, Zinnia dove for Aster's sword, which lay just out of her reach, but Fletcher was quicker. Taking three steps forward he thrust his staff at the sword, knocking it underneath the melted bell.

Having recovered some of her strength, Kara clawed and bit through the strands of hair, but her progress was slow. She needed to pause often to cough and wipe her eyes. The spores from the creature were all over her face. She pulled up the neck of her shirt to clean her face and keep the cloud from her lungs.

Weaponless, Zinnia reached for the only thing left that she could see, her topaz arrowhead. She crawled forward, but Fletcher responded swiftly, pinning her arm to the floor with the staff.

Blood pooled around her left elbow as her face fell into a pillow of cobalt dust. She stretched her hand forward, grasping for the topaz that was just out of reach.

Fletcher watched as she struggled, then pulled out his ice pick. "You took everything from me."

Fear, desperation, then something else; the will to persist. Zinnia reached out one more time, straining with all her might, wishing to grab hold of anything that could help.

The cobalt dust around her glowed then disappeared, as it had for Fletcher. The stone bricks under her hands flowed, then shaped themselves around her topaz, like a stream of water. Then the stone pulled away, forming a shaft, before solidifying. She lifted the newly-formed spear off the floor, yanking her arm out from Fletcher's staff.

It took all her strength, but Zinnia thrust her spear through Fletcher's shoulder.

He took two steps back, his hand grasped on the stone pole that had pierced his body.

Zinnia pushed harder. Fletcher slid backwards on the dust, leaning off the edge.

"Wait!" His voice was panicked as he grasped the

spear with all his might.

Zinnia let go and Fletcher fell off the clock tower leaving a cobalt cloud behind.

She turned, rushing over to check on Aster. He was pale but breathing. His arm had been cauterized, and was no longer bleeding. She helped Kara next: Ripping strands of mushroom off of her until she was free.

They kicked the squirming creature off the side before going back to Aster.

Kara gasped when she saw him. She crouched down and tried to join the severed limb back to his arm. Panicking, she took off her cloak and wrapped it around him, pinning his limb to his body. Tears flowed down her face.

As the tears hit the floor, the belfry flashed blue.

Zinnia noticed a black mark on Kara's upper arm. "What's that?" They both looked closer at the distinctive outline of a whale skeleton branded on her skin.

"I don't know. It wasn't there yesterday. But that's not important. We need to get Aster to a doctor now. Help me out." She sniffed and wiped the tears from her cheeks with the back of her hand before sliding an arm under Aster's back and beginning to hoist him up.

"Give me a second," Zinnia replied. She bent down, grabbing handfuls of the glowing dust and storing it in the sack that Fletcher had discarded.

"Zinnia!" Kara lifted Aster off the ground and onto her shoulder. His feet dragged on the ground as Kara struggled with Aster's dead weight. Her sputtered breathing didn't help.

Zinnia jumped and secured the bag around her shoulder. "Sorry, I couldn't leave without taking some. It might be important."

She lifted Aster's legs and the two carefully descended the spiral stairs.

When they reached the ground floor, Kara placed Aster down on a stone bench and peered outside. The city streets were still empty. Out of the corner of her eye, she saw an amber light shine. "Zinnia. There."

"My topaz," Zinnia said as she stepped out of the clock tower. The stone spear was broken into pieces and the gem lay loose on the pavement.

Zinnia wrapped it and put it back into her pocket.

"But where are Fletcher and those monsters?" Kara asked as they looked around the tower. "Gone. They aren't here anymore." She answered herself when she saw a spore outline on the ground. "Come on, Zinnia. We need to leave before they come back." She dashed back inside to grab Aster.

"How'd they survive the fall?" Zinnia asked as she helped Kara.

"I don't know... can't say that I understand much of what just happened."

It took an hour, but Kara and Zinnia managed to haul Aster back to Calantha's tower. They were lucky enough to meet no other people on the way. Even the city guards were gone from the eastern gate.

The other crew members hadn't returned yet, so Kara took it upon herself to inspect Aster's condition. She laid him on his bedroll and checked his vitals. His breathing was steady, and color had returned to his face. He had cuts and bruises all over his body.

As she removed the makeshift bandage from Aster's arm, she gasped. It was a sickly white color. Just below his shoulder, a black line of charred flesh joined the decaying limb with the rest of his body.

Kara cringed as she tried to separate the arm and inspect the damage, but it was firmly reattached. She didn't want to risk more bleeding, so she gave up. "I don't think his life's in danger, but I'm worried about this arm. We need to get him to a doctor soon."

"Aster's got a mark too," Zinnia commented from behind. She pointed to a black shape on Aster's other shoulder. A great vulture with spread wings was branded there, in the same style as Kara's.

Kara turned her eyes to Zinnia. "Show me your arms." Zinnia rolled up her sleeves, revealing a similar mark—of a stone golem. "What are these and what do they mean?" Kara asked.

"Mine reminds me of Ochress. Beryl had said that I was her champion."

Just then, Chert burst through the door carrying Peter. Tristram and Calantha were right behind him. Seeing the others, Tristram broke down sobbing. "We couldn't do it. We didn't get the Odyllic Stone. Now Peter's hurt... badly." He lifted his shirt and winced at the bruises and teeth-marks that carpeted his back.

Peter lifted an arm weakly.

"It's fine," Kara said. "We just need to find a doctor. Aster needs one too." She gestured to him, unconscious next to her.

"I hate to be the bearer of bad news." Calantha spoke up. "But our posters are all over the city. There is no way that a reputable doctor will see us in New Portsmith."

"It'll be alright. We just need to find one of the less reputable ones... and bribe them." Kara's eyes blazed in determination.

Calantha frowned and turned back to the door. "With what coin? If I remember correctly, you threw the last of yours into the ocean." Kara cursed while Calantha continued to speak. "I can go find some yarrow plants. A poultice of the leaves will reduce the bleeding. Perhaps we can stabilize them enough to see Doctor Malvin?"

"Yes, that's our best option," Kara conceded. "Tristram, go to the Moonlight. Tell them that we need to depart immediately.

"I just need to rest some," Peter croaked. "Put me down, Chert."

Tristram grimaced and exchanged troubled glances with Kara. "Aye, aye, Captain." He sprinted out the door and towards the city.

Chert placed Peter, who was sweating profusely, next to Aster.

Kara grimaced as she pulled back Peter's pant leg. "You didn't wrap it?"

Chert frowned. "No time."

"Bandages. Now."

The Munayallpan dropped to his knees and rummaged through two different bags before shaking his head and tearing off his own shirt, handing it to Kara.

She tied it tight around his leg, but the blood was already soaking through. "Find more." She tried to keep her voice steady for the others, but she'd never seen someone recover from a wound this bad.

The sun was beginning to set, and the air was whistling through the tower windows. Inside, everyone was rushing back and forth, checking on the wounded or packing supplies for their imminent departure.

The chaos of it all was too much for Zinnia, who backed up into the corner under the stairs, tears pouring down her face.

Between lighting the fire and checking her bag for spare bandages, Kara noticed Zinnia in the corner.

She stopped what she had been doing and sat down on the cold stones beside the crying girl. Wrapping one arm around Zinnia, Kara did her best to comfort her. "I know how you feel. I'm overwhelmed too."

Between Peter's agonizing groans, the unnatural mushroom creatures, fighting with Fletcher, and Aster's severed arm, it was too much. "I... I killed someone for the first time today. Two people, actually."

Zinnia gasped. "What happened?"

"They were guards. Both in my way..." Kara inhaled sharply and put a fist onto her forehead. Tears welled up in her eyes and started to drip onto her shirt. "They probably didn't deserve it. They were just doing their jobs. It's not like they were bad people. But... They stood between me and my crew. I did what I had to do... I hope it wasn't the wrong choice."

After putting her arm around Kara, Zinnia squeezed her, and they cried together for a moment. The light of the fire flickered, casting abstract shadows on the walls.

Chert hunched over the cooking pot, adding vegetables to it. The tower smelled of greenery with a hint of smoke. The quiet was a soothing balm, much needed for the beleaguered group.

Calantha opened the door, bunches of herbs clutched in her hands. Kara gave Zinnia one more firm hug. "We'll get through this. We can talk more on the ship."

Kara got to her feet and helped Calantha crush the herbs into a paste and apply it to Peter's leg. They sat him up to wrap him with fresh bandages, pressing the wound tight. Peter flinched every time one of their hands got close to the red-hot flesh, but Kara was thankful that the bleeding had slowed.

After they finished, things calmed down, giving Zinnia the chance to tell the story of what happened earlier that day. "Fletcher had it. Aster was badly injured and Kara was being held down. I'm not sure how, but I knocked it out of Fletcher's hand, and it cracked on the ground. I jumped on it and wished for a lot of things. I wished for everything that came to mind and then it broke. All I could feel was pain. When things were normal again, there was this giant blue butterfly that melted the bell and then flew off."

"That is quite the tale," Calantha replied. "Please give me a moment to collect my writing supplies and then please repeat your story to me with as much detail as you can recall." Calantha zipped upstairs and was back with reams of paper before Zinnia could catch her breath. "Alright, once more from the beginning."

Calantha listened intently to the story this time, taking detailed notes. She had Zinnia repeat herself in places and asked questions that Zinnia couldn't answer. Near the end of her story, Zinnia mentioned the cobalt dust she had gathered.

"You mean that you possess a quantity of it now,

here?" Calantha's eyes were wide in excitement.

"Yeah, I put it into this bag." For the first time Zinnia arrived in the tower, she removed the satchel from around her shoulder, showing its contents to Calantha. "I grabbed as much as I could before we had to go."

"May I have a sample of this? A byproduct of the Odyllic Stone that had an unusual reaction in relation to the phenomenon." Calantha loomed over Zinnia and her bag in a possessive, almost lustful way.

"Sure, take as much as you want. I just had a feeling about it, is all."

"Please, do not tempt me with such an offer," Calantha replied through gritted teeth. "I will accept half, and no more." She ran upstairs once again and came back holding a glass jar. It had a single wilted leaf stuck to the side, as if its former occupant was hastily removed moments prior. Zinnia poured what she considered half the dust into the container for Calantha.

"Thank you. If anything fruitful comes from this specimen, I shall include you as the second author in my publications, Zinnia Hollyhock."

"Uh... thanks?"

"It is the least I can do." Calantha mumbled and then began taking detailed notes on the substance, becoming oblivious to the room around her. She lit six candles around the table to fend off the darkness.

By then, Chert had finished cooking a vegetable stew. He was successful in getting Peter to hold down a few bites.

Before they had finished eating, the door opened. Tristram had returned, looking downtrodden. He took two paces into the room and then slumped against the wall.

"What's the matter, Tristram?" Kara asked.

"Moonlight's gone. Sunk or confiscated."

"We'll figure it out in the morning," Kara sighed. "Come eat and get some rest. We're all tired after today."

The night was long and filled with nightmares. Kara barely slept a wink and found herself outside watching the waves as the sun rose. *What now,* she thought to herself, alone and shivering in the breeze. *If Pat were here, he'd know what to say. Probably something about breakfast.* She laughed, picturing her friend's silly expression as he danced around his cast iron pan, making her eat his latest creation.

There was something bouncing on the waves far to the east. It was a merchant ship with a square blue sail rippling in the breeze. Kara watched as it got closer to shore. When she recognized the swirling figurehead she gasped. "The Blue Skies... but how?"

She stood, waved her arms in the air and called out to the ship. Slowly it changed directions and sailed straight towards her. Stopping just short of the shallows, it dropped anchor. Their rowboat splashed into the water and slowly came ashore.

There was a rocky path down the cliffs onto the beach below. Kara followed it down as quickly as she could manage without slipping. When she made it to the bottom and saw who their savior was, her heart sank.

"What're you doing here?" Kara said as she pulled out her knife.

"Calm down Kara. Your captain is just here to help," Wilbur Whitlock said as he adjusted his navy-blue coat. "Federyc sent me. He thought you might need some assistance."

"I'm confused. You know Federyc?" Kara said, still gripping her knife.

"Know him? Yeah, I've taken care of his shipping needs since he was a kid. I smuggled the wine in for his parties as king and smuggled him out of town when things went south. Peter never told you?" The look of genuine surprise and concern was incongruous with the image she had built of Whitlock since he'd betrayed them.

Kara frowned and put her knife away. "I guess he didn't." She placed her hands on her hips and glared at him. "But that doesn't let you off the hook for what you did to us."

"C'mon Kara, yer being too harsh on yer old captain." He smiled, showing a new gap in his teeth.

"Tell that to Carter, who died thanks to your stupid plot!"

Whitlock's smile dropped. "That was never the plan. I was tired of living under constant watch. Tired of working that hard for no reason. I just needed enough coin to disappear forever."

"That's not good enough! I looked up to you and you turned against us." Fists clenched; she took an involuntary step towards him.

The overweight man grumbled. "Wasn't going to drag the rest of you down with me."

Kara cursed under her breath. "You're lucky that we desperately need the Blue Skies. Come help me carry our stuff down. We leave for Buckwheat Village immediately."

"Alright, Kara," he said as he hoisted his belt buckle underneath his sizable belly.

"And one more thing," Kara added, "Call me Captain."

"What? No. She's my ship." Whitlock stepped back and glanced lovingly at the ship. "I only just got her back."

"The Blue Skies has been mine for a while now. You'd better respect that."

Whitlock ran his fingers through his scraggly beard. "I see you've done a bit of growin' up since I've been gone."

"More than I'd have liked," Kara said as they rounded the cliffs and broke onto the grassy landing. "I'll need your help carrying Aster and Peter down to the ship."

Tristram was hesitant to accept Whitlock's return. The two went back and forth, arguing about betrayal and intent until Whitlock finally blurted out, "Look, what I did had nothing to do with you all. I was done with the BTC, that's all. In fact, I treated you all rather well. Gave you food and transport after tying you up. I figured you'd escape eventually. Didn't want you to die or nuthin'— honest. Though you did get back surprisingly fast."

Tristram reluctantly accepted his former boss' help, "for now." They gingerly carried Aster and Peter to the rowboat and then lifted them aboard the Blue Skies.

After all the supplies were aboard, Calantha stopped Kara. "I believe it is time for us to go our separate ways."

"What? Why?"

"Chert has been pining for his family back in Munayallpa and I have business in Tembour. Here is the rest of my yarrow for Peter. Keep an eye on his leg. It has a foul scent to it. And please send us a letter when you make it back to Buckwheat. We are ever concerned about his and Aster's conditions." She kept her air of dignity despite the concern on her face.

"I suppose it was only a matter of time. Though I wish you could've stayed with us longer." Kara took the bundle of herbs, unsure of what to do with them or Calantha.

"We are all but insects among the leaves. Our collaboration is far from over. I will surely be contacting you again at some point. There are research topics that require more data. But I digress. How should I say this... I appreciate how you included me as a part of your crew."

Chert gave Kara a tearful look but couldn't find any words to say. Instead, he embraced Kara, squeezing her until she felt certain her insides would turn to jelly. He let go just as she began to gasp for air. "Thanks, Captain," was all he could manage before turning away and wiping his nose.

"Calantha, Chert, you have both helped us greatly. Without you, we would have been beached long ago. I treasure what you've done for Aster and for me." Kara bowed her head, hiding a sniffle with the motion.

Whitlock interrupted with a deep, wet cough. When he had the attention of the others, he said, "Err, don't mean to interrupt, but we'd better get moving before someone notices the Blue Skies. She's not exactly a discreet ship."

"Yes, we should set sail. Farewell, crewmates." Kara bowed to Calantha and Chert and left them on the beach as Whitlock rowed them back to the ship.

Aboard the Blue Skies, a grizzled man greeted them. Kara recognized him immediately and pulled out her knife. "Pirates," she yelled, startling the others.

Whitlock laughed and lowered her blade. "We're all pirates now. This is Liosam. He works for me."

"Didn't I stab you?" She asked the man before muttering under her breath, "I'm not a pirate."

"'Ello Kara. I wondered if I'd run into you again. Didn't expect it to be like this though." The smile he offered her did nothing to help his appearance.

She stared into his scarred face, trying to decide when he would stab her in the back. But it wasn't worth the trouble protesting now, they had more important things to deal with.

"Alright, enough with the chatting. Let's set sail," Whitlock exclaimed and began to order the crew around, much to Kara's displeasure. *But he's right, and the sooner we are out of sight of New Portsmith, the better.*

Tristram pulled up the anchor and the Blue Skies began to move towards the Haverhein River and Buckwheat Village.

Calantha Coronatus,

It is wonderful that you have finally accepted our proposal. We have been anticipating your integration with the Collective for some time now. You must return immediately to the Boscage School of Benia and begin the ritual to become a full-fledged professor. Do not arrive later than the festival for Viridus's bloom.

It is unfortunate that Emme has remained the Elder of Tradition. We were the correct choice, but Viridus must not have willed it to happen yet. When you arrive, we can discuss further. It is always sad to see a wayward student like Emme, but she will rejoin the thicket eventually.

As for your special request—we have located the journal that you mentioned. It is translated and transcribed below.

Sincerely,
Grovemother Lucinda

Day 105 – Found it! Onyx chalice sits in lap. It is mystery still, but discover true purpose one day.

...

Day 145 – Returned. Chert happy and asked about adventures. Plans to open rock shop. Sienna grown too big.

...

Day 150 – Presented the chalice to Mogul. Promised me fame and riches for my discovery. Talcium gives celebratory feast soon. Excited to eat peppers once more. Food abroad been bland.

...

Day 154 – Talcium not who he says. Ian found out. Return to ruins to keep chalice safe. Chert should know. Something may happen to Slate, Ochress forbid. Must leave today.

...

Day 192 – Chalice back in resting spot. Joining Ian in search for Odyllic Stone. Let things calm down. He has special map. We leave for Kaleenmunda desert after supplies in Tembour. Need new journal.

14 A SOMBER RETURN

Aster awakened to a guttural groan and a twinge in his bicep. At first he thought that the groan was his own, but quickly determined that it was coming from the next bunk over. Even below deck, the air was cold enough to give him goosebumps.

"You alright?" Aster lifted himself up on his left elbow, straining his eyes in the dim light.

"Aster?" The reply was weak. "I'm sorry… we thought… Emmeline would have it… now it's gone."

"Peter?" Aster clenched his eyes for a moment. His head spun as he remembered what had happened the day before. "What about Kara?"

"Better than us… everyone is." Peter groaned twice more, shallow and dry.

Aster swung his legs over the side of the bunk and tried to balance himself, but found his right arm was strapped tightly across his chest. He gingerly prodded the bandage but felt nothing. *Fletcher really did a number on me. I swore I heard Zinnia on the tower for a moment. I'd better ask Kara about it.* He stumbled over to Peter as the ship slowly rocked back and forth.

Light from the nearest porthole illuminated Peter's pale face. Tiny beads of sweat glistened on his brow and there was an unbearable stench.

"Aster... what are you... gunna do... 'bout Buckwheat?"

His stomach ached as if he hadn't eaten in a week. The Odyllic Stone had been his last hope and it flew out of his grasp. He couldn't help but picture his sickly father wasting away in bed. Gritting his teeth, he said, "It'll be fine. We'll figure something out."

"Good." Peter's voice was barely audible. "Can you... do me a favor?"

A favor? Peter has never asked for anything from anyone—beyond booze or coin drop. The request made Aster nervous. "Sure, what is it?"

Peter sucked in air. "Tell Federyc... tell him that... that I loved him."

"I will... if I see him again."

"And tell Kara... that it's not... her fault."

The Blue Skies traveled up the Haverhein River, passing chunks of ice from the shallows. The trees on the shore were barren. The ground was littered with rotting leaves. Zinnia shivered as a frigid wind blew from the east. It was better than going below deck.

"We're stopping soon," Kara said from behind the wheel. "Whitlock and Liosam, go gather wood when ashore. We'll need twice the usual." She turned to Zinnia. "You'll help me with dinner."

Strands of brown hair whipped in front of Zinnia's eyes. "I'll go check on Aster first," She cleared the hair out of her face. "I guess this is why you braid your hair."

Kara's laugh was hollow and forced. "You've got to keep it short or long and tied back. It can be a distraction... or worse, caught in a pulley." She spotted something on shore and called out. "Tristram, drop anchor."

Zinnia jumped down the stairs two at a time. She slid into the living quarters, nearly crashing into Aster.

"What're you doing out of bed?" She asked, eyeing him closely. His right arm was bandaged from shoulder to fingers and bound close to his chest. He smelled like old pork.

"I feel fine. I told you yesterday," he snapped back, steadying himself on the door frame.

"But your arm." Her hands hovered over his. She wanted to investigate but his tone was a warning.

"My arm is fine too," he replied, lifting the bandaged limb in front of her face, and wiggling his fingers. "See?"

"Then why does it stink so bad?"

Aster scowled.

Zinnia bit her tongue. *Don't pick a fight. Not when he's just woken up.* "We've arrived. Kara says we'll eat, warm up, and you know..."

Aster grabbed his cloak and followed Zinnia back on deck. "I'll help collect firewood."

"No," Kara called from the wheel. "If you'd like to help, you can cook with us. You're still recovering."

He frowned but didn't argue.

Zinnia knew why. Kara had been on a tirade about everyone following the captain's orders since Whitlock had joined. For good reason too. She didn't trust the fat man one bit.

Judging by his sway, Aster could barely keep himself upright. Twice she had to grab his shoulder to keep him from falling off the rope ladder. But they managed to get into the rowboat without incident. Tristram took them ashore.

The ground was barren with patches of ice covering what would be mud in warmer weather. The ruins were eerier than Aster had described. The white pillars looked like the bones of a giant. Though it could've been the missing greenery making them stand out.

Tristram waved them off, then paddled back to the Blue Skies.

Aster led Zinnia through the decaying stone pillars. "Here it is," he said as they arrived at the upright stone slab.

"This is what Kara keeps raving about?" Zinnia asked as she crouched next to the carving of a glowing orb that was radiating otherworldly creatures. "Wait. This is a cockatrice... and that's a boulder beetle," she remarked, pointing at the eroded carvings.

"Here is a lovine. Those wings look like they belong to Quell'est. I wish that part hadn't broken off." Aster continued. "And a few others that I've never seen before."

"What does it all mean?"

Kara walked over, carrying a slab of beef from New Portsmith. "I've been thinking about that for a while now. The object in the center is clearly the Odyllic Stone. It must have created all these monsters. I just don't know why."

Zinnia ruffled her hair. "Somebody's wish? Like Fletcher's mushrooms?"

"Maybe, but there's gotta be something more. I bet Quell'est would know," she said, laying the utensils down on the flattest stone. "Help me start cooking. You'll have plenty of time to ponder the Odyllic Stone later."

Aster and Zinnia cleared the ashes out of the old fire pit and set the cooking pot on top. As they finished setting up, Whitlock and the others returned with wood.

The food was cooked quickly and their meal was unusually quiet. No topic lasted more than a few words. When they had finished eating, Kara stood with a sigh. "Alright, let's begin. Tristram, get Peter."

He returned from the far side of the ruins, holding Peter upright. "It's for your own good," he said between breaths.

When they got to Kara, she handed him a shaved stick, a few fingers across. "Had your fill?" she asked.

"Eaten more than I've had in weeks." Peter's usual fierceness was gone. He had thinned out, too, like a beggar from New Portsmith.

"Good. You'll need the energy."

"I'm havin' second thoughts."

"The leg's gone. And the rot is spreading." She guided him onto the flat stone, propping up his lame leg.

"Can't be more than a few days from Buckwheat. Doctor Malvin—"

"Doctor Malvin would tell you what you already know."

"Kara, I…" His voice was quiet. "I'll be useless without it."

"You'll find something."

"Will I?" He gripped his thigh, wincing at the slightest touch. "Can't walk. Can't fight. Can't sail."

"Don't make me say it."

Peter stood up and limped towards the ship.

"Captain's orders," she whispered.

Tristram ducked under Peter's arm and stopped him from collapsing to the ground. "It's the best option. We've tried everything else." He led Peter back to the stone.

"Fine. But Tristram, promise you'll help me end it if I can't manage."

Kara unraveled thin rope. "Don't talk like that."

"Promise."

"Fine. Whatever," Tristram replied as he held the first mate's leg steady.

Kara wrapped the rope around his thigh, pulling tight.

"Good." Peter clamped his teeth around the stick and Tristram lifted the saw.

Zinnia covered her ears but couldn't entirely muffle the screams. She'd never seen someone in this much pain. At least Aster had been unconscious when she'd found him.

Peter howled. It was animalistic. Primal. *Mom.* The bear materialized, poking it's snout though a bush.

Aster rubbed her back, pulling her back to the present. He glared at the operation with a fierceness that she didn't understand and occasionally flexed his bandaged left hand.

"Now we cauterize," Kara said gently.

Zinnia flinched. She didn't expect the sizzle to be so loud.

When it was over, Peter called for liquor. His voice was shallow and defeated.

She looked over to see Whitlock pulling out a waterskin he'd hidden in his coat. He took a swig before passing it to Peter. "Let us know when yer ready. But don't take too long. Be bad if we get stuck in the ice."

Winter weather was the last thing on Zinnia's mind. She was worried for Aster and all of Buckwheat for. She never mustered up the courage to tell Aster about Hugo's episode. That was months ago.

The Blue Skies crunched through a thin layer of ice to reach the docks of Buckwheat Village. Night had fallen and the crew was eager to get out of the cold air and warm up inside the Toasted Oak.

Aster's stomach growled as he thought of Whitney Fulton's cooking. He had just enough copper left for a round of mead. He owed Kara and the others much more than that, but it would have to do for now. Truth be told, Aster was nervous to be back home. He never expected that his trip to find a doctor in New Portsmith would have turned into a journey that took the better part of a year.

Inside, the crew crowded around a single table to order their meals from Don. The familiar smokey smell of the room made Aster smile. This place was the same. He looked up at the boxy lamps that hung over the patrons, glad to be back in Buckwheat—his home.

"Wait, are you Aster Rutherford? Churn my butter, I almost didn't recognize you." Don excitedly waved Whitney over to say hello. "And Zinnia Hollyhock, too. We thought you weren't going to make it home before the lake froze over. It'll probably happen any day now."

Whitney added, "Yes, we should let Mayor Gilroy know you're both home. I'm sure he'll arrange a feast to celebrate. The mood around here has been grim since... oh." She put a hand over her mouth, horrified, then gave

Don a tearful look.

He adopted a somber expression and his voice fell flat. "Aster, Zinnia, there was a tragedy in the village while you were gone."

Aster's stomach dropped and he lost his appetite. *Fires of Conflag, I'm tired of bad news.* He was hoping to be home in time to save his father, but after Lavender's passing, he knew that it was already too late. And even then, they were not sure if Zinnia's wish to save Buckwheat had even worked. Aster had just wanted one more night in blissful ignorance.

Zinnia reached across the table and grabbed Aster's left hand tightly. They talked on the Blue Skies about the possible outcomes of what they would find when returning to the village. She wanted to support Aster, regardless of what happened.

"I don't know how to put this... Watson Hollyhock is no longer with us. There was a monster at the General Store."

Zinnia went pale, her body tensing at the words, fingers clutching tightly around Aster's. "Wait... what happened?"

"It must've come down from the mountains. A bird with leathery black wings, as big as a cow. Two weeks ago, we caught it eating some of the livestock. Watson, Conflag warm him, lured it away, trapping it in the basement of the General Store.

"He kept it down there for a few days while the rest of us discussed how to get rid of it, but somehow it broke through the hatch and escaped into the shop itself. Several of us…well we barred the door, trapping it inside." Don looked at the floor in shame. "Nobody's seen Watson since. And I'm too much of a coward to check on him. Every time somebody goes past the window, that beast glares at you through the glass. It's unsettling. Gilroy tried yelling for him around back, but never got a response. I'm sure that the monster ate him whole."

Whitney smacked her husband on the arm and

scowled. Zinnia was in tears and Aster just sat there with his mouth open.

Kara broke the awkward silence. "I'm so sorry, Zinnia. I'll go with you to check the General Store. We've encountered so many monsters in the last year, what's one more? Aster, you'll come with us, right?"

Zinnia was trembling in her chair. Aster knew exactly what monster had killed her father—the same one that has haunted her dreams since the Pelware Mines: a cockatrice.

"Yeah, I'll help. Zin, are you okay?"

Her face had gone pale. She stared at the wall.

Aster and Kara discussed the situation at the General Store for a bit longer while Whitney disappeared into the kitchen to bring their food.

After they had agreed on a plan, Aster turned to Don once more. "And what about my father—how's he faring?"

Don opened his mouth but Whitney jumped in first, returning with fresh mugs of mead for the table. "You are fortunate to have come home when you did. Hugo hasn't been able to leave his bed for some time now. He's had about a dozen episodes so far. Doctor Malvin says he's only got a couple of weeks left. He checks on your father every day."

"Oh," Aster replied glumly.

"He will be thrilled to see you once again. I visited him last week and you're all he would talk about. He must be proud of all you are doing for our village."

"Maybe." Aster looked towards Zinnia for reassurance, but she was staring at her lap. "Is there anybody that's cured of the illness? Has Malvin said anything about a miracle?"

Whitney shook her head. "Afraid not. "Deacon Arnit holds prayers to Conflag thrice a week now, but nothing yet. The others lost faith when Lavender passed... but not us. We're being tested. I'll hold my faith until my last breath."

"I see," Aster replied glumly. He looked down at the

plate of fish chowder that had just been placed in front of him. After prodding it with his fork, he gave up on eating. At least the cold, dry mead was comforting.

Across the table, and oblivious to the somber tone of the room, Whitlock cried out, "Why's the food in this backwater village always so tasty? Never got it..."

"Pretty good," Liosam added, bringing a bowl to his lips and making a horrid slurping sound.

Zinnia didn't say another word or touch her food for the rest of the evening.

When Kara had finished eating, she nodded to Aster and the two solemnly readied themselves, checking their weapons and kindling their resolve. Kara stepped over to Zinnia and gently helped her to her feet. "It's time."

Zinnia reluctantly grabbed her things and followed Aster and Kara out of the Toasted Oak, trembling ever so slightly.

They hadn't gone more than a few paces when they bumped into Doctor Malvin, who was on his way to have dinner with Mayor Gilroy.

"Doctor Malvin, I have a question for you." Aster asked after greeting him. "There hasn't been anyone who has been cured recently, has there?"

"No, can't say that there has. I took your father's vitals yesterday, actually. He is a tenacious man. By Conflag's mercy, his decline has been slow. But it's good that you've returned when you have."

That wasn't what Aster wanted to hear. He thanked the doctor and continued down the dirt path with his head down. As they approached the General Store, he could only think about how much time he wasted searching for a cure. Time he could've spent with his father.

Aster and Kara peered into the yellowing windows, looking for any sign of the cockatrice. Zinnia cowered behind them, clutching her bag of cobalt powder like a good luck charm. The shop was in disarray. Broken bottles were scattered about the floor and the dried meat that usually hung in the window was gone. The candles had reddish-brown feathers stuck in the wax. In the far corner, partially hidden by the counter, Aster could see a scaly black wing folded over the top of a massive creature.

Zinnia piped up from behind Aster. "Do you see it?"

"Yeah. It's a cockatrice, like we thought." He whispered back, never taking his eyes from the hulking form.

"What now?"

"Now we get rid of the beast." Aster stepped over to the hefty front door and pushed it open with a familiar *DING* of the bell, releasing a horrible stink from inside. The air was thick with the smell of rotting flesh and spoiled milk.

Kara was the first to enter, bow fixed on the sleeping cockatrice. Aster was behind her, sword in hand. Per their plan, Zinnia stood behind the bulky door, out of sight, holding it open. Aster and Kara crept forward until they could see over the front desk. Cowering underneath was Watson Hollyhock, petrified. Fear forever etched on his gray face.

Kara motioned forward and Aster hopped onto the counter. He puffed out his cloak as much as he could manage with one elbow, trying to appear threatening. Kara loosed her arrow.

It pierced through the creature's leathery wing and into its neck. The cockatrice screeched and jumped to its feet.

Aster hooted and howled, waving his cloak as he stepped forward.

Kara shot another arrow. This one embedded itself in the creature's feathery thigh.

With a spiteful eye, it turned to Kara.

Aster jumped around, and howled some more, but the cockatrice was not interested in him. It hissed and locked eyes with Kara, who screamed and fell to the floor.

Before he could think, his sword was out—gripped awkwardly in his off hand. He crashed into the bird, knocking it to the floor. Aster plunged the sword into its breast over and over again as it slashed at him with its talons.

Then a familiar feeling; his body burned, a hot, dry sensation flowed through him, and his head started to swim.

Zinnia cowered behind the door, watching Kara pull herself off the floor. Aster sluggishly thrust his blade at the creature once more. Then he stopped moving altogether. Kara knocked another arrow and carefully aimed. It tore through the cockatrice's eye, pinning the monster against the wall.

The creature struggled for another moment, then fell limp, black wings draped over Aster.

Zinnia peaked around the door. "Is it dead?"

"Things didn't go as planned," Kara replied. "But I think it's safe now. You alright over there, Aster?"

There was no response.

Zinnia let the door close and cautiously edged around the room, keeping the corpse of the cockatrice in her sight. "Aster?"

Kara rushed forwards and flung the creature's wings aside. Aster stood, unmoving, sword embedded in the bloody chest of the cockatrice. His skin was pale gray. Kara threw her arms around him and burst into tears. "No, no, no, no."

Zinnia nearly tripped on her feet as she stumbled over. He was petrified, the stony surface of his body still warm to the touch. Zinnia wasn't upset: She felt empty. After everything that had happened, she had expected this. Whenever she had asked herself if it could get any worse, this is what she had pictured. *Pat, Peter, her father, and now Aster. It's just too much.*

Her left arm itched, then stung. She lifted her sleeve and saw that the tattoo of Ochress was hot to the touch and faintly glowing blue. It wasn't the only thing; the dust in her bag was giving off light, too. *The dust. If it's anything like the Odyllic Stone, it could save him.* Zinnia reached down and grabbed a handful of dust and pushed it onto Aster's body.

"Please help him," she muttered as she pictured the miners she had saved with the Odyllic Stone. The dust glowed brightly before disappearing. Zinnia felt faint as Aster's stone skin began to ripple. As she moved her hand away, like pulling a thread from a cotton shirt, the stone flowed through the air and into her palm. The process took a full minute as Zinnia coaxed the stone out of her friend. When she finally collapsed to the ground, he was flesh and blood once more.

Aster pulled away from them, gasping for air, eyes wide with fear. He spun around and saw the cockatrice pinned to the wall, then fell to his knees.

Kara's hands settled across her heart. "What happened? How'd you cure him?"

Zinnia opened her palm. Inside there was a stone the size of a peach pit. Something else escaped her view and dripped to the floor. "It felt like I could pull the rock out of him. It has something to do with Ochress and this cobalt dust."

Aster coughed and sputtered, and Kara wiped her eyes. "Zin, your dad." He pointed behind the counter.

Zinnia placed the stone on a nearby shelf and then stepped to the cowering figure of her father. Grabbing another handful of dust from out of her bag, she placed it atop his head and closed her eyes. Again she felt a flowing sensation as the color returned to Watson's face. The strain was too much for Zinnia who crumpled against the counter.

Watson hacked and cleared his throat. "Watch out, there's a monster!" Then he noticed his daughter.

"Not anymore," she replied, weakly embracing him. "We took care of it. Are you alright?"

He patted himself down and scowled at the toppled shelves and broken bottles in the room. "Better than ever. Except the store's a mess."

She pulled back and opened her hand. Another pit-sized stone sat atop a small pool of mirrored liquid.

"Quicksilver!" Aster gasped from over the counter. "Did you pull this out of him? Does that mean that you can cure the others?"

"I can try," she replied, still unsure of what had happened.

"Kara, go find Doctor Malvin and meet me at my house. Let's find out for sure."

Zinnia dumped the contents of her hand on the counter and followed Aster outside, leaving her confused father surveying the wreckage of his shop, shaking his head at the cockatrice corpse pinned to his wall.

Aster slowly opened the door to his father's room, checking to see if he was awake. It was musty with a hint of ammonia—most likely from poppy tea. His father would never admit it, but he was probably dealing with a great deal of pain.

"Malvin?" Hugo asked. Two deep coughs followed.

"No Dad, it's me."

"Aster, thank the light of Conflag you're home. Open the window so I can see you."

Aster crossed the room and pulled back the curtains. He cracked the window to allow a bit of fresh air into the room. Seeing Hugo lying in bed caused his chest to tighten. His father had been replaced with a frail, emaciated man. His face was stretched thin over cheekbones that were no longer hidden by the fruit pies he loved to eat.

Before he could stop himself, Aster's tears splashed on the floor. "You were right... about everything." He held up his bandaged arm. "I was naive and careless and got hurt. In your stories, they always seem to skip over the uncertainty. Out there, nothing is black and white, so how do you know that you're doing the right thing... that it's worth the risk?"

Hugo looked his son up and down. "You don't. You will always question your choices. Take your mother. There's not a day that goes by where I don't ask myself if I did the right thing leaving her. I think that's why we are drawn to those heroes. Unwavering resolve is something unachievable but worth striving for." He coughed, flinching from the pain.

Kara, Zinnia, and Malvin burst into the bedroom. Doctor Malvin had honey stuck to his chin, remnants of a half-eaten meal. Grumpily he said, "Yes, your father is still sick. There's nothing we can do at this point. Make the most of your final days together."

Aster pointed to Zinnia, who was now hovering over Hugo. He was clearly uncomfortable that so many people were in his bedroom, but he found himself as curious as the others.

Zinnia's hand dove into her cloth bag and pulled out a handful of the cobalt dust. Then she turned bright red. "Your chest... I need to touch skin."

Hugo grumbled, but with a little help from Aster he lifted off his shirt, revealing curly brown hair on his chest.

Zinnia placed her hand atop it and the room glowed blue. Hugo groaned and grabbed the sheets to keep from screaming out. When the light faded, Zinnia had a pool of silvery liquid in her hand. She nearly crashed to the ground from exhaustion, but Kara steadied her.

"Is that it?" Aster asked. "That's what's been causing all of these problems? It's so small."

"What just happened?" Malvin adjusted his glasses and pushed on the liquid with a metal tool. He instructed Zinnia to dump it into a glass vial. After taking a sample of blood from Hugo, he mixed it with a few chemicals and shook his head. "This is highly unusual. There is no trace of quicksilver left in his system. How did you do that?"

Kara answered. "She is blessed by Ochress. I guess your wish came true, Zinnia... just not in the way we expected."

Malvin paced back and forth for a second and then said, "Well, I think that Hugo will get better now, though it will take time. His kidneys are still damaged, but I don't see why they wouldn't be able to heal now. There's one thing though..." He stopped pacing and looked directly at Zinnia, causing his ponytail to flick back and forth. "You'll need to do this again. Perhaps once a season. To keep expelling the quicksilver since it is pervasive in this village."

Zinnia opened her bag and peered at the remaining butterfly dust. "I think there's enough for the villagers once, but not for any repeats. And not today—I don't think I could manage another."

Aster placed his hand on Zinnia's shoulder. He wiped his watering eyes and said, "We will get more. I'll make sure that you never run out. Do what you can with what you have and once the ice melts, we'll collect barrels full of the stuff.

Over the next few days, Zinnia moved from house to house removing the metal from each of the villagers' bodies. Mayor Gilroy was the last person—he insisted that everyone else receive the treatment first. Gilroy cleared his throat. "I speak on behalf of the entire village. Thank you for what you've done for us. I know it isn't much, but I'd like to bestow on you all the honorary title—the Saviors of Buckwheat. Aster and Zinnia, I'm so proud of both of you. I remember when I used to catch you rummaging through my apple fields, but now you've done something truly amazing. Thank you."

Their celebration lasted late into the night. Every villager who could get out of bed, bought the crew another round of mead at the Toasted Oak. Two by two the crowd dispersed until only Aster, Zinnia, and Kara remained under the warm glow of the lanterns.

"You finally did it, Aster." Kara smiled as she rubbed her tired eyes.

"It was all Zinnia. I'm not sure I actually did anything," he replied.

"You brought Malvin and inspired Zinnia."

"I guess. So where do we go from here?"

"Dunno. But the Haverhein is already starting to freeze over. I reckon that we're stuck in Buckwheat Village until spring."

Zinnia frowned. "And what will we do about all the trouble we caused?"

Aster rubbed the back of his neck. "What trouble? You saved everyone. You're a hero."

"That's not true," Zinnia snapped back. "Yes, they're better now, but the river is still contaminated, and the mine is still polluting."

"And Arathanon is on the brink of war. What will happen to Benia—especially since the Council of Elders lost the Odyllic Stone?" Kara pulled out her compass and absentmindedly flicked it open and closed. "And Fletcher is still out there somewhere. Not to mention the monsters created by the Odyllic Stone. All of that is our fault. If only I had been an adequate captain…"

"Don't say that, Kara." Zinnia pulled up her sleeve. "And what about these tattoos? Every time I see mine, I'm reminded of my stupid wish that broke the Odyllic Stone."

Aster drank his last swing of mead. "You both are being too hard on yourselves. It's not like we asked for any of that. Besides, I've had enough adventures for now. There's nothing we can do until the river opens back up, anyway. I say we relax and enjoy the simple things here."

"You can be so clueless, Aster." Zinnia sighed and hopped off her stool. "But you're right, we have some time. No point in stressing about it now." She rubbed her eyes and glanced at the door.

Kara followed her lead, sliding off the stool and shuffling towards her room. "I'll make things right. I owe that to both Pat and Peter. But not today." She put her hand over her mouth to stifle a yawn.

When he finally got into bed, Aster couldn't sleep. For the first time in over a year, he was happy. He never truly realized how much stress had been building up in his mind, until it was gone. Except for the one thing that still bothered him.

He carefully unwrapped the bandage around his right arm, releasing a putrid stench. Chunks of flesh were missing, leaving only bones underneath. His pinky and ring finger were entirely unsheathed; two white protrusions from his yellowing hand. Even the ligaments had rotted away, yet somehow the fingers remained attached. Aster flexed them once more out of habit, then replaced the bandage with a fresh one. A problem for another day.

Aster Rutherford,

I was glad to hear that you are doing well. I wanted to say goodbye but did not have the chance. Chert and I have both been thinking about you. He is safely home in Strongfair with his brother and sister.

If you have not heard, Munayallpa has surrendered to Benia, forsaking their goddess, Ochress. I hope this means that we have avoided conflict for now, but I do not believe we will be as lucky with the other countries.

I have settled into my new role at the Boscage School. They have not come up with a proper title for it yet, but I will be leading the department of enigmatic beasts. I would like it if you would be one of my field researchers. There will be a small stipend, but the reward will mostly be in the discoveries themselves. I believe you are one of the more experienced and trustworthy men I have come across, so a perfect fit for the job.

I will be the first to announce it; we have witnessed the emergence of the Fifth Age. The Odyllic Stone was the catalyst. Not a tool, it was an egg. Zinnia Hollyhock's actions gave birth to it—to the Cobalt Emperor of Arathanon.

There have been reports from the small villages of central Benia. Sightings of the Emperor correlated with miracles, along with the cobalt dust it leaves behind. It reminds me of the bone meal that I acquired from the Kaleenmunda Desert, with some unknown property that enhances materials. I need to study it further, but I recommend that you collect more if you get the opportunity. There is much to learn and no time to lose in finding out its secrets. Word will get out soon enough, so we must not spoil our lead.

Do stay in touch. Once winter is over, I expect the world will be more active than it has been in some time. Take care.

Sincerely,
Calantha Coronatus

ABOUT THE AUTHOR

Alex Scheuermann is a budding novelist working on his premier fantasy trilogy The Odyllic Stone. By trade he is an electrical engineer designing semiconductors (computer chips) for autonomous vehicles and factory robots. Alex loves fantasy novels and games, so he decided to create a new magical world for others to enjoy.

Publishing is hard. Like really hard. If you liked this story please post a review. It could just be a mention of your favorite character or scene (no spoilers). This helps authors more than you know. Thanks!